VOL I
"STARTING IN THE MIDDLE"

STEVEN NEMEROVSKI

Wasteland Press
Shelbyville, KY USA
www.wastelandpress.net

E Party: Vol I "Starting in the Middle"
by Steven H. Nemerovski

First Printing – April 2010
ISBN: 978-1-60047-427-9

Cover Artwork: "Eagle"
Original Oil Painting by Majid Kahhak, (30" x 40", 2009)
Kahhak Fine Arts & School
411 Main Street
Carbondale, CO 81623
970-704-0622
www.mkahhak.com

Printed in the U.S.A.

0 1 2

For My Nancy
With All My Love

ACKNOWLEGEMENT

In writing *E Party*, I was fortunate to have an exceedingly talented and dedicated group of family and friends that volunteered to assist with editing. Ed fact-checked, Mark and Poppa word-smithed, Barb attacked grammar, Eiso took the 10,000 foot level, Mike kicked the tires on political strategies, Scot brought the attitude of a twenty-something, and my wife, Nancy, tearfully gave the final nod of approval. Their recommendations, across the board, made me a better writer and enabled me to create a greatly improved product. I am forever grateful to them for helping me climb this mountain.

I also thank my assistant, Dawn, for her usual excellent support, along with the professional editors, Susan and Casey, and Wasteland Publishing for their help in making *E Party* the best it could be.

PROLOGUE

Ever since Aspen had become his permanent residence, Fridays meant one thing: rise at five thirty; exercycle with CNN; a light breakfast of yogurt, granola, and juice; peruse the morning e-mails from Liz; quickly respond as required; grab the backpack. Estimated time of departure: 7 a.m.

With foliage at its peak, there is one clear choice for his weekly hike. From his home on Red Mountain, it is approximately fifteen minutes by car to the trail head in Snowmass Village, just off Horseranch Drive at the Crossings. Mountain bikers tend to embark the Rim Trail from the west where access off Sinclair Road makes the ascent less taxing. Most hikers start from the east where the early switchbacks, surrounded by flowing prairie grasses and natural flowers, are the easy choice over pavement. More importantly, beginning with the seventh switchback, the early views of Mt. Daly and beyond offer a pleasing tease of the majesty ahead.

With a moderate aerobic pace, forty minutes in brings the birch tree line, a grouping of picnic tables, and a chance to rest. The view is so spectacular, first timers often quit here and head back down after prematurely exhausting their water bottles and cameras. To the experienced, this is only the hors d'oeuvre.

The next length of trail covers fifteen to twenty minutes. The terrain is moderately steep and scrub oak begins to dominate. In mid-September, the relatively mundane plant turns supermodel, exploding in a range and depth of colors that few plants can surpass. During this last push to the top, the path curves around to expose a southerly view facing the Snowmass Mountain ski range and a westerly view facing Mt. Sopris, the king of the valley. At the epicenter of the viewing splendor sits an old-fashioned park bench created out of split tree trunk segments. Though the picnic tables seemed bizarre to him, he thought the bench was genius. With almost 300 degrees of unobstructed views at 10,000 feet, it was this spot, and this bench, that had years ago sealed the deal to make this area his home.

People come to Aspen from all over the world for myriad reasons. Sportsmen come for skiing, fishing, hiking, biking, camping, golf, and more recently, X-games. The arts are plentiful. Shopping is expensive and exclusive. Politicians, celebrities and wannabes can see and be seen. For non-skiers, cool, crisp summers kick off with the Harley-led Fourth of July parade and transition to Labor Day with one festival after another. All of this, and more, presented in a charming, welcoming, yet sophisticated package that most visitors grasp immediately.

That he ever traveled to Aspen was a historical anomaly. In 1949, Chicago industrialist Walter Paepcke and the University of Chicago staged the Goethe Bicentennial Convocation and Music Festival. The main draw was Dr. Albert Schweitzer, along with other international leaders, artists and musicians. He accompanied his parents to the convocation and the experience created lasting memories. His next trip, roughly twenty years later, was to ski. The following summer was a longish weekend of hiking and biking; thereafter, and occasionally, for all of the above. As he thought back to his late forties and early fifties, he would grudgingly concede the occasional impulse to see and be seen. Though not a celebrity in the magazine cover sense, he had become one of the most accomplished and wealthiest men in the world.

It's not that one starts out to become a billionaire. He would freely admit that independent wealth was generally on his pubescent to-do list, but it was with an "M" not a "B." Looking back on his career, the day-to-day and year-to-year quest had been about the pursuit of excellence, not wealth. However, his unique brand of excellence and genius had produced assets on a galactic scale.

He was already well-known and highly respected in his field. But once the tabloids announced his membership in the billionaire's club, he was not just labeled; he was incarcerated. At least he felt that way. Friends became tentative, whereas strangers sought him out. His business acquaintances re-evaluated their relationships, while anyone with a get-rich-quick scheme pressed for access. He was even more highly sought after by the legitimate press and news media. Given his bachelor status, he also became a target of the paparazzi.

It was then he discovered a new meaning for Aspen. It was a place where he could be normal and inconspicuous. Although by any demographic it is among the wealthiest communities in the world, for all its enticements and sophistication, Aspen is also a very small town. As a local, it presented the most relaxed pace he had ever encountered. The only thing people hurried to do was ski fresh powder or otherwise enjoy the outdoors. With the exception of an extreme minority, none of this was competitive. Work was conducted at a Southern Comfort pace, just short of mañana. People were genuinely friendly. On any given day, he could walk the streets, grab a brew and, for the most part, be a regular guy.

In short order, his newfound relaxation transitioned to playing hooky for hikes and bike rides in the summer, and skiing in the winter. The Rim Trail bench was the one place where he could sit for extended periods of time, relax, and, as he called it, "escape think."

From an early age he had great insight to his mind. He knew it was always switched on, even when he slept. Like any high-end computer, it could multi-task, handle complex equations, and operate at very high speeds. He also knew it could escape think, put everything aside, and switch to planning, to theory, to outside the box. Until Aspen, until the bench, his capacity to escape think had noticeably diminished over the years. He was thrilled to reacquire this skill because once the question was asked, he was driven by the challenge. The grind of his 24/7 pace conspired against him. The bench was the antidote. And, within a reasonable amount of time, the answer became clear.

CHAPTER ONE

E-MAIL

To: Atlas
From: Liz
Sent: 9/18 9:00 a.m. (CST)
Subject: Kickoff

Good morning. Your guests arrive between 10:10 and 11:05. Two commercial, two private. All transport is arranged and Clay has the itineraries. Lunch at 12:30. Dinner is your call depending on the pace of the day. Usual notice required. Good luck.

* * * * * * * * * * * * * * * *

At the first sighting of Highway 82 at Glenwood Springs, the Gulfstream banked left and began a gradual descent past Carbondale, Basalt, and Snowmass into the Aspen/Pitkin County Airport. Its lone passenger, the General, had flown this leg myriad times, yet each landing presented its own unique vista of the local beauty, and this mid-September trip did not disappoint. This was easily his favorite time of year to visit Colorado, and Aspen was his favorite destination. As he stepped off the plane, the cool, crisp, clean air, the sparkling blue sky, and the Hallmark card surroundings begged their usual inquiry. Why didn't he come more often? Better yet—why didn't he follow the lead of his best friend and live here year-round?

The staff of the fixed base operator is uniquely efficient at the task of fielding dignitaries and this landing was no different. The General was whisked to the private lounge to freshen up. His bags were quickly loaded into the black Range Rover, the status car du jour, and the driver graciously inquired as to his state of readiness. It was a short ride to his friend's home, roughly two miles east on

82 where it becomes Main Street, and a left at the Hotel Jerome onto Mill Street for the two minute journey up Red Mountain.

All on schedule, the other three guests touched down over the course of the next hour. The Rover transporting Tom Robinson, the last to arrive, pulled into the compound at 11:40 a.m.

Upon hearing, "amazing, isn't it?" his guests turned in unison as Atlas greeted them on the main terrace. This is where he generally chose to meet his guests, especially first-timers, and especially on days when the views could not adequately be reduced to words or film.

"Please, as you were," offered Atlas as he joined them at the guard rail overlooking downtown Aspen, the four mountain ski area, and with the aid of his trusty telescope, a staggering portion of western Colorado by day and untold celestial bodies by night.

"General," said Atlas, reaching to shake his hand, "it's wonderful to see you. You're looking well." He turned to K.C. and gave her a hug. "And you look as radiant as ever." Then, in a lowered voice, "How is Pat doing?"

K.C. looked at him intently and shrugged. Atlas held her gaze for a moment before turning to greet Lauren and Tom. He offered "it's been way too long" to both of them and " I trust you've all met? " to the entire group.

They had, in fact, all exchanged greetings and pleasantries during the ten minutes that Atlas had fashionably kept them waiting. But Atlas also knew that, with the possible exception of K.C. and Tom, his guests had probably met before. Although they came from mutually exclusive geographic and ethnic origins, they all traveled in Olympiad style overlapping circles of business and philanthropy.

"Tom, you've never made it out here. Let me show you a few points of interest." Atlas believed there was no limit to the grandeur afforded from his terrace, and with appropriate humility and awe he would spend the first fifteen to thirty minutes with first-time guests regaling in the surrounds. Nor was Atlas unique in his approach or pride. The great majority of Aspen residents understood that no matter how hard they tried to embellish with their lifestyles and possessions, the magic of the place always began and ended with its geography.

On days such as this, with an unending canopy of radiant blue overhead, guests were served lunch in his living solarium; a large hexagonal-like space forming the center of the complex. It was the linchpin of his architectural vision. The home was actually a series of connecting pods that shared this common space. The eight pods consisted of five master suites, a four-car garage, a conference venue and a kitchen/food staging area. It had no defined shape because the pods were situated to maximize views and function, and the solarium was the residual between and among the pods. Whereas the pods had conventional metal roofing, the solarium consisted of a series of thermopane panels, electronically synchronized to climate and temperature to allow maximum growth of the vegetation within, most of which had been preserved during construction. In its simplest functionality, it was an indoor park. In its practical functionality, it was the main entrance, living room, dining room, reading room and billiard room, all divided and shaped by trees, plants, water feature and stone passages.

In keeping with the ambience of his live-in park, the dining table was more along the lines of a circular picnic table. Unlike the vanilla picnic table on the Rim Trail, this item was cut in a singular slice from a fallen California redwood. It seated eight comfortably. Atlas liked the fact that he was not positioned at the head of the table and that the bench-style seating created proximity, thereby facilitating conversation. "Please, everyone," he entreated, "find a seat at the table. Clay tells me we are in for a special treat."

He often invited small, eclectic groups of friends, business associates, and dignitaries to experience Aspen. Liz, his long-time executive assistant, became the social chairman, scheduling monthly gatherings matching guests' interests to Aspen's seasonal offerings. She planned and coordinated all activities while Clay, the property manager and jack-of-all-trades, served as butler and chauffeur. The result was a series of five-star getaways that rivaled anything the finest travelogues could conjure.

"If you will indulge me while you begin to eat, I would like to make a few introductory comments," Atlas began his canned presentation. "First, a few simple ground rules. As my guests, I hope to indulge your complete enjoyment, comfort, and relaxation. You have already briefed Liz on your needs and wants and I trust your quarters are appointed accordingly. Clay, who you've met, is on site and Liz is also available at all times. Clay can be reached by dialing *1 on your villa phones and Liz can be reached by dialing *2. I would appreciate your presence at lunch and dinner each day, with the expectation that the meals will adjourn to discussion sessions lasting approximately one hour. The remainder of your time should be spent enjoying Aspen. My schedule is posted in your kitchenettes and I welcome you to join me on any or all of my outdoor activities. I have also booked brief one-on-one sessions with each of you. Any questions?"

The General, his closest friend, was among the more frequent guests, and over time understood his cue to help put new guests at complete ease. "Atlas," he started, "I'm excited as always to be here. I can't imagine what trap you plan to spring on us. But for the benefit of K.C., Lauren and Tom, I would like to suggest a hike to the Maroon Bells, a bike ride on the Rio Grande Trail down to Woody Creek, and for some adventure, a shot at kayaking or fly fishing. There are also some great late-night spots for which I will be happy to serve as guide once our host accomplishes his usual 9 p.m. disappearing act."

Atlas did usually adjourn relatively early in the evening. Liz fielded his evening briefing call, after which he checked e-mails, including all scanned and electronically forwarded documents. He customarily spent the next three to five hours analyzing the events and data of the day while planning for tomorrow and beyond.

Atlas freely conceded that his success was due in great measure to his ability to function at high levels on less than four hours of sleep. He once calculated that his nocturnal work sessions over the past forty years were the equivalent of an extra 60,000 hours dedicated to his business pursuits—well above and beyond the nine-to-five weekday pace generally practiced. Daytime was for meetings, dialogue, and execution; the bonus hours for preparation and planning. He knew there were not many people blessed with this gift of time and that he was among the even smaller subset that effectively harnessed the opportunity.

"If you don't mind," began Atlas, "it is my intention to monopolize today's luncheon. I have a fair amount of information to lay out for you, which you can then digest along with your lunch during an afternoon break. I have been waiting to host this event for quite some time and now that you're here, I find myself uncharacteristically giddy.

"Three years ago, almost to the day, I was interviewed by *Fortune* magazine. I had unfortunately gained excessive notoriety a few years earlier when I was added to the *Forbes* annual announcement as one of its newest billionaires. A fact, General, for which I hold you primarily responsible. I granted the interview because I knew the reporter, Lisa Boudreau, would give me a fair shake and, with that, I was hoping to arrest the ambulance chasers who were constantly after 'my story.' The plan pretty much worked.

"During the interview, I was noticeably caught off guard when she asked about corporate succession and the ultimate distribution of my personal wealth. How had I planned my estate? Had I, similar to other vastly wealthy people of late, planned to contribute the majority of my resources to charitable causes? If so, what had I chosen? She pointed out that, being unmarried and without issue, I was arguably the world's most eligible philanthropist.

"Fact is, although I had a well defined corporate succession plan in place, until that moment I had not given the personal side serious consideration. I was only in my late sixties, and at least mentally, wouldn't yet admit to being on the back nine. I had always been charitable, but not in any sufficiently organized or planned fashion.

"Her inquiry has been branded into my brain ever since. It became quite an exhausting burden, dominating my thought process and consuming an enormous portion of my time. I've learned the hard way that it's one thing to gain wealth, but entirely another thing to dispose of it responsibly.

"Early in the process I established a baseline. The bulk of any gift should be unique and independent, and most importantly, I hoped to see results during my lifetime. I also concluded that I would like to be involved; not merely pass along a symbolic check at a symbolic press conference before riding off into the sunset.

"My somewhat infamous retreats here in Aspen are an outgrowth of that interview. Scientists, political and business leaders, philosophers and religious leaders—you name it—I asked all of them the same question: 'If you had a personal estate in excess of one billion dollars and no living family, how would you choose to utilize your wealth?' The discussions were as fascinating as they were totally meaningless. The best answers arose from deep personal passion, causing me to fear that I would never experience that epiphany. My work has been my life's passion. My passion created this wealth, but until very recently, I had no capacity or urgency to consume or distribute it.

"I came to the realization that, in the event of an accidental death, my laissez-faire approach could result in huge sums being negligently paid to Uncle Sam. As a fallback, a few years ago I drew up a list of worthy scientific and philanthropic endeavors and assigned arbitrary values in the case of my premature death.

"Since no one in their right mind should ever give the government one cent too many, I began to wonder how we got here. How did we reach the point where government—federal, state, whatever—had become fiscally irresponsible? I know I'm over-generalizing, but let's face it, our country is the world's greatest economic engine in history and has been for a while. Yet we don't adequately educate our children, we experience intolerable rates of crime and poverty, and we appear to be inextricably in debt.

"We're not talking billions, but trillions. Imagine the possibilities if we could bring a semblance of fiscal responsibility to this process. Imagine the possibilities if, in any year, we managed to salvage just two percent of government waste.

"This sidetrack of mine became a yearlong crusade to examine how we got here and how to change course. I read voraciously, but kept coming back to one document, the Constitution. It's all there. It's supposed to be about checks and balances, about compromise and about individual liberties. That's what we've lost and that's what we have to regain. Congress as the most democratic, little d, was arguably to be the most powerful branch of government. I would suggest it is now a distant third. And states were supposed to have rights. Political parties and special interests weren't a consideration. But it did not take long for their cancer to appear.

"As you may be aware, George Washington felt the need to issue a warning about political parties in his farewell address. Almost 175 years ago, James Fenimore Cooper devoted a chapter to the evils of party in his book *The American Democrat*. Alexis de

Tocqueville, in *Democracy in America*, also focuses on parties, concluding that parties dedicated to principles over consequences, and ideas over men, can lead nations to great things, while parties devoted to self-interest are disruptive. He also found that, in America in 1840, only the latter were in existence. Imagine how he would react to today's political landscape?

"Around the same time, the talking heads on the political shows were fixated regarding whether or not Democrats would gain control of Congress. In reviewing the history of the Constitutional Convention I found no reference to control of Congress by parties. Imagine how the founding fathers would react to the scenario in which the executive, legislative and judicial branches are dominated by one force, one power, as in political parties. But this very scenario has played out repeatedly throughout the twentieth century, with perhaps the worst triangulation occurring over the past six years. From all this, I have concluded that the most egregious abuses of power occur when all branches of government are controlled by one party. No checks and no balances.

"As an outgrowth, I commissioned within my company, Atlas Strategic Consulting, a new area of research. As you may know, the majority of my early work supported and supplemented government functions, first in education and then in the military. We branched out to many commercial applications, but I remained intrigued with government decision making; to some, the ultimate oxymoron.

Our new research quickly morphed into the implications of how public officials view the public psyche and that research morphed into new ways to read this collective psyche. With all due respect to political pollsters, we quickly found that current sampling models are greatly flawed. You see this incompetence play out when news services attempt to predict elections. And it's basically the same modeling used to poll on issues; quite flawed, superficial, and incomplete. The main flaw is that the pollsters are limited to the universe of what was and what is. Even when they pose theoretical questions, they are still limited by the parameters of what current government and current political parties can consider.

"Then I realized it's not about any research, it's about what's inside. The older I get, the more my most important ideas are visceral. I have come to trust the gut over the brain on almost all major decisions—the stomach leads and the brain follows."

"Well," barked the General, "at your age I'm glad you're not trying to lead with your dick."

The subsequent burst of laughter helped to create a relaxed mood for the remainder of the visit. It was a well-timed interruption from an old friend.

Atlas grinned. "You make a good point, General, so I'll try to wrap this up. It's not that I am laying the entire blame for inept governing at the feet of the parties and special interests. Yet I have come to believe that an effective solution to inept governing can come from an upheaval within the two-party system. Let's face it, our society abhors monopolies and would not tolerate such a duopoly in almost any other scenario.

"So the confluence of my thinking is this: I plan to take the majority of my personal wealth and use it to support third-party activities. And, most importantly, I plan to start a new political party."

"I don't mean to burst your bubble," said K.C. shaking her head, "but this has been tried before, and rather unsuccessfully, I may add. Teddy Roosevelt couldn't pull it off and he was beloved. Ross Perot couldn't pull it off. He had more money than you and a nation clamoring for change."

"You're right," Atlas responded calmly. "This has been tried and there have been many failures. Roosevelt got just over 27 percent of the vote and Perot, 19. Not much to write home about. If you look throughout history you will see hundreds of political parties, yet very few have achieved any significant success. In fact, across America today there are dozens of parties and they are lucky to hit a bunt single every cycle or two. The few successes, such as Jesse Ventura winning the governorship in Minnesota, or Joe Lieberman's recent run in Connecticut, have been about individuals. They could not, and did not, translate to party continuity.

"I have spent the better part of the past eighteen months contemplating this idea and it is my hope that at the conclusion of our meetings, you will join me in this effort. Lauren, you have more experience than anyone I know in I.T. General, you have spent your entire life organizing and leading troops and then workers. K.C., you have dedicated your life to the advancement of critical social issues, some of which are more mainstream today than ever before. And, Thomas, if you will indulge me for the time being, you are my secret weapon. Each of you has impeccable reputations for honesty and the highest ethical standards; above all else, our research shows these to be the most important qualities that Americans covet in government.

"What I propose at this time is that we adjourn to a more comfortable venue. I have a bit more to share before we break. That will afford each of you the opportunity to consider and react. I am hoping you will be in a position to start tearing me apart over dinner. Assuming you don't pick the carcass too clean, we can spend the rest of our time together forging our plan."

Atlas mentally stepped back and surveyed his guests. He wasn't sure if they were inspired, in shock, or maybe some of each—but he knew they were totally engaged. In the case of K.C. and the General, it was certainly not the first time he had caught either off guard with a revolutionary idea.

CHAPTER TWO

Alexander "Atlas" Stein was born in Chicago, Illinois, in 1937. He was the first and only American-born member of his family following on the heels of their flight from Nazi Germany. His father, from the second tier of Jewish banking and merchant families in their home country, had managed to liquidate sufficient assets to achieve an equivalent status in America. With the exception of the Friday night Sabbath meal ritual, guilt for those left behind turned his parents from religion. Although Alex always considered himself to be Jewish, his family's spiritual aversion was accompanied by an aggressive cultural assimilation into Winnetka, Illinois, a deliberately chosen non-Jewish community just north of Chicago.

He was a gifted student and athlete, but with the urging of his parents spent the majority of his K-12 years focused on intellectual pursuits. Although he inherited a warm, loving nature and a keen sense of humor from his mother, his parents' unrelenting push to attain academic excellence created a veneer of German stiffness that isolated him socially during high school. His grades and academic awards assured him admission to virtually any college. Although his parents pushed for the nearby University of Chicago, their prodding could not compete with a full scholarship to Harvard and the greater opportunity for cord-cutting provided by geographic separation.

The year 1955 turned out to be a great time for this leave-taking. The wars had ended. The country was in the midst of an economic upswing and Americans felt good about themselves. Later in life, he counted this timing among his blessings. He understood that if he had been born a handful of years earlier or later, his college pursuits would have become intensely political, or the military might have interceded, and either dynamic would have inevitably sent him on a different path. Most importantly, he may have never discovered the person beneath his veneer.

Freshman year was the year of Patrick Covington. They were roommates and opposites. Alex was midwestern reserved and conservative, whereas Patrick was a free-spirited, fun-loving Massachusetts liberal. Alex's hard work had led to a scholarship. Though equally brilliant, Patrick was a three-sport athlete and homecoming king who skated by with grades just good enough to allow dad's alumni pedigree, connections, and contribution potential to secure his placement.

Arriving late for the dorm check-in and finding his roommate deeply engrossed in study in his well organized and compartmentalized half of the room, Patrick's introductory reaction was, "Hello, I'm Patrick Covington," and while extending his hand asked, "What the hell are you doing? Let's grab a beer." Alex shortly found himself dragged to a nearby rowhouse inhabited by several upperclassmen Patrick knew from prep school who kept their kegs cold and continuous. Neither had much recollection of that first day and night together. But as with Bogart and Rains, it was the beginning of a beautiful friendship.

By the end of their freshman year, Alex had emerged from his intellectual cocoon, sprouting social wings on which he would fly throughout his career. He also discovered his night owl genes provided enough time to excel in his pre-MBA curriculum. After Alex kicked his butt on the first round of midterms, Patrick's admiration for his sidekick and his own ultra-competitive nature awakened an untapped intellectual capacity that fueled an award-winning career at Harvard and in future business.

The first test of their bond came late in the year when Patrick became the fourth generation of his family asked to join a prestigious final club. There were expectations in the Covington's Harvard genealogy and final club life was among the more cherished.

Upon arriving at the first club invite with Alex as his guest, Patrick was abruptly taken aside, asked where the friend's name appeared on his engraved invitation, and tersely advised that no Jews were allowed. It was a wake-up call for both of them that led to the mutual realization that Patrick could join the club and fulfill his family duty, while the dynamic duo would flourish outside these unfriendly confines. Their friendship would endure other tests, but would never wane.

Julie Kersten, an enrollee at Harvard's sister school, Radcliffe, was as New York and as Jewish liberal feminist as any movie stereotype. To Alex this was initially disturbing, but ultimately endearing. Unbeknownst to him, she had targeted and virtually stalked him since the first session of their Introduction to Psychology class. Her quest was made all the more challenging by the fact that Alex and Patrick were inseparable, and despite all normal hormonal instincts, the residue of their collective immaturity toward coeds was an inaugural college season dedicated solely to beer, books and baseball, both participant and spectator.

Accordingly, it was not until early spring, on a day when Patrick was conveniently absent from class, that she made her move. "Excuse me," she called to Alex as they left the lecture hall, "I think you dropped this." Having had over four months to hatch her plot, it was rather lame to offer a five-cent pen as a conversation starter. Yet it worked. "No, I don't think so," he blandly responded. But she used the opportunity to introduce herself and make small talk for the next few minutes as she escorted him to wherever he was headed. "Well, this is my dorm," he signaled, and disengaged in one quick motion. While the entire episode was a millisecond, it was long enough for her to leverage into subsequent glances and exchanges for the rest of the year. Not the stuff of romance novels, but her instincts correctly told her that she had started a marathon and not a sprint.

The prior year, Alex's curriculum included the psych class in which they had been seated one row apart. On the first day of sophomore classes, Julie wasted no time in grabbing the seat next to Alex, sans Patrick. He did not initially notice her and then he did not quite recognize her. A summer of camp counseling had provided a tan the Boston winter had drained prior to the pen gambit and, more importantly, the crock pot-like camp food had been the perfect tonic for her to lose the freshman fifteen. Her mother's insistence on a haircut and a modicum of makeup also gave a finished, sophisticated look that last season's ponytail had avoided. He glanced her way when roll was called, and always a quick study, he put two and two together rather nicely during Introduction to Economics.

She patiently waited a few weeks before asking Alex for help understanding the intricacies of supply and demand. Over coffee she quickly moved past economics to "What other classes are you taking?" to "How was your summer?" to "Where are you living this year?" The next class led to an extended cup of coffee. "How did you choose Harvard?" led to a cursory exchange of family backgrounds leading to "You must consider yourself so lucky to have escaped!" Through this discussion, Alex put some revealing and intriguing puzzle pieces on the table. Before parting that day, she secured a commitment from Alex to worship with her at the Hillel during Rosh Hashanah and Yom Kippur. She was from a very devout family and Judaism was her fulcrum. Upon learning the history of Alex's family, she had instinctively formulated plan 1-A.

As the air began to cool, their relationship began to warm. By the end of the year, Julie and Alex developed a deeply emotional yet platonic relationship. Patrick had awakened Alex's social self and Julie had awakened the spiritual. Throughout the year, Alex struck a delicate, fulfilling, and exciting balance of Patrick, Julie and study.

Toward the end of the term, Julie shared her intention to spend the summer on a kibbutz in Israel and asked Alex to share part of the experience. She was well aware that he was scheduled to work with his father to gain exposure to the world of finance, but quickly convinced him this could be a once in a lifetime opportunity. Israel was a young, exciting, pioneering country. Kibbutz life, though physically demanding, promised a dimension of character building and ruggedness quite foreign to life in Cambridge and the northern suburbs of Chicago. After thinking it over and checking with his parents, Alex surprised Julie by accepting her offer. By the end of the summer, he surprised himself by falling in love with her; a place she had found long before.

As juniors, Patrick and Alex moved to an apartment near Boston Common. Julie maintained an address at a women's dorm, but for all intents and purposes, quickly took up residence with them. A situation that could have severely tested two tight relationships, rather quickly and seamlessly evolved into a three-way bond.

Alex correctly sensed that an uncharacteristic Wednesday evening phone call from his mother meant awful news. His father had suffered a heart attack at the office and was in stable but critical condition. "How quickly," she asked, "can you get to Chicago?" As it turned out, not quickly enough.

His father's death stirred troubling emotions for Alex. He wondered if things might have been different if he had stayed in Chicago for school. He felt guilty for missing a summer with his father to travel overseas. He worried about his mother and suddenly had anxious thoughts about losing her too.

Nor did his mother need to ask the most obvious question. She had been a fish out of water in America. Whereas his father was Americanized through his business dealings, she never adequately adapted to the language or the culture. A few days after the funeral he announced to his mother that he had decided to leave Harvard and take up study at the University of Chicago. In addition, he would move back home for the time being. Her tears were all the answer he needed to solidify that he'd made the right decision.

No matter how many permutations she could concoct, Julie could not convince her parents to support relocation to Chicago. She did extort a commitment from them for graduate school, but after waiting one year just to inquire about a lost pen, two years to graduation seemed an eternity.

Julie moved back to her dorm and threw herself into her studies. Patrick moved in with some final club buddies and threw himself into their kegs. They would occasionally grab a cup of coffee when either of them had an Alex update to share. Patrick visited Chicago over spring break and was then able to fill in the blanks for Julie. If Alex wasn't corresponding frequently, it was because his burden was staggering. In addition to maintaining a full load at the U. of C.—not to mention a one hour commute in each direction—caring for his mother was a full-time job and he was desperately over his head when it came to unwinding and settling his father's business affairs.

What Patrick did not share with Julie was the state of despair in which he had found their good buddy. He quickly convinced Alex that his mother needed help with the household. Neither Alex nor Patrick was remotely familiar with the necessary qualifications, but they were savvy enough to locate an excellent agency for live-in domestic help. His father's business affairs were not as easily reconciled, because the solution necessitated Alex confronting his own stubbornness. With the help of Patrick's father, trustworthy and competent connections were made in Chicago with an attorney and an accountant who would work in tandem with Alex.

The surprisingly difficult problem was school. On the last night of the visit, after they were well on their way to passing out over beers, Alex totally broke down. For the first time in his life he was failing in school. His dad had been the inspiration for his pre-MBA studies and he was now questioning and rethinking his career. Bottom line, his motivation had been sucked out by the vacuum his father's death had created. Patrick was out of time and almost out of brain cells, but he was clear thinking enough to convince Alex to open up to his academic advisor.

Alex's advisor had seen the symptoms many times before. A brilliant, accomplished student awakens to the reality that his chosen major, for whatever reason, is not the answer. Although with Alex, the complications of his father's death, his mother's dependency, his exile from the Julie-Patrick safety net, and the change of schools did not lead to a simple prognosis. After a few meetings they reached an accommodation. Alex's midterm grades would be expunged and he would take a leave of absence until the fall. Upon re-entering school, he would devote the next semester, and possibly the entire year, to a well-rounded program of humanities designed to help him locate his educational compass. The advisor also suggested spending the summer anywhere but mommy-sitting in Chicago.

A more focused Alex could easily see that his mother was improving under the guidance of her housekeeper/cook/nanny/female companion. He reasoned that time away would do them both good and he got quite excited thinking about time with Julie, perhaps again on the kibbutz.

If only his breakthrough had occurred sooner. Patrick, playing his new role of counselor, had a month earlier also aided a despondent Julie. Given her passion for politics and causes, he invited her to an early organizational meeting for the junior U.S.

Senator from Massachusetts as he contemplated a run for the White House. Patrick's father was among the financial advisors and had volunteered Patrick to spend his summer on the campaign. Patrick had no interest in politics, but attended some of the preliminary meetings to humor his father until a better offer came along. It did not take much arm-twisting for Julie to accept Patrick's invitation and his instincts were instantly rewarded.

Julie had fallen in love with Alex at first sight and she proceeded to fall in love with the message of Jack Kennedy at first stump speech. Alex might be her future, but the presidential campaign became her present. As phenomenal and unexpected as was Alex's suggestion, she had cast her lot for eighteen months. Alex, kibbutz, and Harvard would have to wait. Under almost any other circumstances, Alex would have also committed to the campaign, the chance to summer with Julie being reason enough. But these weren't any other circumstances and the need to escape to a familiar safe house again lead him to the Promised Land.

Upon his return, Alex was relieved to find his mother considerably stronger, although she did not react well when he suggested he might return to Harvard. Alex also realized that, for all intents and purposes, he was starting college over. He knew it would be challenging to find ways to share time with Patrick, who would be in his senior year. So, a relaxed and invigorated Alex re-enrolled at the U. of C.

Julie had taken leave and returned to New York to second chair the Empire State campaign effort. At twenty-two, she had demonstrated the political instincts of a seasoned veteran. Combined with her boundless energy and chutzpah, she had quickly risen up the ranks, and her home state represented a plethora of electoral votes.

Deep down, Alex had expected to awaken from his educational doldrums and reboard the business world express. However, these expectations were never realized after thriving on the advisor's choice of classes and teachers. Above all, he was fascinated by Professor Joseph Mann's class in child psychology, and by applying the old Alex dedication and drive, he equally fascinated the professor with his potential.

It was early in the second semester that Professor Mann asked Alex to join a group of third and fourth year psychology majors in a project of massive and delicate proportions. Alex was totally unprepared substantively, but his maturity, potential, and energy were more important in this instance.

The professor convened this group of his top students and explained, "As I am sure you are aware, a few weeks ago there was a tragic fire at a local elementary school. I recently discovered that a significant majority of the surviving children are suffering deeply, unable to function in school, and I suspect at home as well. I also suspect the great majority of parents are not coping either. Because of my expertise in child psychology, I approached the school board and volunteered to work with these children on an intensive level to speed their recovery. I need at least six to eight volunteers to assist me and I have chosen this group for that purpose."

Alex raised his hand just as "purpose" entered the air. He could never have guessed the course upon which this gesture would set his life. In just three short years, he would graduate with highest honors with a Masters in Psychology; co-author with Professor Mann the definitive paper on "Stress Disorders of Children Surviving Large-Scale Group Trauma," and receive an offer to join the faculty. In those same three years Patrick would graduate with honors and join a silk stocking Wall Street investment firm, while Julie would forsake graduation for a chance to join the president's White House staff in communications.

Whereas Alex and Patrick would always have the guy thing, Alex was uncertain regarding his geographically undesirable love affair, assuming you could call it that. There had been no one else, particularly given the intensity he had devoted to his degree and research. Having closed the college chapter of the book, he decided to relocate to the East Coast where he could consult, teach and most importantly, rekindle his relationship with Julie. Unfortunately, time worked against him once again as the letter outlining his plan crossed in the mail with Julie's 'Dear John' letter.

When his father died there was regret and second-guessing, but with this letter there was despair and self recrimination. There was no blame with death, but in this instance the blame and the burden were his alone. Fortunately, the best path to recovery was found in his new profession, his new love. He became rededicated and consumed. Over the next few years he built a reputation for himself as the rising star of research and methodology regarding emotional fatigue resulting from large-scale trauma. When he wasn't researching he was speaking, writing, and teaching, all at his twenty hours per day pace.

His reputation grew from national to international and he traveled the globe assisting with large-scale tragedies: mining collapses, plane crashes, chemical plant explosions, and earthquakes, among others. He was hired by governments and large corporations; entities that needed to rapidly address situations and achieve relative normalcy as soon as possible. If nothing else, the job survival of the elected officials and corporate officers who engaged him depended upon his ability to succeed, and to succeed quickly. In addition to the unique research and applications he had devised over the years, he assembled a talented swat team that could travel with him on a moment's notice. He originally marketed his services under the pedestrian banner of Alex Stein Consulting. But as the scope of the assignments ballooned, the size of his team exploded and travel requirements broadened worldwide. At that point, he transitioned to Atlas Strategic Consulting (ASC).

In early 1968, Alex received a call from Major Efriam Salomon of the Israeli Army. Salomon was a fairly common Israeli name, but in this case it belonged to a former acquaintance from his kibbutz travels. The connection was made rather early in the conversation when Alex invoked his time in Israel as an icebreaker. Alex was eager to get caught up with his old friend and the conversation became relaxed and nostalgic for almost thirty minutes. Finally, the major regrouped to his original purpose.

The Six Day War had been a resounding military success, but the thrill of victory had only temporarily overshadowed the casualty and fatality lists. In a country of only a few million people, the six steps of separation from death and suffering had overtaken the population, particularly the children. The major was calling on behalf of the prime minister to seek Alex's guidance on an action plan. Once the connection was made, the major also knew that Alex's presence was imperative and he extended the invitation as an order that Alex was fully prepared to obey.

Although no two assignments bore any resemblance, this one was way outside his box. Whereas most disasters were finite, one-time events, this was the Middle East. Although it was called a war, it was part of a never-ending cycle of fighting occasionally interrupted by peace. Yet for an entire generation, this was the first experience with the atrocities of military conflict. ASC would be up to the challenge, but there would be no simple solution.

Patience was not in Alex's vocabulary, but it was the only term of engagement he negotiated and his client grudgingly acquiesced. Most assignments lasted weeks; this one lasted years. His team first dealt with the children, moved to the adults, and ultimately took on the bureaucracy. Alex quickly understood that he was dealing with both the past and the future. The children and their families would reconcile the past, but the bureaucracy needed to prepare for the future, as the next battle was a certainty. Nothing of this magnitude had been attempted or achieved and his work earned him a nomination for the Nobel Peace Prize.

The next call from Israel came in 1973. Thanks to Alex, years of preparation had avoided a repeat of the civilian trauma that followed the Six Day War, but the price of victory from the Yom Kipper War was an emotional wound to its soldiers. "Alex," his old friend was inquiring, "would you consider using your talents to address the residual trauma of war on our armed forces?"

This time the request came with a large measure of humility and Alex's acceptance came after days of soul searching. It was one thing to rehabilitate the victims of trauma from random disaster, yet an entirely different matter to deal with those trained in military aggression. There was no need to request patience. But because he was uneasy with his subjects, for the first time in his brief career he insisted on confidentiality.

Three long years later, on the final flight back to the states, Alex made a critical personal decision to stop in New York City. He had helped thousands of people recover from trauma and now he desired a personal catharsis.

"Alex! Oh my God! What are you doing here? Come in, come in," announced a hurried, surprised, frantic and wonderfully happy Julie "K.C." Kersten-Covington. "Patrick, Patrick, come quickly, it's Alex." And with hugs, tears, sufficient quantities of alcohol, and then laughs, Alex came to terms with K.C. and Patrick

Covington over the course of the weekend. No one left the house, and of course, no one slept much.

As hard as it had been to write and send, the Dear John letter was the culmination of K.C. and Patrick's sudden and unexpected affair during Kennedy's Camelot. News of the marriage that would follow their elopement could not be avoided and Alex deserved to hear it from them. Patrick had considered traveling to Chicago the chivalrous thing to do, but a letter with each co-conspirator baring their soul was the chosen course. Neither had expected Alex's crossing volley announcing his intentions to relocate to be with Julie, and neither had contemplated spending years in exile from their best friend.

Exile, however, had not meant indifference. They had closely followed Alex's career, with K.C. being most attentive to his work in Israel. She had a network of friends from her time on the kibbutz and was very well informed.

Alex, too, had found it difficult to impose complete separation. Liz was charged with responsibility for tracking the Covington family. To that end, he was well aware of her success in the brief Kennedy administration and her exploits since, particularly her groundbreaking efforts on environmental issues. Patrick had been no slouch, but Alex could not attribute much emotion to the accumulation of great wealth from Wall Street wheelings and dealings.

Their only child, Patrick Covington Jr., was away at school. Harvard, of course! From the pictures and parental bragging, Alex happily came away with the notion that he was the perfect blend of two exceptional people.

The next military call did not come from Major Salomon. It came from General Samuel Huntington Smith, United States Department of Defense, Pentagon, Washington, D.C. The General was the youngest son of a career military officer. He chose the family business and graduated West Point at the top of his class in 1961. A born leader and strategic thinker, he rose quickly through the ranks, and following service with distinction in Vietnam, became among the youngest generals in U.S. history. "We need you in D.C. by noon tomorrow. Can you make it?" This question again sounded like an order and Alex agreed.

His nondisclosure agreement with the Israelis had not run to the rank and file and Alex's supplement to their training manuals became fair game during joint U.S./Israeli military exercises. From there, it did not take much effort to identify or track down the author.

Not totally dissimilar to the Yom Kipper War syndrome was the emotional baggage U.S. soldiers had carried home from Vietnam. To the dispassionate in command, it was decimating the career ranks and obliterating enrollment. To the compassionate minority, there was an obligation to repay a debt for honorable service by providing veterans a successful transition to civilian life. But this was not Israel with a manageable number of soldiers; nor was this a tiny country. Alex and his team required massive resources and, once again, a patient client. Resources were easy for the Pentagon, but patience was not in their vocabulary. Hostilities with the Soviet Bloc were on the horizon.

The next call from General Smith was years later. This time he contacted Alex in his capacity as president and CEO of Freedom Corp., a mid-cap defense contractor. The outcome of the 1976 elections had not been favorable to his politics or career advancement. He had also seen his father hang on too long and he well understood all the sacrifices it imposed on the family, one being financial. Having already qualified for voluntary retirement and an ample pension, he rolled the dice when a headhunter called.

The transition had not been as difficult as expected. His predecessor had also been army trained and, in running the corporation, had borrowed heavily from the military playbook. Unfortunately, his predecessor had died suddenly, and at a very inopportune time, given difficulties surrounding a recent merger. Freedom Corp. had swallowed a larger concern in a hostile transaction and it was not going well.

The General had an intuitive sense for talent, a critical survival skill in combat, and was pleasantly surprised with the quality of his new administrative and management team. But the same could not be said for the team being acquired, and their lack of commitment to the merger was filtering down to rank and file. In the first quarter of the fiscal year, productivity had fallen precipitously and the General correctly sensed that morale was not far behind.

The General had not needed a sense for talent with Atlas Strategic Consulting. Outside the military, no other entity had come close when it came to skills and execution. They hit the ground running and were beyond reproach in drive, dedication, and results. The General also had the good fortune to work personally with Alex and thought him to be among the most gifted and trustworthy people he had ever met. To Alex's pleasant surprise, it became the first meaningful personal friendship he had developed in almost twenty years. The timing was also fortuitous because his mother passed away during the assignment. K.C. and Patrick were there for him emotionally, but the General was also there physically and became surrogate family. Alex had no regrets this time; but that didn't mean he had no sorrow. His work and the General saw him through.

The General understood the connection between his needs and Alex's skills. Corporate mergers are quite traumatic, and even for the survivors, the impact is not unlike the Victorious Soldier Syndrome, as coined by Alex. In this case, Alex discovered that union rank and file bore a unique psychological resemblance to other large-scale trauma victims, specifically including the military. One more unique challenge for his unique talents.

The General also proved to be a shrewd business operative and posed a creative compensation plan that Alex embraced and which, coincidentally, facilitated his meteoric financial rise. The General proposed to pay ASC in phantom stock based on a percentage of the value created for shareholders. Alex, demonstrating his own business acumen, reserved the right to convert the value of these phantom holdings to common stock at a favorable exchange rate. Whereas productivity had, on average, fallen 7 percent in the quarter before ASC arrived, it increased over 20 percent in the year after the assignment was completed. More important to the General and Alex, market capitalization increased more than $350 million. Alex's 1 percent contingency was worth $3.5 million, an amount he converted to common at a two-to-one exchange.

Pleased with the success of their most recent transaction, the General's board of directors set off on an aggressive acquisition program. Rather than wait for issues to arise, the General engaged Alex for each deal from square one. The financial growth of the company was staggering over the next twenty years and Alex and ASC benefited handsomely. Because the unions involved also grew to appreciate gains for their workers, they often brought ASC to the table during mergers and acquisitions.

Against Alex's better judgment, but at the insistence of his management team, Atlas Strategic Consulting went public in the mid-'90s. The value of Alex's shares in this transaction alone were in excess of $400 million.

It was during this financial run up that Alex became better known as "Atlas." Some thought the name stuck because Alex was the heart and soul of his company. Others guessed it was his constant globetrotting. But the simple truth was that his friend, the General, jokingly referred to him as the Atlas of psychologists during an introduction at a speaking engagement. "And, I give you Atlas," was all it took.

CHAPTER THREE

"I hope everyone had a pleasant afternoon, Atlas said brightly. "General, what kind of trouble did you get into?"

"I commandeered Lauren and Thomas and we took a walk down the Rio Grande trail. Not too far. You know how easily I run out of gas my first day here. Each year it takes me a bit longer to get acclimated to the altitude. I might not have ventured out at all if this wasn't such a short visit. Then Clay ran us into town for a quick beer at Little Annie's. Of course, I found time for a few winks when we got back."

"Lauren, Thomas, I don't think either of you has been to Aspen before. How did you enjoy the town?"

Lauren jumped in first. "Great spot! At first blush, it certainly lives up to the hype. I've been throughout the Rockies, but this is the first place that feels like a real town. The other ski resorts are too suburban, too contrived, for my tastes. The smaller fishing holes are just that, smaller and lacking charm. Don't get me wrong, they're all beautiful. I haven't been out during the fall before and I can't get over the panorama. Those aspens set against the evergreens are breathtaking; never seen anything like it."

"I've never been in the mountains and I am simply amazed," added Thomas. "We played at Mile High Stadium each season and I have to confess that it never crossed my mind to head up this way. One of my teammates was from Montana and he always raved about mountain life. Never held much interest for this Southerner, cold weather and all. But, now I know what he meant. I also know what the General means about the altitude. I drank a lot of water, just as Liz instructed. I also crashed."

"K.C.," inquired Atlas, "no hiking for you?"

"Heavens, no," she shot back. "I decided it's never too early to start the holiday shopping. I have always been particularly enchanted by Explore Booksellers and ultimately found myself captive there for over an hour. One of my favorite escape authors has a new book out. I sat down in one of the comfy chairs and next thing I knew, time had flown. We'll call that my nap.

"I also started thinking about your luncheon soliloquy. To my surprise, the bookstore had nothing on third party politics. On my way back, I stopped off at the Pitkin County Library. Again, not much. They were kind enough to provide Internet time and I quickly browsed a few web sites—practically nothing. When I checked Wikipedia, I was caught off guard. I never imagined there are so many political parties currently active in the United States. Other than the Green Party and the Libertarians, and the Liberal and Conservative parties in New York, I've never heard of any of them. I guess that's part of the point you're making; domination by the duopoly as you called it."

"I thought we might at least have the coffee poured before starting on politics," Atlas laughed, "but you present such an inviting segue, K.C. And you're right, at both the federal and state levels, I have found dozens of legitimate, yet totally ineffective third parties. My personal favorites are the Boston Tea Party and the Marijuana Party. If you look at Europe, Israel, and various emerging democracies, there may be dominant parties, usually under some semblance of liberal versus conservative, but there are also plenty of alternatives that have enjoyed electoral success. That's a big difference; our third parties exist on paper, but are almost entirely winless.

"Take Israel's system. Today, their Knesset is represented by twelve different parties out of over thirty that fielded candidates in their last election and they only have three and a half million voters."

"Interesting," the General cut in. "I am thinking about some of my military stops. There is almost an expectation of a multifaceted government. But isn't most of that parliamentary in nature?"

"Yes, it is," responded Atlas. "And there are some key elements of that system that facilitate multiple parties. The fact that the dominant party forms the government compels them to cut deals, particularly when they only have a plurality. When a third party can bargain to provide the votes necessary for a majority, depending upon the margin, they can pick up cabinet positions and jobs. Among other things, that enhances their power base and, I suspect, increases both its public visibility and fundraising capability. With our independently elected executive branch, all the spoils go to the victor. How ironic that one of the factors thought to foster checks and balances may actually thwart it. I have concluded that our winner-take-all philosophy for the presidency and governorships is the single largest factor contributing to the failings of the two-party system. But, that's never changing either.

"The only way I can see for a third party to get a lasting seat at the table is to build its base slowly, but surely, the old-fashioned way; one step at a time. Most importantly, it has to be a legislature-based focus, not executive. If you get lucky, you can pick off enough seats to tip the balance from majority to plurality. While it doesn't offer the same leverage as with our parliamentary cousins, our legislatures contain some very important winner-take-all features that follow majority control. The most important are the elections of Speaker of the House and president of the Senate, respectively. A clear commandment of political power: Thou shall not cross party lines when it comes to voting for Speaker or Senate president. With that comes control of the process, the agenda, and the committees—all the way down to parking spaces."

"But, Alex," interrupted K.C.—as one of his oldest friends, she had never migrated to Atlas—"it's too heavy a lift. The system is designed to inhibit third parties. It's almost impossible to get on the ballot in the first place and with constraints on fundraising, you can't catch up. No money, no media. No media, no votes. No votes, no power. No power, no money. I think that completes the losers' tautology."

"Nicely put, K.C.," said Atlas. "As usual, you get right to the crux of it. And yes, getting on the ballot is quite difficult for third parties. However, for the sake of simplicity, let's assume getting on the ballot is purely a function of manpower. If that's the case, and I believe it is, then money is the only issue. Petition circulators can be bought and managed. And while it is currently impossible to crack the federal system of campaign finance, that is not necessarily true at the state level. There are a few states with enough loopholes to allow for single source, unrestricted funding, particularly for funds contributed at the party level. And, there is one state in particular, Illinois, where there are no contribution limits at any level. For that, and many other reasons we shall discuss, Illinois shall be the petri dish.

"Since I sense K.C.'s wheels spinning again, let me jump ahead a few squares. What I plan to do is fund a trust that will be dedicated to the development and advancement of third party politics. This structure, like most things in business, is tax driven. The trust will fund candidates throughout the United States who meet a predetermined set of standards. At the same time, the trust will devote a significant portion of its assets to the creation of a new third party in Illinois. It is my belief that the success of that party will stimulate and drive the same model in other states and at that point, breed success that overcomes your losers' tautology. If that success can be sustained for just a few election cycles, then the congressional barricade can be assaulted. I don't know if it can all play out in my lifetime, but I plan to be around long enough to enjoy the toddler years. And, I am willing to devote my entire fortune. My initial contribution to the trust will be a minimum of $250 million!"

"Holy shit," the newly animated General exclaimed. "I didn't quite grasp where you were going this afternoon. This is revolutionary. I think you've read too much John Adams and not enough Ben Franklin. Bottom line, Atlas, they will never let you get away with this. They're ruthless and vicious. Your world is about helping people survive. Their world is about gutter combat, tearing people down. As a friend, I advise you to reconsider very carefully."

"Thank you," said Atlas. "I am glad you put that on the table. Before I respond, I would like to get all of your reactions."

"Well," K.C. volunteered, "I am still working on my list of why nots. I agree with the General. This is not your milieu. As you know, I was there for the Kennedy-Nixon television debates. I've been active ever since and it only gets uglier every year. You've obviously thought about my ballot and funding concerns, but they're just the threshold. You need to build an infrastructure, attract quality candidates, develop positions, actually conduct the campaigns—media, press, debates, polling, get-out-the-vote, and on and on. None of this happens overnight, and assuming you're thinking about the next round of general elections, you're only fourteen months out. And that's just the obvious. Give me 'til tomorrow and I will find plenty more nails for your party's coffin."

"Thomas, want to pile on?"

"This is out of my league. Literally and figuratively," replied Thomas. "As a former athlete, I've seen many rich people own teams. Most of the time, they overpay to get in the game. The ones that win stay out of the way, hire good GM's and managers, and build balanced, talented teams. And most win with defense. Politics, that's just not my game."

"Obviously my old friends K.C. and the General don't think it's my game either," Atlas responded graciously. "Lauren, how about you?"

"Not sure. As the General said, this is revolutionary—and it's also scary. But maybe it's kind of good scary. I'm hoping you can pull it off. Why not try? I'm probably part of the silent majority and I think a lot of us would not be so silent if we felt we could make a difference; if our vote made a difference. Most of the time I feel as though I'm just throwing it away. That it just doesn't matter.

"And that's so sad because I feel as though there are so many ways to make a difference, to really do something. The Democrats and Republicans just keep offering more of the same. They talk change, but that just means changing from one party in power to another. What kind of change is that? Are our schools getting any better? Are our tax dollars being spent more wisely? Are we finding the answers? I don't think so.

"The other day I was listening to public radio and there was a feature quoting a range of politicians on how to deal with the latest energy crisis. All of the quotes sounded reasonable. At least until we learned that the quotes were from the early seventies. Over thirty years of doing nothing. It really pissed me off! So, how do I sign up?"

"That's not even it," the General charged in. "Read any of the credible literature and one conclusion screams at you—it's all about short term promises and pleasures designed to get incumbents re-elected. We've dumbed down the electorate, created entitlement after entitlement, and lack the will to do the right, or even credible thing in almost any situation until it festers and boils over. Then it's blame the other guy, march out the talking heads, and above all, obfuscate. It's beyond sickening."

"Well," offered Atlas with a pregnant pause, "I guess Thomas would say I'm batting 250. I was hoping for at least 500. Your points are all well taken. I particularly like the 'revolutionary' part. And K.C., General, you're absolutely right, I am not up to the task. However, as Thomas says, I increase my chances if I bring in some good GM's and managers. And, K.C.'s comments notwithstanding, I have some ideas about where to find them and I think they can be corralled in short order.

"Thomas also raises an interesting standard when he talks about winning. Winning in politics currently means getting the most votes and controlling the most power. General, as you know, winning for me, at least professionally, has meant finding a way to eliminate or at least minimize pain so trauma victims can resume their lives, function again. That's the win I am looking for, at least in the short term. I believe the political system is essentially broken. Although trauma may not best describe our current condition, I think that economically, environmentally, educationally, and for certain ethically, it is in crisis.

"One of the ways third parties win is to have their issues co-opted. And depending how it plays out, that could be our victory. What if, for instance, we lead with ethics and civility and drive reform of government? What price would you put on that? Better yet, what if this new party forces balanced budgeting, addresses global warming, or revitalizes our educational system? I'll bet any of you would have me wager $250 million on that.

"Well, General, you're on! As you predicted, I am calling it an early night. This has been a wonderfully exhausting day. I look forward to seeing all of you at noon tomorrow. Enjoy the balance of the evening and rest well. Thomas, I understand you and I have a relatively early hike scheduled so, General, go easy on him. Good night everyone."

* * * * * * * * * * * * * * * *

The knock at the door was rather gentle, leaving out the possibility that it was Clay. And by now, the General was most likely in his element somewhere in town. Atlas opened the door to find an anxious K.C. "I am sorry to trouble you Alex, may I please come in?"

"K.C., yes, of course." Atlas gestured for her to come in. "What a pleasant surprise! Can I get you anything?"

"No thanks, I'm afraid it will put me to sleep and we need to talk. First of all, I hope you don't mind my coming down on you rather hard earlier. Believe me, I've been there. Any list of horribles I proffer will pale in comparison to what they will concoct.

"But I also want you to know that this idea of yours is absolutely inspired and I completely agree with your closing argument at dinner. If you win by losing and manage to significantly move the established order on any of the day's most pressing issues, there will be no way to adequately measure the accomplishment.

"Alex," she paused as tears began to well up in her eyes, "if only I could help you."

"I don't understand," he frowned.

She took a deep breath and continued. "I know you well enough. Our small weekend group is too neatly packaged. The General is a brilliant choice to lead your campaign, at least in the field. He is seasoned in combat and is renowned for his strategic thinking and leadership skills. I am not completely familiar with Lauren, but by reputation she is an Internet genius. And the Internet is the future for political campaigns. It's not totally clear what Thomas brings to the table, but he is the only minority here. His name is golden in the black community, not to mention sports fans across the country. As for me, Alex, there was a time when no one could have out-compassioned me on the environment or education. How am I doing so far?"

"Not bad for a self-proclaimed has-been," he gently teased her.

"Well, here's where I'm stumped. How do you plan to spend a quarter of a billion dollars? That's presidential election numbers spread over fifty states. I don't think you could spend that in a decade—unless, of course, you're headed to the land of the 527 organization."

"We could be," he conceded. "Sometimes you take what you're given. Congress allows the formation of 527 organizations to influence elections as long as they advocate for issues, not candidates. John Kerry found out the hard way during his presidential campaign. If the special interest groups use them against us, I suspect we'll counter appropriately. But if you ask me, they're all part of the same train wreck, so I'd rather not go there.

"The reality, however, is that only a small portion of the commitment will be spent on third party politics. I intend to create various support organizations to advance the cause. For example, and for lack of a better term, there will be a 'think tank' for issue development and we will sponsor masters and doctorate level studies at key universities. I also envision a candidate training program focused on public policy. Another project, one that really gets the juices flowing, is creation of a totally independent watchdog function intended to help eviscerate business-as-usual campaign tactics. Imagine a group with the stature and resources to effectively monitor and influence the content of campaign messaging.

"I'm guessing as little as $100 million, maybe more like $50 million, will land in campaigns. I plan to provide the seed money for the first election cycle or two, but at the end of the day the party dies quickly if voters do not contribute at the individual level.

"And that's part of why you're here, K.C. Define an opportunity and run with it. There is no one better than you to oversee the development of policy."

"Alex," she said, shaking her head, "it's brilliant, it's amazing, but I can't be a part of it. Patrick has deteriorated significantly. It wasn't supposed to be like this. They said there would be time. And I can't tell how much he knows or suspects. I had no intention of coming out here, but he insisted. I had resolved to keep this from you, but I am now consumed with insurmountable guilt. I can't help Patrick and I can't help you." She pursed her lips in an effort to control her quivering mouth.

"Please, Julie," he startled himself with a name from the past, "it's OK, it's OK." He gave her a warm hug. "There's no guilt. You had nothing to do with Patrick's illness and his level of care has been flawless. As for my plan, we both understand and agree with where your priorities lie." Hoping to comfort K.C., he offered her a nightcap.

He then quickly shifted gears. They talked about old times and worked in a few laughs. They avoided talk of Patrick's illness and imminent death, but it was independently foremost in their thoughts. Atlas still could not believe that his vital, active, and robust friend had fallen victim to ALS.

In the end, they struck a deal. K.C. would help in any way possible as long as no travel was involved. Alex would reach out when he encountered an issue for which he needed the blunt, unadulterated opinion of a trusted friend. She also agreed to sit on the board of the trust along with Alex and the General. Her Democratic party leaning would be an appropriate foil to the General's Republican bent. She would follow the third party plan as it rolled out and call when she could offer constructive criticism. Finally, she would consider his offer to lead the think tank.

The next knock, the General's signature shave-and-a-haircut, came shortly after midnight. The General wasn't much of a night owl anymore, but on visits to Aspen he was capable of a good three-day binge. Despite his good natured kidding earlier in the day, he was quite familiar with Atlas' habits and, over the years, they had done some of their best drinking and soul talking late into the early morning.

"So, how did the kids do?" begged an inquiring Atlas as he opened the door.

"Just fine," answered the General as he entered. "Actually, I like them both. They're quiet, especially Robinson, but they did loosen up. You totally blew them away. Then again, you totally blew me away. And listen asshole, a little heads up would have gone a long way!"

"I know, I'm sorry," Atlas apologized. "I went back and forth quite a few times. In the end, I decided the baseline plan had to be all mine. As much as I value your judgment, I wanted and needed a one hundred percent comfort factor before discussing with you and K.C. Also, by keeping you out of the initial decision, it frees you up to be totally independent in your critique. So, fuck you."

"OK," said a laughing General, sipping his bourbon. "Let's get down to it. What do you need from me?"

"Not much," Atlas responded tongue-in-cheek. "I just need you to serve as a co-trustee of the funds and honcho the day-to-day field operations. The entire effort requires military precision, maybe not military style. I'll leave that to you. But definitely precision."

"You never said no to me. If you need me, I'm yours. But I don't know shit about politics. Hell, I might be head of the Joint Chiefs by now if I did."

"Well, I don't agree. You're confusing politics, little p, with political parties, big P. You understand the politics of ordinary life better than anyone I have ever met. And you're a great leader. The people around you understand that you do not confuse bullshit politics with the agenda. It's one thing to translate that in the military, but entirely another in corporate America. You've done both with great success."

"Thanks," said the General. "You could be right. But at the same time it's not like I haven't been around the block. I've seen what these people do. They'd rather start a fucking war than lose an election. They don't give a shit about how many die on their watch for the wrong reasons. They get to a point of self-righteousness that allows them to justify almost any action. You know the absolute power cliché. What I'm trying to tell you is that you can never blink. They will attack you personally; they'll attack me. They'll go after anyone and anything in their way. You have to be ready to fail, to be disgraced, and to be wiped out. I can get there because I've been there. I've had men die because of my mistakes.

"More than ideas and elections will be at stake. It may only be death by reputation or financial ruin, but that's what your troops will be up against. Can you handle that responsibility? And I'm not telling you not to. In fact, and I didn't come ready to say this, the whole thing excites the hell out of me. What kind of General would I be if I turned down this war? I was born for this.

"I've got my own solution," he concluded. "It's called leadership. It's called trust. Where are the Washingtons and Lincolns when you need them? My friend, get all the checks and balances you want. But, at the end of the day, let's get some fucking leaders, too."

"I hear you," Atlas said. "Trust me, I hear you. Let's pick it up tomorrow, only…," he burst out laughing, "try not to hold back anymore. And just so you know, K.C. beat you here by almost two hours."

They were the two people in the world he trusted with his life and their reaction was identical. They were talking about a cost he had not totally considered, at least not yet.

CHAPTER FOUR

"Good morning, Thomas. How did you sleep?" inquired Atlas cheerfully. "Actually, that's not a fair question. The altitude makes people sleepy and a night out with the General has been known to set back many a biological clock."

"I slept very well, thank you, whether it was the altitude or the General. But I also woke early and never fell back. You got me thinking yesterday. I can't say one way or the other about your ideas. I have a bit put away myself and I'll be damned if I've given my own affairs enough thought. At least now I know how you felt when you got done with that reporter."

It was another beautiful day in paradise and without giving the matter much thought, Atlas decided Thomas could handle the Rim Trail. He might not make it the whole way, but as this might be his first and last trip to Colorado, there was no better memory to create for his guest.

Thomas proved to be in great shape. One of his earliest mentors had counseled him on keeping in shape year-round during his playing days. Said too many guys lost it during the off season. The older they got, the harder it was to spring back. Staying in shape year-round had the advantage of losing less and extending the career. Thomas found this reasoning compelling and attributed that advice to his career's longevity.

Following retirement, he had resolved to maintain his regimen. He had seen too many retired colleagues looking six months pregnant after a few years. And, he intended to remain an ambassador for the sport. How, he asked himself, can you preach the value of sports if you look like a couch potato?

His initial foray into the world of kids was to endorse and sponsor a city-wide little league program in Chicago, his adopted home town. He reasoned, correctly, that it would help keep the kids off the streets during the summer months. Besides, he still loved the game and he actively participated in coaching, clinics, and an occasional umpiring stint. At the end of each season, he put together an all-star team and sponsored their entry and travels to the national championships. All great fun, but not enough to keep him feeling sufficiently active or engaged. However, he turned down offers to coach in the minors. The lifestyle was marginal at best and he had no aspirations of playing out that particular string.

At one of the many banquet tributes he attended, he was asked to introduce one of his former teammates; normally the kind of situation that would buckle the knees of this proud gladiator. The circumstances forced his hand and he acquiesced. He had last faced a similar challenge a few years earlier when serving as his cousin's best man. At least that crowd was family and, more significantly, he had time to prepare. Fortunately, he recalled some safe jokes that fit the mood of the tribute and it served to loosen him to the point of appearing semi-glib for his two minutes of waxing extemporaneously. On both occasions, a few preparatory shots of whiskey hadn't hurt either.

Seated in the crowd was a lieutenant from the Commissioner's office who came away impressed with both the brief performance and the crowd's obvious and undying affection. Within a matter of days, he was officially recruited into the Commissioner's Ambassador Club; a feel good, do good, PR program consisting of retired major leaguers willing to travel the country, sign autographs, and talk baseball. A star had been reincarnated. Eventually, this became a full time avocation and, with training and coaching, he ultimately came into demand as a speaker.

After a while, he felt the need to expand his repertoire. It was wonderful to share some jokes and humorous anecdotes from his playing days, but he wanted the kids in the audience to take away his appreciation for the non-athletic elements that had shaped his emotional and intellectual growth. With the blessing of the commissioner and the aid of a speechwriter, he crafted a message of teamwork, sacrifice, and striving for excellence that shortly made him the most requested ambassador in the program.

His rise to prominence as a promotional speaker caught the attention of the corporate world and he shortly found himself on the B level speaking tour for corporate outings and their customary golf, spa, five-star trappings. In hindsight, he often wondered why it took him almost four years to realize it was a total waste. Gone were the kids, the parent-child bonding and the only audiences that took home the message. And although there wasn't a prejudiced bone in his body, the corporate stuff was all fifty-plus white guys. He did a quick one-eighty from rubber chickens and recommitted his efforts to kids, especially those living in poverty.

"I hope I did not embarrass you with my secret weapon wisecrack," Atlas apologized, "but I needed to meet with you one-on-one and being cutesy seemed like an adequate diversion. I think it worked because both the General and K.C. cornered me last night and neither seemed too focused on your place at the table. I imagine most people are thrilled to be in the presence of a baseball icon, at least I always am."

"Think nothing of it," said Thomas. "Your friends have been quite gracious. The refreshing part is that no one asked for an autograph and our sidebars yesterday were about anything but sports. When I got your invitation, I figured this would be about more than hikes and pinot noir."

"By the way, I've been curious for some time. Where does 'Jackie Jr.' come from?" Although they had known each other for almost twenty years and talked baseball incessantly, he had always been Thomas, and Atlas had never inquired. Actually, it was Liz who wanted to know.

They had become great friends and Thomas never missed taking a quick shot. "Even though you white guys think we all look alike, in this case I guess we do. My first manager played with the real Jackie and insisted on the resemblance from the get-go. Our common surname didn't hurt either. Since all rookies need a nickname, it fit like a proverbial baseball glove."

"Thomas 'Jackie Jr.' Robinson, welcome to my favorite spot in the entire world," Alex said when they reached the bench. "I come here maybe fifteen times a year. I come to escape and I come to think."

In the blink of an eye, Thomas understood the special nature of their destination. They had reached the top of the world. He also knew there was no need to state the obvious; that he had never seen anything like it in his entire life.

* * * * * * * * * * * * * * * *

Thomas Robinson was born in Camden, New Jersey, in 1954. His family was somewhere between lower middle class, according to his father, and upper lower class, according to his mother. Although he had not been raised Catholic, his parents sent him to parochial school to better his education. In the Robinson household, education and 'love thy neighbor' were always stressed. With his mother's untimely death from lung cancer, his father moved the family to Texas where a support network from his father's side was ready, willing, and able. When it became apparent that the educational opportunities were lacking, his father supplemented with a tutor. The tutor discovered that Thomas was quite intelligent and delighted in the opportunity to advance his skills far beyond his grade equivalent.

About the time that Thomas was displaying his academic prowess, his gym teacher was discovering his marvelous athleticism. All students in Texas were tested in the sixth grade across a wide range of skills measuring strength, speed, and endurance. Thomas' scores were off the charts. He had never participated in organized sports, but the scores prompted a further assessment by the athletic coach and, by the eighth grade, he was excelling at track in the fall, basketball in the winter, and baseball in the spring. As with most teenage males, Thomas gravitated to sports over scholastics. By his sophomore year, he was on pace for all-state status in all three sports. College coaches started sniffing around, and by the spring of his junior year, they were in full court press mode. He was conflicted at every level; whether to go in-state or out-of-state; whether to emphasize basketball or baseball or track; big vs. small; etc. His father, not overly warming to the process, insisted on the best educational choice.

Suddenly, there was another option. A scout from Chicago came calling with an offer that made young Thomas Robinson breathless. It included more money than he could imagine and lofty predictions of playing major league ball. Much to his father's dismay and disappointment, college was bypassed for a one-way ticket that ended up covering his travel for the next twenty-two years. Final destination: Cooperstown. But it also came with a price. Despite his promises to his father, he never made it back to school. Further, he never could square the traveling and playing schedule with marriage or a normal family life.

* * * * * * * * * * * * * * * *

They sat quietly on the bench for some time. Atlas knew there was no rush and Thomas was taking it all in, slowly and deliberately.

"I've brought my digital camera," said Atlas, finally interrupting the moment. "Please help yourself to a memory or two."

"Thank you," said Thomas. "I'm not much of a camera person. Most of my life I've been on the other side of the lens."

"Now that you mention it, maybe I should snap a few with you included. Which direction is your favorite?"

"How about all of them?" Thomas quipped.

"I tend to agree, but I'm partial to Mt. Sopris," said Atlas pointing due west. "Roughly 13,000 feet of Mother Nature's finest, and quite majestic, don't you think?"

"Yes, but can't we both get in one?" asked Thomas.

"Sure, let's wait 'til someone passes through. In the meantime, let's talk. Have a seat.

"As I mentioned yesterday, I have spent a great deal of time researching the political history of our country. In doing so, my attention has continuously been diverted to the convoluted evolution of race relations, particularly in politics; from slavery to emancipation to civil rights to voting rights. And that's obviously skipping huge chapters. Lincoln is regarded by many as the greatest president because he freed the slaves. And, thanks to any number of people from Rosa Parks to Martin Luther King Jr. to President Johnson, we have a recent legacy of civil rights."

"And let's not leave out the Supreme Court," Thomas was quick to add.

"But," Alex continued, "when I try to equate freedom and civil rights to educational and economic gains, I don't see where enough has changed. At best, there are smatterings of wealthy blacks and my guess is that the majority of that cohort is from entertainers and athletes, such as you. Peel back another layer, and there are pockets of professionals and businessmen, but certainly no such thing as a significant black middle class. By comparison, almost every other group that came to America after the Civil War, whether by ethnicity or race, has found greater economic power.

"I sometimes wonder how Atlas Strategic Consulting would have responded to certain situations. Imagine trying to cope with the trauma of the Chicago fire or the Titanic? Hiroshima? The Holocaust? Unimaginable! But the granddaddy of them all would have been the Civil War. I guess what I am trying to say is that our country never came to grips with the trauma of that war. It never came to grips with the trauma of millions of people being set free."

"I have a sense of where you're trying to go," Thomas assured him. "I've spent most of my retirement trying to give back and I have a message that resonates one-on-one. But it just seems like a drop in the bucket. I get kids for twenty minutes of their life. So what?"

"Well at least you're trying. Giving back. You should take comfort in the effort. And that's why you're my secret weapon. Black voters are, by far, the greatest voting bloc in America. As I see it, that means they are either the most powerful force in politics or the most taken for granted. And I think we both know the answer to that one.

"So if we borrow from my approach to goal setting in the context of this third party, by better educating, empowering, and emancipating the black voter, we force the current party structure, in this case the Democrats, to legitimately earn the black vote. In the alternative, we earn the black vote and use that leverage to drive the agenda. To that end, I am specifically suggesting educational gains as the fulcrum of the party's initial platform. My personal view is that the educational system has not been sufficiently responsive to the black community and that some innovative, yet relatively simple fixes will go a long way."

"Amen to that," Thomas acknowledged.

CHAPTER FIVE

Atlas had hoped to do less talking and more listening at lunch, but was surprised with his guests' apparent edginess. Not even the General seemed poised to volley and, after exchanging daily pleasantries about how everyone slept, what they had done in the morning, and other idle chitchat, no one bothered to push any pawns into the open. Atlas, never one to let pregnant pauses languish, made the first move.

"With all of fifteen hours of reflection, although you have identified some legitimate hurdles, I remain committed to my third party aspirations. There is obviously much to be done and I hope you will all be with me. Today, I think our time can be best utilized if I expand on two items: why Illinois, and, ideas about establishing the third party. We can discuss Illinois at lunch and save the platform for dinner.

"The political climate in the Land of Lincoln is as dysfunctional as any place in the world. And that may be an understatement. Although you are the first friends with whom I have discussed my plans, I did engage a political consulting firm to assess the political landscape in a variety of states. I've asked Clay to leave a complete copy of the Illinois report in your rooms this afternoon. What I think will blow you away is that the report predates any of the allegations surrounding Blagojevich and his cronies.

"The plan is based on a go-slow approach predicated on creating a legislative beachhead in the first election cycle. Our research suggests that, to the extent voters are willing to take a chance on a new party, it is more likely to occur on a less highly regarded office such as state senator or state representative; 'down ballot' as they call it. Illinois helps in that regard because they did away with straight party voting. It also registers quite high on the corruption meter.

"Not long ago, on a trip that unfortunately took me through O'Hare Airport, an editorial in the *Chicago Tribune* caught my eye. It was lamenting the plethora of criminal investigations then reportedly being conducted by grand juries, primarily federal, across a wide range of governmental entities. The state's former governor, name's Ryan, had been indicted and ultimately convicted. Chicago had a major trucking scandal with alleged tentacles throughout city government. Upon digging further, I learned these were just the veritable tips of the iceberg."

"You know," interrupted K.C., "I read about Governor Ryan. Interesting character. As I recall, he was found guilty of a variety of financial fraud type issues, but at the same time he was apparently being considered for a Nobel Prize. How's that for controversial? He imposed a moratorium on the death penalty and ultimately commuted the death sentence of more than 150 convicts on Death Row. Some say it was an inspired, bold move and others speculate it was part of a longer range strategy to either avoid his own trial or at least greatly reduce his sentence. Personally, I don't care. I have no issue with the death sentence as the ultimate club so to speak, but our justice system appears to be sorely lacking. Statistically, if you're rich, you get the right counsel and avoid the harsh result; if you're poor, particularly a minority, you're cooked—pun regrettably intended."

"K.C., I totally agree with you," Thomas jumped in. "I am not as well versed on the death sentence, but our prisons are disproportionately filled with young black males. Blacks made up 13 percent of the population and 37.5 percent of all state and federal prisoners. I mention those numbers all the time when I talk to kids. Atlas, what does your third party plan to do about them apples?"

"Thomas, those are terrifying statistics. Along the same lines, there are three other key statistics that I recently saw that grossly offended me. One in six Americans does not have health insurance, one in four Americans does not graduate from high school on time, and one in five American children live in poverty. Sadly, I have subsequently seen articles from other highly respected journals suggesting these numbers are all too low. At the risk of being insultingly simplistic, I think the third party can help immensely in two critical areas—education and jobs, particularly for minorities. What hope is there for the 25 percent that doesn't finish high school or the shocking percentage of teens having kids out of wedlock—not to mention the babies—the next generation of burdening statistics.

"When I read Jared Diamond's book, *Collapse: On The Downfall Of Civilizations*, one of my take-aways was the failure to both recognize and act upon compelling threats in a timely fashion. So unless we want to go the way of Easter Island…"

"Easter Island?" quizzed Lauren.

"Yes," answered Atlas. "Death of a society by deforestation. Exactly where we're headed if we fail to nurture and grow the youth of America instead of maintaining the human forest needed to sustain us. We are creating an intellectual and emotional wasteland. Our political system defers difficult issues to times of monumental crisis and the failures of our educational system are not perceived that way."

"That's where I was going yesterday," Lauren piped in excitedly. "Whether it's energy, education, global warming…you name it. I look at our political leaders. I see interchangeable bobble heads that have collectively failed over the course of my adult life. We squander too many resources and too many opportunities. It makes me sick just thinking about it."

"You're not alone," confided Atlas. "Unfortunately, your great silent majority is too silent. Our research shows two significant, yet opposing outcomes. There is enormous pent-up energy waiting to break down all barriers to effective government. But, at the same time, the political structure keeps this energy harnessed. Voters have been totally emasculated. Actually, it's more like they are in a politically induced coma. To your question, Thomas, awakening this sleeping electoral giant is, alone, a crucial part of the remedy.

I apologize, but Clay is signaling that we need to break at this point. If you have time this afternoon, please peruse the memorandum on Illinois. Lauren, still up for fly fishing?"

"Actually," inserted K.C., "before we break I'd like to put a thought on the table. And contrary to Alex, I have no research to support my position. But I have often wondered this—what is behind all of the negativity in politics? The constant attacking, the constant undercurrent of darkness and futility. And how much of this is also about deflating expectations, deflating turnout, and therein perpetuating the status quo? General, how do you attack such an enemy without sinking to their level? If I were them, the quicker I could bring the third party to the lowest common denominator, the quicker I could write its epitaph."

"K.C., I know better than to cut you off, but negativity in politics is a topic for which we will need considerable time to address."

"Maybe so," she conceded. "But if you truly want to distinguish your party from the others, I suggest you add some civility to the recipe."

* * * * * * * * * * * * * * * *

MEMORANDUM

TO: Atlas
FROM: Mark Stone
SUBJECT: Political Analysis Regarding Third Parties—Illinois

One of the toughest hurdles in Illinois politics is getting on the ballot. The Republicans and Democrats have ridiculously low petition requirements, whereas third parties have ridiculously high requirements. By way of example, as "established" parties, Republican and Democratic candidates for governor each need 5,000 signatures, whereas a "non-established" party needs 25,000. Assuming you obtain ballot status, more or less a function of manpower, the news gets much better. Polling shows that the political climate in Illinois has reached new depths for distrust and disdain. There are many reasons for this:

1. The actual and perceived corruption at all levels of government is off the charts; particularly as measured by the totality of politically related indictments and convictions. According to a *Tribune* article referencing work by political scientists at the University of Chicago, since 1970, 1,000 public officials and businessmen were convicted of public corruption in Illinois, including three governors, nineteen Cook County judges, and thirty Chicago aldermen. And it reaches all levels of government. If only a portion of the current rumors of potential indictments are accurate, the trend shows no signs of abating. One of the things I find totally inconceivable is the number of political crooks who concocted and perpetrated crimes when the U.S. attorney was known to be aggressively on the attack.

2. Political nepotism is rampant. Sitting politicians blatantly stock the employment rolls with every known variety of relative. Further set forth

in the printout, there are hundreds of high ranking second and third generation office holders who were virtually bequeathed their spot. Politics in Illinois, particularly in Cook County, is a family business. No politician will rock the system because it's a bipartisan trough. But, an independent third party could totally rock this world.

3. Illinois has no limits on campaign contributions and "pay to play" politics has achieved new levels of legal extortion. It's so ironic that politicians and their cronies are going to jail in record numbers when the legitimate system is so efficient. The only requirement is public reporting. The number of associations and unions contributing high six (and occasionally seven) figures in an election circle is stunning. Six figure gifts from individuals and families are also commonplace.

4. Illinois is a fiscal disaster at all levels of government, a result of which is a unique vulnerability in recessionary times. The state is beyond broke using any economic or accounting lens. This has just begun to play out; particularly in cuts to essential services and massive amounts of deferred payments.

All this is well documented by the press and adds to a growing stress that the voter has no voice in government. Ironically, it is reflected in meager registration and turnout because the two-party system does not project a solution. Any third party that can reverse the apathy and drive turnout can be successful. This is, in fact, the venting that occasionally produces personality driven victories for independent candidates. However, it has yet to be sufficiently harnessed by a third party organization.

By no stretch of the imagination should you think that victory is easily achieved. As a political consultant, I continuously marvel at how effectively the two-party system has dumbed down the voters and their expectations. The amount and quality of information used to decide elections is paltry. Even the best-intended and well-founded third party faces a daunting task to engage the electorate in the blink of any election season. Apathy is so embedded that it generally takes some seismic event, such as a recession or military threat, to awaken the beast and such events are neither predictable nor staged; except, of course, by Robert DeNiro and Dustin Hoffman.

Finally, and curiously, Illinois is better attacked by a new political party during a presidential election year, such as next year. At the presidential level, Illinois has not been competitive for at least twenty years. All Democrat all day, when it comes to the White House. Conversely, Illinois elects its statewide officers, such as governor, during the non-presidential election cycle.

What all this means to a new party is that, with sufficient funding, their message can be adequately voiced. If Illinois were to be in play for president, a nascent third party could shout their message from every rooftop and still not be heard. They would never get the air time or attention from the media necessary to compete.

CHAPTER SIX

Fly fishing is not your Tom Sawyer pole, string and worm exercise. It requires split-second reaction time once the fish offers at the synthetic, simulated insect. It requires cunning, balance, and agility to ford the swiftly moving stream and its slippery bottom while quietly stalking. It requires timing and touch to cast. Much to Atlas' chagrin, it also requires keen eyesight to coordinate the entire activity. Regardless, it had become one of his favorite escapes.

Lauren Chevez de la Rosa had never been fly fishing and, as Liz would report, her reaction to the suggestion was far less than enthusiastic. But Atlas instructed Liz to persist. He knew Lauren exceedingly well and understood that, like him, an afternoon of trout failure would excite the hell out of her.

She may not have been born with the competition gene, but being the youngest, and the only female, out of seven siblings certainly sharpened her survival skills. Her family had emigrated from Argentina, slowly but surely, over a period of twelve years during the sixties and seventies. Dad came first, working in Southern California. Her brothers followed, sequentially by age, whenever finances permitted. Baby Lauren came with mom in 1978 at age thirteen.

Not unlike many American immigrant success stories, the family found education. All seven children graduated from high school. She and two brothers graduated from college. They were also instilled with an insatiable work ethic.

Notwithstanding the explosive potential she exhibited, family tradition kept her tied to failing parents. Her undergraduate degree was in computer sciences, but her graduate program was tending to sickly parents and overseeing the family's hosteria in a moderate sized Southern California town.

The fact that she had never exhibited any culinary talents whatsoever soon became her greatest asset. Any self-respecting cook could replicate the family recipes, leaving management and marketing to her. With her parents content to enjoy their remaining sunsets, she was free to experiment with the many ideas they had so quickly dismissed over the years. In short order, she was overseeing seven establishments.

The growth of the family business did not escape the attention of a food service industry constantly seeking a new taste and a new spin. A six-month-long series of family negotiations culminated in an agreement to sell, provided Lauren's role in the conglomerate would insure the integrity of their product and, more importantly, the family name on the door.

Very few are blessed with the talent to do it all, but she was extraordinary. The whirlwind of the next fifteen years included both a nationwide launch and a loving, well-nurtured family. She had once thought she would match her parents, but stopping at a boy and a girl was an easy decision. Because of her gifts, whether at home, in business, philanthropy, whatever, her challenges rarely became much other than opportunities.

The one challenge that did not result in an opportunity was the episode that brought Atlas Strategic Consulting into her life. A unique bacteria had traveled from Argentina to the states in one of their food shipments and an unprepared inspection regimen had failed to guard against the threat. To compound matters, this particular bacteria only presented after weeks in the blood stream, long after voluminous sales of their signature dish that relied on the infected ingredient.

Without the quick and decisive actions of Lauren and ASC, the unfortunate deaths and illness would have been equally fatal to the family brand. Mistakes, whether avoidable or not, were publicly acknowledged. The cause was quickly determined and isolated. Following the ASC model, all aspects of the matter were handled with dignity, compassion and a great deal of doing unto others. Perhaps the most stunning aspect was the total absence of litigation.

Although she was nationally acclaimed in the restaurant world for her response, and the family name took on new meaning for quality and integrity, she brought this chapter of her business life to an abrupt close. At a personal level, the deceased patrons were an insurmountable burden. Accordingly, she abruptly retired to devote herself to her husband and children.

Atlas had developed the utmost respect for her considerable talents and was certain that her self-imposed retirement would not be an adequate response. Family time and a loving environment would provide healing; but the total cure required newfound success and achievement to restore confidence lost. Although she declined his reasonably persistent offer of employment, he was able to periodically entice her to assist with short-term consulting projects.

Her hiatus also coincided with the explosion of the Internet. She immediately grasped the potential of the new medium and, divorced from the rigors of business, had ample opportunity to homeschool herself in the intricacies of this new world. The inspiration for a new business model was shortly upon her and she brought her concept to the one person she could trust—Atlas.

* * * * * * * * * * * * * * * *

"Well, let's go," offered a very chipper Lauren to Atlas and Clay. She was dutifully adorned in the fishing attire and paraphernalia that had been placed in her room. Clay had already packed the car with other necessary equipment and they quickly set off.

"I never expected such an emotional response from you to my ideas," Atlas noted. "You are always so measured and controlled in business, even in the most trying circumstances."

"I think it's the mother in me doing the talking," she said. "Over the past few stay-at-home years, like you, I have started to view the world more viscerally, or should I say hormonally, than through balance sheet colored glasses. Our business was heavily regulated, but it was generally translatable into quantifiable cost items. No smoking in restaurants. I can take that on. Checking workers' papers, providing health coverage; O.K., what's it cost? And can I raise prices to cover it?

"Of late, I'm more focused on the world my kids will grow into. Despite all the technology and individualization, their schools produce a product inferior to the learn-through-repetition crap I suffered through. I want my kids having it better than me. They are financially set for life, but seem to face many more daunting obstacles than we did. And we lived in poverty, separated by continents. So sure, I can get emotional."

"Well, I need that focused, calculating business woman," Atlas pushed. "Your Internet applications will be critical to our new party. I need you to come on board full-time and help develop the next generation of interactive communication for political campaign application. Imagine the ability to have the public instantaneously participate in the process. Imagine our elected officials being able to canvass electronically on any issue before they vote. We're talking about the ultimate tool in democracy."

Lauren's eyes widened. "Wow," she said, "I'll have to think about it. But if I get where you're headed with this, then yes, the Internet is clearly the way to go."

"Sorry to interrupt," Clay offered. "We're about to turn off Highway 82 and pass through Basalt on our way up the Frying Pan. I was born here and the Frying Pan is still my favorite fishin' hole. Basalt's smaller and quieter than Aspen. More like Aspen was before the billionaires threw out the millionaires. Sorry, Atlas, you know what I mean."

"No offense taken as long as we catch lots of fish!"

"Can't guarantee. But we always try. Lauren, you'll have to hop out here. We need to get you a fishing license."

* * * * * * * * * * * * * * * *

"I'm happy to announce that Aspen has its newest convert," proclaimed a proud Atlas later that afternoon to the assembled guests. "Not only did Lauren out-fish Clay and me combined, but she had us detour to an outfitter on the way back and now owns half their inventory."

"Maybe only a third," offered a blushing Lauren. "There is no doubt that I also got hooked today. Can't wait to turn on Jack and the kids. I don't know if it was the serenity or the fly fishing. Considering I can't tie any of the knots, can't tell one fly from the other, and couldn't cross the cascading water alone, it was still amazing. Thanks again."

"You're welcome," said Atlas. " And in your honor, we're blowing off Liz and drinking tequila tonight. When you get home, you'll now have two fish tales. The one about kicking our butts and the one about creating a third party. What do you say we get dinner? General? K.C.? Thomas? How did you spend the afternoon?"

"I'm happy to report," said the General, "that I got these two on horses and we took a very scenic trail ride out to the Maroon Bells. We caught a break and arrived to clear skies. Any photographer worth his Nikon would have killed to be with us."

"I hadn't ridden since my childhood days in Texas," followed an obviously pleased Thomas. "Makes you wonder where the time goes."

"Wonderful, Thomas. That makes me happy. And K.C.," said Atlas, "I'm not sure what could have brought a bigger smile to my face today. Lauren's first catch or you on a horse."

K.C. grinned. "I still don't know how they conned me. I didn't fall off, which may have been the best part. But I am indebted to the General because the scene at the Bells was truly a once in a lifetime experience. My sentiments run with Thomas. Atlas, you're a lucky man."

"I am unbelievably lucky and grateful. But please, let's dig in. Bon appetite!

"I'm sensing not too many brain cells were devoted to thoughts of Illinois today. So, rather than get bogged down in politics, I've had Liz dig up seats for tonight's performance at Aspen's Theater in the Park. I don't know what's playing, but any show I've ever seen there has been excellent."

* * * * * * * * * * * * * * * *

"Well, children," began an excited Atlas, as they convened on their getaway morning, "today is graduation day from Third Party 101. Best of all, there will be no final exam. But you must promise to be good boys and girls and participate in class. Liz tells me the first wheels are up at one thirty. That should give us just enough time.

"In case you hadn't noticed, I've managed to avoid the toughest issue facing any political party. Just as it's easier to buy than sell, in our political world, it is significantly easier to win elections than to govern. Even the most gifted elected official will lose sufficient credibility over time to suffer defeat. That is particularly true the higher the office and in the world of television-facilitated, sound bite, attack ads. K.C., that negativity you wanted to address.

"The hard part is in governing. Not just governing to the polls, but governing to achieve goals; to stand for something. The Democrats and Republicans set meaningless party platforms to assuage their donor base. But they generally end up on the cutting room floor right after the election results are tabulated. The platforms bring in the contributions, but they do not bring reform. Nothing can either irritate or make me chuckle more than the candidates who run on change when their party's platform is virtually identical to its siblings. You know that old expression, 'the more things change, the more they remain the same'? Well, bingo.

"The new party has to stand for something, and I insist it be measurable. Thomas, we touched on this the other day; education has to be the centerpiece. In addition, ethics and the economy. By the economy, I mean the whole nine yards: the budget, capital, jobs; making sure the public gets value for its tax dollars. I am convinced that improvements in public education can be adequately measured, although for me, it has got to be more than grades and test scores. Similarly, there are myriad ways to measure taxes versus value. The tough one is ethics. With major ethics reform, I'm not sure you ever know if what you're measuring is accurate."

"Atlas," started an impatient K.C., "I was wondering when we would get around to, as you call it, standing for something. But you've gone for the wrong, low-hanging fruit. Everyone running in the Illinois legislature will be running on education and taxes. That's the circular soap opera to which Lauren referred. When it comes to Democrats and Republicans, the expectations are set so low that it doesn't matter that they aren't worth the paper they're written on. When it comes to education and economics, there are lots of reasons nothing gets done. And ethics? Good luck with those leopard spots.

"If you're stuck on the letter E, I'd lead with the environment. It's more timely than ever with global warming and the price of gas. And, its very measurable. Every windmill, every hybrid car, every fluorescent light bulb has a calculable, positive impact on the carbon footprint. Best of all, the technology is ready, willing, and able once government gets its act in gear."

"Points all well worth taking, K.C." said Atlas. "A good addition as long as the message isn't too watered down. Up until now, the Green Party has the issue staked out. But they have never had the resources to take a real political run. On the other hand, please know our research also shows that it isn't high on the voter's screen. Sure it's timely when gas prices spike, but that phenomenon unfortunately, at least from a political perspective, fades rather quickly once prices stabilize. Having said that, if and when your time permits, it's part of the program.

"Most importantly, no matter what issues we focus on, we can't run from diluted expectations. My thinking may be convoluted in the world of American politics, but it's standing for something, and the legitimate raising of expectations that will set us apart.

"Let the Democrats and Republicans have the left and the right; to me, it's about starting in the middle. We branch out once we create core strength. If we pick the right spots, we can totally ambush the status quo. General, what would SunTzu say about this?"

"I don't know without looking it up, but his book does sit on my nightstand. Nothing like well orchestrated guerilla warfare. But on the issues, I'm with Thomas. Our criminal justice system downright sucks. If you have the personal resources or status, you can beat the system. If not, it's throw-away-the-key time. Speaking of economics, ever read the statistics on the cost of incarceration?"

"Guilty. But, now you're on the other side of the political spectrum. To me, criminal justice issues play out more at the local level than the state level. I'd like to also get there as quickly as possible. But it may be difficult in a state as diverse as Illinois. Our analysis shows that gun control would tear us apart before we learn to crawl."

"To that end," the General responded, "can't we free up our candidates to take positions based on local dynamics?"

"Candidates?" burst K.C. "What a great idea," she added sarcastically. "We've spent the better part of three days talking about a party without knowing who's invited. How do you propose to identify and attract viable candidates?"

"As usual K.C., you're ahead of the curve," Atlas complimented her. "And in that regard, I think the emphasis is definitely on viable. We make or break depending upon those fortunate enough to win seats. On the bright side, I will tell you the process has already begun and I have great hope.

"I was concerned until I saw an article in the *Chicago Sun Times* identifying fifty people in Chicago who were making a difference. The stories of unsung heroes are normally buried, or should I say ignored, in our glamour-seeking tabloid world. It was about people who get inner-city kids into college, help keep kids out of gangs, foster communication between cops and at-risk kids, and work to address sex-based street violence against young women. I actually called a few and flew to Chicago to meet them.

"Here's the take-away. They all succeeded. They all dearly believed in their mission. And they were all told by the bureaucracy it couldn't be done, wouldn't work, whatever. They just persevered. So that's our candidate; focused on mission and with the physical and mental capacity to persevere.

"They also need a dash of pioneer spirit. About the same time I saw that article, I heard Condoleezza Rice speak in Aspen. She was reflecting on her goals for life after the Bush administration and said she wanted to work to preserve the log cabin, anyone-can-succeed mentality that made our country great. That's also what I want this to be about."

"Easy on the apple pie, Grandma Moses," said the General. "This is about finding soldiers. Give me the right skills and I'll build you Marines. Too much emphasis on pioneers and log cabins and you'll all end up with a herd of cats. Give me thirty minutes with each and I'll tell you which of your pioneers will circle the wagons and which ones will head for the hills."

"Done!" Atlas exclaimed.

"Sorry," Clay interjected. "Tom, wheels up in thirty minutes. You're loaded and ready to roll. K.C., out in forty-five. Lauren, noon sharp. And General, the mountain bike's outside. You and the boss have just enough time for a Woody Creek run."

* * * * * * * * * * * * * * * *

The Rio Grande trail stretches from Aspen to Glenwood Springs; forty miles of enticing, scenic bike path that essentially parallels the Roaring Fork River on its westward journey to the Colorado. The main tourist segment is the initial eight-mile leg down to Woody Creek. Aspen provides the tourists and the bike rentals; the Woody Creek Tavern provides the burgers, onion rings, and cold ones. Over the past umpteen years, the General and Atlas had developed many social traditions and, weather permitting, this ride had become the culminating activity of the General's visits. First one there earns the right to buy. The trail is sufficiently wide for two abreast and the ride back usually continues whatever debate their beers have inspired.

"So we're set," continued Atlas on the ride back. "I'll meet you in Chicago mid to late November, early December at the latest. At that point, we should be ready to finalize the candidates and start circulating petitions to get them on the ballot. The field team needs to be readied. I leave that entirely to you, just as long as all efforts are local. We cannot afford to be labeled as carpetbaggers. Remember what Tip O'Neil said?"

"Absolutely," said the General spiritedly. " 'All politics is local.' No problem. I have every confidence my past relationships can be sufficiently drawn upon. We're all mercenaries or whores, depending on the perspective. And, every veteran I know has an 'I hate politicians' itch just waiting to be scratched. The fees we just agreed upon will more than catch their attention."

"I fully expect to get challenged in court," admitted Atlas. "They need to all meet the Caesar's wife standard. No shortcuts."

"Not to worry on that," the General confirmed. "We set a target completion date three weeks out and take them all to the wood shed. If we can't convince ourselves after a thorough review, we still have time to regroup. Then you should welcome the challenges and the free publicity."

"Normally, yes. But the first time out I want to sneak up on them. More stealth campaign than anything else. I do not want to be perceived as a threat. If we're challenged and go to the lengths necessary to survive challenges, and by that I mean some son-of-a-bitch lawyers, then they'll be on to us way too early.

"That's also why we will not run in every district. Just enough to achieve our majority breaking caucus. We'll need at least eleven Senate candidates with an expectation of taking seven seats and at least twenty-one representative candidates for thirteen seats."

"Atlas, you've got this old man's blood boiling again," beamed the General. "I can't wait to get to Chicago."

CHAPTER SEVEN

E-MAIL

To: Alex
From: K.C.
Sent: 10/2 10:12 p.m. (EST)
Subject: Thanks

Thank you again for a lovely and intellectually stimulating getaway. I'm sorry if I did not meet your expectations regarding my participation. As it was, I found myself drifting in and out between thoughts/worries for Patrick.

Turns out, my trepidations were misplaced. His weekend was totally uneventful. That marvelous Covington support network was at its best. Having Pat Jr. there with all the grandkids was quite a plus. And I know the staff greatly enjoyed a break from my anal, micro-managing self. I'm lucky they didn't change the locks.

Your home and surrounds are spectacular…and, as I needed, quite cathartic. In the spring, I'd like to bring Patrick out for a short stay. I think the clean, crisp air and abundant sunshine will be good for him.

As it turns out, I spent the entire flight home scribbling endless thoughts about your adventure. Since then, I find myself awakening at all hours with ideas popping like corn.

Patrick's initial reaction was one, you're crazy, and two, if anyone can pull it off it's you, particularly in league with the General. He also picked up on my enthusiasm and has pressed me to expand my role. Still not likely, however.

As you move forward, I want you to consider engaging someone to watch your back. Probably a public relations/press type. I'm sticking to my initial reaction that you do not understand this game. While you try to reinvent politics, your opponents will be constrained by the world they know. Please find someone who can anticipate and help counter their moves.

* * * * * * * * * * * * * * * *

E-MAIL
To: K.C.
From: Alex
Sent: 10/2 8:46 p.m. (MST)
Subject: You're Welcome

Thank you for your thoughts. I am glad your anxiety was misplaced. It was, as always, great to see you.

Things are moving along nicely. As to your recommendation, back watching will be a priority. Once again, you and the General have attacked the same point from different directions. He wants their playbooks to plot offense, while you stress defense.

Happy New Year. Best wishes to Patrick.

* * * * * * * * * * * * * * * *

E-MAIL
To: Atlas
From: Lauren
Sent: 10/11 7:15 p.m. (PST)
Subject: Ready To Go

I am prepared to move ahead. I have created a separate timeline to support both the campaign and the post-election effort. I have also identified staffing needs (including some I already want to steal) and other logistics, i.e., space requirements, I.T. support, blah, blah, blah. You won't like the budget. See attached.

Is this being done under the auspices of ASC? If not, what? And, if not, what role do you anticipate for ASC?

Can be up and running within two to three weeks. Productive in two to three months?

* * * * * * * * * * * * * * * *

E-MAIL
To: Lauren
From: Atlas
Sent: 10/11 8:22 p.m. (MST)
Subject: Go!

Go! Funds will be wired on 48 hours notice. I do not anticipate any direct involvement with ASC unless you request it. But, third party consultants, primarily legal, are available. Work through Liz.

I haven't yet fixed on your umbrella organization. Give the lawyers and me one more week. I assume there's no objection to a totally independent entity under your control?

* * * * * * * * * * * * * * * *

E-MAIL
To: Atlas
From: General
Sent: 10/19 6:48 a.m. (CST)
Subject: Recruiting

Field recruiting should be complete in a few weeks. Training is scheduled to run for two weeks, mid-November. Conversely, candidate recruiting is off to a slow start. Anything on the churches? Glad to hear about K.C./Patrick.

* * * * * * * * * * * * * * * *

E-MAIL
To: General
From: Atlas
Sent: 10/19 6:13 a.m. (MST)
Subject: Churches

No churches. Wanted to give Tom some time. I'll call him next week. Want to make the pitch in person, in Chicago. Should I be concerned about candidate recruiting?

* * * * * * * * * * * * * * * *

E-MAIL
To: Atlas
From: General
Sent: 10/19 9:11 a.m. (CST)
Subject: Candidates

I wouldn't be concerned at this point. We'll take a snapshot when you get here and refocus if necessary.

* * * * * * * * * * * * * * * *

"Thomas?"

"Well, if it isn't my long lost friend, Atlas. I was wondering when I'd hear from you. I thought an old fly fisherman like you would not let the hook set for this long."

"My friend, I was wondering when a savvy old fish like you might come to the surface. I'm obviously not using the right bait."

"We'll see. How've you been?"

"Busy. Spending all my waking moments trying to move forward. Things are going well, but I need my secret weapon."

"Well, for those of us not living at 8,000 feet, a little thing called the baseball playoffs is in full swing. Damn Yankees. They look like a lock on the series. I'm doing my thing for the Commissioner and, since you can never rule out a game seven in any series, my plate is full 'til late in the month."

"Let me know when you can meet, preferably in Chicago."

"Sure, I've been expecting the question and I'm ready to talk."

"Great. I'll have Liz set it up."

* * * * * * * * * * * * * * * *

E-MAIL
To: Tom, K.C., Lauren and Mark
From: Atlas
Sent: 10/30 9:11 p.m. (MST)
Subject: Chicago

FYI—Despite my chomping at the bit, the General asks that I push back my trip to Chicago until after Thanksgiving.

* * * * * * * * * * * * * * * *

E-MAIL
To: Liz
From: Atlas
Sent: 11/11 5:30 a.m. (MST)
Subject: Chicago

Let's get cracking on the second week of December. I'll need a day with Tom and one with Lauren. Dinners are optional, but book the General across the board. Let Tom and Lauren choose the restaurants if either has a favorite. Otherwise, I'm sure the General has scoped out his steak and pasta favorites by now.

I also need one to two days with Mark. Schedule him up front and include the General. For that dinner, find an out-of-the-way location.

I doubt she'll come, but also check with K.C. If not, see if she will consider dinner in New York on either end of the trip.

* * * * * * * * * * * * * * * *

If Atlas could have handpicked the stage for his political play, it would have been Chicago. Where else? The home of his youth, the resting place of his parents, the roots of his professional career. Chicago always made sense. Although Aspen was his home, Chicago held a nostalgic tug on his heart. It was therefore quite satisfying that, by any rational measure, Illinois was chosen to be the incubator.

Knowing well the political history of Chicago, he symbolically selected the near South Side for their headquarters. The South Side meant the Daley family and most other political dynasties from Chicago's Irish political mafia. So, where better to launch his first political satellite?

Upon arriving, he found the General well ensconced in the matters of the day. Similar to his corporate style, the General had situated his cubicle in the center of the work room. Troops needed to know their leader was about and the flow of information needed to be crisp and efficient. He saw no reason to operate his business dealings any other way. In the General's world, a corner office was for the least strategic of functions. Views be damned. It also endeared him to his troops and, later, to his corporate colleagues. Actions spoke louder than words.

"You're late, as usual," was the warm greeting he bestowed upon Atlas.

"Nice to see you too," he responded. "I just love what you've done to the place. Was it always this stark or did you have to work at it?"

"If you want trappings," retorted the General, "then you and Liz can waste your time. My guys only come here to report. The work is in the field. When I want pampering, I'll check into the Peninsula."

"You win," surrendered Atlas. "Let's get to work. After today's touring, we've got the political consultant tonight; Tom, Wednesday; and Lauren, Thursday."

They may have been 180 degrees apart when it came to ambiance, but they were Siamese twins when it came to work ethic. The week ahead was crammed with meetings, reports, field trips, and endless strategy sessions.

"Give me an hour with you alone," the General commanded. "Then we'll head into the field." With that, he put his arm around his good friend and led him to the war room. "I trust you've had time to examine the candidate dossiers. I've done phone interviews with all and have personally met with most. That should be done by Christmas. It's been tough to spend sufficient time in the downstate districts. They're far more geographically dispersed than I imagined. In Chicago, I can often work in four to five interviews a day. Downstate it's two to three; often just one or two. Most have jobs so we're generally meeting after hours; occasionally a military start. For second interviews, I'm focusing on weekends when we can also do some walking and driving to get acclimated with the districts as well. Easy in the city, tough in the burbs, and impossible downstate. Downstate districts are generally bigger than Cook County."

"I've studied the dossiers," Atlas acknowledged. "You've done an amazing job. How many have committed at this point?"

"Unfortunately, none. But I'd prefer to discuss that issue later."

The General's capacity for efficiency and organization had never ceased to amaze Atlas. Once his third party idea had evolved, it was ordained that his good friend would serve as Commander in Chief. Atlas knew that at sixty-eight years young, the General was still fit for such a daunting task, physically and mentally.

Luckily, some of the best men the General had ever served with had significant roots in Chicago and throughout Illinois. Within weeks of arriving, he had worked the phones, reminisced endlessly over coffees early and beers late, and started to build his political army. Finding and training troops to circulate petitions had proven so successful that, of late, he had to slow down the pace. The proposed pay was good, the training and work was short-term, on weekends, and his former military buddies had done well producing children and grandchildren for the task.

Identifying candidates was considerably more time consuming and considerably more difficult. Initially, he was drilling too many dry holes. It was Atlas who hit upon the idea of contacting school principals and superintendents to request nominations for the annual ASC award, given to Illinois teachers most dedicated to community service. No one seemed to care that they had never heard of this prestigious award nor did they subsequently notice that no such award was ever bestowed. However, the inquiry had produced a wealth of prized resumes.

Back in September, over burgers and beers at Woody Creek, they had quickly formulated the rules of engagement. Candidates needed to possess certain non-negotiable attributes:

1. Education backgrounds were a top priority with current teachers being preferred. But not just any educators. From their own life's experiences, they knew each school, each vocational setting, contained at least one teacher known for truly making a difference; the ones who, much later in life, still resonated. They were the ones that should set policy because they understand what it takes to help people succeed. With education being among government's most precious functions, particularly at the state level, Atlas was stunned to learn how few educators enter politics. On the flip side, the dominance of lawyers was startling and frightening. How sad to leave the job of governing to a profession that, for the most part, could never be accused of producing ideas to advance humankind.

   Scientists and engineers also ranked high on their list. However, time was an initial concern. They would be harder to find and even harder to enlist; not that they would turn down a Ben Franklin if one were to appear.

2. Neither Atlas nor the General was the epitome of family values, nor did either appreciate the pandering done by the Republican party. However, they both agreed there was a certain "we'll know it when we see it" standard for candidates who were well adjusted and grounded. They referred to it as the "no bullshit quality."

3. Age was not considered a relevant consideration, but a certain measure of life's experience was. They wanted the kind of person who went above and beyond the world of nine-to-five whether that be volunteers for causes, world travelers, or just those with solid hobbies that combined energy, drive, and a touch of wanting, in the words of the Army commercial, "to be the best they can be."

It wasn't the longest of lists, but they never agreed on a fourth point. The General offered military experience and just as quickly withdrew it. Neither felt that gender or race would have value as a selection criterion. Although, it was also agreed that male and white was not to be a preference. The demographics of each district would, however, be considered if compelling.

Seeing as how they were both of the politically unfashionable white male fraternity, they ran the checklist past K.C. She agreed in concept, but suggested adding some quantifiable elements and characteristics to the no bullshit category. She thought the experience of parenting should be a prerequisite as well as practicing religion. Her adult life had, ironically, lacked both and she understood the void. Recalling Alex's reference to the pioneer spirit, she suggested looking for entrepreneurs. She also contributed a fourth criterion. No one should be chosen if they had previously participated in Republican or Democratic politics—too much baggage.

Armed with the four corner offense, as it jokingly came to be known, the General had been scouting candidates for well over a month.

* * * * * * * * * * * * * * * *

Chicago is a city of amazing cuisine. For Atlas, it wasn't about five stars, but rather the local favorites and their ethnic specialties. No trip was ever complete without some deep-dish pizza. It could be Gino's, Uno's, Due's, Barnaby's, Nancy's—whatever. They all hit the same gastronomic sweet spot. For this trip, Connie's got the nod given the proximity to their headquarters. The only complicating factor with Connie's was the spectacular stuffed pizza alternative. No problem—onc of each never hurt anyone.

"General, allow me to introduce you to Mark Stone. Mark, this is my best friend and mentor, General Samuel Huntington Smith."

They exchanged the usual "heard a lot of great things about you from Atlas," and, "you must know what's his name" and a few "how 'bout them" sports teams. After the pies and vino were ordered, Atlas quickly got down to business.

"As you know, Mark authored the paper on Illinois and the preliminary strategic plan. His analytics to identify the optimum mix of Senate and House districts are driving your efforts to identify and field candidates."

"I like your work," said the General. "Easy to see why you've gained my friend's confidence," he added with a nod to Atlas.

"Thanks, General," said Mark. "Fortunately, in this game, preparation goes a long way. And equally fortunate, if we do it right, and I have no reason to think we won't, our opponents will not be prepared for us. We're new and we're not anticipated. How goes the planning for the petition drives?"

"Excellent! As you recommend in your report, we are scheduled to obtain at least two signatures for each one required. Also per your report, we will complete petitioning not less than ten days out, at which time we will conduct an internal audit to validate signatures and registrations. In any district for which we cannot certify the audit to at least 150 percent of the statutory requirement, we will still have enough time to go back into the field."

"And the candidates?" Mark inquired.

"The good news is that the targets meet your consensus of attributes by district and by priority. In most cases, we should hit on at least seven out of ten. We also layered your modeling with the criteria Atlas, K.C., and I developed. Of the thirty-seven potential candidates, I think only three failed to match a significant majority of the checklist. At the end of the day, those three are all aces."

"I've read their backgrounds," responded Mark. "But you've met them and spent time with them. I've worked with many a candidate that passed the beauty contest compulsories only to lose in the talent portion."

"Problem is, Mark," the General hesitated, "how to lock them in. Atlas and I have been commiserating most of the day and we're hoping you can connect some of the dots."

"I'm not sure I can," Mark apologized. "From my personal experience, the majority of the time there's been a farm system, so to speak. The party system is fairly regimented that way. Municipal officials, community activists and school board members usually aspire to become state representatives. State representatives aspire to join the state Senate, and both state representatives and senators aspire to congress and statewide offices. Most of the time there's a likely suspect waiting in the wings. Sure, there's an occasional maverick, but even those candidates generally have a history of working within the party structure."

"But what's the motivation?" Atlas asked.

"Motivation?" Mark hesitated.

"Yes," Atlas attempted to clarify. "What's bringing them to the table? Why are they taking the risk?"

"I'd have to give that some thought," said Mark. "It's definitely not a one-size-fits-all answer if that's where you're going."

"I was afraid you'd say that," shrugged an obviously frustrated General. "Frankly, I was hoping I was missing something. In the military, most of the recruits share common threads. For some it's the career, for others the training, and there's always the macho types. Understanding that, we know how to close the deal.

"We've identified great candidates, at least I think we have, and they all seem genuinely excited about the possibilities of a third party. But at this point, not one is committed to running. I understand their hesitancy. They all have jobs, security, and a healthy distrust of the political system. One big fucking 'do not pass go,' if you'll pardon my French."

"Know this," added Mark. "No matter how perfect you perceive the candidate to be, if you have to work too hard to 'close the deal' as you called it, you will not have a candidate with the necessary drive for the grind of an election. They have to want it and it has to come from within. That's your common thread. Final answer."

"In that case," Atlas shook his head, "we're about to blow every deadline in the strategic plan. And we all agreed that our best chance lies in the upcoming presidential election cycle. It's now or never."

* * * * * * * * * * * * * * * *

The General waited for the obligatory nightcap to inquire of Atlas, "So how'd you meet Mark? Very impressive."

"Internet all the way. In fact, I hired him over the Internet and never met him face-to-face until he'd produced significant work product. I was convinced the usual outlets would not be productive, so I assigned a couple of my best researchers to monitor the more prominent political blogs. Political peacocks love to spread their feathers. As it turned out, if you're patient and thorough, those with the brightest arrays stick out. We contacted a half-dozen or so and Mark won out. One of the few to have successfully worked both sides. That's what clinched it.

"He was originally a dyed-in-the-wool Democrat; from Jersey, as if you couldn't tell. Ended up following a very promising young congressman to D.C. When the Republicans gained control of Congress during Clinton's first mid-term, his protégé calls him one night to say he's flipping. Can't stand Clinton, has heard the Lewinsky banter and knows he'll be lucky to escape the carnage.

"Mark cuts a very lucrative campaign funding deal and flips, too. The toughest election is the one post-flip and Mark's guy, due in large measure to Mark, not only survives but flourishes. Years later, he goes for the gold but loses a close race for the U.S. Senate. The protégé becomes a gazillionaire lobbyist in D.C.; helps Mark when he can. But, our guy is a man without a party…'til now. It's truly a fascinating story. I'll leave the juicier details for him to share with you.

"If you don't mind, I may be an hour behind, but I'm still beat. Sorry. See you tomorrow with Tom."

* * * * * * * * * * * * * * * *

E-MAIL

To: Tom
From: Atlas
Sent: 12/9 2:26 p.m. (MST)
Subject: Thanks Again

Thanks again for the day in Chi-town. I can't say the E Party will have all the answers. But at the same time, someone's got to step up to the plate (pun intended).

Take your time, but if you can commit by late spring, we can work up your tour schedule. Mark thinks you can make a significant difference in almost half the races.

Always great to see you. Please give my best holiday wishes to the extended Robinson family.

* * * * * * * * * * * * * * * *

E-MAIL
To: Lauren
From: Atlas
Sent: 12/9 2:29 p.m. (MST)
Subject: Thanks Again

Thanks again for the day in Chi-town. Sorry you had to schlep all that equipment. I know the General and Mark were impressed with the demonstration.

* * * * * * * * * * * * * * * *

E-MAIL
To: Atlas, General
From: Mark
Sent: 12/17 8:19 p.m. (CST)
Subject: Revised Schedule

As we discussed in Chicago, the failure to timely complete the candidate selection process has put the entire campaign in jeopardy. Accordingly, I've spent the last week revising the schedule. It's all laid out in the attachment. However, please note that our attorneys have not yet blessed the change. Even if it's legal, it's also very unorthodox.

Notwithstanding, in some ways, this could work to our benefit. As you know, the original plan called for the party to be formed in early January. If counsel confirms that we can skip the February primary and push back our organizational filings to June, we keep off the radar screen for an additional four months. Also, if the General's hunch is correct, those potential candidates who are currently teaching will be more comfortable committing to run if they can avoid the limelight until after the winter/spring semester. To that end, under the revised timetable their petitions will not be circulated and filed until after the school year concludes.

The significant downside risk is that we will have no wiggle room on the back end, particularly if there is a successful challenge to any one candidate's petition. At that point, it will be virtually impossible to place any substitutes on the ballot.

The remaining hurdle is allowing sufficient time for issue development and training. With the summer months dedicated to campaigning, we either have to double up and work the candidates that much harder, or we stick to the original script and start platform development in the spring before we know who's on the ballot.

* * * * * * * * * * * * * * * *

E-MAIL

To: Mark
From: General
Sent: 12/22 2:51 p.m. (CST)
cc: Atlas
Subject: Revised Schedule

I like it! That is, assuming counsel confirms the legality of deferring both creation of the party and the filing of the candidate petitions.

Having almost five additional month's time to lock in candidates is a real difference maker. In a few cases, it will allow me to tinker with and expand the target group.

Otherwise, I'm convinced the great majority of the group will "want it," when they better understand the program. To that end, let's keep the issue development and training in the spring. For any potential candidate who is still hesitant at that point, devoting time to the issues process should solidify their decision one way or the other. And, if some decide to drop out, we've still got up to two months to find a replacement.

* * * * * * * * * * * * * * * *

E-MAIL

To: General, Mark
From: Atlas
Sent: 12/27 4:04 p.m. (MST)
Subject: Filing Dates

I just got off the phone with our election counsel. He confirms that we can delay formation of the party to June. However, our candidate petitions MUST be filed between June 14 and June 21.

It's too tight on the back end for my tastes. But, I do not see that we have any choice in the matter.

* * * * * * * * * * * * * * * *

E-MAIL

To: K.C.
From: Alex
Sent: 2/01 11:15 a.m. (MST)
Subject: Easter Break

Can you give me three to four days in Chicago around Easter? The General has recruited an excellent class of potential candidates and we need to get started on issues during the break in the school schedule. Bring Patrick.

* * * * * * * * * * * * * * * *

E-MAIL
To: Alex
From: K.C.
Sent: 2/02 1:27 p.m. (EST)
Subject: Easter In NYC

Patrick would love to come to Chicago. At this point, he would be happy just to leave the house, as would I. Depending on his condition at the time, I can give you parts of three to four days. But, it has to be in New York City. Sorry for any inconvenience.

* * * * * * * * * * * * * * * *

E-MAIL
To: K.C.
From: Alex
Sent: 2/03 11:30 a.m. (MST)
Subject: Easter In NYC

Consider it done. I assume the General can coax the majority of his group to make the trip east. Liz will be in touch. Looking forward to seeing you and Patrick.

* * * * * * * * * * * * * * * *

E-MAIL
To: K.C.
From: Liz
Sent: 2/08 2:17 p.m. (CST)
Subject: Candidate Conference

Atlas has instructed me to move the candidate conference to New York City. I have booked the Plaza for April 6, 7, 8 and 9. Most of the teacher candidates have Easter break from school and the General is confirming their availability. What is your best and worst case scenarios on those dates?

Attached is a list of proposed lecturers/facilitators. Atlas says you have total veto power over agenda and participants. Leave the rest to me.

* * * * * * * * * * * * * * * *

E-MAIL

To: Alex
From: K.C.
Sent: 4/10 1:22 a.m. (EST)
Subject: Camelot #2

Put a check mark. I was very pleased with the results of the conference. Still not clear to me why you abstained.

First of all, the candidates are terrific. Kudos to the General.

Initially, I was concerned that, with their median age in the mid-thirties, they would lack the necessary sophistication and seasoning. Not only is this a savvy crowd, but their collective creativity and energy is very refreshing and a little humbling—my second Camelot.

Kudos to Mark as well. His sessions on Politics 101 and Elections 101 were quite effective. K.I.S.S. at its best.

Given the make-up of the group, we abandoned the script and focused almost entirely on education. I'm probably overly optimistic, but the initial white paper should be done by late May/early June. To that end, we now have an education working group and I'd like to bring them back when school ends.

'The economy,' as you call it, is off to a slower start. The good news is that any setback relates more to the quality of the questions and not to lack of (at least not yet) answers. The Friedman scholar you found has a gift for putting complicated financial concepts into laymen's terms. Instead of scheduling a time to bring this group back, I think a series of weekend conference calls to foster the learning curve is more in order. We can do the next group thing in late June if that won't mess with the schedule too much.

Best news of all. Patrick came to a few of the sessions. Had a look of enthusiasm in his eyes that's been absent for a long time.

* * * * * * * * * * * * * * * *

E-MAIL

To: Atlas, Mark, K.C.
From: General
Sent: 4/18 9:02 p.m. (CST)
Subject: Candidates

Things are finally looking up. Thanks in large measure to K.C.'s issue magic, we now have commitments from 17 out of the 24 who made the trip to New York. No matter how much "talking the talk" occurred on my end, it was the hands-on "walking the walk" that got our recruits to finally see how real and exciting this experiment in democracy can be. K.C. turned them into believers. By the time those 17 finish working on the last 7, I'm convinced they'll all be in the fold.

We're still short the 13 that dropped out before the conference, but I have some solid leads and I'm certainly not stressing like I was in early December when faced with the original deadlines.

* * * * * * * * * * * * * * * *

E-MAIL

To: Atlas, General
From: Mark
Sent: 4/19 9:03 a.m. (CST)
Subject: Candidates

I am not comfortable at 17 candidates, but we will need to start passing petitions if we are to meet our June deadlines. Our original minimum target was 27, 18 in the House and 9 in the Senate. I cannot foresee any success unless we can get to 21 candidates, 14 House and 7 Senate. As it is, that is cutting it very close, particularly in the House.

Working backwards, we have to start petition drives no later than mid-May. That gives us just over three weeks to confirm at least four of the remaining seven and/or find new talent. You cannot assume victory in every race—it just doesn't happen.

* * * * * * * * * * * * * * * *

E-MAIL

To: Mark, General
From: Atlas
Sent: 4/19 10:10 a.m. (MST)
Subject: Candidates

I agree that 17 is unworkable. At the same time, the thought of waiting two years for the next election cycle is unthinkable and unbearable.

I am proposing a bit of divide and conquer. K.C. has agreed to lobby the undecideds. She believes her rapport with at least four of the seven is excellent. I have also reached out to Tom Robinson. Depending upon K.C.'s progress over the next week, he has agreed to meet one-on-one in those cases where K.C. and the General think his assistance can make the difference.

The General will focus his energy on identifying three to five new recruits. Once identified, we can use our base of 17 plus Tom to put on a full court press.

* * * * * * * * * * * * * * * *

E-MAIL
To: Alex, General, Mark, Tom
From: K.C.
Sent: 4/29 11:00 a.m. (EST)
Subject: Candidate Update

It's very frustrating to be sitting at 20. I thought for sure we would be at 22 to 23.

At this point, I think we should write off Benske and Morison to concentrate on Emerson, Cooper and Snapp. Of those three, I think Tom should meet with Emerson and Snapp.

Cooper's big hang-up is family and, at this point, I'm not sure what it will take. Turns out her uncle once served in the Oklahoma legislature and the strain on the family led to a divorce and kid problems. She says there was too much time away. Mark, any ideas on how to deal with that issue?

* * * * * * * * * * * * * * * *

E-MAIL
To: K.C.
From: Mark
Sent: 4/30 3:17 p.m. (CST)
cc: Atlas
Subject: Cooper

I have definitely seen life in politics put a strain on the family. But, it's usually guys with big egos hitting on secretaries. I'm guessing that uncle what's-his-name was playing around.

Regardless, it is not unheard of for legislators with districts in close proximity to Springfield to go home each night. Fortunately, Cooper's district is not much more than an hour's drive away. If it would help, I can call her to discuss travel and scheduling options.

* * * * * * * * * * * * * * * *

E-MAIL
To: General, Mark, K.C., Tom
From: Atlas
Sent: 5/4 1:14 p.m. (MST)
Subject: Candidates

Thanks to Tom's cavalry charge, Emerson committed last night. That gets us to Mark's minimum magic number of 21. The General's field team will begin passing petitions as soon as possible.

In addition, Mark has hope that his conversations with Cooper are progressing and the General thinks he may have a few on the line.

* * * * * * * * * * * * * * * *

E-MAIL
To: Atlas, K.C., General
From: Mark
Sent: 5/11 8:25 p.m. (CST)
Subject: Cooper

I just left Cooper's house. Funny how it can take so long to ferret the real problem. In fact, I should have figured it out after my first visit to their home.

They are a one car family and couldn't possibly afford two on their combined salaries. The light bulb lit quite brightly once I made it clear that the party can provide a car for campaign duties and she will receive expense reimbursement from the state for travel to and from their home.

My only hesitation was making the campaign commitment without your blessings.

* * * * * * * * * * * * * * * *

E-MAIL
To: Mark
From: Atlas
Sent: 5/11 7:37 p.m. (MST)
Subject: Cooper

Done! Let's get her petitions circulated ASAP!

* * * * * * * * * * * * * * * *

E-MAIL
To: Mark, General, K.C.
From: Atlas
Sent: 6/02 10:15 a.m. (CST)
Subject: Update

As set forth in detail in the attachment from our legal counsel, we have completed the first round of organizational matters as follows:

1. The E Party has been officially established in Illinois. The General is the initial organizer and Sylvia Rose from the law firm has been temporarily designated as treasurer. No further filings are due until early July, at which time the first set of expenditure reports are required.

2. We have not filed organizational papers for the E Party in other states, but have taken the steps necessary to reserve use of the name for future

activity. The attachment includes a sequential itemization of the dates through which the registrations are valid.

3. We have also taken steps necessary to protect use of the name E Party for Internet communications, including a variety of web address/domain choices.

4. We have created and registered three additional entities:

   (a)The Atlas Trust. This will serve as the primary vehicle for all funding. Julie Kersten-Covington, the General, and Lauren de la Rosa are trustees.
   (b)The Atlas Foundation of Colorado. This will serve as the primary funding vehicle for educational purposes in support of E Party policy development, think tank organization.
   (c)The Chevez de la Rosa Corporation. This is the company formed to support Lauren's I.T. efforts.

* * * * * * * * * * * * * * * *

E-MAIL

To: Atlas
From: General
Sent: 6/18 4:52 p.m. (CST)
cc: Mark, K.C.
Subject: Petitions

Ready or not—all petitions have been filed.

CHAPTER EIGHT

"What do you make of this?" asked an inquiring Democratic party staffer handing a small stack of papers to his supervisor. "Ever heard of the E Party before?"

"No, but it's a great name. I'll bet some guy just made himself a small bundle selling it off an Internet name registry."

The papers in question were the organizational filings of the E Party. As with all Forms D-1, it contained the date the committee was created, amount of funds available for campaign expenditures, indication of this being a new committee, and purpose and area of activity. In this case, the answers staring back were (a) June 1, (b) $2,800, (c) new committee, and (d) statewide political party. The E Party of Illinois was born.

"Never heard of Samuel Smith. Have you?"

"Can't say I have, but check him."

The staffer spent the next hour Googling. There were hundreds of results for the name Samuel Smith, none of which tied to the given address in Chicago, Illinois. The rights to the name "E Party" had been sold to him for $10,000. The transaction was handled by a Chicago-based law firm.

"I know a few people at that firm," added the supervisor, "and there's not one that I would normally associate with political activity. Probably acting as agent for someone who wants to be careful. See if Roger Bauer has any ideas how to check this out. I'm guessing it's a bunch of liberal geeks out to set the world on its ear."

Since an almost identical non-reaction was occurring at Republican headquarters, it meant that Atlas and the General had guessed correctly. The apparent insignificance of the party would buy them months of anonymity. The element of surprise, as much as preparation and execution, was critical to their effort.

In most cases, opposition to the Republicans and Democrats was a token, underfunded effort. No third party would ever be taken seriously until their filings showed financial staying power and, at least in Illinois, they never had. At $500,000 for a contested House race and at least twice that for a Senate seat, no third party had ever come close. Depending on the circumstances, third parties were actually welcomed.

For incumbents, the absence of major party opposition makes it difficult to convince potential donors of the need to either make or increase contributions to their campaigns. However, party leaders would still demand their exaction. Having an opponent, no matter how insignificant the challenge, creates the pretense of urgency needed to shake the contributor bushes. It also helps maintain a political operation, particularly important for House members facing the biennial election cycle.

Even more convoluted is the benefit to the other major party. They may have been otherwise compelled to field their own token candidates. Attract some schlub promoting dreams of changing the world. Promise financial and staff support and possibly even deliver short term. When the first poll is taken and the inevitable die has been cast, cut 'em loose. The mope has put his good name on the ballot so he or she stays the course. The incumbent has done the same polling. But ego and fear of showing vulnerability, or worse yet, the occasional lightening strike, keeps them engaged. Money is raised, but is now pinned down in district. All part of the game.

The supervisor in this case was Daniel "Danny" Ryan, a highly revered, long standing Cook County Democrat operative. Danny was born on the South Side in the late sixties and, in addition to the political genes imbedded in Chicago Irishmen, he was also fortunate enough to be born and raised in the Tenth Ward. With union labor being the default option, at the time there were only two other respected career paths for Tenth Ward progeny, and the priesthood was never an option for Danny. That left politics.

While his dad had achieved a modicum of success as a union laborer, his parents were of the "our kids need to graduate college to get ahead" generation. Lacking the wherewithal, they connected

Danny's intellectual prowess with the necessary neighborhood chieftains and he was rewarded with a path to the political pinnacle. A scholarship to Notre Dame was arranged in exchange for a commitment to work politics during his summers and vacations. After graduating, an appropriate job with the City of Chicago was arranged; this time with the understanding that political work on nights and weekends were his real assignment.

It never occurred to Danny that he was making a Faustian deal. He thrived on politics. In fact, he was among the best they had ever seen. From the mundane—knocking on doors for votes; to the compulsory—arranging jobs for lasting fealty; to the strategic—organizing and running campaigns; it was a symphony and he was a Beethoven.

For the better part of the last decade, Danny had been anointed executive director of the Democratic Party of Cook County, the most influential non-elected political position in Illinois. Under his tutelage, there had never been an electoral setback, not one.

Danny possessed every skill and instinct needed to excel in politics. He was brilliant, cunning, disciplined and licensed to kill. He could charm major contributors, manipulate elected officials of any stature, and welcomely get drunk with the patronage army. He was admired and feared. He was the total package.

* * * * * * * * * * * * * * * *

"Danny, its Bauer. The report from the law firm was benign. Apparently, a gentleman by the name of Samuel Smith called to interview the firm. He was representing a group of disgruntled ex-executives from high-tech companies. They had achieved great financial success during the Internet explosion in the nineties, primarily through stock bonuses. The bursting of the tech bubble had created unforseen tax issues that wiped them out. They had created a nationwide blog of similarly situated, angry taxpayers, and had unsuccessfully lobbied Congress and certain key state legislatures for redress under the respective tax codes. They were now aligned on a variety of business/tax issues related to the Internet and were forming a political party to take their message public.

"The firm of Yura, Mix & Eisenstat was hired to assist with various organizational issues. Other than a reasonable retainer, they had yet to be paid in full and the aging of the receivable was becoming a cause for concern. Of late, Mr. Smith had not returned their calls."

Danny made a mental note. He was right about the geeks. No need to worry about some lunatics forming a political party that wasn't paying its lawyers. The lawyers would fuck with them long before he had to.

* * * * * * * * * * * * * * * *

E-MAIL
To: General
From: Yura
Sent: 6/21 11:11 a.m. (CST)
Subject: You Were Right

General, as you predicted, our firm had an inquiry regarding the origins of the E Party. I am positive it was on behalf of the Cook County Democratic organization. The pre-arranged response was sent yesterday.

* * * * * * * * * * * * * * * *

E-MAIL
To: Atlas
From: General
Sent: 6/21 11:16 a.m. (CST)
Subject: We're On The Map

See attached from Yura. Even a blind pig…

* * * * * * * * * * * * * * * *

Hating lawyers was one of the General's favorite pastimes. He avoided them like the plague, with the exception of the ones who, of necessity, were assigned to him in the Army, and later, corporate life. It boiled down to one thing; his training was getting to victory. Lawyers were trained in avoiding defeat. He was about "yes sir" and they were about "no sir."

Atlas did not exactly hold lawyers with any measure of esteem, but understood the necessity of their evil, particularly in the political world. His resentment grew more out of the pretense.

ASC would work its magic in resolving the emotional side of trauma only to find, more often than not, that attorneys would cut apart his sutures with their litigation scalpels. Over time, he grew disgusted by their "take-no-prisoners-in-the-name-of-monetary-reward" approach. It hadn't always been that way, but he could no longer remember when it wasn't.

Early on, the General and Atlas set parameters they felt would ameliorate the unavoidable. They would look for younger lawyers, hoping that their idealism had not yet been totally sucked out, and they would work with smaller firms in the hope that their sense of obligation to the client remained somewhat intact. While they had also intended to spread their work around to maintain some competitive balance, that prerequisite was cut loose when Yura, Mix & Eisenstat sold them on the expediency of one stop shopping.

Y, M & E was a young, aggressive, talented law firm, and though loyalty would never be expected, the General sensed the ability to control and dominate. In that regard, the promise of a handsome, recurring retainer went a long way.

They were from the finest law schools. Some clerked, others went right to silk stocking firms, and most did both. At the urging of Keith Mix, they came together with the joint mission of setting the legal world on fire. Within only eight years, the original three musketeers had exploded to over fifty lawyers. With one exception, they had the world by the balls. That exception was politics. They had been unable to cultivate relationships to catapult themselves into the sphere of pinstripe patronage.

They sought the one thing that the great, powerful and influential firms all had—clout. Rolling the dice on the General and his third party became an easy choice. Worst case, they'd run up a ridiculous number of billable hours.

* * * * * * * * * * * * * * * *

E-MAIL

To: Atlas
From: General
Sent: 6/28 5:10 p.m. (CST)
cc: Mark
Subject: Challenges

Today was the deadline to challenge petitions. As Mark predicted, no bites in any of the three-way races. In the two-ways, we've got challenges in the 8th, 14th, 21st. 38th, 53rd and 58th House Districts and the 14th, 15th, 20th and 31st Senate Districts. Our counsel has reviewed the petitions in each and thinks these are just fishing expeditions. The candidates in question have been fully briefed on alternative scenarios. Written statements for the press have been prepared should anyone have a slow news day.

* * * * * * * * * * * * * * * *

E-MAIL

To: Atlas, Mark, K.C., Tom, Lauren
From: General
Sent: 7/12 2:18 p.m. (CST)
Subject: Man Down

We lost Vicki Lynn Peterson's petition challenge in the 21st House District. At the end of the day, we did not have an adequate cushion of excess signatures to cover the ones found deficient. I'll take the blame. Just too tight adding her at the last minute. Lesson learned for next time.

Now, get me out of this town. Haven't seen the sun in months and my ass still hasn't thawed from the Chicago winter. Let's go fishing!

* * * * * * * * * * * * * * * *

E-MAIL

To: Atlas, General
From: Mark
Sent: 7/12 6:16 p.m. (CST)
Subject: Final Plan

Now that all slates are set, I can finalize our strategic plan. If I'm the Democrats or Republicans, I won't be overly concerned with our candidates. That changes, however, once they detect a pulse. A rogue reporter or two may seek out our candidates on a slow news day. I'm comfortable the non-story-story we've prepared and rehearsed will arrest any such outreach.

* * * * * * * * * * * * * * * *

E-MAIL
To: Staff
From: Danny
Sent: 7/15 8:14 p.m. (CST)
Subject: E Party Candidates

The geeks remaining on the ballot (22 total) now have my full attention. Attached is a list of their candidates, by district. Within two weeks, I want background papers. And, I want more than w, w, w, w, w and h. Dig deep.

* * * * * * * * * * * * * * * *

Whereas the Democratic political hierarchy emanates from Chicago, the Republican base consists of the collar counties just outside Cook along with pockets of rural Illinois. The collar counties were once bastions of the fiscally conservative, white suburban voter, while the downstate Republicans tend to the family values and "don't-take-my-guns" wing of the party. Because the demographics of the collar counties had shifted with the migration of Democratic yuppies from the city, the last thing the Republicans needed was further dilution.

Prior to the E Party, women held 18 percent of the Democratic seats in the Illinois Legislature, but Republican women held 41 percent of their seats. At the leadership level, the demagogues were 85 percent white male. The Republicans weren't better at 75 percent, save for one thing: Elizabeth DiMaggio was their puppet master.

Scratch younger suburban Republicans and you'll find a Democrat somewhere. In most cases, only one generation removed from the city. Elizabeth DiMaggio was prototypical in this respect. The daughter of a Chicago precinct captain, she married her college sweetheart and relocated to the burbs. Equally prototypical was her ascent in politics: college educated stay-at-home mom becomes active in the schools, gets elected to the school board, needs more as the kids grow and start leaving—runs for office. In Elizabeth's case, that was twenty years ago and included mayor, state representative and, for the last six years, state senator. Along the way it also included committeewoman, member of the State Central Committee and, for the last four years, chairperson of the State Central Committee. She was a big tent person with a pinch of street fighter. She was also a tenacious fundraiser and her husband's ascension to the upper echelon of the investment banking world didn't hurt. Most assumed she had not yet peaked politically, with governor or U.S. senator next on the drawing board.

CHAPTER NINE

E-MAIL

To: General, Atlas
From: Mark
Sent: 7/16 6:00 a.m. (CST)
Subject: Ready Or Not

Gentlemen, start your engines. The phase we are entering is a lot like the Indy 500—a long journey, at full speed.

I've spent the past few months updating data and fine-tuning our campaign plans. As you know, we are in eight three-way races (four with Democratic incumbents, two with Republican incumbents, and two with open seats formerly held by Republicans). We are in fourteen two-way races (nine with Democrats, five with Republicans and none representing open seats). Attachment A includes a breakout of all the candidates and their affiliations.

In a package I'm Fed-Exing today, I have also included background pieces on the incumbents—complete histories of their terms in office, voting records, election results, fundraising, cash on hand, yada, yada, yada.

You'll note that none of the loyal opposition has more than $25,000 in the bank at this time. For the incumbents, this is indicative of their nonchalance. That will change once they take polls and find we are active. For the open seats, it may also signal lack of organization. To that end, I reviewed the primaries and, in all cases, they were uncontested.

In addition to tracking funding through the Board of Election reports, we have an effective, yet unscientific monitoring system for opposition fundraisers. In the case of incumbents, their events are predictable. For those incumbents with sufficient repetition, by tracking attendance we can at least gauge significant deviation from prior efforts and predict financial outcomes. All of which is a long way of saying we can react to outliers if and when necessary.

The key date becomes September 30. At that point, we will get the next round of campaign disclosure reports, the D-2 filings.

I have also prepared comprehensive strategic plans by district. General, please review as soon as possible, particularly the sections for field operations. I highly recommend they be fully staffed by Labor Day. If I understand correctly, interim staffing is already in place.

I have deliberately saved the best for last. Recent polling reconfirms all trends we have tracked since early last year. Voter dissatisfaction continues its upward trajectory. It's almost scary how favorable the unfavorables are. Individual ratings for statewide and federal officials also continue to trend negative. As previously discussed, we will not poll for our races until two, four and six weeks into our respective campaigns unless circumstances dictate otherwise and then on a district by district basis.

General, let me know when you are prepared to finalize the campaign plans, at which point we will be ready for the next round of candidate briefings/training.

* * * * * * * * * * * * * * * *

E-MAIL
To: Mark
From: General
Sent: 7/17 4:02 p.m. (CST)
cc: Atlas
Subject: G.O.T.V.?

I have reviewed the plans and compliment you on their thoroughness. Unfortunately, the sections entitled G.O.T.V. appear beyond my pay grade. Can you please enlighten the old man?

* * * * * * * * * * * * * * * *

E-MAIL
To: General
From: Mark
Sent: 7/17 5:55 p.m. (CST)
cc: Atlas
Subject: G.O.T.V.?

My apologies. Politics is the land of acronyms. "G.O.T.V." stands for "Get Out The Vote" and refers to the effort expended at the very end of the campaign, pursuant to which, each candidate's field operation attempts to make sure the voters they expect to support their candidates (as identified in their various canvassing efforts) either get to the polls or submit absentee ballots. It represents one of the most important tenets of winning campaigns. Identify your supporters and make sure they all vote!

* * * * * * * * * * * * * * * *

E-MAIL
To: Danny
From: Roger Bauer
Sent: 7/19 10:10 a.m. (CST)
Subject: E Party D-2's

I have reviewed the E Party expenditure report for the period ending June 30. Nothing unusual.

The report indicates no contributions and a loan from Smith of $30,000. Most of their expenditures are for office, telephone, etc. The only thing a bit out of the ordinary is no report of expenses for their petitions. Either they had a massive volunteer organization or, more likely, held off paying until July 1 so we couldn't see the scope of their operation. That should all be in the September 30 D-2's.

* * * * * * * * * * * * * * * *

E-MAIL
To: Mark, Atlas
From: General
Sent: 8/7 8:03 a.m. (CST)
Subject: CSI Chicago

Well, Gentlemen, we've been baptized. Not that it wasn't expected—but maybe not this soon.

Very nice work, too. No discernable finger prints. And, they very efficiently corrupted all the PC's at the headquarters. Lauren's crew did an amazing job of encrypting all of our false data so, at this point, I'm guessing they're collectively cursing the 'fucking geeks.'

They never looked for the camera, however. So either they think their shit doesn't stink or they figure us for AAA ball; probably both. Regardless, I've got a nice home video for Chicago's finest if and when the time comes.

Did not leave any bugs, either. Wish they had so we could run some additional misdirection. Would love to fuck with 'em. From this point forward, we will need to sweep all the campaign offices at least weekly.

* * * * * * * * * * * * * * * *

E-MAIL
To: Atlas
From: K.C.
Sent: 8/8 9:09 a.m. (EST)
Subject: Policy Papers

Have sent the draft policy papers via overnight delivery—in all cases inclusive of talking paper dot points, press releases, executive summaries, and web site content. Your idea of using grad level poli-sci types was joyous. It felt like I was operating a summer camp for brain cells.

As you know from our chats, Patrick sat through many of the brainstorming sessions and, while his skills continue to diminish, his intensity spoke volumes. We both thank you.

Thanks to Lauren, our candidates kept engaged through a variety of web-based tools. They continue to bring great enthusiasm and creativity to the challenge.

Once you have completed your review and submitted comments, the candidates will return to New York for another 2-3 day session before school starts. As we agreed, they get the last word(s) on all positions.

The goal is for all working documents to be available to the respective campaigns no later than October 1. Mark indicates the timing is acceptable.

* * * * * * * * * * * * * * * *

E-MAIL

To: K.C.
From: Atlas
Sent: 8/11 4:59 p.m. (MST)
Subject: Policy Papers

Liz will be returning the marked drafts. Imagine the thrill of legislating and implementing this package. You and your team give new meaning to "outside the box." I'm jealous of our candidates. Thanks.

* * * * * * * * * * * * * * * *

E-MAIL

To: Atlas
From: Mark
Sent: 9/6 7:46 a.m. (CST)
cc: General
Subject: Labor Day Update

We've had a terrific summer. All campaign offices were staffed and operational, as I'm sure the General has briefed you. Our candidates have proven to be a capable and energetic bunch. They have all stayed on plan; meeting with all key local constituencies and actively engaging in each district's target activities/events. Once we start polling, I am confident we will hit our preliminary name recognition and favorability rating targets.

For the most part (and to the extent we can rely upon our reports) a significant number of our opponents have underperformed—especially with respect to fundraising. As you are well aware, the next meaningful candidate expenditure and fundraising reports will soon be filed for the period ending September 30.

This should be a relatively quiet month. Our teacher candidates will be back in school and their political activities will be relegated to weekends. Most have applied for and received grants of leave from October 8 through the election. Never thought I would ever come to appreciate the loosely drawn family leave regulations that the unions successfully fought for during the Clinton administration.

Otherwise, all PR/campaign materials are being finalized. A complete draft package should be on your desk within the next week to ten days.

* * * * * * * * * * * * * * * *

"What have we got?" asked an edgy Danny Ryan of his staff.

His team was all assembled at Cook County Democratic Headquarters for the finale of the campaign season. They had already worked endlessly for nine months. Post Labor Day, it was crack the whip, all-out sprint mode. He was obsessed with the significance of the end game, and with his track record, who could fault his approach and reasoning? He had concluded years back that extending campaigns beyond the Labor Day to Election Day bookends was of no consequence. It might stroke political egos, but he did not relish circle jerks.

His candidates were invariably incumbents possessing superior funding and field organizations. His priority races also tended to be down-ballot, out of the glamour that comes with races for statewide and federal offices. If a candidate for president sneezes, their campaign catches cold. If a candidate for state representative dies, they still might win.

Besides, no one pays attention until at least Labor Day and, these days, more likely Halloween. He knew the statistics. Only 24 percent of the population can name their state representative or senator and Danny prided himself on finding and delivering that 24 percent on Election Day. Nothing else mattered. One of the little known hypocrisies of American democracy is that only sixty-some percent of eligible voters register and only fifty-some percent of those actually vote. If you capture 51 percent of those voters—roughly 18 to 20 percent of those originally eligible—you win. A sad commentary that, in the end, the knowing of which drives campaigns.

It was a seasoned staff and they knew the drill: representatives first, then senators. Reports were chronological by district number.

Vital statistics were opponents' cash on hand, polling results, precincts walked, precincts remaining to walk, and plus/minus tallies; pluses for voters who will vote for their candidate and minuses for those who won't. It was a bi-weekly exercise from Labor Day until the October D-2's were analyzed and weekly thereafter. Detailed weekly polling also began in early October. No holds barred until the polls told Danny he had his Red Auerbach moment in a particular race. At that point, the campaign would go to cruise control and resources would be shifted to other campaigns where the outcome remained in doubt.

Mark Stone knew this sequence all too well. It was legend in the political community for its simplicity and its effectiveness. Everybody knew Jim Brown was going to carry the Cleveland Brown's offense. Just try to stop him.

Danny's team had completed its third go-round of the current campaign season when the itch began. The E Party was in twenty-two races, was trending naggingly positive in all races, but otherwise showed no apparent energy or financial capacity. Nothing to worry about. In each case, his incumbent was favored with over 50 percent positives from likely voters—the ultimate political safe harbor. Nothing to worry about. And in each case, he was fully funded and adequately staffed for the necessary mailings and G.O.T.V. Nothing to worry about. So why the itch?

In the Republican hemisphere, Elizabeth DiMaggio wasn't itchy; she was agitated. The Dems controlled the House 66 - 52 and the Senate by 32 - 27. In her dream scenario she could close to fifty-eight and twenty-nine respectively; but in her nightmare scenario she was down three to four seats in each chamber. That spelled D-I-S-A-S-T-E-R. In a year when she thought the political stars might align, the last thing she needed was a maverick third party dictating an unexpected diversion of resources.

The difference was in the social genes. Danny's incumbents were soldiers. Hers were prima donnas. If a Ryan soldier lost they were rewarded with a patronage position and a second pension. When her guys lost, their social standing dropped a notch and things could get unpleasant at the country club. When you're in the minority to begin with, notch dropping was U-N-T-E-N-A-B-L-E. Especially getting notched by an unknown, third party assassin.

She now, quite unexpectedly, had seven whining incumbents in need of babysitting and money. This drain on the party's staffing and financial resources, although not yet compelling, was just enough to suggest a revamping of her original game plan. A cycle designed for offense, and a net gain in seats, was teetering on defense.

* * * * * * * * * * * * * * * *

E-MAIL
To: Atlas
From: Mark
Sent: 10/5 6:47 p.m. (CST)
cc: General
Subject: Still On Target

A review of our opponents D-2's confirms no significant fundraising since the June 30 reports. All of which can change in the blink of an eye, and will, once we make our October surprise. For now, it strongly suggests we remain under their radar. Our opponents would be actively fundraising and reporting bigger cash on hand totals if a threat were suspected.

I suggest we set an all hands conference call for next week to review and finalize the next phase.

* * * * * * * * * * * * * * * *

E-MAIL
To: K.C., Mark, Tom and Lauren
From: Liz
Sent: 10/6 10:14 a.m. (CST)
Subject: Video Conference

The video conference call has been set for next Thursday, October 12, at 1 p.m. (MST). Each of you will receive your briefing books by Wednesday. The General has elected to attend in person and Atlas asks me to again extend an invitation for all of you to do so. I respectfully request two, preferably three, days notice to arrange your flights to Aspen.

* * * * * * * * * * * * * * * *

Atlas did not welcome video conferencing for important meetings such as the final all hands election prep. But with Patrick's health, Tom's reluctance during the playoffs, Mark's preference to be surrounded with all his analytics, and Lauren's concern with traveling in the face of pending deadlines, there was no viable option.

"Good afternoon everyone. And, as always, thank you for your time," Atlas began. "The General and I regret that you cannot be with us in Aspen, but I trust your local video conferencing venues are suitably comfortable.

"As you know, we're twenty-six days out and, pending any significant strategic deviations that we agree upon today, we will be fully operational on October 18. I've asked Mark to quarterback this session. Mark?"

"Thank you, Atlas. I trust you all have the updated campaign binders. I'd like to skip the overview, unless anyone has any questions, and go right to the section on ground game. General, unless you tell me otherwise, all candidates are on leave from their jobs and the troops, as you call them, are fully trained and scheduled for door-to-door canvass and other activities."

"Check," affirmed the General.

"We have four weekends left," continued Mark. "For those of you unfamiliar with the door-to-door canvass, it is still, in my estimation, the best way to identify our voters. We will use the old fashioned plus/minus scoring to designate who's with us and who's not. In each district we have targets for plus totals based on historic voter turnout algorithms. If we hit the targets and then get our pluses to the polls, we win.

"If you have enough volunteers, door-to-door gives you the best read. I know ASC has perfected phone polling research, but I'm a big believer in having the voter commit with their eyes and body language. Too easy to weasel over the phone. We will still poll by phone, but as a supplement.

"Thanks to Lauren's team, we're experimenting with bar code coupons for our pluses. Each canvasser will have a hand held device that will produce these coupons on site. Voters will be instructed to bring them to the polls to qualify for prizes for voting. I know it's tacky, but it's legal and has been shown to work. In doing so, we gain several tactical advantages.

"First, since we know who has received coupons, we will be able to electronically monitor our base on Election Day. This will allow us to identify who we still need to coax to the polls as the election unfolds. The system will be pre-programmed to generate calls to voters' homes urging their vote and will suggest site visits, if necessary. As you might guess, these last minute voter appeals can spell the difference in close races. And I dare to venture that we will find ourselves in many squeakers.

"Second, it will also be the first organizational step to party building. Anyone identified during the canvass who not only votes, but seeks out our pole watcher to redeem their coupon, will be prime targets for subsequent election organizing and fundraising.

"With respect to messaging, our mail campaign will kick off first. In your packet, you have generic puff pieces regarding why anyone should vote third party and specific issue pieces on education, the economy and ethics. Depending on our subsequent issue polling, we will roll out environment and energy.

"One of the decisions we need to finalize is the graphics and coloration. Anyone?"

"Mark, on these bullshit issues, you and Atlas have my proxy," snapped the General. "If you think anyone really gives a damn, I say pick 'em and move on."

"I'm not quite as impartial as the General," joined Lauren, "although I agree the graphics are fungible. I like the purple. It's a strong shade and I think mixing red and blue fits our message, at least as I see it."

"I'm partial to the purple myself," Tom agreed. "When it came to uniforms, I was always taken by the Lakers and Vikings. Different and strong."

"OK," said Atlas, "we're purple. Lauren, I also like the symbolism. And I agree, Mark you pick the graphics—just no gothic."

"So, I don't get a vote?" K.C. asked belatedly. "In that case, I vote purple. If nothing else, I always have a very negative visceral reaction to candidates who pick green. Anyway, here's my idea for symbolism. If they're donkeys and elephants, as long as we're the E Party, our symbol should be the American bald eagle."

"Outstanding," proclaimed Atlas. "Hearing no objections, we just became the Purple Eagles. All kidding aside, the eagle is truly inspired, K.C.," he said approvingly. "Thanks."

"With that settled," said Mark, "let's move on to the advertising, radio and TV. The video I'm about to play lasts thirty minutes. Afterwards, I propose to re-run and separately discuss each piece. The candidates will also view it over the next few days and comment electronically, after which we will finalize our package and media buy."

An invigorating two hours later, Mark turned the meeting over to the General for a detailed walk-through of the on-the-ground effort, including Tom's speaking tour. Lauren updated the I.T. toys in development and K.C. recapped the position papers.

As the call ended, Atlas and the General broke for dinner where they optimistically toasted to a victory that suddenly seemed plausible.

* * * * * * * * * * * * * * * *

"Keith, it's Atlas. We are set to transfer $150 million: $100 million to the trust and $50 million to the foundation. The trust will then transfer $25 million to the E Party upon Mark's direction. I expect him to request an immediate draw of $10 to $15 million, and in no event later than October 16. Please prepare any necessary resolutions to authorize the respective transfers. Please also contact the General to coordinate all disbursements and all necessary political and/or financial reporting for the E Party. As always, thanks for your help."

"Consider it done."

* * * * * * * * * * * * * * * *

E-MAIL

To:	Mark
From:	Atlas
Sent:	10/13 3:37 p.m. (MST)
cc:	General
Subject:	Transfers

Keith Mix has been advised to respond to your direction to transfer up to $25 million to the E Party campaign fund. Keith and the General will coordinate all disbursements and state filings. All vouchers will clear through Liz. Have fun.

* * * * * * * * * * * * * * * *

"Holy fucking shit! Holy fucking shit! This better be a typo. And what the hell is the Atlas Trust?"

It was not the first, nor the last time Danny Ryan would utter the politically incorrect HFS. For the staff present at that time, it was certainly the loudest, most animated version in unrecorded history.

Illinois law requires all contributions after October 1 in excess of $500 to be reported within twenty-four hours. Mark's direction to Keith Mix was delivered on October 14. The funds were wired on the 16th and Danny Ryan had been dutifully advised by staff within minutes of the daily election reporting update hitting the Internet.

Elizabeth DiMaggio received her report at roughly the same moment through an e-mail update on her Blackberry. Though not one to conjure up an HFS, her reaction was unequivocally on par, as was her stream of e-mail orders to staff.

* * * * * * * * * * * * * * * *

Nathaniel "Nat" Carson was the only other person in Illinois as facile with election reports as Mr. Ryan and Ms. DiMaggio. He was, beyond a doubt, the most savvy member of Illinois' third estate; a thirty-five-year veteran of its political wars and the official keeper of all political skeletons and gossip. He was also quite the entrepreneur, having launched one of America's most successful and influential political rags, "*The Back Bench*." For the most part unfairly characterized, as it grew in popularity, so did the use of its nickname—the Stench.

Nat was a seasoned journalist and his HFS moment was followed by the intuitive expectation of a phenomenal story. Just as Danny and Elizabeth were pushing their staffs for an instant analysis and revised plans, Nat was working every phone and every source he could muster. There would be no losing out to the *Tribune* or *Sun-Times* on this one.

* * * * * * * * * * * * * * * *

THE BACK BENCH
"If you let it slip, we catch it"

October 16
Special Internet edition

EXTRA EXTRA EXTRA EXTRA

An obscure political party, known only in Illinois, made history today with a deposit of $15 million to its campaign coffers. The contribution was made by an entity calling itself the "Atlas Trust."

The "E Party" was formed in June, listing Samuel Smith as its founder. In early June, it filed a slate of candidates for state Senate and House seats.

Officials of both the Democratic and Republican parties declined to comment on this story. Full details will be provided in tomorrow's regular edition.

* * * * * * * * * * * * * * * *

<u>E-MAIL</u>
To: State Central Committeemen
From: Danny
Sent: 10/16 7:00 p.m. (CST)
Subject: E Party Funding

STRICTLY CONFIDENTIAL

The E Party has submitted a D-2, dated today, indicating a contribution of $15 million from something called the Atlas Trust. This amount is almost three times our current budget for 87 races. If you do the math, they have an average budget of $1.5 million per Senate race and $1 million per House race.

Little is known about the E Party. They are running twenty-two candidates, of which thirteen are running against Democratic incumbents; four in the Senate and nine in the House. The attachment identifies the districts and candidates.

Our initial intelligence indicated an underfunded group of techno-geeks bitching about taxes. Underfunding is obviously off the table.

A call is set for tomorrow at 4 p.m. Please be prepared to address concerns for immediate, significant fundraising. Shoot any intelligence on E candidates to staff.

* * * * * * * * * * * * * * * *

THE BACK BENCH

"If you let it slip, we catch it"

October 17

As reported in yesterday's extra edition, the E Party of Illinois is reporting a contribution of $15 million from an entity called the "Atlas Trust." To put this in perspective, based on October 1 filings, the sum total of cash on hand for all other Senate and Republican races, combining resources for all Republicans and Democrats, sits at just under $6 million.

So who are these guys and who are their benefactors?

E Party candidates are currently running for eight Senate (four Democrats and four Republicans) and fourteen House seats (nine Democrat and five Republican). In a related story below, we list their candidates by district and opponent.

As we went to press, we have confirmed that a significant portion of the E Party candidates are educators. Whether or not "E" stands for education remains to be seen. Calls to all candidate offices have been met with "no comment."

A person named Samuel Smith is the titular head of this new party, but he remains an unknown.

The party is headquartered on Chicago's Southwest Side, giving rise to speculation that it could be some sort of new twist from Danny Ryan. Let's face it, who else could fund such an operation? And his ongoing war with the teachers' unions is widely known to have escalated. Efforts to reach Mr. Ryan were also met with "no comment."

Elizabeth DiMaggio reports that she has been suspicious of this new party, particularly since they filed against some of the Republican party's longest standing incumbents, normally the ones who get a pass from the Democrats as part of their non-aggression treaty for certain key legislators. She gave Mr. Ryan the temporary benefit of the doubt, saying "Let's see how these funds get allocated heading into the election. If the disproportionate share is used in races against Republicans, that will speak for itself."

Needless to say, sources all over Illinois report the anxiety meter has rapidly hit levels unseen by this reporter in decades.

In other news…

* * * * * * * * * * * * * * * *

E-MAIL

To: State Central Committeemen
From: Danny
Sent: 10/17 11:00 a.m. (CST)
Subject: Today's Call

STRICTLY CONFIDENTIAL

In preparation for today's call, I am forwarding all staff backgrounders on E Party candidates. Someone has assembled an impressive, hard-working, intelligent slate. Predominantly award-winning educators; each highly respected in their communities. The rest are best classified as entrepreneurs; successful in their fields and also highly regarded locally.

Given yesterday's funding, their effort presents a real threat to our majorities in both chambers, particularly given the political environment in Illinois.

We have organized an additional $5 million media buy that will need your approval no later than the close of today's call. The attachment includes a breakout, by district, of the points and the schedule.

We are developing content and will present the full campaign within 72 hours.

We are currently in the field with a comprehensive poll of all affected districts and the results will also dictate our messaging. Keep your fingers crossed that our incumbents' favorability ratings remain over 50 percent. We have no time for rehab assignments.

Our call is at 4 p.m. NO SPEAKER PHONES!!

* * * * * * * * * * * * * * * *

E-MAIL

To: General, Atlas
From: Mark
Sent: 10/17 4:22 p.m. (CST)
Subject: Hello Stench

As you can see from the attached articles, the stench is on us—literally and figuratively. Per our plan, I will contact him and begin leaking the E Party story. General, you can expect a call no later than Friday. Remember to keep your comments "off the record" and "for background purposes only" unless you review any stories pre-publication.

And, remember, Nat is only reputable to a degree. He is less inclined to fabricate "high ranking sources" but will cave on his principles to beat the *Trib*. They're all over this as well and have seemingly infinite resources when the story demands. But, with our help, Nat will always be at least one day ahead and, for the most part, should be spinning things our way. We're in the sprint phase of the election so a 24 to 48 hour press lead should be sufficient.

* * * * * * * * * * * * * * * *

"Nat, its Mark Stone."

"Mark Stone, how the hell are you? It's been at least a month of Sundays."

"I'm in Chicago and I was hoping we can get together. Among other things, I think I can keep you out front regarding the E Party until the election."

"You just made my year! You name it, I'll buy."

"Great. How 'bout six-thirty tomorrow for breakfast at Lou's."

"Six-thirty in the morning? This better be good."

"If it's not, I'll buy."

Lou Mitchell's, like deep-dish pizza, is another Chicago classic. The best breakfast in town, primarily home to the early birds—the traders, lawyers and construction workers. Always an eclectic scene; suits interspersed with hard hats. It opens at 5 a.m. and stays jammed until closing. It is not usually visited by reporters, given their night owl tendencies and, therefore, was a perfect rendezvous for Messrs. Stone and Carson.

"You look great," Mark said with his best suck-up opener.

"If you think I look great now, see me at 1 p.m. today when I wake up," Nat retorted.

"If you don't mind, I'll pass. Thanks for coming."

"No problem, as long as I end up buying. What have you got?"

"For the time being, no questions. I can feed this to you in a way that works. If, at any time, you can show me that I'm moving too slow we'll change the rules. Deal?"

"Deal for now, but if the *Tribune* scoops me; someone pays. And I don't mean for breakfast. I know where all the bodies are buried. Comprendé?"

"Comprendé! And, if the *Trib* or any other paper looks to have a scoop, call me as soon as possible and we'll work it through. I can pretty much guarantee you it will be a fabrication because I know from whence the E Party comes and it's an extremely short list of fiercely loyal people.

"The envelope I'm giving you today contains bios on all of the E Party candidates. It also contains the first E Party white papers on a variety of issues. The full content will hit the web next week.

For that matter, the E Party web site goes live this weekend. I'd like your feedback. I didn't put it together, but from what I've seen it's as good as any."

"Thanks. But, gimme a mulligan. Who's Samuel Smith?"

"No questions. But we can talk day after tomorrow. For now, it's all about the candidates."

* * * * * * * * * * * * * * * *

THE BACK BENCH

"If you let it slip, we catch it"

October 19

> Until today, the names of the E Party candidates were public, but not much else. *The Back Bench* has obtained exclusive background stories on all twenty-two E Party candidates. They're posted on the blog.
>
> On the surface, it's an impressive group. Mostly educators and all highly regarded in their communities. None of them have any prior political involvement, although they all have excellent voting records in general elections.
>
> In other words, no hacks. Isn't that a breath of fresh air?
>
> In other news…

* * * * * * * * * * * * * * * *

"Nat, Mark. Great story today. If I'm Danny Ryan, I'm in your pants."

"Well, you're right about Danny. Had one goon, one elected official and one union hack each call me within an hour of publication. Classic Ryan—multiple flanks. Report back to headquarters and compare notes. I'll never understand why the asshole can't pick up the phone himself. Too much 007 for me."

"And, DiMaggio?"

"Yeah, she called. By the way, I assume you scrubbed those backgrounders because I'm passing them out to both parties. Gotta feed the beast."

"We're OK. Anything I give you can be used however you choose. Let's do another round of omelets tomorrow and we'll talk about Mr. Smith."

"See you there. How about seven-thirty this time? No? Fuck, you're killing me."

* * * * * * * * * * * * * * * *

"So, who's Samuel Smith? If the competition had anything, it would be out. And, I don't think Danny's got it or they'd stop pumpin' me."

"Envelope number two. The complete dossier for General Samuel Huntington "Hunt" Smith, retired Army, retired CEO of Freedom Corp., and current chairman of the E Party of Illinois."

"*The* Hunt Smith?" asked Nat.

"*The*," answered Mark.

"Wow, this gets better every day. Decorated war hero, boardroom guru, friend to presidents and kings, and now running a political start-up. Either someone has goat pictures or there are suddenly 15 million reasons for this to get interesting."

"There may be goat pictures—but there are at least 15 million reasons to think this gets interesting. Have fun."

* * * * * * * * * * * * * * * *

THE BACK BENCH
"If you let it slip, we catch it"

October 20

General Samuel Huntington "Hunt" Smith was a war hero when I was growing up. There was once talk of a presidential bid à la Eisenhower. He retired with distinction and went on to build Freedom Corp. into one of the nation's most highly respected defense contractors. His reputation in the military and the boardroom are impeccable. Last this reporter heard of him, he was retiring to count his money.

Well, he may be done counting because, according to well placed sources, General Smith is the one and only Samuel Smith heading the E Party efforts in Illinois.

This could get interesting. The General is clearly up to doing battle with the likes of Danny Ryan and Senator DiMaggio. I never counted his money, but he retired with 2.5 million shares of Freedom Corp. common stock and when I checked, it was trading on the New York Stock Exchange at 37. You do the math!

In other news…

* * * * * * * * * * * * * * * *

E-MAIL

To: State Central Committeemen
From: Danny
Sent: 10/20 11:01 a.m. (CST)
Subject: Updated Polling

STRICTLY CONFIDENTIAL

The updated polling is attached. As you are well aware, news of the E Party has been flooding the television and newspapers since their funding became public. As I suspected, it seems to have unleashed a knee-jerk, pro-third party reaction, all of which predates the Hunt Smith announcement. Read it and weep!

Eleven out of our thirteen at-risk candidates now have favorability ratings under 50 percent; nine are under 40 percent. To the contrary, all of the E candidates exceed the magic number.

With the exception of the race for president, our entire line-up is weakly rated across the board. I trust you will reach the same conclusion after digesting the cross tabs—negative, negative, negative. Fasten your seatbelts!

Finally, the revised field campaign is fully operational. But we need additional bodies. Get us your lists of usual suspects. The Chairman has begun discussions with the unions for at least 100 additional workers per district.

* * * * * * * * * * * * * * * *

E-MAIL

To: Atlas, General
From: Mark
Sent: 10/21 9:30 a.m. (CST)
Subject: Pop Goes The Weasel

Grand slam! All leading papers in Illinois ran the story on the General and our overnight polling jumped big-time. E Party name recognition has passed the critical 50 percent level, and across the board our candidates' favorable/unfavorable ratings are averaging eight to one.

If I'm Danny Ryan, I don't know where to go first. Do I hit the General and the E Party or the individual candidates? By now, he should be in the can with attack pieces on our candidates, but this has to set him back.

Tom's next up to bat.

Atlas, I'd like you to consider making that call we discussed.

* * * * * * * * * * * * * * * *

"Nat, Mark. If it's okay with you, let's skip the eggs. Ever heard of Thomas Robinson?"

"Sure, but there are more Tom Robinsons than Samuel Smiths."

"Touché. But who's the most famous, highly respected Tom Robinson you've ever known or heard of?"

"We're not talking Jackie Jr. are we?"

"Let's just say you should do some checking around to see what he's up to lately."

"Holy Shit—this *is* right out of 007. Can't wait to meet the Bond girls. Thanks for the tip."

* * * * * * * * * * * * * * * *

THE BACK BENCH

"If you let it slip, we catch it"

October 23

Remember Tom "Jackie Jr." Robinson? Last time I saw him, he was sweet swinging himself into the Hall of Fame. Last time I heard, he was an ambassador for youth baseball; a mentor and father figure to countless underprivileged kids.

It appears Jackie Jr. is now batting clean-up for the E Party. Sources tell me he's been appearing before black churches and community groups across Illinois talking up education and E Party candidates.

Even before learning this information, I heard that the Democrat's polling has the E Party candidates on a rocket trajectory. Favorables are running at least five to one over unfavorables and that's just what they're admitting to.

The Republicans don't appear to have the resources to poll this late, but they can undoubtedly read the papers and the tea leaves.

In other news…

CHAPTER TEN

Filed under the category of "it's better to be lucky than good" was the relationship between Don Colletti and Atlas.

Colletti was the national head of the most powerful union in the country. While union membership across the country was either down or stagnant, his numbers were up. While indexed wages were also down or stagnant—his were up. Not tons, but enough.

On speaking engagements, he offered the canned presentation about hard work, dedication, efficiency, and of course, team work. Behind closed doors, off the record, he talked about his days as a union steward and the impact that Alex "Atlas" Stein had on his path to the top.

They still traveled together on occasion and he would drop his entire schedule on a chance call from Liz offering time in Aspen. Liz never forgot a birthday, and as luck would have it, Don Colletti was born on October 24.

"Mr. Colletti, this is Liz calling for Atlas. Can you take the call?"

"Take the call? Is the Pope Catholic?"

"Don, how's my favorite union boss?"

"Atlas, old buddy, you just made my year! When I grow up I want to be you—retired in Aspen, drinking beer at those great taverns, enjoying the good life."

"How many times do I need to remind you? I'm not retired. In fact, I outwork your entire day by 9 a.m. Once a union guy, always a union guy."

"Well, if you're not retired, you're a stupid asshole. Give me your money and I'm sitting on my island sipping beer—like in those commercials."

"On an actuarial basis, I think your bullshit pension is worth more than anything I own. Anyway, I called to say happy birthday. And I'd love to see you. I'll call your bluff and have Liz drop us into the Caribbean whenever you're ready."

"I'll see that bet and raise you to two weeks away. Just get me past the elections. As you might expect, we're balls out in the presidential race."

"Then it's a deal. I'll put Liz to work and you owe me fourteen days after the election. Bring some of the boys and I'll bring the General."

"Speaking of which, what's this I hear about old Hunt causing trouble in Illinois?"

"I'll fill you in on the trip. But he did want me to ask you a favor."

"Name it."

"When the political leaders in Illinois ask the unions to help kick his third party butt, insist that the game gets played straight."

"Know what? I can do you one better. That Shakespearean tragedy they call the Democratic Party in Illinois has cost us big time. If the call comes, I can serve up some serious lip service. And, I'll also quietly put out the word. Just promise me I won't get bit in the ass."

"Done! Thanks! You're the best!"

"No, old friend, you're the best! Tell Liz to bug the crap out of me. I'm already mentally packing my bags."

* * * * * * * * * * * * * * * *

E-MAIL

To: State Central Committee
From: Elizabeth DiMaggio
Sent: 10/25 4:30 p.m. (CST)
Subject: Staying The Course

The E Party's well-timed and well-financed run at a minority stake in both Houses is projected to produce a seismic shift in the electorate.

However, after careful analysis, I am recommending that we make no changes in our campaign strategy. The exception will be if any one candidate experiences a precipitous drop in polling, in which case we will cut bait and reallocate resources, both field and financial.

Unfortunately, in sticking to plan, we will also be placing members in serious jeopardy. Notwithstanding, our analysis suggests that the financial lift to remain viable is too heavy and would, at best, remain a risky proposition.

There is a silver lining. If the polling for the E Party holds, they will crack the Democrats' majority. This positions us to leverage our votes to create majority positions on issues for which we would otherwise face a brick wall.

More importantly, if we preserve and marshal resources, we position ourselves for a gubernatorial run in two years. The chance to capture the 800 pound gorilla seat at the table is quite enticing.

Please make every effort to participate in this evening's conference call. We will allow one hour for discussion and vote at 9 p.m. sharp.

Thank you.

* * * * * * * * * * * * * * * *

E-MAIL

To: Atlas, General
From: Mark
Sent: 10/26 9:14 p.m. (CST)
Subject: Thank You Stench

Thanks to Mr. Carson and the trailing stories across the state, we have hit our polling targets.

According to Lauren, the web site is getting a gazillion hits from web surfers looking for E Party, the General and Tom. That should explode once Nat goes public with the latest polling.

General, we need to step up the canvass. Now that our PR is out there, the last two weekends are critical. Unless I'm totally off base, we will be the headline story in each daily on multiple occasions over the next two weeks. We're working to schedule T.V. appearances. But, we have to give them the General or Tom to capture their imagination. As you can guess, the loyal opposition is going all-out to suppress.

* * * * * * * * * * * * * * * *

"Elizabeth, it's Danny Ryan."

"Mr. Ryan, to what do I owe this honor. Last time you called me the Cubs were in the World Series."

"I'm calling because I have information that you may find very beneficial to your at-risk incumbents."

"I'm listening."

"My polling has the E Party up at least six points across the board. And, well, my guys are not looking for any new kids at the playground. Remember, 'we don't want nobody that nobody sent,' and we surely didn't send for General Smith or Tom Robinson."

"So, you're saying I'm the lesser of the evils."

"Not exactly, but we can leave it there. Anyway, I'm going all-out negative from now until the election and I'm offering you our complete package—mail, radio, TV.—you want it, you got it."

"Danny, let me give this some thought. After all these years, I need to think through this Trojan horse of yours. But I'm definitely interested. I'll call you tomorrow. Thanks."

* * * * * * * * * * * * * * * *

THE BACK BENCH

"If you let it slip, we catch it"

October 28

If you have followed my rantings on a somewhat regular basis, you are no doubt aware of my disdain for the circus atmosphere surrounding our elections. I am particularly critical of the fifteen to thirty second sound bite character assassination pieces whose only redeeming feature is fat returns for the network executives.

With their gobs of cash on hand, I have awaited the inevitable television/cable roll-out of the E Party. It began yesterday. And while one day's viewing does not an upheaval make, I was stunned by the clarity and earnestness of their pieces.

The first piece dealt with ethics. Rather than attack the unseemly culture of modern Illinois politics, it spoke to the paternal aspect of government and the value of civility. I especially enjoyed the link between Washington and Lincoln regarding their greatness and the fact that their reputations are predicated on honesty. It gave me pause as I consider which president in my lifetime, if any, was worthy of that distinction.

The next piece dealt with the economy. It may have been too professorial in style for the voters' second grade attention span, but at the same time it avoided condescension or attitude. The message, once again, was clear and succinct—focused on the cancerous effect of under-budgeting and overspending, particularly on future generations.

Both commercials ran a surprising two to two-and-a-half minutes and were superbly choreographed. I don't know about

Joe Six Pack and his soccer wife, but I found them refreshing, stunning and compelling.

In other news…

THE BACK BENCH

"If you let it slip, we catch it"

October 30

With only one week until the election, the E Party polling shows tight races across the board.

Danny Ryan has launched a vicious counter-attack campaign. Sources indicate he has gone to all major party donors in an effort to support an additional $5 million media campaign. All negative.

In other news…

* * * * * * * * * * * * * * * *

The Senator never returned Danny's call. It was clear that he had much more to lose and she did not see enough upside in being complicit in his ruthless campaign. To the contrary, when she looked a few moves ahead on the chess board, her pawns were not worth putting her knights and bishops at risk. And, if the E Party caught fire, there would be deals to cut. Her silence was deafening. And when the Carson story broke on Danny going negative only one thought coursed through his brain—*You fucking bitch.*

* * * * * * * * * * * * * * * *

E-MAIL

To: Atlas, General
From: Mark
Sent: 10/30 8:28 p.m. (CST)
Subject: Going Negative

This will be a very difficult last week for our candidates. They may buckle under the fabricated, personal attacks Danny Ryan has unleashed. General, you will need to work your magic. I know you have counseled many a soldier facing heavy artillery. Atlas, when this is over, anyone who loses may need some ASC counseling as well.

However, unless the polling drops precipitously, at the individual campaign level our posture must remain 'no response.' At the party level, we will update the website with appropriate response messaging. General, you need to be ready to break silence and handle press inquiries. For those papers endorsing our candidates, we may reach for editorial board support.

* * * * * * * * * * * * * * * *

E-MAIL
To: Atlas, General Mark
From: Lauren
Sent: 10/30 10:00 p.m. (PST)
Subject: E Party Web At Ten Days

I am very pleased with the initial rollout of the E Party web site. Thanks to your Mr. Carson, we are now approaching 500,000 hits per day and growing. I am particularly fascinated by data showing that inquiries outside of Illinois constitute almost half of our traffic. That phenomenon has required us to quickly rewrite our registration software to segregate potential Illinois voters.

That's another surprising fact. Of the Illinois based hits, there are huge numbers of un-registered voters. In the next go round, we will segue this cohort to our voter registration application.

The best news is the response to our E-Back feature. In excess of 90 percent of the registered voters expressing interest are linking to the candidate directed sites and spending significant quality time analyzing backgrounds and positions.

Atlas, you'll be happy to learn that education is far and away the issue garnering the most attention. In a separate e-mail, I am forwarding all data from the completed questionnaires. General, I am also forwarding an e-mail to you with breakouts of all likely voters expressing interest in a specific candidate or whose questionnaires suggest a statistically significant issue preference profile. We can phone bank for plusses from these lists.

You would be literally kicking yourself if you knew how many inquiries we are fielding with an expression of interest in contributing. The software is ready when you are.

* * * * * * * * * * * * * * * *

THE BACK BENCH

"If you let it slip, we catch it"

October 31

I've seen some slick web sites in my day, but the E Party has broken the mold. I clicked on around 6 p.m. last evening and it was well after 9:30 when I realized I had blown through dinner.

I was especially drawn to the candidate pages. Kind of like Facebook meets YouTube. If any of their candidates get elected, I can't wait for the candidate interface feature they describe. Democracy will never be the same.

I also had this "Big Brother is watching" sensation. After answering multiple questionnaires, prioritizing issues, and playing simulation games, I realized that they had me share some very personal information.

Watching the E Party in action, I think back to the posse chase scene in *Butch Cassidy and the Sundance Kid.* The Democrats and Republicans around Illinois have got to be asking themselves "who are those guys?"

In other news…

THE BACK BENCH

"If you let it slip, we catch it"

November 2

With the election only five days away, the big question remains whether the Democratic party onslaught has sufficiently wounded the E Party players. I don't know where Danny Ryan gets this stuff, but calling it deplorable is too kind.

One wonders if negative campaigning will finally backfire. The General and Jackie Jr. seem ubiquitous in their response. They're such class acts. I think that explains why attacking the individual candidates was the Democrats' only hope.

Editorials around the state are unanimous in their condemnation. And since editors can sometimes be human, that probably explains why the E Party slate received the lion's share of endorsements. I don't know how much weight endorsements carry these days, but it's generating tons of free press for the new kids. Stuff you can't buy.

Since the media doesn't generally poll in down ballot races, the only data I'm receiving is party-based. That means it's too skewed to be consistently reliable. But if Mr. Ryan or Ms. DiMaggio and their minions had happy news, they'd be leaking it all over town. That's not happening.

In other news…

* * * * * * * * * * * * * * * *

E-MAIL
To: Atlas, General
From: Mark
Sent: 11/3 10:00 p.m. (CST)
Subject: Final Polling

Keep your fingers crossed gentlemen. That stuff the Democrats are using is hitting us hard. Never saw such flagrantly fabricated personal attacks. General, some day you'll have to tell me how our guys have managed to demonstrate such restraint and poise.

Against that backdrop, it's almost impossible to poll accurately. In this environment, the voter won't trust the voice on the other end. Answers to the softball test questions call the entire poll into question.

Notwithstanding, as the attached data shows, we lead in seven out of eight Senate seats and twelve out of fourteen House seats. Those in which we do not have leads are basically dead heats. I am equally encouraged by the results of the canvass to date. Our plusses exceed our goals in all districts and that's without interlacing Lauren's Internet polling.

General, if our G.O.T.V. efforts are successful, your infantry will have put us on the map. To that end, I will call you tomorrow night for our final walk-through before the field team conference call.

* * * * * * * * * * * * * * * *

"Good evening ladies and gentlemen. This is General Samuel Huntington Smith, and with me via simulcast, is Mark Stone.

"Thanks to our magnificent technical staff, you should be watching and listening on either your computer or television. You should also be capable of communicating directly with us and each other through your cells.

"Over the course of the next hour, we will review the procedures for mobilizing our voter base on Election Day. As you know, it is essential that we get all our identified supporters to the polls.

"Captains, you should have reviewed all scheduling sequences with your teams. Poll watchers, you may have the toughest job of the day because we anticipate every play in the dirty tricks book to be used. You've seen their attack ads. Need I say more? For the G.O.T.V. teams, we will start feeding data to the captains around one-thirty in the afternoon.

"Let me thank all of you for the amazing effort during the canvass. If you bring that drive and dedication to the field on Tuesday, your candidate is going to win. I repeat—victory is in our grasp as long as we execute. And with that, Mark will walk you through election eve and Election Day in great detail. Good luck. Let's get a victory!"

* * * * * * * * * * * * * * * *

E-MAIL

To: General, Liz, Tom, Lauren, Mark, K.C.
From: Atlas
Sent: 11/8 3:00 a.m. (MST)
Subject: Congratulations!!!!!!

UNBELIEVABLE! I LOOK FORWARD TO SEEING ALL OF YOU IN ASPEN LATER THIS MONTH FOR AN EXTENDED CELEBRATION.

* * * * * * * * * * * * * * * *

THE BACK BENCH

"If you let it slip, we catch it"

November 8

I've been at this crazy game of politics for more than twenty years and, until the last six weeks, I thought I had seen everything. But the E Party tsunami was as spectacular as it was unforeseeable. We have all complained for years about the inadequacies of the two-party system. I never thought I would live to see a truly successful third party effort, particularly in the Prairie State.

After all, who are these guys? A retired Army General, a former big leaguer and a band of school teachers. My comment is not intended, in any way, as a slight on their respective career achievements, as they are all quite accomplished. But to take on Mr. Ryan and the vaunted Democratic Party of Cook County, not to mention a none too slouchy Ms. DiMaggio, you're talking Daniel beats Goliath; U.S. hockey beats Russia; Red Sox come back from down three to beat the Yanks.

What is even more staggering is the way it was done. They withstood some of the ugliest, meanest personal attacks this reporter has ever seen. And, at no time did they lower themselves to respond in kind. Could it be the even greater victory yesterday was the repeal of negative campaigning?

They also did some good ol' fashioned stuff. They chose leaders, primarily educators, who had already earned the respect of their community. No lawyers—imagine that. And no get-rich-quick millionaires looking to buy their way to celebrity and power.

They also worked hard to promote their message of education, economy and ethics. Most took leaves of absence and campaigned, in-your-face style, for months. Their position papers were straightforward and refreshingly honest. They did not promise the world, rather some back-to-basics ideas that just may work. Nothing wrong with a little humble pie.

Congratulations E Party. Only now you have to show us what you're really made of. As anyone in politics knows, the toughest campaign is the first one for re-election. You will no longer have the element of surprise. You will all have voting records and you will have slogged in the legislative mud of Springfield. Mr. Ryan and Ms. DiMaggio will be waiting this time and they will be very well prepared.

In other news…

CHAPTER ELEVEN

The scene and celebrants were essentially the same as their initial meeting. Mark Stone was new to Aspen, but not the group. The lone absentee was Tom Robinson, keeping a previous commitment to a youth group.

The warmth of the late afternoon winter sun allowed for champagne toasts on the terrace where it had all started. "Well, my friends," Atlas saluted, flute held high, "we have much to celebrate and much to do."

The General cleared his throat. "A toast to Mark," he said. "Your strategy was flawless. As to you, my great friend," gesturing to Atlas, "thanks for giving this old warhorse the ride of his life."

"Some old warhorse," Mark began. "You and Atlas are the closest I've seen to non-stop energy. You both need to have your thyroids examined. I've never seen such attention to detail, organization and anticipation of adversarial moves. Danny Ryan is a certified mastermind and you reduced him to third grade playground antics. He's still looking for his non-existent union reserves. As for K.C. and Lauren, you blow me away. K.C., I see you as the tin man in this journey—all heart, and Lauren, absolutely the scarecrow—all brains."

"Well, I'll be the lion," said the General. "Atlas, you can be Dorothy."

* * * * * * * * * * * * * * * *

"Morning," began a groggy Atlas. "Sorry to start so early, but I have every confidence that Mr. Ryan awoke hours ago as part of his daily vendetta regime. Mark, am I off base?"

"Nope, I doubt he even took off for Thanksgiving. He's got November fifth circled on the calendar twenty-three months from now and he won't rest until our candidates are literally six feet under. However, I draw comfort from believing that Mr. Ryan and his henchmen will remain captive to the old playbook while we continue to reinvent the game. As we've already shown, staying at least one step ahead is essential. That's also why the negotiations for our votes regarding Speaker and Senate president are so critical."

"Whoa, horsey," said K.C. "I think you just skipped a few steps on the yellow brick road."

"Right, sorry. Thanks to you, K.C., our team has developed well conceived positions on a variety of topics. But it's all meaningless unless we are allowed to advance our agenda in the legislature. What most people fail to understand about our system of government is that control of process in the legislature is concentrated in the hands of two people—the Speaker of the House of Representatives and the president of the Senate. Especially in Illinois, in their respective chambers they are virtual dictators.

"Each new session of the General Assembly starts with critical votes in the respective Houses, for Speaker and president. Once elected, our beneficent dictators propose and the representatives and senators respectively vote to adopt rules of conduct that protect their fiefdoms. So that's what we're negotiating. In the Senate, the scoring is now 28 Democrats, 23 Republicans and 8 E-sters. It takes thirty votes to elect the president. In the House, it's now 57 Democrats, 47 Republicans and 14 E-sters. It takes sixty in the House to elect the Speaker.

"As our fearless leader set out to accomplish, we now arguably control the balance of power in each chamber. Our votes can give either the Democrats or the Republicans the majority needed to choose the leaders and the rules."

"But Mark," K.C. challenged, "can't the D's and R's, as you call them, cut us out?"

"Absolutely, but I seriously doubt they will. The Democrats have, with limited exception, controlled the Illinois legislature since anyone here was born. I doubt they give a sufficient share of control to the Republicans just to avoid us. As for the Republicans, their leadership should have figured out by now that the E Party is their ticket to the Promised Land, not a chance to become happier mushrooms."

"Very fascinating," said K.C. "And you're right. I'd like to think I'm an educated voter. Yet until today, I have never understood the power scenario you just described. I assume that's how it works in my state too."

"I'm not that familiar with New York. But from Congress on down, most legislative bodies wield power and process in the same way. The one exception, and it's unique to my knowledge, is the opportunity of the minority to filibuster in the U.S. Senate."

"So what do you propose?" the General asked Mark.

"That depends, in part, on our agenda. Once we know our plans for the two year General Assembly, we approach both parties and offer enough votes for their Speaker and Senate president candidates in exchange for whatever."

"If I'm the Democrats," the General began, "I don't deal unless I keep control of both chambers. How do you see that playing out?"

"Haven't thought that far ahead," answered Mark. "It's definitely the right question. I guess it depends on how they view the next election. The Speaker's the key. If he views the Senate as disposable, in the end I think he cuts the deal. But if he perceives the split will prevent him from re-establishing majority control, then it's a package deal."

"Well, if you're right," posed the General, "the way it plays out will give us insight as to how the Speaker perceives us."

"I don't know about that," said Mark, shaking his head. "We haven't spent much time talking about the Speaker. Be forewarned. He is one of the most brilliant political strategists in the entire country. A grandmaster of political chess. Staying a move ahead of Danny Ryan is one thing. The Speaker will set his checkmate many moves ahead."

"Mark," cautioned Atlas. "I'm sensing the need for a major sidebar on this topic. Let's move on. As I see it, we need to identify our agenda first with the negotiating strategy close behind."

"Maybe, but I don't think that's for us to say," said K.C. "We just helped elect twenty-two people who need to make that decision."

"I couldn't agree more," said Atlas. "It has got to be their agenda. As we all know, we've done this backassword. We elected candidates and called it a political party. Now we need to form the E Party underneath our elected officials. Mark, how much time do we have?"

"Not enough, I'm afraid. The new legislature convenes in early January. Traditionally, the Speaker and Senate president are elected as the first order of business in each chamber. But in reality, not much gets done in the General Assembly before mid-February. Assuming we never want to play the Newt Gingrich card and be portrayed as the ones shutting down the government, that buys us an extra six weeks. Let's call it mid-February. That's the over/under.

"Regardless, I believe the better course is to have our legislators set a very limited agenda for the spring session. The party complex can be completed over the summer and a more robust agenda can be set for the following year. The next election will grade us on the two-year cycle anyway. There's no advantage to an early sprint. In fact, there is likely a disadvantage. Our guys will be lucky to find the bathrooms before they have to vote on a budget in May. Better to be tortoises than hares in this marathon."

"In that case," offered Atlas, "I propose that K.C. convene another policy session to work on agenda building based on a two-year plan. K.C.?"

"Sure. Usual terms?"

"No problem. I'll have Liz start planning as soon as possible. It will be tight, given the calendar. But we should be able to squeeze it in after the holidays and before the swearing in.

"K.C., since we only have you for the one day, I'd like to devote some time to the think tank."

"Thanks. Since we last spoke," K.C. began, "I have been thinking about the concept of a policy think tank to support the E Party and I have come to the conclusion that we need to shift our focus. Unfortunately, the think tank concept is a throwback that does not appropriately reflect our message. To me, think tank connotes a sense of elitism and closed-end fraternity—a repository of smart people who can't find their individual voices.

"We need a revolving door to keep new ideas and people flowing. More like a university without tenure. We need to also blend doers with thinkers. Most importantly, our product should be people, not papers. I'd go so far as to suggest that future candidates not carry the E Party banner without graduating the E Party University. In many ways, it's what our current crop did in micro-fashion during their sessions in New York and the tutorials in between."

"A candidate school?" asked Mark.

"Well, yes, in a sense. Except the students, if you will, are engaged in creating and implementing the curriculum, which ultimately feeds the political agenda."

"Sorry, K.C., but I'm either dense or I'm just not on board," Lauren suggested. "We won this election because we are not them. As we move forward, we will need an identity or at least a solid core of principles. What I'm hearing you say is that we are more of a moving target."

"No, not really. Let's take education. Our identity, and core principle for that matter, can and will be that education is our top priority. We get there by staking out a platform that sets a series of goals, such as maximizing pre-school education programs. But from there, we just sound like your Democrats and Republicans if we don't constantly push the envelope. The point is to always be on the outlook for new and fresh solutions. And to that end, we can point to our institute as the laboratory that makes it possible."

"Then our institute needs to be without walls," added Lauren. "I'm thinking about Internet universities. Atlas asked me to develop an interactive platform to support our candidates. That same system can be expanded to serve the purposes you describe."

"I actually think it's both," said Atlas. "K.C. can create her institute and your platform can be used to facilitate, support and implement. Love it. But can it come together in time to meet the summer schedule we discussed earlier?"

Everyone nodded.

"If you don't mind," Mark began. "There is a segue here. My unscientific observation is that the average legislator spends almost no time doing the job he or she was hired to do. By that I mean finding out what makes the lives of their constituents better, and facilitating that betterment through government, when appropriate.

"Most legislators spend an inordinate amount of time raising money and campaigning, particularly congressmen for whom the burdens of raising money are staggering. At the state level, where fundraising is not quite so dominant, many legislators have careers to which they devote significant time. Others, some of whom we just defeated, just get lazy because they have safe districts. Either their party makes no demands on them to produce ideas or they learn to ignore their constituents without consequence; usually both.

"Regardless, the ideas they end up legislating come from interest groups pushing their agenda or an occasional forum, such as the NCSL, which hosts regional and national conferences."

"NCSL?" asked Atlas.

"I'm sorry. The National Conference of State Legislators. Or ALEC, the American Legislative Exchange Council.

"So, even if these ideas are the next sliced bread, and they're usually not, they tend to be the equivalent of loss leaders in a store, driving volume and sales—in this case contributions and votes. You'd be amazed how the system is gamed to allow legislators to boast about the bills they file or the votes they take, all the while knowing their bills and votes don't have a snowball's chance in hell of becoming law or producing public benefit.

"Look at the average session in Illinois. Five thousand or more pieces of legislation are proposed and very few pass. While some would say that represents effective and efficient government, it's just theater. Scratch the bills introduced and you'll find a startling lack of substance. Scratch the bills that pass and you'll find a startling lack of utility or creativity.

"The E Party has a chance to break that cycle. Thanks to Atlas, our legislators have no fundraising obligations. They can be totally devoted to their jobs. Thanks to the program K.C. and Lauren just conceived, they can be leaders of ideas, not followers.

"The missing puzzle piece is implementation. When the E Party can transition from idea to result, that's when it will have created value. And, that's when there will be a sustainable party."

"Then one of the things we need to address," added Atlas, "is how we transition our newly elected legislators to this role and how we build a party base to create and sustain the value system. I think this is also a good break point. The sun's out and the slopes are calling. All work and no play makes the General cranky. Let's pick this up at dinner."

* * * * * * * * * * * * * * * *

E-MAIL

To: Tom
From: Atlas
Sent: 12/9 7:14 a.m. (MST)
Subject: You Were Sorely Missed

It was such a shame that you were unable to join us for the celebration/retreat. Please know that we offered many toasts in your honor. We drank hard and skied hard. We also worked hard in anticipation of the challenges ahead.

You also missed learning that Lisa Boudreau will be joining our cause. If you recall, it was her interview that jump-started this journey. I have since enlightened her to that end and have hijacked her to join our crazy ride as our public relations guru. She's already cooking up some goodwill missions for you and others. How does an appearance on *Conversations with Kathryn Collins* sound? Might as well dream big.

I'm very satisfied with our plan to shape and finalize a legislative agenda for the next two years. To that end, I'm expecting you to weigh in big-time with ideas for keeping kids in school. Notwithstanding our teacher-legislators, the ideas you've shared with me are among the most straight-forward, imaginative and encouraging. At the end of the day, you can never substitute experience.

K.C. will be hosting another session with our senators/representatives over the Christmas break. I hope you can join them, even if you can only squeeze in a day. I'll have Liz call you to coordinate.

Just so you have the up-to-date status, in addition to K.C.'s work sessions, Mark and the General are mapping a strategy to negotiate the terms under which we will cast our votes for Senate president and Speaker of the House. The General will conduct the negotiations in conjunction with our leader designates. To that end, based on your work to date with our team, who do you see being our captains in the Senate and House? That all needs to get worked out in New York. All the more reason for you to make the trip.

Lauren continues to improve the web site and is focused on our platform for intra-party communications. The launch is scheduled for the summer. I'm learning that, in this nutty business, the two year election cycle for representatives is a whirlwind. There's not even a full year between the election and petitioning for the next term. What madness.

The General has also begun mapping out the rules of engagement for the E Party. Next time around, it will not be about five crazy people and twenty-two candidates. Unavoidably, there will be a political party with rules and structure. Not sure how I'm going to feel when the cord gets cut.

Speaking of whirlwinds, Mark is 24/7 politics and prepping for the next election. It's definitely a young person's game. I have trouble just keeping up with the reports he generates. Speaking of which, he has done an analysis on turnout in the districts where you worked the churches, etc. Claims you increased turnout by 5 to 10 percent and that, without you, we're too close to call in those elections. That makes you a cinch first ballot selection for the E Party Hall of Fame.

Best wishes to you and the entire family for the holidays and the new year. Hope to see you soon.

* * * * * * * * * * * * * * * *

E-MAIL

To: Atlas
From: Mark, General
Sent: 12/22 10:00 a.m. (CST)
Subject: Talking Points

Attached is the proposed framework for negotiations. The overriding strategy is to control the Education Committee and make sure our legislative initiatives get called for votes. Let us know when you're ready to discuss.

CHAPTER TWELVE

THE BACK BENCH

"If you let it slip, we catch it"

January 4

Great to be back from the long holiday break. I am waiting with baited breath to see how the new General Assembly plays out. The scenarios have been bouncing around in my brain.

For anyone who took the trouble to count, the E Party captured enough seats to block the Democrats bi-annual coronations in each chamber. I know Senator DiMaggio caught that in a nanosecond.

My spies tell me the midnight oil has been burning at both Republican and Democrat headquarters. The Speaker allegedly cut short his annual fishing trip to New Zealand. The possibility of there actually being a Republican in the Speaker's chair is right up there with Santa Claus and the Tooth Fairy. But every time I add 47 Republican House members to 14 E Party seatholders, I come up with enough votes for that to happen.

Republicans in control of process in both chambers? Snow in August?

And when it comes to legislation, how will the E Partiers vote? Taxes? Gun control? Abortion? Union issues? Women's issues? Legalizing marijuana? Death penalty? And, the hits keep coming.

Get yourself a good seat and a scorecard.

In other news…

* * * * * * * * * * * * * * * *

The Capitol building in Springfield, Illinois is a majestic beauty, embodying the classic lines of the 1868 architecture it proudly represents. It was never home to young State Senator Abraham Lincoln, but it warmly cradled many great thinkers and statesmen, including the 44th president of the United States.

Not unlike similarly styled models across the nation, it has withstood the onslaught of elevators, air conditioning ducts and incalculable miles of information technology conduit. All sorts of machinery invade catacombs initially designed for horse and buggy. And once grandiose meeting chambers have been decapitated to accommodate mezzanines and office space for armies of bureaucrats.

To the credit of its curators, the strength and inner beauty of its primary passageways and stairways have been meticulously preserved, along with historic art treasures depicting the history of the Prairie State. The cupola of the crown is a wonder of color and style rarely attempted, let alone captured, in the glass and steel of twentieth century architecture. Finally, despite the introduction of computers, electronic tote boards and big screen depictions of democracy in action, the original style and ambience of the legislative chambers reminds visitors of a time when the process was synonymous with civility and decorum.

It was a typically cold, gray Illinois January day when General Samuel Huntington Smith paid his first and only visit. Normally, he would relish an opportunity to partake of the cook's tour to feast upon the beauty and history characteristic of such a magnificent edifice. Unfortunately, his mission was too critical and focused for distractions; four meetings, one hour allotted to each.

Participation in each session was limited to the General and one invitee. Meeting requests had been sent under the auspices of the E Party of Illinois, addressed respectively to the Speaker of the House, the president of the Senate, the minority leader in the House, and the minority leader in the Senate. Each request set forth a concise and cordial outline of purpose, including the parameters pursuant to which the E Party legislators were prepared to cast votes for leadership. Finally, in an effort to avoid attention, the meetings were all scheduled on Sunday. The General insisted on the Capitol as both a sop to authority and a convenient way to accomplish his schedule.

Mark and the General had seesawed regarding the sequence of the meetings before settling on the Speaker being first. It was the most pivotal and would set the tone and tenor of those to follow. The Senate president would be second. Mark pushed for at least one Democrat to fall to last in order to assimilate Republican sentiment; whereas the General, ever battle-ready, did not want to afford an opportunity for interim collaboration between Speaker and president. Divide and conquer eventually won out over playing with a full deck.

David Kennedy had been Speaker of the House for eighteen consecutive years, a record of accomplishment in politics on par with Joe DiMaggio's 56-game hitting streak. Many attributed the streak to his unparalled brilliance, others, to his uncanny political instincts. But what most failed to grasp was the fact that his intelligence and instincts combined to yield his true gift—the ability to read trends before anyone else and make all necessary adaptations. He was always at least two steps ahead of the herd, and it had made all the difference. That he was a charismatic and gifted leader, and being born and bred a Chicago Democrat, completed this political David.

Had he chosen to do so, he could have at least been governor or U.S. senator. But the niche he carved suited his ambitions and allowed him to keep his equilibrium.

Similar to Danny Ryan, the dramatic onslaught of the E Party caught him off guard and the experience had been uniquely unsettling. Unlike most, he had anticipated the possibilities of a well funded third party emerging at the historically appropriate moment. But he had expected an emotional victory, more akin to a Jesse Ventura type of phenomenon, not a well orchestrated, fully funded, perfectly timed opponent emerging and succeeding—especially at the General Assembly level.

In hindsight, this is exactly how he would have launched an attack were he in the General's shoes. He admired the achievement. But the enemy was upon him and the element of surprise was exhausted. He totally understood where they had to go next and he would stop them. He was measuring the end of days and this would not be his legacy.

* * * * * * * * * * * * * * * *

E-MAIL
To: Atlas, Mark, Lisa
From: General
Sent: 1/5 4:30 p.m. (CST)
Subject: Meetings

The meetings went well, and for the most part, as expected.

The Speaker is terrific—exactly as advertised. So is Elizabeth DiMaggio. Were she in a Republican state with decent resources, she would be the dominant force.

They seemed to both state their positions a bit too quickly. But at this point, they're obviously on their own Machiavellian trajectories. And it's quite clear they still don't know who we are.

I'll give you the blow-by-blow when we talk tonight.

* * * * * * * * * * * * * * * *

"Atlas, this is Liz. I have the General, Mark, Lisa, and K.C. all ready for the conference call."

"Thank you, Liz.

"Hello all. I'm glad you were all available on short notice. As you all know, the General has met separately with Democrat and Republican leadership to discuss the E Party terms and conditions required in exchange for our votes for Speaker of the House and Senate president. General, it's your show."

"Thanks and good evening everyone. As Atlas indicated, earlier today I had a series of one hour meetings with the respective legislative leaders. Not much happened.

"As I guess we could have anticipated, the president of the Senate deferred completely to the Speaker. Conversely, the two Republican leaders indicated that all future negotiations had to include both of them. In each case, I told them I would respect their wishes. However, negotiating simultaneously with both Republican leaders will make it difficult to have one party control each House should we favor that outcome. However, that is not our current intention, nor do I think either party would want that result unless they see a distinct advantage in a two-year cycle of open warfare and minimal results. The Democrats might conclude that two years of inaction will vindicate their argument to return to the good old days, but I don't see the Speaker going in that direction unless it is his only alternative. He is just as likely to conclude that another two years of ineffective government strengthens our case for change. He doesn't strike me as someone who ever bets on the come.

"He also didn't say much. He congratulated us on a brilliant campaign, looks forward to working with us, small talked about fishing and the like, and listened intently to my pitch. His response was a very cordial 'let me get back to you.'

"The session with the Senate president was almost identical. The exceptions were that he's quite the Chatty Cathy and his response was essentially, 'I defer to the Speaker.'

"Both Republicans wanted to get right down to business. Having been in the minority for so long, this unexpected opportunity to grab the brass ring appears to have them spinning. They each asked very detailed questions about our proposal and took copious notes. Each also probed deeply into our party's decision-making apparatus, wanting to confirm that we can be trusted, and that we can deliver what we promise. As much as the prospect of governing excites them, wearing the jacket for two years of inept governing is not an acceptable scenario.

"I hadn't gone into the meeting expecting them to be so open about their downside risk. But, as I later thought about it, I totally understand their point. We could cede control to them, but cast our votes in ways that undermines their leadership and then attempt to leverage their failures in the next election. No trust. No partnership."

"So, who has the ball as of now?" Atlas wanted to know.

"Well," the General paused, "I guess the Democrats have the ball versus us and we have the ball versus the Republicans."

"That's what I thought."

"I propose," the General volleyed, "that we try to close the deal with the Republicans. Assuming they're willing to accept our entire package, that's our ticket to turn Illinois upside down and get some things done. Although trust is a difficult commodity to sell to strangers, this is literally a once-in-a-lifetime change they can't afford to pass up."

"I hear what you're saying General," Mark cautioned. "But we don't want this to be our once-in-a-lifetime chance. If we work with the Republicans and they push for legislation we can't tolerate, we will be taking votes that could cost us the next election. Even if we collaborate on meaningful legislation, the governor can impose his veto and pick us apart with spin. Either outcome could be a slippery slope.

"On the other hand, by keeping the Democrats in control, we are positioned to pass a few laws. I'm not trying to suggest they will let us hit anything out of the park. But we can build on a few singles and doubles."

"I hadn't thought about the governor's veto," Atlas conceded. "If I understand Mark correctly, he is the Democratic backstop against anything we hope to get done."

"But, Mark," K.C. chimed in, "can't we override?"

"Sure, but that takes seventy-one votes in the House and thirty-six in the Senate. Can't get there between us and the Republicans."

"Then I'm leaning toward a deal with the Democrats. Only…how do we know they'll take our deal? A full deal with the Republicans might be preferable to a half deal with the Speaker. How's that for waffling?"

"I've never known you to waffle, K.C.," said Atlas. "Lisa, what's your take?"

"I have a different slant on waffling. When it comes to PR, I can defend almost anything if we have the budget. And Atlas tells me we do. Therefore, your anti-Republican scenarios don't scare me. On the other hand, I clearly see the benefit to keeping the Democrats in power. That leaves me voting for whichever side gives us the better deal."

"General?" K.C. asked. "Have we set any deadlines for negotiating?"

"Good question, K.C. I told each side that if I did not have a deal in one week, for the following week I would negotiate exclusively with the other. Now we have to decide which one I lied to."

"Maybe it won't come to that," Atlas theorized. "Unless something breaks, let's plan a call for two to three days from now to update status. I'll have Liz contact all of you to set that up. Thanks again. Good night everyone."

* * * * * * * * * * * * * * * *

E-MAIL

To: General and K.C.
From: Atlas
Sent: 1/5 8:02 p.m. (MST)
Subject: Tonight's Call

Didn't want to pick a fight during the call, but I found Mark's argument compelling. With the Democrats, we might get something done. With the Republicans, we might win the PR battle, but lose the war in the respect that nothing ends up getting done. Should we falter in the next election cycle, I do not want our only accomplishments to have been PR victories. If we could be assured that our PR victories will lead to electoral victories, I would deal with the Republicans. I just don't see us needing to take that chance.

* * * * * * * * * * * * * * * *

E-MAIL

To: Atlas and K.C.
From: General
Sent: 1/5 9:17 p.m. (CST)
Subject: Tonight's Call

I get where you're coming from. Let's not rush to judgment until the Speaker responds.

* * * * * * * * * * * * * * * *

E-MAIL

To: State Central Committee
From: Senator DiMaggio
Sent: 1/6 8:30 a.m. (CST)
Subject: Mission Accomplished

The meeting with the General went well. As was our primary goal, we have established clear lines of communication. He has promised to respond quickly through designated go-betweens and a procedure is in place for direct contact, if and when necessary. Consistent with his reputation, I believe he and the E Party will shoot straight.

* * * * * * * * * * * * * * * *

E-MAIL

To: Atlas, Mark, Lisa, K.C.
From: General
Sent: 1/7 4:01 p.m. (CST)
Subject: Negotiations Update

There must be something in the Springfield drinking water because I was contacted today by both Speaker Kennedy and the Republican twins. Here's a brief summary:

A. Conversation with the Speaker (11:02 a.m.):

1. We asked for chairmanships of two out of three committees in each House from among Education, Education Appropriations, and Environmental. He said we can have only one in each and we cannot have the Appropriations Committee.

2. We asked to have all appropriations bills be public for two weeks before being voted on. He said we can have five days in each chamber and only three full days if the scheduled adjournment date has passed.

3. We asked to have all of our bills guaranteed to be passed out of committee and put to a vote on the floor. He will only guarantee bills can come out of the committee for which our representative/senator is the chairperson and, although he will allow a floor vote, he does not agree to block hostile amendments. But, if our bill is amended, we have the right to have it not called for a vote.

4. There were a few minor tweaks not worth discussing.

B. Conversation with the Republicans (2:56 p.m.):

1. Similar to the Speaker, they will not offer chairmanship of an appropriations committee. They said they've been in the desert for too long and their own members want the most prestigious chairmanships. However, their counter is to offer three chairmanships in each House; one can be either Education or Environment, and we can choose the other two from a group of five less desired committees to be determined once their members' priorities have been met. But, they will not canvass their members until a deal is cut. They do not want to create false expectations (totally understandable).

2. They will allow the two weeks of "sunshine" (as they call it) for appropriations bills in the House of origin. But, only one week in the second House. They also add another layer. If there is a need for the

House of origin to reconsider, that vote only gets one day of "sunshine."

3. Most troubling is that they will not guarantee any of our bills will be called for a vote on the floor. They will, however, let all of our bills out of committee.

4. Minor tweaks.

* * * * * * * * * * * * * * * *

E-MAIL
To: Atlas, General, K.C., Lisa
From: Mark
Sent: 1/8 12:14 p.m. (CST)
Subject: Negotiations Update

Curious!?

I am surprised by the Speaker's response, but mostly because he gave away more than I would have suspected. Was this 'take it or leave it' or is there room for negotiation?

I am equally surprised by the Republicans, but in the reverse. They pushed back much harder than expected. The biggest concern is their being unwilling to give us votes on our bills by the entire chamber. Letting bills out of committee is worth nothing if that's the end of the trail. This goes back to their concern that, on the floor, we can join with the Democrats to pass things they don't like.

The Speaker's offer on that issue, although appearing to be moderate on its face, highlights the fact that we can expect hostile amendments. Since he has control of the rules committee, rest assured he will find ways to tweak us to death by amendment.

As for chairmanships, if education is to be one of our primary issues, having control of that committee's chairmanship in both Houses is all we need. The extra committees offered by the Republicans don't excite me.

At this point, I think the Speaker has come far enough and may give more. I remain convinced that the all Democratic leadership strategy is the way to go!

* * * * * * * * * * * * * * * *

E-MAIL
To: General
From: Atlas
Sent: 1/8 6:16 p.m. (MST)
Subject: Negotiations

You seem to be outvoted 4 to 1. Before you respond to the Speaker, see how hard you can push the Republicans to give us <u>everything</u> we want.

If you cannot get them to agree, let's push back on the Speaker and cut the deal once you determine you've got as much as he will give.

By the way, great job! Some day when we elect our first president, you can be secretary of state.

* * * * * * * * * * * * * * * *

E-MAIL

To: State Central Committee
From: Elizabeth DiMaggio
Sent: 1/10 12:14 p.m. (CST)
Subject: Leadership Negotiations

We withdrew from consideration today. The voting requirements were too onerous. Although the thought of having Republicans sitting as Speaker of the House and Senate president was extremely exciting, I am more convinced than ever that taking a shot at governor in the next election is significantly more important to our long term interests.

* * * * * * * * * * * * * * * *

"Nat? It's Mark. Let me wish you a belated Happy New Year! I hope you and your family enjoyed the holidays and that the new year will be good to all of you."

"Thank you and same to you," Nat answered. He had not spoken to his E Party mole since the election and had hoped that his usefulness was not fleeting. He sat up a little straighter.

"How about some breakfast?"

It was exactly the question he was hoping for.

"You name it. I'm buying."

* * * * * * * * * * * * * * * *

E-MAIL

To: Alex
From: K.C.
Sent: 1/10 10:11 p.m. (EST)
Subject: Strategy Session Update

The final strategic policy session with Team Atlas was a smashing success. Sending Thomas once again solidified your uncanny insight to group psychology as he greatly facilitated our team building.

Team E also has a renewed dedication, having survived the personal onslaught of the Democratic attack campaign. That, and the Thomas touch, have forged lasting bonds.

The sessions on education were outright fun. There is a rapidly building synergy and they feed on each other. Although the entire effort remains a work in progress, early childhood education and reducing high school dropouts are their primary focus. We now have working groups for each topic and the collective sense is to work one issue in the House and the other in the Senate.

With Thomas' help, Representative Jenkins has been selected team captain (God bless Thomas and his sports analogies). Senator Madeline Martin has been selected head of the E Party Senate Caucus and Representative Harris Kubik was chosen on the House side. Not exactly the selections I would have made, but the choices are solid—no reason to second guess. Finally, assuming the General works his magic, Senator Mona Benjamin will chair the Senate Education Committee and Representative Perle Abernathy will chair the House Education Committee. Jenkins is spectacular and will be an outstanding leader. Tell the General to get the baton ready.

Sorry to end on a down note, but Patrick couldn't make the sessions. I'm not sure what's up, but he's on a bit of a downward spiral and his physicians thought the commotion of moving about would be too disruptive. He does, however, have me brief him in detail. And, he still "gets it."

* * * * * * * * * * * * * * * *

THE BACK BENCH
"If you let it slip, we catch it"

January 11

Reliable sources have confirmed that, when the new Illinois General Assembly convenes, the same old faces will be sitting in their respective seats of power.

In a series of high level negotiations recently conducted at the Capitol, the Speaker and General Smith have reached an arrangement, the terms of which have not been made public. Since the General holds no elected office, until the deal is confirmed and announced, there is no public entitlement under the Freedom of Information Act.

We have confirmed that the General met separately with leaders from both sides of the aisle and from both Houses. Consistent with past practices, it is easy to conclude that the Speaker made the General an offer he could not refuse. Or, perhaps, vice versa.

In other news…

THE BACK BENCH
"If you let it slip, we catch it"

January 12

The inauguration of the new General Assembly was a day for history. To the untrained eye, it was business as usual with David Kennedy elected Speaker for the tenth consecutive two-year term. Senator Welk was elected Senate president. In addition, rules of procedure for each chamber were adopted.

The E Party contingent showed all the enthusiasm and trepidation of first day kindergarteners. Surrounded by loved ones, they beamed with pride as they raised their hands for the swearing-in ceremony.

Although the terms of the deal with the devil have not been publicly disclosed, to the "trained eye" there were some significant and telling developments. For the first time in the 18-plus years that Kennedy has been Speaker, committee chairmanships have been awarded to minority party members. Senator Benjamin and Representative Abernathy of the E Party will each chair the respective Education Committees.

On a more subtle, but totally shocking note, Rule 5-2 in the Senate and Rule 38 in the House have been amended. These respective rules now require (are you sitting down?) that budget bills must wait one week before being called for a vote on final passage. Because the rule applies independently in the House and Senate, the budget for the state of Illinois will now be open to public scrutiny for at least two weeks. This is a beautiful thing—transparency on steroids. Certainly a big change from the "slam-bam-thank-you-ma'am" budgets negotiated in last minute deals and passed with almost no analysis or reflection.

Thank you, General Smith. Thank you, E Party.

Efforts to discuss today's events with E Party representatives were met with their familiar "no comment" mantra. We understand the E Party has engaged a soon-to-be announced press spokesperson to handle media inquiries from this point forward.

In other news…

THE BACK BENCH
"If you let it slip, we catch it"

January 15

EXTRA EXTRA EXTRA EXTRA

In a press release late this afternoon, the E Party announced that Lisa Boudreau, formerly of *Fortune* magazine, will be serving as their media spokesperson. Lisa may not be a household name, but she is an award-winning journalist and very highly respected in the financial community. Once again, the E Party has attracted a nationally renowned figure to its leadership team.

In other news…

THE BACK BENCH
"If you let it slip, we catch it"

January 18

At her official introduction as the E Party spokesperson, Lisa Boudreau quickly threw down the gauntlet.

She announced that the E Party representatives and senators will not vote on any initiatives (including all legislation, rules, regulations, resolutions) until the legislature passes and the governor signs ethics legislation containing a set of principles to be released.

In response to questioning, Ms. Boudreau explained that the atmosphere of sleaze encompassing Illinois politics has tainted the entire process. In her words, "from this day forth, the citizens of Illinois are entitled to know that legislation is free of any and all corrupting influence."

When pressed to offer specifics, Ms. Boudreau refused to cite any individual examples, referring instead to the "myriad of notches in the U.S. attorney's belt over the last decade."

She left the door open a bit for emergency matters, but declined to specify how they would be determined.

In the absence of E Party votes, Democrats and Republicans collectively possess sufficient voting potential to pass any measure. It remains to be seen how they will react to this announcement.

In other news…

* * * * * * * * * * * * * * * *

"Hello Daniel."

To Danny Ryan, these two words had the equivalent impact of "this is nurse Jones, the doctor asks that you come in today to review the results of the biopsy" or "this is the ABC school, there's been an accident." To the best of his recollection, there were only three people to have ever called him Daniel and his parents were both dead.

The last time the Speaker called to discuss election results, the Republicans had come within an unacceptable margin of three seats in the House and just one in the Senate. It mattered not that the economy had tanked or that the Democratic president and congress were at all-time lows for job approval. It mattered not that several of the defeated incumbents had been involved in the worst sex scandal to hit Springfield in decades. And, it mattered not that other Democratic stronghold states had seen the first capture of a legislative chamber by Republicans in, respectively, 22, 18 and 16 years. This was Illinois.

The last such call came within two days of the general election. It was a measured, terse, effective warning. That this call had taken until February, creating a false sense of security that had allowed him to disengage his mental air bag, made the psychological whiplash all the more painful.

"Hello Daniel."

Even in the best of times, these two words had never preceded "How are you?" "Congratulations," "Merry Christmas," or any other common salutation.

It mattered not that he had earned a national reputation for excellence, had accumulated untold reservoirs of respect and gratitude for his party and its leaders across the country, or that his commitment and dedication had come at such great personal sacrifice.

"Hello Daniel. I need three things. I need to know where their money comes from. I need to know all members of their inner circle. And I need to know when and where they begin recruiting for the next election. I know you have been plotting your revenge. Stop! You're wasting valuable time and energy. I expect a report on the money by the end of session. Thank you. Good-bye Daniel."

Well, at least "Thank you" and "Good-bye Daniel" beat a purposeful click. "Thank you," and "Good-bye Daniel" beat, "I can't begin to express my disappointment. Your efforts are tantamount to failure." Most importantly, unlike the last time, it beat "You have placed us in extreme jeopardy. You have failed our trust. I think you understand the consequences in the event this outcome is repeated."

Repeated? He had just failed miserably. The inevitable "Hello Daniel" had arrived, but the guillotine had not been dropped.

Thank you, Mr. Speaker, he jokingly thought to himself.

* * * * * * * * * * * * * * * *

THE BACK BENCH
"If you let it slip, we catch it"

March 22

Well, we have reached Spring Break. The traditional half-time of the legislative season. To date, the most potentially contentious session in the history of the Illinois General Assembly hasn't produced so much as a whimper of controversy. Did they call a truce in the Middle-East and forget to alert the press?

The E Party threw down the ethics gauntlet in January and, true to their word, their member legislators have voted present on every bill. They have made a lot of noise in committee but, as yet, have not offered meaningful ethics legislation. The Speaker should be hoisting them on their petard of inaction. The Democrats and Republicans are all kissy face, passing the usual 'this is bound to make me look good with the voters' legislation. Having earned their press releases, these good for nothing ideas will dutifully die when they cross over to the second chamber. My favorite so far is creation of the "*Retail Sale and Distribution of Novelty Lighters Distribution Act*," prohibiting the sale of such lighters and imposing a petty offense of not to exceed $500 for each violation.

Is the E Party a paper tiger?

Too quiet. Too neat. Scary.

I would like to wish all my readers a Happy Easter or a Happy Passover. Enjoy the time with your families. Might as well enjoy it while it lasts. My kishkees tell me we're in for a long hot summer.

In other news…

* * * * * * * * * * * * * * * *

E-MAIL
To: Atlas, General
From: Mark
Sent: 3/24 5:16 p.m. (CST)
Subject: Spring Break

It would appear our actively planned inaction has worked well. The troops have set out all we hoped to accomplish. They are all now steeped in process.

The pretense of waiting for an ethics bill to pass has given them the cover to observe and avoid rookie mistakes. I'm somewhat surprised that the press has tolerated the charade, but Lisa has done a masterful job of deflecting. Feeding Nat an occasional scoop has avoided any pestering on his behalf.

We will introduce our ethics bill on the first session day after the break. It will be an amendment to Senate Bill 986. Although it will be considered a hostile amendment, the Speaker will be taking a risk if he holds it in rules. It has too many goodies the liberals have been clamoring for.

If we don't move now, we run the risk of being cast as spoilers, especially if and when the session runs into overtime. We do not want to be seen as the ones shutting down government.

Last item. I'm told Danny's field envoys are leaving no stone unturned in an attempt to identify the funding source for the Atlas Trust as well as the "real" E Party players. The General's traps must be holding or we'd be seeing leaks to the press. Here's hoping our luck holds out until after adjournment.

* * * * * * * * * * * * * * * *

There had been no surprises in the Speaker's ask. In fact, Danny had set his staff on that same path shortly after the election.

To date, chasing the money and the inner circle had borne no fruit and the candidate ferreting season was months away. With respect to the money, the path of least resistance should have been through an arranged leak at the Yura, Mix & Eisenstat firm. But at the General's insistence, all files had been moved off-site and the assigned attorneys were taking their "Chinese wall" quite seriously.

Determining the inner circle was an equally daunting endeavor. The General had employed very sophisticated anti-bugging strategies to prevent phone and Internet surveillance. To avoid any wiretapping risk, all vital communication was relegated to e-mail and e-mail addresses were scrambled frequently. Both the

General and Thomas had been regularly followed. But since this was post election, they had resumed fairly normal patterns for which no discernable links presented themselves. Neither had traveled to a common destination and, among their individual travels, neither had visited the same location more than once. Dead end after dead end.

Had the Speaker not imposed a premature deadline, Danny may not have thought to engage Nancy Rae.

* * * * * * * * * * * * * * * *

Nancy Rae Mitchell, known as the "Black Pearl" long before Johnny Depp turned pirate, was Danny Ryan's political assassin. They had worked together for almost twenty years, which was difficult to square in his mind given that she was only then in her mid-thirties, resembled a college coed, and was as beautiful as ever.

Born into a broken home in Southern Alabama, her upbringing mirrored any bigoted stereotype: constant relocating, physical abuse, abject poverty and a failed education. How and why she landed in a foster home in Chicago, Illinois, was not a topic she had ever shared with Danny. Fortunately, she had never been subjected to drugs and, despite many unfortunate episodes starting at a very young age, had never become pregnant.

Her beauty, grace and allure were a devastating package. Throughout her youth, it was a curse. Après Danny Ryan, it was both a blessing and a weapon.

Her Chicago foster dad had stumbled into precinct work at a young age and had parlayed his dedication into a steady but unspectacular career of menial labor for the city. When his legs could no longer tolerate precinct work, he figured the angles on foster parenting, and sent his revolving brood to fulfill his obligations. If for no other reason than her stunning good looks, Nancy Rae became a favorite of the local ward boss. Yet, it was her equally stunning mind and sassy self-confidence that catapulted her to the upper echelons of the Democratic machine.

When she first met Danny Ryan, she was just short of seventeen, but armed with her degree from the college of hard knocks, she presented as a sophisticated twenty-something.

Danny's first reaction was as visceral as any man's to this young seductress. However, as his one and only true love was politics, he was the only man she ever met who chose to enter her brain. Under Danny's tutelage, she became quite the package. Over time, she gained the majority of her victories through strategy and hard work. Only occasionally did she use her sexual charms to complete a conquest.

Eventually, she became Danny's right hand person and most trusted confidant. Although there had never been the slightest amorous moment, the long hours and proximity drove the jealousy that ended with Danny's divorce. His spouse was convinced and he could never prove the negative. Just as well, he rationalized. Borrowing from *The Godfather*, he well understood the personal consequences of the life he had chosen. He was also genuinely happy for his ex when she remarried and ultimately gave the Speaker a grandson.

Rather than subject Nancy Rae to his fate, he pushed her from the nest and presented her with two, six figure, politically induced lobbying contracts; a part-time career that she quickly grew to a seven figure annual income. At the end of the day, the brains/sex package was even more powerful for achieving results in her new pursuits.

When the call came from Danny, she jumped at the opportunity to help her best buddy. That Thomas Robinson Jr. was her target was an enticing frosting.

* * * * * * * * * * * * * * * *

All legislature-based press conferences at the Capitol in Springfield are held in the "Blue Room," a non-descript auditorium for up to fifty or so press and gawkers on the mezzanine level. It's available to any statewide officer, legislator, caucus, press secretary, or constituent group needing to fill the papers and airwaves with the vital propaganda of the moment. On any given session day, there will be anywhere from one to five planned spoutings and, occasionally, they rise to the level of newsworthiness. Of somewhat less significance, if there is such a thing, are the endless stream of press releases —generally targeted for the respective legislators' local newspapers where their stories have a better chance of appearing above the fold.

If pressed, Nat Carson could have tallied over 20,000 press conferences and more than half-million press releases during his career. If pressed further, he could remember a handful of each that had made a difference. But, at least on most days, the system kept him from actually having to break a sweat chasing the news.

Nat was also spoiled by Mark's clandestine tips, so he was as miffed as he was excited to learn that Lisa Boudreau had called a press conference to announce the E Party ethics proposal.

* * * * * * * * * * * * * * * *

THE BACK BENCH

"If you let it slip, we catch it"

April 6

An unusual event occurred at the Illinois Capitol yesterday. The E Party held its first press conference of the session, for the purpose of introducing their ethics bill.

I was totally unprepared to have their party spokesperson, Lisa Boudreau, and its caucus chair, Representative Barbara Jenkins, present the most comprehensive, well organized proposal in this reporter's memory. The supporting press release was distributed an unheard of day ahead to allow the press to prepare. Even more startling, each question was answered in context. When was the last time that happened? If there was a sound bite, I missed it.

The full release is posted on the blog. The essence of the initiative is this year's most politically exploited noun, "transparency." However, when elected officials call for transparency, it usually refers to others. In this case, it refers to the legislators themselves.

To that end, the plan requires: (1) all legislators to post weekly on the Internet their schedules for the preceding week, as it occurred, and the upcoming week, as it is expected; (2) before voting on any measure, a legislator needs to post a log indicating all persons with whom contact was made concerning that initiative and indicate if any contributions were received from the contact or any client they represent; (3) lobbyists must regularly identify each specific piece of legislation with respect to which they are lobbying and on whose behalf.

Related transparency provisions are proposed for all statewide officeholders and key executive branch administrators.

There is a total block on all political contributions by any lobbyists and clients on whose behalf they are registered during the time the legislature is in session, until thirty days after adjournment. Contrary to existing measures and rules, the ban on contributions is not just limited to specific days on which the legislature meets.

Finally, there are strict limits placed on nepotism, at all levels of government across the state. No relative of any elected office holder inclusive through first cousin, can be an employee of government. The proposal would grandfather any such current employee for five years.

I doubt this proposal flies, but it gives the E Team the credibility they need to stand behind their pledge to not vote on bills until meaningful ethics legislation passes.

We have finally seen the first aggressive move on this year's legislative chess board. The next move is the Speaker's.

In other news…

THE BACK BENCH

"If you let it slip, we catch it"

April 8

That did not take long!

Only two days following the E Party's shot over his bow, the Speaker responded with his own ethics package. Although it doesn't go quite as far, it adds some bells and whistles that the public will like.

His sell job is to find enough Democrats or Republicans to get it passed. Someone will be left standing when the music stops.

In other news…

* * * * * * * * * * * * * * * *

E-MAIL
To: Atlas, General
From: Mark
Sent: 4/8 4:52 p.m. (CST)
Subject: Ethics Package

Gentlemen, you moved a mountain today. The Speaker's ethics package goes further, by leaps and bounds, than anything the Illinois General Assembly has contemplated, let alone passed.

If you notice the subtlety with respect to contributions, he leaves the door open for the party to receive funds at all times. As party chairman, that actually increases his stranglehold. At the same time, a big win for those pressing for campaign reform. The E Party can declare victory for driving the agenda.

The Speaker must have other plans for dealing with the Atlas Trust. However, as we anticipated, he's going after our previously undisclosed sources by requiring identification of all contributors to trusts making political contributions. Since this legislation has an immediate effective date, your role, Atlas, will be public within ten days of your next contribution following passage by the General Assembly and application of the governor's John Hancock.

Even though he removed the bar on nepotism, I suggest we unblock our members so they can vote for the Speaker's package when it's called. As you know, he owns the timing.

* * * * * * * * * * * * * * * *

THE BACK BENCH
"If you let it slip, we catch it"

April 22

Fresh off its ethics victory, the E Party today announced a yearlong campaign leading to passage of major education reform next year.

Representative Abernathy and Senator Benjamin, the respective chairwomen of the House and Senate Education Committees have announced an ambitious schedule of hearings and symposiums focusing on both improvements to early childhood education and our troubling high school dropout rate. The House committee will focus on early childhood while the senate committee will focus on what it will take to dramatically improve the dropout rate.

In other news…

* * * * * * * * * * * * * * * *

E-MAIL
To: General
From: Atlas
Sent: 5/2 8:26 p.m. (MST)
Subject: Meeting with Don Colletti

I contacted Don Colletti to request a private audience for you. As you know, I previously asked him to cut you and the party a wide berth.

He remains uncomfortable with the E Party's toehold. Labor unions and Democrats in Illinois have scratched each other's backs quite nicely. Until they better understand the E agenda, they are braced for the worst.

At the same time, the Democrats dismal handling of the state's economy has greatly limited the union agenda and recent job cuts have made the rank and file nervous.

I doubt you will remember him, but Don remembers you well from the Knell Enterprises merger. Your tolerance for, and ultimate acceptance of, the workout has created a level of respect that should survive the initial shock of our proposal.

* * * * * * * * * * * * * * * *

E-MAIL
To: K.C.
From: Atlas
Sent: 5/8 2:16 a.m. (MST)
Subject: PR Campaign

I hope your head hasn't swollen from all the clippings Liz has been sending. The intelligencia has totally embraced the issues, presenters, and content for the education policy rollout.

As the chairperson of the foundation, Lisa wants to have you do some National Public Radio spots. I know Patrick is not well, so it's totally your call.

Thank you for all your help in these difficult times.

* * * * * * * * * * * * * * * *

E-MAIL
To: Alex
From: K.C.
Sent: 5/9 11:46 a.m. (EST)
Subject: PR Campaign

Patrick has failed considerably of late and any quality of life seems to have evaporated. I know he would cherish a visit from you, as would I. Please hurry.

CHAPTER THIRTEEN

Fuck!

A word that rarely, if ever, crossed the Speaker's lips. Or, as in this case, cursed through his mind.

He was in Washington Park, arguably Springfield's finest token to Mother Nature, partaking in an early stroll on a crisp, cool spring morning. Not unlike Atlas' version of escape thinking, it was his one respite from the brutal pace and stress of the legislative season. It was also the only non-sleeping moment in his schedule without phone, people, and interruption.

His thoughts harkened to election night and his subsequent post-mortem. He remained convinced that the E Party phenomenon had a predictable end game, but their subsequent moves belied the rollout he had anticipated.

The price for him to remain Speaker still seemed to be a bargain: ethics reform, education committee chairmanships, and ordained scheduling breaks prior to bill passage. The ethics battle had gone his way. They demanded transparency in a non-threatening way. He massaged it enough to get the lion's share of the credit.

Now they were off and running on the bluest of all blue ribbon education task force boondoggles. What were they smoking? The educational system in the United States couldn't be fixed if Jesus Christ himself came back to lead the effort. Even if the E Party found the magic elixir, by ceding the process to him, he would always outflank him. Yet, for the first time in years, there was an ember of doubt regarding his ability to stay ahead, to stay in control.

* * * * * * * * * * * * * * * *

"Hello, Daniel. I don't know how far along you are, but with the language I added to the ethics legislation, I'll soon learn the funding source of the E Party. *You* get me the key people."

Daniel heard a click and then the line went dead.

* * * * * * * * * * * * * * * *

E-MAIL
To: Black Pearl
From: Danny
Sent: 5/10 9:09 p.m. (CST)
Subject: Status

Anything???? How soon????

* * * * * * * * * * * * * * * *

E-MAIL
To: Danny
From: Black Pearl
Sent: 5/10 9:12 p.m. (CST)
Subject: Status

The ballplayer and I are still in the early innings. No score. Patience.

* * * * * * * * * * * * * * * *

Nancy Rae had two basic strategies and countless variations.

For those situations that called for domination and control, when she needed to own a politician, it was the vampire. If they thought with their dicks, all the better, just as long as she stayed in control. For the average political mope, very little stroking was required. Blood sucking, optional.

For those situations that necessitated a political death sentence, when she needed to break someone, it was the "python." Squeeze them a little harder, literally and figuratively, after each breath. Devour them when they were spent. Pictures were often involved, although it never actually rose to blackmail. Retaining their pension and the offer of a soft landing from Danny kept them on life support.

Thomas Robinson. Hall of Famer. Beloved in the community. Bachelor. Not exactly your average Mr. "Political Sleaze Bucket."

Not exactly your average Mr. "I'm the big fucking gorilla to whom the rules don't apply." Not exactly your average Mr. "Vows, what vows, if she doesn't like it, let her hit the road." Not exactly your average Nancy Rae assignment.

Like the vampire, she clearly needed to gain and stay in control. Unlike the cobra, it remained to be seen if crushing her prey was the preferred outcome. Regardless, with Thomas Robinson, it took planning and patience.

* * * * * * * * * * * * * * * *

E-MAIL

To: General
From: Liz
Sent: 5/11 7:16 a.m. (CST)
Subject: Colletti Meeting

Your meeting with Don Colletti is confirmed for noon on May 13 at the Bellagio Hotel in Vegas. I have booked the Grand Lakeview Suite for your accommodation and the meeting location. Lunch and dinner will be catered. You leave Chicago via Southwest at four-thirty tomorrow afternoon. Atlas has instructed me to hold the suite for one week in the event you choose to stay on.

* * * * * * * * * * * * * * * *

Don Colletti loved Vegas. He loved the glitz, the shows, the food, the girls, the poker and the fact that it is a great union town. He could invent an excuse to land there anytime he wanted. His friend Atlas had asked him to meet with General Smith at the Bellagio. And when a good friend asks a favor, no sacrifice is too small.

He remembered meeting the General when Freedom Corp. acquired Knell Enterprises, a 100 percent union shop. He was then Regional Coordinator for the AFL/CIO, with responsibility for negotiations in situations involving 1,000 employees or more. What had originally looked to be a friendly merger took a sudden and drastic turn when the General announced his intentions of introducing robots to the assembly line. When the transition was fully implemented, the work force reduction was estimated at 38 percent, at an annual savings to Freedom in excess of $50 million. Robots do not require overtime or benefits!

In conjunction with the work of Atlas and his ASC team, a rather quick and amicable solution was negotiated. Apropos to his friend's most recent ask, as a result of the negotiations, Colletti had found the General to be creative, honest, trustworthy and, surprisingly, quite caring.

Consistent with Atlas' prediction, the General was able to immediately place Don, notwithstanding the gray, the paunch, and some obviously unfortunate denture work since their last encounter. The General made an immediate mental note to never see a union dentist.

"Don, if I can call you that, it's been awhile, but now that I'm connecting the face and name, you obviously haven't changed much. At least you kept your hair."

"You look great," added an equally patronizing Don Colletti, "hair is overrated. What's more important, you don't appear to have aged."

"Like my doc says, don't smoke, don't fret and buy Viagra by the gross," was the General's usual response to age related comments.

"It's not the buying," quipped Colletti, "it's the using."

"Come on in," offered the General. "We cut a good deal last time around. I'm interested in a sequel. Have a seat. Liz ordered us a great lunch and I understand we've got all the time we need."

* * * * * * * * * * * * * * * *

E-MAIL

To: Atlas
From: General
Sent: 5/14 2:22 a.m. (PST)
Subject: Vegas

I must be learning from you after all these years. Don Colletti and I reached the framework for a deal. That is, assuming the lawyers don't fuck it up.

As soon as the i's are dotted and t's are crossed for the legislation, we will hold a joint press conference.

I also took a page from your playbook. To seal the deal, I let him kick my ass at hold 'em.

* * * * * * * * * * * * * * * *

E-MAIL

To: General Smith
From: Atlas
Sent: 5/14 5:47 a.m. (MST)
Subject: Vegas

Congratulations! Your e-mail and Don's arrived within minutes of each other. I think we're going to have some fun in June, if not July.

* * * * * * * * * * * * * * * *

THE BACK BENCH

"If you let it slip, we catch it"

May 14

In another death defying act, the E Party is again refusing to engage in the legislative process. Earlier this year, they announced that E partiers would refrain from voting until an ethics bill was passed. That was accomplished on April 8, with all E legislators voting in support.

Today, E Party spokesperson, Lisa Boudreau, issued a statement proclaiming another voting hiatus, this time until a truly balanced budget is presented for consideration, as in no gimmicks as usual. According to Ms. Boudreau, the party is concerned that, with only fourteen scheduled session dates to adjournment, inadequate attention has been focused on the most important bill in any session.

In pointing to House and Senate rules, Ms. Boudreau notes that the budget has to be presented by May 16, only two days from now, if the budget is to be passed on schedule. Both of these rules were apparently the outgrowth of E Party negotiations when the Speaker and Senate president were elected.

Historically, the budget has miraculously and mysteriously appeared on the final day of the session, still reeking from the "smoke filled" room in which the ink dried. Legislators issue press releases griping about lack of input and then vote to pass a 1000-plus-page document they've never read.

The alternative is to miss the deadline, at which point the constitution requires a super majority vote and the minority party gains leverage. For the Democrats, it has always been better to pass a bill you haven't read, but has been blessed by the Speaker, than risk an overtime session. Hell hath no fury like a spouse in the heat of summer, with kids out of school and no one around to share the carpool duties.

Thanks to the E Party, the voting configuration in both Houses is such that minority party votes are immediately necessary to meet the traditional adjournment. There is a distinct advantage to whichever minority party makes their deal first. That will totally cut out the other.

Whereas the ethics play was softball, the E Party has now moved up to hardball. No one is more astute than the Speaker at end of session wizardry. If this heads to overtime, it will be because he has decided that's the winning strategy. We'll find out on May 16.

In other news…

THE BACK BENCH

"If you let it slip, we catch it"

May 16

May 16 and the trains are running on time.

When the Senators arrived for the opening of the daily session, Senate Bill 234, the annual budget, was sitting on their desks. Under Senate rules, it has to sit for seven days before it can be called for a vote and moved to the House.

The Senate president, obviously wary of the E Party maneuvering, and no doubt in league with the Speaker, has scheduled a rigorous series of hearings. Of course, his designated appropriation chairs will control the parade of witnesses.

However, the budget needs thirty votes in the Senate. Accordingly, it stalls without either Republican or E Party votes. Both of the minority players may decide to let the budget fail. Conversely, either can cut a deal and complete a timely adjournment.

In other news…

* * * * * * * * * * * * * * * *

"Elizabeth, it's David."

"Hello Mr. Speaker. I was thinking I might be hearing from your side of the aisle. Is the Senate president's phone out of order?"

"If you prefer, I can have him call instead."

"No, that's okay. I assume we're talking budget."

"You assume correctly," the Speaker confirmed.

"First of all," she began, "we appreciate the seven day window. It sure beats the seven minutes we usually get. Unfortunately, my staff has not completed its analysis. We've got six days left. I think we can get serious day after tomorrow. Does that work for you?"

"We'll make it work. I'll call you in the afternoon."

"One thing, David. I trust you've given an old nemesis the benefit of the first option. If I even suspect you're double-dealing with General Smith, prepare for a long, hot summer. Understood?"

"Understood. You have my word. Thank you."

* * * * * * * * * * * * * * * *

THE BACK BENCH

"If you let it slip, we catch it"

May 20

Welcome to let's make a deal, Springfield style. In a stunning but predictable vote, the Senate yesterday passed an amended budget. Eleven Republicans joined twenty-five Democrats to reach thirty-six votes. In typical fashion, the vote was structured to allow members in targeted districts to avoid a controversial vote.

In this case, the controversy avoiding nostrum is pork. There is $147 million in capital projects for Republican districts. In combination with capital goodies for Democrats in the original bill, we're talking over $400 million of honey roasted finest.

The package includes sufficient oink oink for Republican House members to insure passage by the Speaker as well.

By virtue of the amendment, to fully comply with the new sunshine rules, session will require four days of overtime. Not to worry, however. The thirty-six votes in the Senate insure that a super majority vote of Republicans and Democrats in each House will be reached.

In other news…

THE BACK BENCH
"If you let it slip, we catch it"

May 26

EXTRA EXTRA EXTRA EXTRA

The Back Bench has been advised that the E Party will launch a multi-million dollar media campaign to advise the public of the intricacies (i.e., failures) of the State's proposed budget.

General Smith has apparently met with editorial boards across the state.

In addition, at 9 a.m. tomorrow, the E Party will post a complete analysis of the budget on its web site.

Now that both Democrats and Republicans have signaled their support, the E Party is attempting to spring a trap.

In other news…

THE BACK BENCH
"If you let it slip, we catch it"

May 28

The E Party had to be scratching their collective heads yesterday. General Smith apparently met with editorial boards across the state and their web site put out an exceedingly slick piece on why the about-to-pass state budget is a disaster waiting to happen. The result—absolutely nothing.

Today we learned why. Leading papers across the state all came out in favor of the proposed budget and attacked the E Party. Replete with quotes from the Speaker and Senator DiMaggio, the E Party was chastised for its laissez-faire "we don't vote" stance during the Session.

"It's easy to criticize," said the *Tribune*. "However, the E Party has not brought one constructive budget idea to the table. Until that happens, they remain unproductive obstructionists." "The E Party appears to be a one trick pony," adds the *Alton Telegraph*. "Their non-voting stance was cute for a while, but the Democrats and Republicans have stepped up at a time when responsibility trumps inactivity."

Of course, the editorials were replete with spoon-fed sound bites of this budget's virtues, from increased education spending to new healthcare initiatives. It would appear the Speaker has won this round.

In other news…

THE BACK BENCH
"If you let it slip, we catch it"

May 29

When it comes to the budget, the Speaker decisively won the battle of the editorial boards. However, the buzz around the Capitol yesterday was about members' phones ringing off the hook with calls from angry constituents.

The E Party's Internet prowess is apparently driving an unprecedented voter backlash. Their site specifically ties each legislator to the pork they received for their vote. This reporter thought he had seen everything, but this year's list redefines absurd. Representative Resnik, what were you thinking when you requested $2 million to heat the community pool for winter swimming? Senator Artola, are you kidding? $500,000 to your local library for a proof set of the Harry Potter series?

Round two to E Party.

In other news…

THE BACK BENCH
"If you let it slip, we catch it"

May 30

Numbers don't lie.

The Back Bench has learned that an unprecedented, rushed poll, co-sponsored by the Democrats and Republicans, indicates the budget passed by the Senate is opposed by a whopping 78 percent of likely voters. Don't order those Harry Potter books just yet.

The E Party web site has apparently taken on cult status for independent voters, receiving in excess of 250,000 hits per day in the last few days. Among other things, the site generates instant e-mail and letter quality responses to the writer's state senator and representative. In a rather unique twist on the normal click to send uniform batch communication, the site offers a simple path to producing sender specific correspondence and e-mails, varying both content and tone.

The spectrum ranges from a rather outraged mood to a more objective approach while offering a cafeteria plan of budget elements with which the sender is concerned.

To add insult to injury, with only a modest amount of additional effort, each constituent can create individualized robocalls to their legislators.

One legislator told me she had received the most constituent-based correspondence on a single issue in her seven terms in office. I am not at liberty to print the quote attributed to the robocalling.

With the House vote approaching, this is making the natives very restless. We are advised that neither the Democrat nor the Republican caucus went well. In the case of the Republicans, an extremely rare joint House/Senate meeting was held.

The Democrat leadership team met into the wee hours of the morning and did not take press questions afterwards.

In other news…

THE BACK BENCH

"If you let it slip, we catch it"

May 31

Not resting on yesterday's polling results nor its Internet barrage, the E Party has launched a comprehensive, statewide television buy attacking the proposed state budget. Consistent with the last elections, the ads are comprehensive, yet concise, and extremely informative. They seem to again favor the two-minute, not-your- average-sound-bite, format.

The Back Bench understands the posted 800 number voting line is running over 80 percent opposed. Even more damning than the poll results.

This has become another E Party tsunami!

In other news…

THE BACK BENCH
"If you let it slip, we catch it"

May 31

EXTRA EXTRA EXTRA EXTRA

In virtually identical press releases this afternoon, the Democratic Party of Illinois and the Republican Party of Illinois respectively denounced the pork in the proposed state budget.

This takes the budget completely back to square one. Overtime session, here we come.

In other news…

* * * * * * * * * * * * * * * *

E-MAIL

To: Mark, Atlas, General
From: Lauren
Sent: 5/31 8:21 p.m. (PST)
Subject: Scary Stuff

Your most recent vintage Internet communication schemes are unbelievable. The personalized robocalling feature is scary.

In the 24-hour period from noon, May 29, to noon, May 30, the system generated in excess of 300,000 e-mails, an equal number of letters, and over 80,000 automated calls. Although the calling feature ran glitch free, given the drop off, the additional steps may have proved either too challenging or time consuming. On average, the e-mail/letter sequencing ran under three minutes per attempt, whereas the calls were running up to seven minutes from the time the user completed the pre-screen until the send button was clicked.

The introduction of the blog was also a numerical success. Among other things, we are seeing greater percentage of users completing their profiles than just before the election.

Gentlemen, I know this is a tease, but I think they'll have to pick you each up off the floor when we send you the data sets for people indicating a willingness to run on the E Party ticket next year.

* * * * * * * * * * * * * * * *

Dawn Eckersley had served as the Speaker's secretary since his first term in office. She was proper, professional, and efficient to a fault. She carried untold volumes of politically sensitive information in her cranium and would take it all to the grave. As the Speaker's gatekeeper, her polite yet firm "no" was not to be challenged, while her ability to juggle an endless stream of must-sees and must-do's was a marvel. The Speaker held her performance in the highest esteem, recognizing that her quiet, effective style was the daily linchpin to the inner workings of his staff.

Up until the last few days, she thought she had seen his every mood and nuance. The passage of the budget in the Senate and the manipulation of the editorial boards had unleashed an unprecedented spike in endorphins. Just as quickly, the E Party Internet assault and the overnight polling results created an equally unprecedented and disturbing flirtation with depression.

Well aware of his obsession with identifying the brains behind the E Party curtain, she stumbled upon a simple, yet brilliant idea. That evening she presented her analysis to the Speaker. It did not take long for the winning glint to form on his face. Before he could give the initial order, she advised him that a call with Danny Ryan would take place in fifteen minutes.

* * * * * * * * * * * * * * * *

The assignment was presenting new and exciting challenges that filled her with uncharacteristic anxiety. This was not the usual "show up in a bar and time the sexual entreaty with a stop watch." Tom Robinson was not a political egomaniac; he was a beloved Hall of Famer. His accomplishments were on a wall in Cooperstown, not a series of fabricated dot point hyperbole on a constituent mail piece. His mission was helping kids, not helping himself. Although sufficiently into middle age, he was trim and dapper, not paunchy and dressed for traffic court. For the first time in a very long time, this was both exciting and challenging for Nancy Rae.

Tom Robinson, political evangelist, had returned to mentoring big league wannabees. During the campaign, he had discovered the draw of the church. Continuing to work with the Chicagoland pastoral network, he adjusted from the E Party message to the virtues of baseball and education, while avoiding the temptations of the street.

Given Nancy Rae's vocation, she had surmised that the extremes of either regular observance and confession or none at all were the only realistic options and she had chosen the latter. When she arrived for Tom Robinson's presentation at the 56th Street Baptist Church, she was jolted into the realization that she had not visited a house of worship in over ten years.

She arrived early to gain her seat of choice. Not too close to draw attention, but close enough to draw attention. Normally, attention gathering was a non-issue, especially when clad in her usual come hither attire. Tonight she carefully selected a Prada number that cried out classic and educated. After all, she was now Nicollette Lawson, a reporter for *National Politics Quarterly* preparing an in-depth article on this sports hero turned policy wonk.

With his first quick scan of the crowd, warm-blooded male Tom Robinson spotted Nancy Rae. It was much to his later chagrin to learn that this enticing member of the audience had departed before he could complete the autograph session.

The sequence was repeated four times at four churches before he happily found her lingering one evening. Dressed in a slightly more provocative outfit chosen specifically for her opening salvo, she approached at the precise moment the receding crowd would tolerate her monopolizing his attention. With outstretched hand and appropriately firm handshake, she offered her nom de gare and her well conceived fraud. Focusing more on her eyes than her words, he accepted the luncheon invitation despite having missed her statement of intention. Who cared?

Lunch led to lunch, which led to dinner, which led to a weeklong tour of his life, which led back to dinner. He was totally consumed with Nancy Rae and was grateful that some magazine he had never read had chosen him for a feature. No matter how fleeting, it was a wonderful opportunity to spread the messages that defined his life to a nationwide audience.

The assignment was having an equally profound effect on Nancy Rae. "TR" as she had come to call him, was proving to be only the second man to discover and embrace her mind. Their conversations started about him, but often wandered onto tangents and vectors about her. Having spent her entire adult life with political leaders that society had unwittingly assigned expectations for great policy and leadership, she found them for the frauds they were or quickly became. Here was a guy who achieved fame by hitting balls with sticks and yet, other than Danny, was the most thoughtful, inspiring person to have entered her world.

He talked to her about hoping to reach at least one kid at each stop. She was convinced he got them all. She watched them watch. The kids were fixated and uplifted; the parents rejuvenated and hopeful. Surely, the message would resonate in them as it had in her.

The irony was punishing. Her normal brand of "professionalism" revolved around sex without meaning. She had now spent two months of unexpected and fulfilling meaning and desperately yearned for a sexual relationship. And here they were, both showing the utmost respect for her make-believe occupation and assignment.

Danny was pressing, but she hadn't passed "Go." He was so refreshingly lacking in ego that he never came close to divulging the information she sought. Twice, her questions had ventured directly to the source code of the E Party and twice she had been smoothly diverted. Once again, how unlike the talking heads who spewed state secrets in the sack to further demonstrate their power and superiority. Too late to play the whore, Nancy Rae Mitchell found herself in virgin territory.

* * * * * * * * * * * * * * * *

THE BACK BENCH

"If you let it slip, we catch it"

June 12

The E Party Internet, television, and radio assault continues. Having initially attacked the low hanging pork barrel fruit, they are now deep into the root structure.

Three University of Chicago Nobel Prize winning economists have been turned loose on the budget package. Their full report is on the web and, continuing with our tree theme, all of the branches have been shaken.

The E Party brain trust has taken the full report and translated the major findings into compelling, fifth grade terminology. There are two major themes of contention. One, the budget is structurally out of balance, which they eloquently and simply translate into a fraud on the taxpayer. Two, promises made to fund education are not accurate and the children of Illinois are suffering from the charade.

Tom Robinson has been tapped as the public face of the E Party for these purposes and his presentation is succinct, believable, and compelling. He is featured in one of the E Party's now characteristic two-minute infomercials tying the budget's inadequacies to entrenched poverty. His message is strong, credible, and straight from the heart.

I suspect the E Party is winning the political battle. I know they are winning the substantive battle because no one else is showing up.

In other news…

* * * * * * * * * * * * * * * *

E-MAIL

To:	Black Pearl
From:	Danny
Sent:	6/19 6:30 a.m. (CST)
Subject:	You're Killing Me

Robinson is killing us. Where's my cobra? All I know is "he who shall not be named" in Springfield is squeezing my nuts. I'm done with patience. I need results. Fast!

* * * * * * * * * * * * * * * *

Danny needed results. Speaker Voldemort needed results. And, Nancy Rae Mitchell—she of the 1000 batting average—was striking out.

CHAPTER FOURTEEN

THE BACK BENCH

"If you let it slip, we catch it"

June 30

Here we sit at June 30—thirty days into the budget stalemate and one day from the start of the state's fiscal year.

For those readers who don't remember budget battles past, when the clock strikes midnight on June 30 and there is no budget, anyone providing services to the state, including over 40,000 employees, cannot be paid until the budget gets passed. The first week is traditionally dedicated to "don't blame me" bantering and Fourth of July parades. Things will start to heat up the second week when the comptroller fails to issue bi-weekly paychecks. By the third week, all state workers will have missed one cycle and all non-essential services are curtailed.

Legislators grow more stressed and weary with each passing day. State employee constituents, the ones that vote, are banging hard. Spouses are home with the kids who are not being babysat in school. It's hot. Vacations are postponed. They're stuck in Springfield. It's very hot. No per diems are paid. Spouses are spewing four letter ultimatums. It's very, very hot.

It eventually comes down to blame and cahones.

Scripts of budget battles past were generally predictable. The Speaker would measure the pressure with his unique visceral gauge and ultimately buy votes with Manhattan-style trinkets. It appeared to work six weeks ago when he bestowed sufficient largess to attract the needed Republican votes. But the E Party rallied to block passage.

The Republicans now appear to be sitting this out, hoping the Speaker and the General duel to the death. At the same time, they run the risk of becoming irrelevant.

It will be interesting to see who makes the first move.
In other news…

THE BACK BENCH
"If you let it slip, we catch it"

July 9

It's day nine of the budget strike. The first significant pressure point arrives tomorrow. Roughly 25,000 state workers will fail to get paid. In years past, one month temporary budgets were adopted to avoid payless paydays. This year the votes do not exist.

The Speaker, seemingly without much in the way of options, appears to be waiting for the inevitable pressure necessary to force concessions and consensus. That pressure, which ostensibly begins when paydays turn empty, culminates on July 15, at which point all state workers, including the legislators themselves, will have missed at least one such bi-weekly event.

Vendors will be similarly pinched. But, they are better prepared for the vagaries of slowed state receivables having been there many times. Their flashpoint is likely in the 45-90 day range.

In other news…

* * * * * * * * * * * * * * * *

E-MAIL

To: Atlas, General
From: Yura
Sent: 7/12 4:16 p.m. (CST)
Subject: Legislative Package

We have concluded our documentation of the proposed legislation and the union's legal counsel has received sign-off from his client. There are two pivotal documents: draft legislation implementing the new pension system and a memorandum of understanding (MOU) to be signed by the E Party legislators acknowledging their support for the legislation if called for a vote.

Once the MOU has been executed, the union leaders will present the package to the Speaker. As required under the MOU, he will be allowed no more than 24 hours to accept the same terms and conditions and obtain the requisite number of member signatures in each chamber to insure passage.

If the Speaker agrees, we will have a joint press conference to announce the budget solution. If he declines, the E Party is freed up to announce the package with full and complete union support or take it to the Republicans to form a voting majority, but forfeit the union's public support.

The completed documentation is attached hereto. I leave the politics to you gentlemen. Good luck.

* * * * * * * * * * * * * * * *

THE BACK BENCH

"If you let it slip, we catch it"

July 14

In an obviously choreographed and ceremonial gesture, leaders of the state's major employee unions descended on the Speaker's office yesterday. There were also a few new elders in attendance, reportedly from national.

Although the display was clearly designed to draw attention, it was placid in contrast to the infantry of disgruntled, unpaid workers customarily sent to create commotion and nightly news pictorials when budget battles heat up. Nothing intimidates Democrat legislators more than angry union members—especially angry, unpaid union members. So much so, I've often wondered if the Speaker calls union leaders and has them send in the troops to facilitate his budget end games.

Regardless, the union's new tactics bear watching. Over the years, the Speaker has masterfully worked a series of bait and switch tactics to plug budget holes. After all, it's not as if they're running to befriend the Republicans.

Perhaps the E Party has altered the calculus. It was recently pointed out to me that the great majority of the E Party legislators are union members and, while wearing his corporate beret, the General negotiated some very crafty union supported mergers and acquisitions.

In other news…

* * * * * * * * * * * * * * * *

With her strategy a failure on all fronts, Nancy Rae decided to revert to the old playbook. She concluded that a sex-based solution would enable her to probe more deeply into Mr. Robinson's personal world, while most assuredly meeting her libido's growing needs.

She selected the most provocative Dolce & Gabbana number from her wardrobe and suggested a quiet, mood-inducing restaurant for their dinner. After sufficient chit-chat, she announced that her research was concluded and that she would be returning to New York to complete the article.

Happily, Thomas was noticeably upset with the thought of her departure, offering that he might soon find an excuse to travel to the commissioner's office. Although he was brilliant at communicating with his target audiences, she had come to understand him well enough to know that his response was as romantic as the situation would allow. But not to worry, for she was also a Hall of Famer.

She maneuvered the evening to a nightcap at the Four Seasons hotel, complete with smooth jazz and soothing scotch. From the moment of her well-timed bombshell, his sixth grade sadness over her pending departure was sweetly received. It was the positive reinforcement she had hoped for.

When she asked him to escort her to her room, he wagged his tail and left an exorbitant tip in his hurry to move along. Driven by lust, other victims had made similar gestures. She had despised their carelessness and welcomed their eagerness as a sign of weakness. Conversely, TR's out-of-character exuberance left her glowing.

Upon arriving at her door, she unleashed an embrace that was unmistakenably suggestive. Caught somewhat off guard by the advance, he responded in a way that triggered her Richter scale. Then, just as quickly, he pulled back.

Quickly realizing that a public display of affection was too awkward for this Southern gentleman and exceedingly private person, she regrouped with an offer to come inside. But, as she turned to open the door, he said, "No thank you, Nicollette. I need to be getting along." And, as she turned back, he was already out of arms length and leaving without so much as "goodnight" or "goodbye."

She couldn't open the door to either the room or the mini-bar quickly enough. Within an hour, the statuette she built from three-inch bottles was only slightly less impressive than the story she had concocted for Danny. Then again, maybe it wasn't a fabrication. Perhaps it was the only aspect of her faked crusade that wasn't.

* * * * * * * * * * * * * * * *

"Alex," K.C. said in a quivering voice. "We lost Patrick last night."

"I don't know what to say," said a stunned Atlas. "After my visit last month, I had no idea it would happen so soon."

"The doctors told me a few weeks ago that things could accelerate. A cruel hoax that disease. A cruel hoax on a strong, vibrant man. Thankfully, the end was peaceful."

"I will leave immediately and..."

"No," she cut him off. "Patrick wanted this handled a certain way. He specifically requested that no one other than the immediate family be in attendance. Let me call you in a few days. Just wanted you to know."

Reluctantly, he had to respect their wishes.

* * * * * * * * * * * * * * * *

E-MAIL

To: General
From: Colletti
Sent: 7/15 7:30 p.m. (CST)
Subject: Budget Deal

We met with the Speaker yesterday and he just called to accept our terms.

There have been some contentious meetings with his highness before, but this one was uncharacteristically personal and nasty. I couldn't tell if he was more upset having his hand forced or learning that the E Party had out-flanked him with labor.

We agreed to a few changes that I trust you can live with.

1. There are to be no E Party legislators present on the podium at the press conference. You are to be the lone attendee and you will not be offered a chance to speak or answer press inquiries.
2. The votes on the floor for the amendment will be voice votes. As such, no E Party legislators will have a record of voting for the amendment.
3. The unions have agreed that they will not endorse any E Party candidates over Democrats in next year's general election.

Your response is requested within the hour.

* * * * * * * * * * * * * * * *

E-MAIL
To: Colletti
From: General
Sent: 7/15 7:12 p.m. (MST)
Subject: Budget Deal

We accept. But Tom Robinson will be there in my place. Since we can't speak, there is no need to park my ass on a plane. Tom's already in Chicago.

* * * * * * * * * * * * * * * *

E-MAIL
To: Atlas, General
From: Mark
Sent: 7/16 11:56 a.m. (CST)
Subject: Budget Deal

Good move by the Speaker. By freezing us out at the podium and without a recorded vote on the amendment, we are hard-pressed to claim a significant role in the budget resolution. We'll just have to chalk it up to another Atlas-style victory. Actually, in your terms, it translates into a $20 billion return to the public on your $50 million investment. Not bad.

I'll bet the unions were also shaken down for big-time financial commitments for the next election. Don't ever think for a second that pay-to-play is dead in Illinois. It makes our other surprise all the more important.

* * * * * * * * * * * * * * * *

THE BACK BENCH
"If you let it slip, we catch it"

July 16

EXTRA EXTRA EXTRA EXTRA

In an afternoon press conference, Speaker Kennedy, flanked by representatives of the state's major unions, announced a resolution to the budget conundrum.

The cornerstone of the Speaker's proposal is a complete overhaul of the state's hiring patterns and related pension obligations, each of which is expected to save tens of billions. Although there is no immediate operating fiscal benefit, the adjustment to the actuarial assumptions and calculations for the various state pensions translates into an immediate adjustment to liabilities that arguably balances the budget.

The proposal contains the following key elements:

- With the exception of exempt positions, including teachers, tenure for all state employees will be limited to ten years.

- Workers unable to transition to the private sector will receive job training.

- There will be a transition program for all current workers under the age of fifty. All current workers over fifty will be offered early retirement as soon as replacements are trained and available.

- By constantly rejuvenating the state's bureaucracy, the average salary base is lowered and the pension obligation related thereto is considerably reduced.

- The state becomes a training ground rather than a burial ground (my interpretation).

- The state is positioned to hire more workers and offer greater training for much less than the cost of sustaining an older and unhealthier work force.

- The current endemic of bureaucratic dependency, job malaise and patronage are minimized.

It almost makes too much sense. How does something this pragmatic happen in 21st century American government? And what took so long?

I see this as a win for the unions. Given the state's dire fiscal status, cuts to either staff or wages were not out of the question once the session went into overtime. As it turns out, they maintain, and may possibly expand, the union employee base. A massive pension crisis is avoided and health benefits are preserved. The 30 to 50 crowd can't be happy, but if the training components are legit and the transition is handled with a modicum of humanity and respect, it could work.

The Speaker wins because the budget is resolved and, instead of him cramming the deal, it literally walks in the door.

Finally, I understand the E Party will give the Speaker the votes needed for passage. Which begs the question: At what price?

In other news…

* * * * * * * * * * * * * * * *

E-MAIL
To: K.C.
From: Atlas
Sent: 7/18 3:17 p.m. (MST)
Subject: How Are You?

How are you? How are you getting along?

The budget fight in Illinois has concluded. The party did well, although the subtleties of the victory are best left to a longer discussion.

I would like permission to come to New York to see you and pay my respects. Liz has cleared my schedule.

* * * * * * * * * * * * * * * *

E-MAIL
To: Atlas
From: K.C.
Sent: 7/20 2:30 a.m. (EST)
Subject: Not A Good Time

My heart is not in it. Give me at least another week. E Party tales might be what the doctor ordered. Thank you for caring.

* * * * * * * * * * * * * * * *

"Danny. It's Nancy Rae. I have some very interesting news for you. How about lunch tomorrow—the usual."

"Sure, that works," he accepted.

"See you then," she concurred.

The usual was Leo & Heather's Irish Deli, home to Chicago's best corned beef and cabbage. A South Side tradition spanning four generations, but with décor and ambience unchanged. The menu also remained unchanged, the recipes remained unchanged, for a generation at a time the wait staff remained unchanged, and the cash-only requirement remained unchanged. For the most part, the neighborhood remained unchanged.

Danny was no longer the regular he had once been, but his customary table was still held every Tuesday and Friday, just in case. Other politicos would be allowed access to the prestigious corner after 12:15. Mere mortals were whisked out of earshot if and when business was being conducted. On the days Danny held court, especially when patronage was more in vogue, a steady stream of staff, friends and wannabees, a la Vito Corleone, could easily extend lunch past 4 p.m. Danny and Nancy Rae had hatched many schemes at Leo & Heather's over Irish coffee and soda bread. All part of the intentional public display that had backfired on his marriage.

"I don't know exactly what it is" opened Danny, "but you look even more radiant than usual. Has bessball been berry berry good to you?" He chuckled, having failed miserably at his Garrett Morris imitation.

"Actually, not as good as we might have wished. But thank you for noticing the subtle changes inspired by my short-lived career in the magazine business," she chuckled back. "I've decided the Prada look suits me better than Victoria's Secret—at least for lunch."

"Well, whatever that means. You're still the best looking woman in Chicago. What'll it be, corned beef and cabbage, corned beef on rye, or should we just split?"

"Let's split. That way you can have one of each while I watch," she chuckled again. A routine they had repeated myriad times over the years. She hated corned beef and he knew it.

It felt great to be with Danny again. "Do you ever wish you could just get away from all this bullshit?" she questioned in an unusually serious tone. "For the past two months I've been living a lie, but there were times when the lie felt real and our day-to-day existence was the fake. Who do you think we were in prior lives? In the next one I want to be normal. Maybe get married and have kids."

"Whoa, you sound like you got beaned a few times lately."

"Maybe I did," she pondered, "maybe I did."

"OK, so you and I exit stage right to the Caribbean after the next election. Only, I've got fifteen months of campaigning between now and then and his highness is all over my ass. He's called me more times in the last month than the last decade. He's fuckin' obsessed. If I didn't know better, I'd think he's slipping. But, I do know better. That brain hasn't slipped in forty years. So, what have we got for the man behind the curtain?"

"I wish it was more. Tom Robinson is all about the E Party. Sees it as a beacon of light that can lead to better outcomes for blacks in a wide array of opportunities. In particular, he talks incessantly about the need to remake education in America. Talks about General Smith ad nauseum. Also talks about a K.C. and a Mark and a Lauren. But he never puts a face on it. Never references meetings, places, discussions. And I could not get him to address the money. It's as if the money doesn't exist. But we know it does. Twenty-five million doesn't just happen."

"Well, that's a start. There's a K.C., a Mark, and a Lauren; or is that a L-o-r-e-n?"

"Good question. They are completely faceless. In his world, it's about team and kids. Gender is not a relevant consideration. E Party is team. Baseball is kids. The end game for each is the Tom Robinson version of the audacity of hope."

"The audacity of hope? You getting soft all of a sudden?"

"No, not soft. But not exactly Ms. Vampire lately either. Been thinking a lot. Thinking about the tiny world you and I live in and the larger universe guys like Tom Robinson live in. But I'm back now. That's all that matters."

"I'll accept that, but I was hoping to feed the beast. Is that all you've got?"

"Maybe not. Turns out our hero is gay. And I'm not talking happy-go-lucky."

"Tom Robinson? Gay? That definitely creates some possibilities. When we get to the Caribbean, I want to hear how the great Nancy Rae dealt with that one."

I'm not sure you ever will, she thought to herself.

* * * * * * * * * * * * * * * *

THE BACK BENCH

"If you let it slip, we catch it"

July 20

Before this cowboy rides off into the sunset, it's time for the annual legislative round-up from the session. Keeping with tradition, we'll stick with the winners and losers format. Although with three parties in the game, I've struggled to find a triangular rating system. Maybe next year.

WINNERS:

1. The Speaker always wins.

First of all, he's still Speaker. And the cost of E Party votes to form the majority was apparently benign. He co-opted the E Party on ethics and otherwise ran his agenda unimpeded.

The budget stalemate could have been disastrous, but he coerced his union friends into a stunning concession. Thanks to his restructuring of the pensions, the state's budget is now more sound than it has been in many years. In doing so, he appears to have escaped collateral damage from the original pork laden budget. Given the final outcome, I'm guessing my press brethren will overlook that toe stubbing.

2. The E Party.

Sometimes you win by not losing. As rookies, they managed to hold their own and at the end of the day, can claim to have kept their word—an unusual political outcome.

They promised ethics reform, budget reform, and education reform. Although the Speaker gets the gold star, the party can point to one indisputable fact—neither ethics reform nor true budget balancing happened until they were on the scene. They may have only hit bloop singles, but they look like line drives in the box score.

Their announced education program could be their home run. It has such introductory fanfare that, in the end, it will be difficult for them not to claim credit for victory. But, see number one above.

3. Taxpayers.

Faced with an almost certain tax increase to fill the budget hole, the taxpayers were big winners. Our budget has screamed for pension reform for decades. Funny what a little third party political opposition can accomplish.

LOSERS:

1. Republicans.

It makes you wonder if they ever get tired of losing. Surely Elizabeth DiMaggio's brood could have offered the E Party sufficient spoils to claim at least the Senate presidency. If they have a strategy, it escapes me.

They voted for plenty mail piece ready initiatives to avoid tar and feathering. But, and it's a big but, they went for the pork. In doing so, they came up totally empty and, whereas the Speaker found a get out of jail free card, they did not. I'd call that the lose-lose scenario.

2. Unions.

Not sure they lost. And, in the long run, they could be big winners. Helping the Speaker win is always a good thing. But, for now, there would appear to be a lot of 'splaining' to do with rank and file.

In other news…

CHAPTER FIFTEEN

The last time he had walked up the steps to the greystone on East 63rd Street, he was justifiably apprehensive, given an eighteen-year hiatus from his former best friends. This time his apprehension resulted from the premature death of one of those friends. Almost fifty years ago, it was Patrick's comforting outreach that had soothed the loss of his father. He was now planning to reciprocate.

Not unlike his previous visits to the Covington home, he was greeted by an emotional K.C. The element of surprise was missing, but the energy and warmth extended with her welcoming embrace was unmistakable. Also not unlike the previous visit, trauma recovery prescribed hours of reminiscing and serious quantities of alcohol. Laughter not optional.

Alex was quite pleased to learn that K.C. was all about the E Party, considering the emotional roller coaster she had been on. The one redeeming aspect of Patrick's debilitating death sentence was that his mind stayed strong to the end. The E Party had been a sort of magic potion for Patrick, providing a source of strength and hope in the darkest hours of his journey. Toward the end, he insisted, and K.C. willingly concurred, that at the appropriate time she would move to Chicago and embrace the cause on a full-time basis.

"Patrick and I had excess opportunity to discuss my life after he was gone," she explained. "We discussed my finding a new mission in life and your E Party fell like manna from heaven. I also had time to mourn a little each day and Patrick's death brought total closure. There is nothing left for me here. So, starting in two weeks, when the education hearings begin, I'm front and center."

* * * * * * * * * * * * * * * *

"Mr. Speaker, Eddie Cobb here," he announced in his finest Texas come on. "How's my favorite political operative?"

Eddie Cobb! Chairman of the Democratic National Committee. Eddie Cobb! The anaconda-sized political snake that had either bought or crushed his way to the top. Eddie Cobb! Survivor of numerous federal investigations from which any change of judicial venue outside of Texas would have translated into more lives in prison than the healthiest cat. Eddie Cobb! Riding high, after having seen his party gain—during his tenure—the presidency, along with control of Congress, and more governorships and state legislatures than ever before. Eddie Cobb! Scumbag millionaire.

"Eddie! What an honor. It's been since the convention, I think." The Speaker cringed. This would either be a financial or patronage shakedown. Eddie never called without a costly or dangerous agenda.

"Since the convention? Hadn't realized! I must get to Chicago more often. Great hospitality. The best outside Texas."

Ouch. The Speaker cringed again—this is going to hurt.

"Mr. Speaker, far be it from me to disrupt the master, but there's a certain energy comin' out of Illinois that has a few members of the committee concerned. I think you might know what I'm referring to."

"Let me guess—E Party?"

"That's right. E Party. What the hell is E Party anyway? When this first broke, we figured it was one big fifteen minutes of fame anomaly and you, being the best, would be all over it. And, believe me, I know you are. If you're not cornering the angles, no one is. But, maybe you can help me help you. There's a creeping nervousness. If this boil festers, well, I'm sure you grasp the consequences." (Translation: What the fuck are you doing back in Illinois you over-the-hill know-it-all?)

"Thanks, Eddie. I appreciate the call. Tell the committee that we're on it. There was a bit of wind in their sails, but I think we're on the right tack now. As I'm sure you know, they instigated the union pension deal. Nice piece of work, I might add. But, that's been headed off. There'll be no more union folks crossing lines in

Illinois. If there's anything we need, it's great to know you're ready to jump in. (Translation: Keep your Southern fried ass out of our business.)

"Well, I'll let 'em know not to worry. And, don't be a stranger," Eddie concluded. (Translation: You're on a short leash, my friend.)

Typical, thought the Speaker. Rome's been burning for eight months and, at the national level, they just smelled smoke. At least the E Party was a rational, worthy adversary. Rational he could defend. Having the national bozos get loose on this spelled disaster. They only know one solution set—trash, burn, run over with a steamroller. Not the right strategy for dealing with the E gang. Not a pleasant thought.

* * * * * * * * * * * * * * * *

E-MAIL

To: Atlas, General, Mark
From: Lisa Boudreau
Sent: 7/26 8:30 a.m. (PST)
Subject: PR Rollout

In conjunction with the rollout of the education hearings, I've arranged a series of interviews, primarily local radio and television. For the time being, the actual hearings will only be tracked by local press—mostly B and C level talent.

The networks haven't yet figured us out. Electing twenty-two representatives and senators and driving the state's agenda isn't sufficiently compelling at this point. To them, we're still no more than an occasional sound bite. The education hearings aren't jazzy enough either. Every political administration for the last century has tried to reinvent education. They are also trying to "get" the General and Tom, but don't see either as Sunday morning talk show material.

I can arrange time on any of the afternoon talking-head chatter shows, but let's not go there unless we have to. Radio spots will allow us to talk up the education agenda in a non-threatening way. In a few cases, there will be call-in, but I doubt there will be anything our guys can't handle—they're pros!

I understand this is a substantive effort, but getting off the ground with a known celeb or two is, in my opinion, critical to a successful run.

* * * * * * * * * * * * * * * *

E-MAIL
To: K.C.
From: Atlas
Sent: 7/28 1:18 p.m. (MST)
Subject: Kickoff

I trust Liz has you comfortably situated in Chicago. Let me know if you need anything.

I have reviewed the plan for the rollout and from a content perspective, it's superb. You, Jenkins, Abernathy and Benjamin have all done an amazing job in a very short time frame. Lisa remains concerned that we are destined to be a tree falling in the forest and I am beginning to share her concern. The talent pool is deep, but lacks that *People* magazine star power.

I agree with you that we can't pander either. Let's keep working this.

* * * * * * * * * * * * * * * *

E-MAIL
To: Atlas
From: K.C.
Sent: 7/28 3:33 p.m. (CST)
Subject: Kickoff

I know. I get it. And we're working it, too. We all want to get off to the right start. And yes, Liz has worked her usual magic. Thanks.

* * * * * * * * * * * * * * * *

THE BACK BENCH

"If you let it slip, we catch it"

August 1

Did you hear that sonic boom across the political skies of Illinois yesterday? If you didn't, you must have spent twenty-four hours on another planet. It made news in every media outlet and the bloggers surely overworked their fingers typing into the wee hours.

The June 30 financial reports are out and the E Party reports raising $50 million.

Let's put that in context. $50 million would be enough to run a full slate of candidates in every legislative district and for every statewide office—for at least two election cycles! It's more than the Democrats and Republicans have ever raised, combined, in any election cycle.

And, did I mention the E Party had an almost $10 million surplus from the last elections?

In other news…

* * * * * * * * * * * * * * * *

"Speaker? Eddie. I know it's only been a few weeks since we spoke. But fifty million? Holy shit! That's one Texas big fucking number. That tells me your E Party has serious expansion plans. I know you're all over this—but it would help me if I knew what you had."

"Well," countered the Speaker, "the funds come from an entity known as the Atlas Trust. Unfortunately, under Illinois law, we don't require additional source information in any public filings. We will under an ethics law that just passed, but this latest contribution neatly predates any disclosure requirements.

"The most likely source was General Smith. But that was based on the $25 million in contributions last year. We've combed his companies' S.E.C. filings pre-retirement, and unless he has the world's greatest broker or bookie, there's not enough there. Tom Robinson has a nice nest egg of his own. But not even the two of them together could pull this off.

"Our current thinking is that someone willing to invest—to use the term loosely—that kind of money, needs a net worth of at least three to four times the amounts contributed. Unfortunately, that census is a lot larger than you'd expect. Guys in your league," said the Speaker taking a shot over Cobb's bow.

"I wish that was my league, but that's a start."

"There are more details that I would rather not get into at this time," the Speaker continued. "We're moving along with our research and I'm expecting a break in the next month. Let's regroup around Labor Day. I don't look for any political damage in the interim. Keep some perspective. The funds can only be used in Illinois and we're a long way from the primaries."

"You're right about one thing. August is our quietest month. Congress will be in recess and the president will be on his annual summer working vacation. Let's plan on September fourth, day after Labor Day. I'll call you. But let me know if anything breaks." (Translation: Better get a hold of this pretty damn quick.)

The Speaker couldn't stand Eddie's belabored drawl. As the conversation wore on, it seemed to get thicker and thicker as though he was ladling sweet syrup. No doubt every conversation with Eddie was wired. Now it was "his" E Party. Nice hand-off Eddie.

* * * * * * * * * * * * * * * *

E-MAIL
To: Atlas, General, Lisa
From: K.C.
Sent: 8/6 8:10 a.m. (CST)
Subject: How's This?

I think Representative Jenkins has hit upon an awesome idea. Details are in the attached memo.

We will have to push back the hearings a bit, but I think this solves the problem we've been struggling with. Atlas, I hope we can afford it?!?

* * * * * * * * * * * * * * * *

E-MAIL
To: K.C., General, Atlas
From: Lisa
Sent: 8/6 9:17 a.m. (CST)
Subject: How's This?

"How's this?" It's spectacular! Assuming Atlas signs off, let's conference this afternoon.

* * * * * * * * * * * * * * * *

E-MAIL
To: K.C., General, Lisa
From: Atlas
Sent: 8/6 8:47 a.m. (MST)
Subject: How's This?

This is a wow! And, yes, we can afford it!

* * * * * * * * * * * * * * * *

"I hate to wake you from your summer hibernation, but I have something you may want to run with. Breakfast?"

"I was wondering what became of the E Party," responded Nat. "Just not too early, okay?"

* * * * * * * * * * * * * * * *

"Speaker, I have Danny on line two."

"Danny, I've been hoping to hear from you. After that $50 million megaton bomb dropped, my best friend Eddie Cobb reinserted himself."

Eddie Cobb. The name coursed through Danny like a bolt of lightening. *That fucking asshole*, he thought to himself. It was one thing to have a strained relationship with the Speaker. At the core there was still a reservoir of deep professional respect. There was no respecting Cobb at any level. Fortunately, Cobb was usually scarce due to the fact that Illinois rarely came into play during presidential elections. He had not foreseen the E Party fiasco as an invitation to Mr. Sleeze. And, he clearly understood the Speaker's total disdain for the man and his modus operandi.

"Mr. Speaker, I had no idea," said Danny. "Does this effect any of our planning?"

"Hopefully not," snapped the Speaker. "That guy can fuck up a wet dream."

Enough said, thought Danny. For the Speaker to invoke the 'F' word was the equivalent of the Mississippi violating the 100-year flood plain.

"Well, I was calling with some lukewarm good news. As you suggested, we hired Michael Jacobson, a private investigator, to tail Nat Carson. I think you said it was Dawn who noticed he had too many E Party news scoops.

"Nothing unusual until a few days ago. Nat meets an unknown person for breakfast at Lou's. The private investigator knows most of the political figures in Illinois, but not this guy. And, no way he's from the Carson family tree. The private investigator gets more curious because he knows that, outside of Springfield, Carson hasn't left his residence before 2 p.m. in over a month. All of a sudden, he has a craving for omelets?

"On a hunch, the private investigator follows the breakfast companion. Turns out to be a guy named Stone from back East. Long political pedigree.

"It gets better. Two days later, Mr. Breakfast is at it again. This time with Lisa Boudreau. No way this Stone is the E Party benefactor, but my stomach tells me he's the political brains."

"Hmmmmm," the Speaker contemplated out loud. "Could be the break we've been hoping for. Good work by the investigator. Let's see where it goes. As for Cobb, if he contacts you, send him right back to me. Put the word out. This guy has to be on a very short leash with a very constraining choker. Thanks Danny."

* * * * * * * * * * * * * * * *

"Morning, sunshine," Mark Stone offered to an obviously wasted Nat Carson. "Am I catching you on the way in?"

"No, but let's just say I'm a few brain cells lighter this morning. Coffee, the high octane version, would go a long way. Waitress! Wasn't sure I'd be hearing from you. You guys seem to be playing the radio card these days."

"Candidly, we're kind of betwixt and between. The extended session threw off the timing of our education program. On the political front, we're gearing up for the primaries. Petitions are right around the corner."

"Late October, right?" Nat answered his own question. "Way too early if you ask me—but, as usual, they didn't. Moved up the primary to accommodate Barack against Hilary. Thought they'd move it back to late March by now. Who wants to freeze their ass off campaigning in Illinois in January? I guess it's all done on TV and through the mail anyway. Speaking of which, that fifty million nest egg of yours should buy tons of airtime. Fifty million dollars—I didn't know whether to laugh or cry when I saw it. Almost called to say what the hell, but I figured we'd eventually commiserate over eggs and toast. So what the hell?"

"In due time, my friend. The election is still fourteen months away. Let's just say it's there for insurance purposes. As in, think through the consequences before you mess with us. But since we haven't spoken in a while, my primary agenda item is to thank you. You honored a handshake deal and the E Party is grateful. I'm hoping we can extend our deal indefinitely."

"Deal?"

"Yes, our deal. We keep you at least one day ahead of the competition and you give us honest reporting in return."

"No problem there—a straight story is the only deal I've ever known. The dailies play it straight, too, as far as I'm concerned. But with the web, well, that's a game changer. More like, all the news that fits in the printer!"

"Thank you just the same. You and I both know the next campaign season will be ugly squared. The E Party will need all the straight shooters it can find. I'm not nominating us for sainthood, but we are determined to stay out of the mud as best we can."

"There is one thing I would like to understand better. What role, if any, did the E Party play in the pension overhaul? It was all a little too neat and too quick. Shit like that just doesn't happen."

"Off the record?"

"Duh."

"OK. The quick and dirty is that General Smith cut that deal with Don Colletti. Colletti sold the unions but the Speaker was given a right of first refusal, which he exercised."

"Colletti and Smith? Whoa! How does that happen?"

"Let's just say it happened."

"Time out! A seismic event occurs in pension reform. You claim the E Party gets it done, but you tee it up for the Speaker! Sorry, doesn't compute."

"It may not compute, but that's how it came down. Nat, my friend, I was as stunned as you. But that's the E Party in the brave new political world. Result oriented, not credit oriented. And there's no arguing with the result—the singularly most spectacular pension reform in American government.

"I've come to realize there is definitely a method to my guys' madness. Let's face it. The General is no stranger to strategy. If this comes across as an E Party deal, no way the bureaucrats buy in and no way it gets implemented, at least not very quickly. This way, it's the Speaker's deal and the bureaucratic rebellion is minimized. As I'm sure you are well aware, legislators, and even presidents, win political victories every day, only to have them banished to bureaucratic purgatory. Legislators and executives come and go; the bureaucracy is the mother of all EverReady batteries."

"Touché! And, in this case, asking bureaucrats to implement pension reforms that diminish their retirement benefits is about as easy as asking George Bush to admit Iraq was a mistake. That's a sharp group you hang with. By the way, I assume we're here for more than thank-yous and java."

"In fact we are. Ever heard of Billy Shakespeare?"

"Billy Shakespeare. As in, ever heard of General Smith or Tom Robinson? As in, who's arguably the biggest name in the recording industry? Is there anyone you can't commandeer to deliver your message?"

"That would be the same Shakespeare. But, his role is somewhat narrower in this case. He will be a surprise presenter at the opening of our education forum and I'm told a brief musical performance is not out of the question."

"A presenter?"

"You heard right. He allegedly attributes a great deal of his success and stardom to Representative Jenkins. As I understand it, he endows a foundation that supports after-school programs for underprivileged kids, primarily in the inner city. Jenkins is on his board."

"Who'd a thunk that one. Thanks for the tip."

* * * * * * * * * * * * * * * *

Representative Barbara Jenkins was born and raised in East St. Louis, Illinois, arguably the most economically challenged municipality in Illinois. A place that time forgot for as long as anyone can remember.

Fortunately for her, children in East St. Louis take the same standardized exams as the rest of the state and having a student in East St. Louis top the charts throughout grammar school is not likely to go unnoticed. Her intellectual prowess prompted a full scholarship to the state's math academy and a valedictory performance there led to similar recognition at M.I.T.

Graduating with honors in physics, she turned down lucrative offers in business and enlisted in the Peace Corps. Four years later, she entered the Masters Program in Education at Columbia.

Notwithstanding all the intellectual horsepower of M.I.T. and Columbia and all the world-beating agendas of her classmates, the

Peace Corps shaped her life's mission: identify ghetto kids born with potential for greatness and find a way to light their path. To the chagrin of her admiring professors and classmates, that led her back to teaching high school math in East St. Louis, Illinois—graduation rate, poverty rate, and teen pregnancy rate all below the Mendoza line.

Her contacts at and through M.I.T. and Columbia, and her unmitigated persistence, resulted in the development and funding of the "Reach For The Moon" program. Children with exponential potential are identified through a unique community based program and their gifts developed to the fullest extent. Whereas other similar programs stress academics or athletics, her vision runs equally to the arts.

William "Billy" Cleveland, later to gain fame and fortune as Billy Shakespeare, was one of Reach For The Moon's earliest success stories. A self-taught percussionist on a variety of second-hand store and junkyard instruments and components, he was a legend-in-waiting at age fourteen. Barbara Jenkins learned of Billy shortly upon his entering high school. She engineered a scholastic and mentoring combination that led to a scholarship at Julliard; it being no coincidence that Columbia graduates are well represented on the board.

William Cleveland is likely to forever be the only person to have played with the New York Philharmonic in the same year he had four platinum rap hits, each at its ghetto rhythmic finest. No less a genius with words than his namesake.

One of the more unique features of the Reach For The Moon program is the pledge she extracts from her protégés, a lifetime commitment to mentoring and philanthropy. Just as she sacrificed in giving back to her hometown, so too, do her beneficiaries. Billy Shakespeare is far and away the greatest financial success, and among the most dedicated, to reciprocating her vision and dedication.

Although her work in East St. Louis has become a model throughout the country, it was General Smith and the E Party that presented her with a platform to institutionalize her vision.

* * * * * * * * * * * * * * * *

THE BACK BENCH

"If you let it slip, we catch it"

September 16

The E Party should have called itself the Magician Party. Every time you turn around, they're pulling a rabbit out of the hat.

The rabbit in this case is one Billy Shakespeare, the rapper par excellence and, as we learned at the kickoff of the E Party's education forum, a man dedicated to excellence in education.

His personal story is very compelling, as is his philanthropic work for inner city kids. It never dawned on me that he was the same Shakespeare as in the "Shakespeare Foundation For Excellence In Education." That Representative Jenkins is his mentor was another unexpected bit of magic.

With the endless list of eminent presenters and the exhausting schedule and agenda, it was already destined to be the most thorough examination of a vital, hot button issue by the Illinois legislature in recent memory. Now that Billy Shakespeare has associated himself with the cause, the forum takes on new meaning.

At the same time, the E Party's taking a huge risk. It would not be the first time an overly ambitious and aggressive agenda, no matter how well intentioned, was headed to political oblivion.

When it comes to pushing other people's ideas over an electoral cliff, the Speaker always has a few tricks up his own sleeve.

In other news…

* * * * * * * * * * * * * * * *

"Nancy, it's Danny. Mr. Shakespeare has again proven the E Party is formidable. This would be a good time to move ahead with your plan."

"No problem, Danny. Consider it done."

CHAPTER SIXTEEN

E-MAIL

To: Atlas
From: Mark
Sent: 9/18 9:44 a.m. (CST)
cc: General
Subject: Candidate Recruiting

I have reviewed the potential candidates identified by the General and our sitting legislators. My comments are highlighted in red.

As with the initial grouping last term, the overall talent level is tremendous. I think we may be weighing too heavily to education at this point, but I am at a loss to offer an alternative mapping.

My primary concern relates to the potential size of the class. If all recruits are deemed viable, we will grow from 22 races to 93; 31 senators and 62 representatives. Coincidentally, were we to run the table, we would control both chambers of the Illinois Legislature. Not likely! But also not desired!

Given that we are comfortable with another session of minority status, I recommend paring the number to between 51 (17/34) and 60 (20/40). I am also wary of clipping too many Republican wings. There is a distinct advantage to keeping them competitive, particularly as we advance issues and need to build coalitions.

As I am sure the General has advised, we need to finalize the list by October 1 in order to assure an efficient and accurate petition process. Nothing worse than getting knocked off the ballot.

* * * * * * * * * * * * * * * *

E-MAIL
To: General, Mark
From: Atlas
Sent: 9/23 4:16 a.m. (MST)
cc: K.C.
Subject: Recruiting

Certainly a great group on paper. At this point, I prefer to set limits based only on the General's capacity to manage the field operation. If we can handle all 93 races, then let's go for it.

Assuming we cannot, by copy to K.C., I am asking her to work with the General to prioritize candidates.

Mark, at the same time, please prioritize, by district, our demographic strengths. If two candidates are considered relatively equal, your political moxie will be the coin flip.

* * * * * * * * * * * * * * * *

E-MAIL
To: Atlas, Mark
From: General
Sent: 9/24 7:12 a.m. (CST)
cc: K.C.
Subject: Recruiting

The final list is attached. I am totally comfortable with the numbers and demographics in all cases. In hindsight, 93 was a stretch. I am comfortable at 67. Unless anyone has an objection, we will start passing petitions in the next few days.

Regarding those not making the cut, K.C. and I will make personal contact. They're all stars in my book and we need to keep them energized.

* * * * * * * * * * * * * * * *

E-MAIL
To: Atlas
From: Lisa
Sent: 10/2 1:16 p.m. (CST)
Subject: Tom's Availability

Thanks to Representative Jenkins and Billy Shakespeare, we are in demand. I am fielding a steady stream of calls from A Level programming. Billy has generously offered to handle a few. Attached is a spot from the local NBC affiliate. I have overnighted the complete collection.

With Billy's limited schedule, I planned to compensate with the General and Tom, occasionally looking to also slowly introduce Representative Jenkins to media. All of a sudden, Tom's begging off. Turned down the last five spots. Fortunately, I was able to fill all but one request.

I do not know Tom well enough to push. Can you please reconfirm his availability? Thanks.

* * * * * * * * * * * * * * * *

E-MAIL
To: Lisa
From: Atlas
Sent: 10/2 12:23 p.m. (MST)
Subject: Tom's Availability

Let's give Tom some space. The baseball playoffs are starting and I'm sure he's swamped with his duties for the Commissioner.

If I remember correctly, he took leave last fall as well.

* * * * * * * * * * * * * * * *

E-MAIL
To: Atlas, Mark
From: General
Sent: 10/23 5:12 p.m. (CST)
Subject: Petitions

All petitions have been filed. Prior to filing, all signatures were verified by the field team and an election attorney. Never say never, but I like our chances if and when challenged.

* * * * * * * * * * * * * * * *

E-MAIL
To: Danny
From: Headquarters Staff
Sent: 10/29 2:22 p.m. (CST)
Subject: Petition Review

We have reviewed all petitions filed by the Republican and E Party challengers. With only three exceptions, all Republican, they are complete and accurate. Please advise if you want to file challenges in those three races.

* * * * * * * * * * * * * * * *

E-MAIL
To: Headquarters Staff
From: Danny
Sent: 10/29 3:27 p.m. (CST)
Subject: Petition Challenges

File against those three. Also, file against the E candidates on the attached list. I do not expect to win, but I want to get a read on how these few candidates and the E Party signal callers respond to the pressure.

* * * * * * * * * * * * * * * *

E-MAIL
To: Atlas, Mark
From: General
Sent: 10/31 11:14 a.m. (CST)
Subject: Petition Challenges

Our friend, Mr. Ryan, has selected an interesting group for his petition challenges. In almost all cases, they are in the races Mark has labeled our greatest challenges. I'm guessing he's looking to identify a few weak links to help determine whether and to what extent to deploy his resources. Very astute on his part. Assuming we hold serve, we will have to find ways to push back quickly in these races.

With Mark's help, along with our incumbents, we've started the opposition research on the candidates they will likely face. There are some interesting early observations: (1) There are relatively few educators. (2) Otherwise, the race, sex and ethnicity match our candidates in almost all cases. No effort at diversity in that respect. (3) The Democrat challengers are all union. This last factor is consistent with Mark's research. If they gain enough seats, they can unwind our pension reforms before the ink dries. (4) Surprisingly, this is not a highly educated group—very few college graduates. Can't figure the angle there yet, but no doubt they have one!

* * * * * * * * * * * * * * * *

"Mr. Speaker, I have Eddie Cobb on line one. It's the fourth time he's called this week."

"Thanks, Dawn. I'll take it this time."

"Hello Eddie. What can I do for you?"

"Well, for one, you can call me back! Obviously, our national party doesn't mean cow shit in Illinois. But I've got obligations and some cooperation could go a long way. If you're too damn good to talk to me, I can have the president call. I'm sure you'll be wanting him to make a few appearances in Illinois next year."

"Relax, Eddie. There's nothing to discuss. And, when there is, I'll call you."

"Nothing to discuss? Nothing to discuss? We've got fifty million reasons to talk. And I'll give you one more reason. I don't like watching the national news and seeing Billy Shakespeare singing his newest hit with the E Party honchos tattooed to his hip. When a man's selling ten million CD's a year and starts rhyming "E" with "we"…well Mr. Speaker, I'm getting nervous. So I expect a return call even to tell me I'm a fucking idiot."

"Eddie, let's try this again. Nothing's happening. Mr. Shakespeare can sing whatever he wants, wherever he wants. The people buying his CD's don't vote. If they don't vote, I'm not interested. If it was Frank Sinatra and the seniors were paying attention, we could talk. But he's dead and so is this issue of yours. As for the $50 million, it was still in the bank last time I checked. If it were buying airtime, we could talk. But it's October and I still don't know who's on the ballot. What else can I do for you today?"

"Mr. Speaker, I've known you since I cut my political teeth. You're the best there is. But your head is too far up your Illinois ass. For your information, the E Party is registered in every state and our sources tell us they are beginning to organize. If you won't talk to me, then tell me how we get some coordination. Because otherwise, we can trip over our own dicks. I don't need that."

"Eddie, I'll get back to you," he heard himself say. But his mind was answering: *That's right Eddie. I can't afford to clean up after you. All fifty states? Hmmmm.*

* * * * * * * * * * * * * * * *

THE BACK BENCH

"If you let it slip, we catch it"

November 6

I do not normally track committee level proceedings. They're predominantly for show; allowing legislators to stake positions and create mail pieces for campaigns on issues going nowhere.

However, there appears to be a very interesting dynamic to the education hearings. They are technically under the auspices of the Senate and House Education Committees, but for all intents and purposes, are all about the E Party. They have become, for lack of a better term—cult like. There is a growing following at many levels and, surprisingly, the Republican and Democrat members of the committee are demonstrating energy and enthusiasm.

A case in point is the recent hearing in Belleville. The topic was "The Impact of Teen Pregnancy on Graduation Rates." Under normal circumstances, the schedule would run from nine to three at most. Less than half the committee would be in attendance, given that it required travel and was subject matter only. One or two experts, predominantly Illinois based, would lead off, to be followed by the usual trade association and union types. Bringing up the rear would be an interested citizen or two. Those committee members in attendance would be out the door once they created sufficient sound bites. Only the chairman and an occasional committee member would make it to adjournment. Once in a blue moon, a meaningful written summary is published.

Not this time, and not with most of the proceedings I have attended. The sessions run a full two days, including evening hearings. Sixteen hours in total. The panel of experts includes nationally renowned presenters. Not that they are better than those to be expected from Illinois, but the variety of opinions and experiences has been greatly broadened. Further, the experts stayed throughout and participated in lively breakout and wrap-up sessions.

The most compelling sessions included young mothers, young women facing difficult choices in high school, and their parents. There were educators, clergy, and business representatives.

Are you sitting? Not only was the entire host committee (in this case the Senate) in attendance, but many local area legislators as well. The Democrats and Republicans were very positive in their approach and independently invited experts and participants. How do I know? If I had a nickel for every twitter message sent by the Republicans and Democrats on the committee, I could start my own political party.

Are you still sitting? Within two weeks a committee report was issued, again with meaningful participation and commentary from all parties.

The E Party is also running video on their ever-expanding web site. Although the videos are produced independently, they are available to all committee members for their campaign web sites. Reality check. A political party in Illinois, in the United States of America, is helping the competition because the message appears to be bigger than politics.

Through today, there have been ten such sequences with another fifteen scheduled. Did someone use the word "renaissance?"

In other news…

* * * * * * * * * * * * * * * *

E-MAIL

To: Atlas, General, Lisa, K.C.
From: Lauren
Sent: 11/9 3:19 p.m. (PST)
Subject: Good News And Bad News

First, the good news. Our web site has been overwhelmed with inquiries related to education pieces. We're not just talking Illinois. Hits are flying in from all over the world. It would appear that Mr. Shakespeare has quite the following. I never expected this in my wildest dreams.

Now the bad news. I'm sensing we're losing control. The blog is replete with demands for action, from people wanting to run as E Party candidates to potential contributors. There are literally millions of well intentioned ideas about where we go next. I fear our little Internet dike cannot withstand this onslaught.

* * * * * * * * * * * * * * * *

E-MAIL

To: Lauren, General, K.C., Lisa
From: Atlas
Sent: 11/9 4:22 p.m. (MST)
Subject: Your "Bad" News

Agreed. It's time to meet as a group.

* * * * * * * * * * * * * * * *

E-MAIL

To: Atlas
From: Liz
Sent: 11/16 8:02 a.m. (CST)
Subject: Meeting Schedule

I have set a two day meeting for December 6 - 8. With the exception of Tom Robinson, all arrive in time for lunch on the sixth. Clay has the complete breakouts of travel schedules, meal requirements, etc.

Tom is unable to attend. Said he had been meaning to call you. Should I schedule a call?

* * * * * * * * * * * * * * * *

"Mr. Robinson. This is Liz. Are you ready for your call with Atlas?"

"Yes, Liz. Thank you."

"Tom, good morning. I'm afraid I forgot to ask Liz where we're calling you."

"Morning to you. I'm down in Texas visiting family. Nothing more depressing than Chicago during the winter. That cold works its way down to my bones and the endless cloudy days—well, you lived there. I don't have to tell you."

"No need to explain. I think we once had three straight weeks without seeing the sun. That's part of the attraction to Aspen. Three hundred plus days a year with appreciable sunshine."

"I'm thinking it still has to get awfully cold at night. I'll take Texas and, of course, once we get past the holidays, I'm already preparing for spring training. Nothing like some good 'ol hot stove to get the blood moving."

"One of these days, I'd love to hook up with you for a week of spring training. Your pick—Florida or Arizona."

"Sounds great. Have Liz call whenever you're in the mood."

"Thanks. In the meantime, we're going to miss you at our December meeting. I can't guarantee warm, but I'll send a plane and promise to get you back the same day if you can make it work."

"Actually, I've been owing you a call. Between my baseball gig and the E Party spokesperson role, well, it's just getting to be too much. I need a break and, well, I didn't know how to handle it. So I've been somewhat avoiding Lisa and all of a sudden Liz was applying her best 'won't take no for an answer' charms."

"I wish you would have said something. I got you into this because of my dreams to upgrade our education system. At the end of the day, it's the answer to so many problems. And, with the hearings and all, I sense we're on the cusp of breaking out. Now is when you're needed the most. In fact, if it makes things easier, back off the politics and just handle education."

"I agree things are moving. But, Billy has a significantly greater reach and more powerful message. If nothing else, I just need some time. Please try to understand that."

"Say no more. Enjoy Texas and, if it's okay, I'll have Liz give you a holler after the New Year to plan that spring training getaway. Tom, thanks for all you've done. None of this happens without you. Take care my friend."

* * * * * * * * * * * * * * * *

E-MAIL

To: General
From: Atlas
Sent: 11/29 11:46 a.m. (MST)
Subject: Tom

I just got off the phone with Tom. Something isn't right. He admits he's been avoiding me. Asking for time off. This is a guy who never took a day off in his life. I've known Tom for almost thirty years and my stomach tells me something is off-kilter. Please gently kick the tires for me and let me know what you find out.

* * * * * * * * * * * * * * * *

E-MAIL

To: Mark
From: Atlas
Sent: 11/30 6:56 a.m. (MST)
cc: General
Subject: Other States

In preparation for our upcoming meetings, please dust off and update your memos on the other states with favorable political and campaign contribution opportunities.

* * * * * * * * * * * * * * * *

E-MAIL
To: General
From: Atlas
Sent: 11/30 6:58 a.m. (MST)
Subject: Other States

Assuming Mark can identify a few new beachheads, can you give some thought to staffing the candidate selection process and field operations? I'll have him shoot you his updated memos, state by state, when available.

* * * * * * * * * * * * * * * *

E-MAIL
To: Elizabeth DiMaggio
From: Bruce Frazier
Sent: 12/1 12:12 p.m. (CST)
Subject: Election Challenge

Attached is the draft petition and supporting memorandum challenging the E Party's ticket, requiring them to run a full slate of statewide constitutional officers. There is no statutory filing deadline for our petition that we can find, as it is not expected under Illinois law that a party will need to be compelled to field candidates. However, with the primary only sixty-eight days out, I am concerned that a judge will toss out the case if, in prevailing, there is insufficient time for them to set their slate. Vacant slots for representatives and senators can be filled relatively quickly. Finding candidates for governor, attorney general and the others does not happen overnight. The judge will want them to have reasonable time. I'm guessing forty-five days minimum. Assuming you are prepared to move ahead, I suggest filing no later than December 15.

* * * * * * * * * * * * * * * *

E-MAIL
To: Bruce Frazier
From: Elizabeth DiMaggio
Sent: 12/3 2:39 p.m. (CST)
Subject: Election Challenge

Your memorandum raises an interesting tactical consideration. As a case of first impression, if the law does not mandate a filing date for our petition, what is the risk of waiting until the primaries have concluded? The issues don't change, but, in waiting, we push back the E Party's window for initiating and running statewide campaigns.

* * * * * * * * * * * * * * * *

E-MAIL
To: Elizabeth DiMaggio
From: Bruce Frazier
Sent: 12/5 4:04 p.m. (CST)
Subject: Election Challenge

We have updated our research. Delay does impose a greater risk that laches (the legal concept of delay) could apply. However, it also avoids a ripeness issue during the primaries that would prematurely announce your strategy. As to timing, we recommend working backwards, at least one hundred days from the date final ballots are printed. Given this is a law issue rather than a fact issue, the briefing schedule and arguments can be accelerated to fit that time frame.

* * * * * * * * * * * * * * * *

The drill was the same as always, planned to perfection by Liz: landings, transport, accommodations, and greetings from Atlas at the stroke of noon.

"Welcome all. Hard to believe it's been almost one year since we were together, basking in the glory of our initial victories. I trust your travel was relaxing and uneventful. We've been having an unusually snowy December and, as recently as last night, I was concerned that some or all of you would not make it in. Maybe the gods are smiling on our E Party. Clay? Are you ready for us? I don't know about anyone else, but I'm starved. Ladies?

"Before we begin, I want to thank Lauren for putting us on alert. I find that sometimes we're so busy sticking to plan that we don't realize events have overtaken us. However, I think we can get back in sync very quickly. Lauren, what would be your priorities at this point?"

"Not really my priorities," she began. "I just do technology, remember? But the messaging on our site, particularly the blog, has been screaming for attention. I have a complete report available, but the three themes that rise to the top are questions regarding when the E Party will offer slates in other states, when it will run congressional candidates, and when it will take contributions from the public. There are also thousands of well-intended ideas for reforming government and for passing legislation. For those, we did the best we could to categorize by subject and content.

"But, if I had to put it in a nutshell, the overriding theme is how to get actively involved in the E Party. How to make a difference. The preponderance of activity on the site is from outside Illinois. And, get this, once the Shakespeare stuff hit, we're running a growing volume of interest from outside the United States."

"Thanks, Lauren. There's so much in there it's hard to know where to begin. I actually came away with a slightly different twist. It's a concern, actually. Have we created an unmanageable aura of expectation? Having spent my career dealing with trauma, it is not clear how to rein in unbridled optimism."

"Why does it need reins?" questioned K.C. "What makes us the repository of wisdom? Similarly, the notion of managing is also too manipulating. Sometimes ideas have to play out. To me, it's a lot more about channeling. Between the technology Lauren has developed and the outlet for expression we've created around educational issues, well, that's two big pieces right there. My concern is the human capital; sustaining the momentum we've built developing a new paradigm for political leadership. Right now, we have Team Atlas and twenty-two legislators operating outside politics as we know it. And, it's working."

"I also have to disagree with you on this one," the General piped in. "I'll take optimism every day of the week. I'll even take irrational exuberance—as long as it's trained. Channeled. Whatever. Winning is attitude and that aura, as you call it, comes from winning. So what if expectations run high. We set our strategy in that context and move on."

"Winning is what my game's about, too," joined Lisa. "The press feeds on winning. While we're winning, they want to be with us. The optimism, the emotions are all part of building public relations. At this point, we've just begun to capture their attention, especially at the national level. I'd rather run the risk of too much than too little. Without having completely digested Lauren's report, I'm ready to blast away. We may have gobs of cash in the bank, but you can't buy the kind of publicity this creates."

"Well, this is an unexpected role reversal. When this all started, it was you cautioning me about the risks. Now, I'm the one in need of convincing," concluded Atlas. "However, as Liz has most of you hitting the slopes this afternoon, let's regroup at dinner. Just come back in one piece."

* * * * * * * * * * * * * * * *

"I hope the skiers fared well today," Atlas opened at dinner.

"I wish I had a better word than unbelievable," said K.C. "My only skiing has been back East. This definitely tops Vermont!"

"My kids would love this," Lauren enthused. "How do we book spring break?"

"You just did," Atlas smiled. "General, did you ski or just après ski?"

"I think you know the answer to that one. Parked myself at The Little Nell in my favorite chair by the fire and après'd away. Also, went back to Lauren's report. And I'm ready to take my chances with that Internet army she's recruited."

"I'm not there yet, but your collective enthusiasm has tempered my anxiety," countered Atlas. "You all know how I define winning in the context of the E Party. The winning you all reference is another flavor. To that end, I'm very interested in what Mark and the General see as our next steps. Mark, any objection to talking your way through dinner?"

"No. In fact, I'm happy to forge ahead. As I doubt we'll get everything covered in one evening, what I'd prefer to do is focus on Illinois tonight. We can regroup tomorrow after skiing to talk about opportunities outside Illinois. I hope you had an opportunity to review the executive summary for this year's political campaign. I'll take those nods for a yes.

"Last time around, most campaign elements were in our favor. We were well financed, the mood of the public was exceedingly anti-incumbent and anti-government, the element of surprise reduced the campaign to a sprint and we had exceptional candidates, all of whom stayed on script. Finally, we were a clean slate—no negatives. The General and Tom Robinson were the public face and, their joint persona, based on their legendary roles in their respective careers, was above reproach.

"Flash forward to tonight. We can again put a check mark next to well financed. But, that's where any resemblance may end. The loyal opposition literally has our $50 million number painted on the wall reminiscent of a charity fundraising thermometer. They are currently only one-third of where I expect them to be next fall. But, they will find the funds no matter how many limbs get broken when they shake their contributor trees.

"The electorate definitely threw some bums out. If anything, there is heightened unrest with the economy, foreign affairs, almost any issue—you name it. But, the Blagojevich impeachment is old news and we also have a new president riding high in the polls, proposing a cascade of new initiatives. There is no way to gauge the political impact and the corresponding public mood one year from now.

"The prudent course is to assume the status quo weighs slightly in favor of the Democrats. In that event, the president is probably worth two to four percentage points to every Democrat candidate we face. Were he to campaign in person or lend his endorsement in a targeted way, without identifying our own game breaker, we lose that race. Fortunately, the chances of the president engaging at the local level are historically remote, even in his home state. However, if Democratic National Committee honchos view the E Party as a downstream threat, which I suspect they will, squashing will be in order. Their efforts will increase exponentially if we venture outside Illinois. And, General, it will definitely be a take no prisoners effort.

"Since I'm good enough at reading body language to note your collective deflation, let me also suggest that history will be on our side. Mid-term elections for newly minted presidents are disasters waiting to happen. In which case, the action will be about control of Congress. In that case, we will not be prominently featured on anyone's radar screen. As you saw in the last election cycle, even though we devoted untold energy, money and human capital to our victories, the average campaign for the state legislature is effectively an off-Broadway production in Podunk. No relentless media buzz like the national level stuff. Remember, most people can't even name their state representatives and senators and, don't kid yourselves, that also applies to the E Party.

"Regarding the element of surprise and sprinting—that would be zip, nada, no way Jose. Danny Ryan, along with every warm-blooded Democrat operative, has been working 24/7 to plot our demise. By now he has dossiers on all of our elected officials and is scrambling to investigate our recently identified farm team. It's not a question of if, only when, the personal attacks and nuanced innuendos will commence. I would be stunned if robo attack calls were not initiated during the next session of the General Assembly. Politics in America is about driving negatives, particularly when our opponents' records are as substantial as quicksand and they know it.

"The Democrats and Republicans will also be working non-stop to get their single issue voters to the polls. Between prolife/choice and gun/no gun, depending on turnout, Illinois can see up to 20 percent single issue voters. If they split evenly among Republicans and Democrats, it's inconsequential to them, but in any one legislative district we start down ten points. In a non-presidential voting year, with reduced turnout, that's a lot to overcome.

"In the last go round, we grabbed 5.6 percent from the various single issue camps. But, we haven't voted on their pet issues and the Speaker has, as usual, brought sufficient voting loss leaders to the floor to energize the faithful. Our failure to acknowledge the single issue causes will cost votes in the fall.

"This may be a good time for me to take questions and comments while I get caught up on this delicious spread."

"Mark, I don't have questions. But I am struck by the fact that you almost totally disregard the Republicans," K.C. remarked. "Particularly if, as you remind us, the mid-terms favor them."

"What mitigates on our behalf is that, at the national level, this is a zero sum game. Just as the national Democrats might give us a pass while protecting their Congressional butts, the Republicans will no doubt use every effort and campaign dollar at that level to gain ground. I don't see the national level Republicans extending themselves to help local Illinois legislators protect an already weakened minority position just because we exist. Conversely, if we go multi-state and become a perceived threat to one of their strongholds, they will similarly launch an all-out offensive. We would prove to be the one issue that unites the Democrats and Republicans. All the more reason to carefully target our multi-state efforts.

"Elizabeth DiMaggio knows the math too. Even with a significant mood swing her way, she picks up only a few seats in each house. However, if I'm Elizabeth, I am all about the governor's race. In fact, if you'll indulge a brief detour, there's some interesting inside baseball behind that comment.

"The census occurs next year, culminating in political redistricting for the following election cycle. With the exception of U.S. senators and one or two congressmen who also run statewide, every legislator in America, federal and state, will be running in newly drawn districts. Whoever controls the redistricting process in each state has the ability to shape political power for the following decade. Until we arrived on the scene, the Democrats held all the cards in Illinois. So, they have an added incentive for regaining majority control of both Houses, while keeping their flag flying over the governor's mansion.

"Without us, the Republicans have no hope of influencing the new map. With us, they can cut a deal to maximize their position. But the game changes dramatically if there should happen to be a Republican governor. Without getting into unnecessary detail, a legislative stalemate results in a coin flip and the governor's party can end up drawing the maps for both state and federal redistricting. Grand slam home run for the Republicans.

"So, where does that leave us? It tells me the Republicans will protect their legislative base but, in the absence of serendipity, will not look to expand. All available resources will go to one race—governor. In fact, you may have noticed, whereas the Democrats have an opponent slated against all our incumbents, the Republicans chose not to do so. Frankly, were I advising them, that's my strategy as well.

"Fortunately, we have not exactly remained stagnant. Thanks to our host, we have a well-stocked capital pond. And thanks to the General, we have excellent candidates and, for a lack of a better phrase, a superb political army. The goal is to again run our field operation with the precision of the last campaign, add a few de la Rosa magic technology upgrades, and aggressively promote voter registration.

"For us to win, it will come down to messaging and content. Lauren, your I.T. blows me away. Whether it's the software and technology you built to support the General, or the bells and whistles supporting the various web applications, we are exactly where we need to be.

"Lisa, I do not understand the voodoo that you do so well, and I'm not sure I want to. But the press and other media seems to be with us. To that end, if I had one wish, it would be that they don't attack us in their own unique way. They see themselves as the paragons of political virtue and, in many instances, work to boost the underdog. With our financial advantage, we may have lost underdog status. The reality is that close elections sell more papers and boost the ratings of the nightly news, virtue or not.

"Which, in total and absolute unfairness to K.C., brings us to the crux of the matter. Can we reverse umpteen years of U.S. political history and win elections on issues?

"We have initially staked our claim on ethics, the economy and education. We hit a few hanging curveballs out of the park last session, but we also ceded bragging rights on ethics reform to the Speaker as well as our pension reform blockbuster. Yes, we will run on these issues again, especially education, but the Speaker will be me-tooing us to death. As my memo explains, Mr. Ryan has assembled a 'me too' Democratic candidate slate against our incumbents. When our candidate is a black female—so is theirs. Where we have a senior, formerly successful Catholic entrepreneur—ditto. It's a classic pattern and not unexpected—the more they look, feel, taste and smell like our guys, the less reason the voter has to think of us as the party of change, particularly when we aren't looking so attractive wearing freshly caked-in mud.

"The one issue they should not be able to copy is education. As you're all well aware, the statistical mountain of inefficiency, mediocrity and waste upon which the politicians have built our educational system is their Gordian knot.

"K.C., everything about the hearings has been brilliant. Certainly better than any bullshit reality TV. The problem will be taking all the hours of testimony, the inspired white papers, and the international following Lauren has documented and turning it into blue ribbon, election winning legislation."

"Mark," began K.C, only to be preempted by Atlas.

"K.C., before you respond, let's call it a night. Go attack the mountain in the morning and we'll attack education in the afternoon."

* * * * * * * * * * * * * * * *

That K.C. and the General managed to arrive at the Atlas pod within five minutes of each other created an uncomfortable triage over nightcaps.

"Why do I have the feeling you two synchronized your watches?" Atlas began with a warming smile.

"The funny thing is," offered the General, "she stays on Eastern Standard and I'm on Central. It's a small miracle we got this right on Mountain. At least give us some credit."

"OK, OK. So to what do I owe this honored sojourn?"

"We're both concerned about your newfound reticence," began the General. "Since neither one of us has ever seen that from you, we thought we'd stop by to slap you out of it!"

"Reticence? Really? Maybe so. But when you combine Lauren's notion of losing control with Mark's analysis of the elections, I'm not exactly feeling warm and fuzzy. No, that's not it either. It's more about letting go. We gave this thing life and before we can enjoy the toddler years we're running, or maybe more like flying. And I'm not sure we're ready to fly. All the things Mark alluded to are great accomplishments, but that was basically seven people. I can't get my arms around the transition—rationally or emotionally."

"That may be the case," said K.C., "but the alternative is unacceptable and unworkable. We cannot exist or survive as a minority party in Illinois with just twenty-two legislators. This business is as much up or out as any. When we met last year, we talked about the need to constantly reinvent ourselves. This is just Reinvention 101."

"I know you've looked down the road. You and I both know what's coming," counseled the General. "Only your ride into the sunset is surprisingly imminent. By next year, this will all require public funding. Let's not forget one of the main reasons we started in Illinois was because of the ridiculously loose campaign funding laws. Any state with an E Party will also need organizational structure and candidates on par with Illinois. So be it, my friend. By then, if we've done our job, we will have forever changed the system. Best of all, those Atlas-style victories you sold us on will be taking place all over the country, at all levels of government. This genie is not going back in the bottle."

* * * * * * * * * * * * * * * *

"No broken limbs that I can see. How was that fresh powder?" asked Atlas upon convening.

"Let's just say," said the General, "that if we had put things to a vote, we'd still be skiing and you'd be meeting alone."

"In that case, I wish you'd have voted. One thing I've learned from the locals since moving here is to never sacrifice a powder day for work. Fortunately, it will still be there tomorrow for anyone wishing to stay. K.C., if I remember correctly from last night, you're up to bat."

"That may be, but I'm bringing in a pinch hitter. More like twenty-two pinch hitters. From Representative Jenkins to Representative D'Alba, those people we elected to form the E Party are the ones who have to embrace and execute Mark's issue challenge. Our forum will produce approximately fifty white papers across a remarkable spectrum of education related issues. But it's their work product, not ours. They have to decide where to go next, not us. We just facilitate this process."

"Well, that makes for a fairly short discussion," laughed Atlas. "How do you propose to facilitate our issue facilitating?"

"Easy. When the Legislature convenes the spring session, our education committee chairmen, in conjunction with our twenty regulars, call for votes on the issues about which they are most passionate. For those that win, Mark has issues to design his campaign. For those that lose, our team decides on which to stand, and we take our case to the voters.

"Mark," K.C. continued, "you gave all of us a great deal to sleep on last night. What I concluded is that winning an issue-based campaign does not mean only pushing issues that can survive the Illinois General Assembly. It's that take-a-poll-to-decide-your-convictions mentality that got us into this mess. We have to stand for our principles, whether we win or lose the election. That's my definition of victory."

"Mark?" challenged Atlas.

"From now on, any time I forget that I work for the E Party, just have K.C. kick me. However, that also means a depth of organization among our group that we have not fully developed. They will need to quickly transition from twenty-two individual legislators to a cohesive caucus. Somehow, I'm guessing that K.C. has that figured out as well."

A quick wink and nod from K.C. was all the answer Mark needed.

* * * * * * * * * * * * * * * *

"Mr. Speaker, sorry to interrupt your meeting preparation. I have Danny Ryan on line one. I asked if this could wait until later, but he's insistent."

"Danny, what's so important that it can't wait?

"Three days ago, our guy Jacobson followed Mark Stone to Chicago Executive Airport. He called me to see if I could get him access to the tower, and I remembered Matt Tristano flies his corporate jet out of there.

"The next day, Jacobson calls and tells me that Stone was flown to Aspen, Colorado, on a private charter. We tried to get him out of there to follow the lead but due to bad weather there were tons of cancelled flights and everything else was booked. Chartering was prohibitive and driving from Denver was dicey.

"Three days after leaving, Stone was back in his apartment. Guess how he got back? Same way.

"I'm checking with you because I still want to send Jacobson to Aspen. But, there's a chance the trail will be cold by now and it's a budget breaker on my end. He says the likelihood of relevant clues diminishes exponentially each day. So, your call."

"Aspen. Doesn't Cobb have a place there?" asked the Speaker.

"Wouldn't know," Danny conceded.

"Lots of money in Aspen," mused the Speaker. "The kind of people that have $50 million to spare. Send him!"

* * * * * * * * * * * * * * * *

E-MAIL
To: Atlas
From: K.C.
Sent: 12/12 10:01 a.m. (CST)
Subject: Follow Up

With Liz's help, we have booked a Team E meeting over the Christmas break. As a treat (your money of course), we're heading to Arizona. Thought the kids could use some rest and relaxation too!

Thanks for trusting me on this one. We will be totally ready to engage when the session opens. Why don't you join us?

* * * * * * * * * * * * * * * *

E-MAIL
To: K.C.
From: Atlas
Sent: 12/12 9:15 a.m. (MST)
Subject: Follow Up

Arizona is a great idea. Get yourself a little rest and relaxation while you're at it. And, ha ha!

* * * * * * * * * * * * * * * *

"Danny, it's Dawn Eckersley. Please hold for the Speaker."

"Danny, I'm returning your call. What's up?"

"Unfortunately, we came up short in Aspen. Too many hotels to cover and the fixed base operations staff had no interest in cooperating. Evidentially, lots of dignitaries and trust fund babies pass through there and protecting identities is part of their job description. Jacobson stayed a few days to snoop around, but this is ski season and there were upwards of 20,000 visitors in town during Stone's stay. I did have him check whether or not Cobb keeps a place in Aspen and, turns out, he does. Also turns out Cobb was there at the same time entertaining a group of senators. Probably a total coincidence, but I thought you should know."

"Next time, if there is one, get our guy out there ASAP. And I agree about Cobb. Just remember what I told you."

CHAPTER SEVENTEEN

THE BACK BENCH
"If you let it slip, we catch it"

January 9

The General Assembly returns to Springfield tomorrow and where this session goes is anyone's guess.

The Democrats are confronting an extremely difficult budget once again. The economy remains weak, with state revenues off as much as 7 percent. If they held their customary majorities in both Houses, they could pass a gimmick-laden budget in May in order to get past the November general election. There's no way they can vote for tax increases in this environment. But their sacred cow constituencies including labor, education and the bleeding hearts, won't be very receptive to program cuts. Also, not a good year to antagonize major contributors.

I am tempted to say the E Party can sit things out again while the Democrats implode. Remember, their coffers are already full. However, they continue to run the risk of being labeled a do-nothing party. The education hearings garnered five-star ratings and stirred up legitimate energy, but there's a long way between schmancy hearings, Internet hocus-pocus and votes in November. The Speaker understands that as well as anyone, so don't look for too many E Party sponsored bills making their way to the governor's desk.

Even though they hold many more seats than the E's, the Republicans appear obsolete. When they were embarrassed over the initial budget deal last spring, they lost bragging rights as the party of fiscal responsibility. They probably lost most of their claim during the Bush years anyway, but their taste for the other white meat was likely the final straw.

They also have a very crowded field of candidates running for governor. With the Democrats in disarray themselves and with the E Party sitting out the statewide candidate dance, the winner of the Republican primary will have the party's proxy to enforce whatever message he or she runs on. The smart money seems to be betting on Healy, at which point their agenda gravitates even farther to the right.

In other news…

THE BACK BENCH
"If you let it slip, we catch it"

January 10

Following a rather classic political gambit, in his opening address to the House of Representatives yesterday, the Speaker pulled the rug out from under the E Party. He graciously acknowledged the work of Representative Abernathy's committee during the fall and offered effusive praise for their work product. He then declared himself to be the education Speaker.

He reminded the assembly that in even-numbered years, with the exception of the budget, only emergency matters are to be considered. He engaged in a lengthy discussion regarding the need to dramatically improve education in Illinois and concluded with a startling announcement. For the entire spring session, the House will sit as a Committee of the Whole with the goal of passing a comprehensive education package. Most surprising of all, while sitting as a Committee of the Whole, Representative Abernathy of the E Party will preside.

I never bet against the Speaker, knowing he has analyzed this move from every angle. Since most third parties are single issue, the traditional majority response is to co-opt their position. I assume that is the guiding principle in this instance.

But, the E Party is not your average third party. They are incredibly well financed and have superb organizational and technological capacity. They also have a six month head start with the media and their work product has set a new standard for excellence.

Until legislation actually passes, the most brilliant ideas have no electoral value. Which leaves two likely outcomes:

1. The Speaker passes a major education package, inclusive of multiple E Party concepts, and he sets the table for the Democrats in November.

2. Nothing passes, but the debate is maneuvered to a draw. The Democrats cannot claim victory, but neither can the E Party, especially with Representative Abernathy chairing the process.

I am certain there are many combinations and permutations and I am equally certain the Speaker has taken full measure of each and every one.

In other news…

* * * * * * * * * * * * * * * *

E-MAIL

To: Atlas, General, K.C.
From: Mark
Sent: 1/10 3:32 p.m. (CST)
Subject: Committee of the Whole

This is a major league curve ball.

* * * * * * * * * * * * * * * *

E-MAIL

To: Mark
From: Atlas
Sent: 1/10 2:36 p.m. (MST)
Subject: Committee of the Whole

Patience.

* * * * * * * * * * * * * * * *

E-MAIL

To: K.C.
From: Atlas
Sent: 1/10 2:38 p.m. (MST)
Subject: Committee of the Whole

I trust we are ready for this?

* * * * * * * * * * * * * * * *

E-MAIL
To: Alex
From: K.C.
Sent: 1/10 3:40 p.m. (CST)
Subject: Committee of the Whole
Yes. I will call you tonight.

* * * * * * * * * * * * * * * *

"Alex. It's K.C. I hope I'm not calling too late. I decided earlier that I might wait until tomorrow, but I can't sleep thinking about the challenges ahead."

"No, it's fine. I don't sleep much lately. I'm down to about three hours a night. Old age I guess. Don't get me in trouble with the General when I tell you this, but I've been sneaking some naps of late. Works against me at night, but sustains me during the day."

"Then I've got all night if you do. First of all, I never met the Speaker and I understand he's a reputed political genius. But you haven't met any of the E kids and they are the real deal.

"Let's not forget how you found them in the first place. All of the teachers were and are award winners; very highly respected in their communities. The others are just as strong. All bright, all leaders, all accomplished—and, for the most part, charismatic.

"As for Representative Abernathy, a total spitfire: strong, vivacious, bright, energetic. If I was the Speaker, no way I'm showcasing her as chairwoman. In short measure, she will become the face of the E Party. I hate to pick on you old guys, but the General and Tom's media days are toast once she struts her stuff.

"There's also a group dynamic that won't be corralled either. When we met in Arizona, they worked and played long and hard. Once I pitched a concept, they ran with it. I was quickly relegated to fly-on-the-wall status.

"Representative Jenkins, you remember her from the Billy Shakespeare plan, has all the talent required of a great leader. She has both an inner strength and a public presence that commands respect. I know I'm running on, but I'm grateful to be associated with this group and, above all, I want you to be proud of your accomplishment."

"I am proud, K.C. This whole escapade, as brief as it has been, has exceeded all expectations which, of course, makes us thirst for more. As for the vicious world of politics, Mark is correct that we face a battle for survival and yes, the Speaker is one tough customer. Let's not forget, you're the one who so adeptly laid out all the risks when the group first met."

"Maybe that's the disconnect here," she pounced. "You sit in your Aspen castle and read reports. We're in Illinois on the front lines. Maybe you should get in the game. You're the one insisting on total separation from the candidates. Who cares if that opens you up to some downstream bullshit what's-in-it-for-Atlas attack ads. You've spent your entire life up front and center and now, in your most important fight, you've boxed yourself into the corner. Join the crowd."

"K.C., we've been through all this. The Chinese wall stays. Let's move on."

"OK, I'm off the soap box. Here's where we stand. The E kids have prioritized their education wish list and, at the same time, have grouped issues by what they're calling the 'sell factor.' That's S-E-L-L factor.

"For example, even though most of them teach in public schools, they are fascinated by the charter school movement. At the same time, they recognize it's a red cape to the education lobby bullies. High priority, low sell factor. You can see where this is going. In the top quadrant are the best matches for priority and sell on down to the bottom with lower priority, lower sell factor. For the foreseeable future, that grouping is entirely off the table. After much debate, and here's my pride showing again, they chose higher priority, lower sell over lesser priority, easier sell as their secondary push. I'm guessing the professional politicians reverse that, assuming they even get that far.

"So, bring on the Speaker. We're ready."

* * * * * * * * * * * * * * * *

E-MAIL
To: Atlas, General
From: Mark
Sent: 1/14 6:27 p.m. (CST)
Subject: The Curve Ball

I have been giving a lot of thought to the Speaker's opening day pitch. It's really an extension of the 'me too' strategy.

I know you are inclined to exchange public policy advances for political gain. In this case, major, meaningful shifts in educational policy are worth the trade. No argument from me.

But, I have concluded that the Speaker's version of educational 'me too' is that nothing meaningful advances; the end game being a blame-the-other-guy stalemate. He wins every time at the game of mutual impotence.

The only way to beat this strategy is to build a constituency that forces his hand. If the education lobby, unions, trial lawyers, bleeding hearts and other major core Democratic contributors demand E style education reform, his indifference or inaction puts campaign funding at risk. With us sitting on $50 million, that's a risk he cannot afford. Chances of a double or triple remain remote, but a few solid line drives will produce a significant Atlas victory and enhance a Stone victory in November. My chicken versus your egg.

The next month to six weeks is critical. Should we fail to create momentum in that time frame, legislative inertia will grind us to a halt. I have a few contacts in the field and I trust the Atlas–General–Tom axis of power has entrees I haven't dreamed of. It's all part of the day-to-day world of government lobbying!

* * * * * * * * * * * * * * * *

E-MAIL
To: Mark, General
From: Atlas
Sent: 1/15 5:25 a.m. (MST)
Subject: Lobbying Support

I've always considered lobbying a four letter word. Let's find an E Party euphemism. Otherwise, your latest e-mail makes total sense.

* * * * * * * * * * * * * * * *

E-MAIL
To: General
From: Atlas
Sent: 1/15 5:28 a.m. (MST)
Subject: Tom

We're going to need Tom. Have you come up with anything?

* * * * * * * * * * * * * * * *

E-MAIL
To: Atlas
From: General
Sent: 1/15 7:30 a.m. (CST)
Subject: Tom

Sorry. That one fell through the cracks. I'll get on it.

* * * * * * * * * * * * * * * *

THE BACK BENCH
"If you let it slip, we catch it"

February 7

The results of yesterday's primary are in and, for the most part, there were few surprises.

As expected, Jeff Stewart will be the Democratic candidate for governor. With solid credentials, including his current eight-year stint as secretary of state, there was a sense of entitlement commonly found in politics. Stick around long enough and it becomes your turn. Early on, he captured endorsements from most state central committeemen, mayors, and other party dignitaries. It also did not hurt that he out-raised his challengers by a wide margin.

In a bit of an upset, Robert Allen will be the Republican nominee. As an outsider, using his personal wealth and business connections for funding, he was able to establish a position in the ideological center of a crowded field. Never having held political office proved to be a big plus in a spirited and decidedly negative campaign. Although not yet sufficiently polished for the general election, exit polling attributed a charismatic quality that will appeal to independents.

The conclusion of the primary also means the legislative session can begin in earnest. With members needing to campaign, the legislature's schedule for the past five weeks has been particularly light. From this point forward, there is a jam packed schedule running through the Easter/Passover recess.

In other news…

* * * * * * * * * * * * * * * *

E-MAIL

To: State Central Committee
From: Elizabeth DiMaggio
Sent: 2/7 10:00 a.m. (CST)
Subject: November

Congratulations to Robert Allen, our candidate for governor. Unfortunately, the campaign was quite un-Reagan-like. Accordingly, we need to immediately mend fences and move forward. Nothing short of a total, cohesive effort will allow us to achieve victory. We all understand the importance of the governorship to our party.

Next Sunday, I will be hosting a unity breakfast in DuPage County. Please make every effort to attend. We must quickly heal our collective wounds and move forward. We are just 266 days from the general election.

* * * * * * * * * * * * * * * *

E-MAIL

To: Atlas, General, Lisa
From: Mark
Sent: 2/12 8:02 p.m. (CST)
Subject: Primary Results

Attached is an analysis of our general election campaign opponents. I believe the Republicans selected the candidate for governor that gives them the best chance in November. This benefits us twofold. It will require the Democrats to divert more resources to the race than if a right-winger had prevailed and it insures the Republicans will disproportionately prioritize the race.

General, we should shortly review with all our candidates the protocol for dealing with robocalls and other attack elements that are certain to surface shortly.

* * * * * * * * * * * * * * * *

E-MAIL

To: Atlas, General, K.C., Mark, Lauren, Tom
From: Lisa
Sent: 2/14 7:22 p.m. (CST)
Subject: ABC Nightly News

Home run! Let's just say it helps to have a friend who has a friend. Tune in to Friday's *ABC Nightly News*. The person of the week is none other than the "E Party of Illinois." I'm told it will be presented just as I wrote it. Keep your fingers crossed!

* * * * * * * * * * * * * * * *

THE BACK BENCH
"If you let it slip, we catch it"

February 17

WEEKEND EXTRA!

Sometimes you report the news and sometimes you let the news report itself. The Illinois education reform movement was put on the map last night by *ABC Nightly News*. Below is their closing feature, "Person of the Week" in its entirety. The video is also featured on the blog.

"Finally, we turn our attention to a little known political party out of Illinois with a fairly catchy name for our times: E Party.

While we have come to expect stories of political corruption and sleaze to be the lead story from Illinois, the E Party may be changing things for the better.

The majority of the twenty-two seats they hold in the Illinois Legislature are held by award-winning educators. For the past six months, the E Party organized an aggressive, innovative series of dialogues on education reform. They produced a series of provocative white papers that can be found at www.epartyofillinois.com. They have so captivated the imagination of their legislative brethren that the Speaker of the Illinois House has devoted a significant portion of the spring legislative agenda to education.

We wish them well. From where we sit, education, like the weather, is something everyone talks about, but no one does anything about. Unlike the weather, education in America can be improved upon dramatically with sufficient effort. We wish the E (as in Education) Party of Illinois great success, and they are our person of the week."

In other news…

* * * * * * * * * * * * * * * *

"Mr. Speaker. Eddie Cobb calling. I hesitate to bother you on the weekend, but your 'don't call me, I'll call you' attitude is not ringing my phone off the hook."

"I'm…"

"Just let me finish! You know what is ringing my phone off the hook? The E Party of Illinois! And why, you might ask? Because the great state of Illinois is launching a major education campaign and the national news has declared the E Party to be the mother of education. Not the Democrats, or my friends the Republicans, but something *ABC News* now calls the Education Party.

Now, I don't know what you have in mind here, but the national committee wants answers. In fact, they want answers fast. Frankly, I don't give two shits about the legislature in Illinois. But, I warned you this could get out of hand and, from where I sit, you're not part of the solution." CLICK!

* * * * * * * * * * * * * * * *

"Hello, Danny," began the Speaker. "I know it's early, but I want to start polling on a weekly basis. Issue tracking will be at a premium through the end of session. At all times, I need to know the weighting of education. In particular, who, if anyone, is tracking the hearings in Springfield, and who's perceived as the winners and losers of that ebb and flow. Once we get past the Easter break, I want detailed tracking of all candidates and…"

"E's *and* R's?" interrupted Danny.

"All candidates," the Speaker answered firmly. "Hold off on your phased attack strategy until the beginning of March. We'll talk one week out to determine if the polling is suggesting a shift in emphasis. I would rather our early focus address ideology. The personal attacks work better late when it is too difficult to respond or the overall noise of the general election drowns them out. Above all else, we need to keep the E Party from grabbing a toe hold on key issues."

* * * * * * * * * * * * * * * *

E-MAIL
To: Atlas
From: Lisa
Sent: 2/17 1:16 p.m. (CST)
Subject: Tom

ABC News might as well have given out my phone number. Remind me to send them a thank you note!

I'm mapping out the spring PR agenda and need to know Tom's availability, if any. If he's in, we can push for more national TV spots. If not, maybe Billy will rethink his role.

* * * * * * * * * * * * * * * *

E-MAIL
To: Liz
From: Atlas
Sent: 2/17 12:52 p.m. (MST)
cc: General
Subject: Tom

Please find Tom. Remind him that we agreed to get together during spring training. Schedule at least three days of games/dinners.

General. Anything yet?

* * * * * * * * * * * * * * * *

E-MAIL
To: Atlas
From: General
Sent: 2/20 8:01 p.m. (CST)
Subject: Tom

Tom's last public appearance was over four months ago. He is usually booked up to one month out and, as far as we know, cancelled at least two weeks of commitments before traveling to Texas. In all cases, he apologized politely and profusely, but offered no specific reason.

Nothing indicates a sudden health issue and he was hitting them out of the park at engagements immediately preceding his hiatus. I'm not even going down the drugs, gambling, or Internet porn route. The man doesn't have a sinister bone in his body.

There's clearly something wrong. I've seen my share of AWOL, but this one's a stumper.

* * * * * * * * * * * * * * * *

E-MAIL
To: General
From: Atlas
Sent: 2/23 11:06 a.m. (MST)
Subject: Tom

Liz has me booked for spring training in Arizona. Tom was reluctant, but too much the gentleman to fend off my pit bull. Get me what you can before then. Let's hope he doesn't cancel. This is becoming much more about a friend in need than anything else.

* * * * * * * * * * * * * * * *

THE BACK BENCH
"If you let it slip, we catch it"

February 26

The Speaker formally began the Committee of the Whole education hearings today. His opening remarks were, as to be expected, comprehensive and focused. Given the recent boost from *ABC Nightly News*, three Chicago based network outlets covered the proceedings.

The E Party was profuse in their support of the project and compliments to the Speaker. Their main departure went to scope. The Speaker was more limited, obviously walking the teacher's union tight rope. Whereas the E Party, with their unfettered imagination, wants to encompass every aspect of their recently completed hearings and white paper series.

To the contrary, the Republicans are betting on this being a do-nothing, grandstanding by the Speaker. They are quick to point out that the hearings started one month late and that the agenda and presenters are of the Casablanca syndrome. In a nice bit of gamesmanship, they trotted out all the blue ribbon reports on education prepared since the Speaker has been in control and juxtaposed this series of circular file proposals against educational performance. It was clearly the sound bite moment of the day and spawned a few editorials.

As might be expected, our two gubernatorial hopefuls are keeping their distance for the time being.

In other news…

* * * * * * * * * * * * * * * *

E-MAIL
To: Atlas
From: General, K.C.
Sent: 3/3 4:44 p.m. (CST)
cc: Mark
Subject: Outreach

We met with our members over the weekend to brainstorm potential outreach to garner support for our education package. The attached list of targeted groups and individuals also details each member's personal assignments for initiating contacts and specific action items.

Given that any legislation is not likely to be voted on until late May, part of the outreach campaign will be an old fashioned, build from the bottom petition drive, conducted one-on-one, teacher-to-teacher. Lauren was instrumental in designing a web application to support this effort. We don't know if it will work, but it's the kind of team building exercise that will create a positive residual for November. We can always retreat quickly if our energy is misdirected.

Those on the Education Committee have decided to also initiate discussions with individual Democrat and Republican members. There was a sense of camaraderie building during the hearings. Evidently, we've excited a sense of potential that hasn't been manifest in quite some time. Lots of tweets between them and us. Our guess is that they all fall into line when the Speaker cracks the whip. In the interim, fomenting a little dissent in their ranks can't hurt.

* * * * * * * * * * * * * * * *

E-MAIL
To: Speaker
From: Danny
Sent: 3/8 10:00 a.m. (CST)
Subject: Polling

Having never polled this early, I am not sure what to measure against. The complete report, with cross tabs, is attached. As you will see, the leading issues are all national. Given the recession, the economy and jobs are the 800 pound gorilla of the day.

Please advise if we should be tracking any different issues or asking push questions at this stage. We're back in the field in six days.

* * * * * * * * * * * * * * * *

E-MAIL
To: General
From: Atlas
Sent: 3/10 11:15 p.m. (MST)
Subject: Tom

I just spent three terrific days at the Cactus League with Tom. Round the clock baseball; BP, games, dogs and beer. Doesn't get any better. Found Tom in his element. Besieged by fans, high-fiving from dawn to dusk and signing autographs until his arm fell off.

Also, snuck in 18 holes the last day. We're on for next year, old buddy. Set your calendar for the first week of March.

Tom's not the same guy I spoke with in December. However, when I finally asked him about coming back, I got a quick, expressive don't-ask-me shrug and a subtle funk clouded the balance of our last night's dinner. Unless you come up with something, and relatively soon, I fear that Tom's out for the season.

* * * * * * * * * * * * * * * *

THE BACK BENCH

"If you let it slip, we catch it"

March 22

With spring break rapidly approaching, it's like déjà vu all over again. This being an election year, I was expecting some old fashioned political fireworks. Was I ever wrong. Up until now, you can hear a pin drop in Springfield.

The only issue in play is education. The Speaker has gone to a four corner stall while he runs out the clock. Representative Abernathy and her E Party cohorts wax eloquent, but scintillating dialogue is not stirring the public's imagination. Unless these Houdinis act quickly, a once and future golden opportunity will just be a dead goose.

The only pulse belongs to the Republicans. Allen hasn't been the most inspiring candidate, but he's the only game in town. Stewart appears unwilling to get out front of the Speaker and who can blame him?

I'm shutting down for two weeks during the break. Happy holidays to all.

In other news…

* * * * * * * * * * * * * * * *

E-MAIL
To: Atlas, General
From: Mark
Sent: 3/24 12:15 p.m. (CST)
Subject: A Few Ideas

All polling remains on track. Our incumbents are significantly above the 50 percent mark in favorability and our new candidates are tracking ahead of last year's pace. That is to be expected given the name recognition our party has built. Stunning marks for integrity and, to that end, we need to keep the market cornered. Danny Ryan is long overdue when it comes to the expected torrent of negative attacks.

Stewart leads in polling over Allen, but his negatives are too high. Although it's early, I'm encouraged if I'm the Republicans. If they can make the campaign about Blago, this one should stay too close to call.

Since Danny has cut us some early slack, I have been thinking about ways to put them back on their heels. The education stuff will hopefully still play out, but it's not generating any energy at this point.

I've attached a few ideas. Let me know what you think.

* * * * * * * * * * * * * * * *

E-MAIL
To: Mark
From: Atlas
Sent: 3/24 2:12 p.m. (MST)
Subject: A Few Ideas

If you weren't on our team, you would be evil. If any of this works, you'll need to have someone start your car in Chicago. Assuming you can break away, Liz will arrange a few days out here as soon as possible.

* * * * * * * * * * * * * * * *

E-MAIL
To: Speaker Kennedy
From: Danny
Sent: 3/29 4:00 p.m. (CST)
Subject: Polling

Attached is the most recent polling heading to the Easter break. With few exceptions, I'm comfortable with the positioning of our legislative candidates.

I am, however, growing concerned with the E Party numbers. It is my continuing recommendation that we take them down a few notches. If for any reason their education stuff gains traction, the cost goes up considerably.

* * * * * * * * * * * * * * * *

"Can't we ever do this at a civilized hour, like three in the afternoon?" asked an unusually grouchy Nat.

"I always thought the early bird got the worm," answered Mark with sufficient indifference.

"What the fuck. You win. I assume we're here because the E team has no interest in sleeping through the entire session. I seem to recall that, in the last go round, you hit the ground running right after the break. Same playbook this year?"

"Perhaps, the difference being last year our guys couldn't walk yet."

"I'll give you that. No reason to get ahead of yourselves."

"This, however, is an election year, and when it comes to playbooks, I know the Speaker and Mr. Ryan well enough to expect major casualties. Do you think, for one minute, Illinois sees the cause of education advancing this year?"

"Actually, no. My money's on the bait and switch. Either nothing passes or whatever does is so watered down as to accomplish absolutely zero. Can't offend the unions you know. The hell with kids. Don't fix what's not politically broken. And, don't get me started, either. This discussion requires large quantities of alcohol, not this cup of caffeine."

"You're right, as usual. And that's why, starting April 6, the E Party will announce a major campaign focused on the state budget."

"The budget? I may need a rewind."

"Yes. Remember Willie Clinton? As far as we're concerned, 'it's still the economy, stupid.'"

"After all that work on education?"

"Mark my words. All that work will come to good purpose, and, if we're right, hopefully this session. Let's just say we're running our own little game of bait and switch. Let me walk you through it."

* * * * * * * * * * * * * * * *

"Mr. Speaker. Danny Ryan on line one."

"Danny. You were on my call list for this afternoon. What's up?"

"Looks as though we've had a major breakthrough. Stone flew to Aspen again last week and our guy Jacobson was out there the next day."

"He did some checking around and came up blank. Worried the target may be leaving town, he camped out at the private side of the airport and got lucky. Not only does he pull up in a big ass Range Rover, but out pops General Smith."

"The driver was more than happy to trade details for a C note. I think we may have identified Daddy Warbucks."

"Great work. Great work. We have to be 200 percent certain on this one. When will your source complete his investigation?"

"In a few weeks, tops."

"That makes my scheduled call a bit premature. Let's get the funding source nailed down and, at that point, go negative; slowly but surely."

* * * * * * * * * * * * * * * *

THE BACK BENCH

"If you let it slip, we catch it"

April 2

EXTRA EXTRA EXTRA EXTRA

The Back Bench has learned that, not unlike last year, the E Party plans to ratchet up the energy level in Springfield when the Legislature returns from its spring break.

Although the E Party has dedicated a major effort to education reform these past eight months, reliable sources indicate they will launch a major campaign focusing on the state's budget.

Even with last year's pension reforms taken into consideration, the E Party estimates the budget shortfall for the state's next fiscal year will exceed $2 billion. The recession has considerably reduced revenues. On the expense side, entitlement escalators, particularly in healthcare related categories, continue to significantly outpace inflation.

When asked if education is now off the table, our source suggested that the E Party will continue to press for meaningful reforms this session. They expect the Speaker to shortly unveil his package and look forward to working with him.

In other news…

* * * * * * * * * * * * * * * *

"Mr. Speaker. Danny Ryan on line two."

"Daniel. This needs to be brief. What's up?"

"No doubt you saw today's extra edition of *The Back Bench*? Turns out Stone met with Nat Carson yesterday. Just one day after his return from Aspen. Thought you'd want to know."

"Yes, thank you. Please call me as soon as you receive the private investigator's report. I need to drop off. Mr. Carson's extra edition has caught our attention for other obvious reasons."

* * * * * * * * * * * * * * * *

THE BACK BENCH

"If you let it slip, we catch it"

April 6

The E Party today launched what they are calling an experiment in democracy. The kickoff was highlighted by a massive advertising campaign coupled with an extremely imaginative, interactive Internet component. To me, it's a combination of reality T.V. meets government in one big game of *Who Wants To Be A Millionaire.*

In a nutshell, they have issued a challenge to all citizens of Illinois to find effective ways to balance the state's budget. Anyone who submits a concept that saves at least $1 million will earn a payment of $1,000; $10 million earns $10,000; and $100,000,000 extra earns $100,000. As I figure things, if the E Party challenge solves the $2 billion budget hole, they will be handing out in excess of $2 million in prizes. As judged by the sitting E Party legislators, the person submitting the most creative solution, regardless of the savings, will earn an additional $1 million.

As you would come to expect from the E Party, this contest has some unique twists. First, in order to compete, a person will have to demonstrate that they are registered to vote. Second, each registered voter will be required to successfully complete a three-hour, on-line educational program akin to state budgeting 101. For anyone who enjoys that kool aid, there is an additional series of one-hour training vignettes of targeted issues such as healthcare and education. Finally, the idea must be incorporated by the legislature into the state budget and enacted into law.

The entire operation was previewed for the media yesterday, complete with hands-on simulation of the on-line primer. Take my word, this is one slick operation.

Politically, it could truly be a game changer. The voter registration requirement is almost certain to boost E Party turnout in the general. The on-line course is an instant classic. Even this old dog walked away with new insight into how our tax dollars get allocated (or should I say wasted). I plan to visit the site this evening to review the one hour supplemental pieces.

To me, the true and simple and most compelling bit of political genius lies in the passage requirement. The E Party will be unleashing an army of E lobbyists; banging on legislators to pass a budget that incorporates their idea. That's a wow!

In other news…

* * * * * * * * * * * * * * * *

E-MAIL

To: Speaker
From: Danny
Sent: 4/20 11:54 a.m. (CST)
Subject: Polling

This latest E Party gimmick is a disaster. Not only have their numbers exploded, their new candidates are also benefiting big time. Conversely, it's driving our negatives in an unexplainable way. Almost as though our incumbents are being punished for not thinking of this idea. The complete report, with crosstabs, is attached. Perhaps we should meet with the State Central Committee to discuss.

* * * * * * * * * * * * * * * *

E-MAIL

To: Atlas, General
From: Lauren
Sent: 4/21 8:21 a.m. (PST)
Subject: Web Traffic

If our site didn't crash last night, it never will. The number of people taking the on-line budget course has surpassed one million in total. Similar to past experience, there is a remarkable percentage from outside Illinois. Surprisingly, although the voter registration aspect is tracking nicely, the majority have not yet registered.

We are now ready to roll out the additional target states whenever you and the General make the call. In each case, 72 hours' notice would be welcomed.

* * * * * * * * * * * * * * * *

E-MAIL

To: Eddie Cobb
From: Dawn
Sent: 4/30 2:30 p.m. (CST)
Subject: Update

Speaker Kennedy asked me to forward the attached report from private investigator, Michael Jacobson. He asks that it be kept confidential. He also asks that I set a call to discuss with you at your earliest convenience.

* * * * * * * * * * * * * * * *

E-MAIL

To: Atlas
From: General
Sent: 5/1 3:15 p.m. (CST)
Subject: Tom

Did not want to discuss the information regarding Tom with you until we could completely verify sources and information. Mr. Ryan is one mean MF. Let's talk tonight.

* * * * * * * * * * * * * * * *

"Mr. Speaker, I want to thank you for the information you sent recently," began a rather subdued Eddie Cobb. "If your man is right, and I have no reason to doubt his report, this situation is extremely dangerous and delicate.

"Mr. Stein is not only one of the wealthiest men in the United States, he is one of the most highly respected. He has done great work for his country and has provided personal counsel to at least three presidents, four chiefs of staff, and countless high ranking elected officials. He is revered by some of our most important contributors and constituents, particularly the unions. He and Don Colletti are close personal friends. Have you taken any action on this?"

"No," answered an uncharacteristically rattled Speaker. The name Alex Stein had meant nothing to him other than an extremely wealthy John Doe living in Aspen, Colorado; not the second coming.

"Then hold tight. I'll get back to you on this."

* * * * * * * * * * * * * * * *

E-MAIL

To: Atlas
From: Mark, General
Sent: 5/2 9:15 a.m. (CST)
Subject: Rollout

We have elected to begin sequencing the four target states over the next month. That allows us to address any speed bumps in a somewhat controlled environment. No need to rush.

* * * * * * * * * * * * * * * *

"Mr. Speaker, Eddie here. I can't share my sources, but first kick at the tires confirms Stein is definitely providing the E Party funding. As of now, he is our concern, not yours. We also have reason to believe the E Party will launch statewide campaigns in at least three other states. At this point, you're the only one who has dealt with them. I need to know everything you have—and no fuckin' around this time."

"Eddie, I don't appreciate your directives or your tone. Take Stein for all I care, but I want to know at least forty-eight hours in advance before you unleash whatever lame brain strategy you're considering. I've got my hands full and don't have time for your bullshit. I will contact you if, and when, I have something to share. And good luck with Stein. From what I've seen so far, you will not enjoy the challenge. He's way beyond your league."

CLICK!

* * * * * * * * * * * * * * * *

"Danny, it's the Speaker. I'm sorry I missed you. Let's meet Saturday at headquarters. Get back to Dawn with times. It's time for the E Party to come down a few notches."

CHAPTER EIGHTEEN

"Rae, Danny. Long time no talk. How's my favorite lobbyist doing this session?"

"Well, between the Speaker and the E Party, this session is a disaster for lobbyists. Even if I had an education client, most lobbyists are afraid to get in the middle of that one. And the budget, what a disaster! The state's broke. Pork went south last year. And now everyone is trying to cut out the next guy. Imagine how it will look when some Joe Public finds the hundred million dollar silver bullet and all the legislators start the recrimination game to deflect responsibility. This is fast becoming the political version of musical chairs. All of which has to be driving you nuts. Not to mention my good buddy, the Speaker."

"Well, shit still rolls downhill. Only now, we've got Eddie Cobb tossing his share of buffalo chips. It's gotten so bad, the Speaker's acting like I'm his new best friend."

"Don't fall for that one, my love. Remember the fool me twice rule."

"Say no more. You can tell me so 'til the cows come home if this ends up in shame on me. But while I have his attention, at least I'm not getting blindsided either."

"So, let me guess. Nancy Rae to the rescue?"

"Thought you'd never ask. And it's right up your alley."

"Well, most of the E Party legislators are women. So don't go there."

"Ha ha, funny. Can we get serious? Bottom line—we're going negative as soon as possible. The usual innuendo, chat room, blog, robocall, push question crap. You know the drill. And that's where you come in."

"I know. No fingerprints, right?"

"Right."

"We've got our package ready to go and need a trusted go-between. That would be you. Think about it and let me know. Only let me know by tomorrow."

"Only for you, Danny. But you better have more than innuendo. These E people have made a strong impression down here. They're fighters. And they've got the bucks to fight back. This will not be one of those deals where the messenger gets shot. Are we in agreement on that?"

"When was the last time I let you get shot?"

"It only takes once. I'll call you tomorrow."

* * * * * * * * * * * * * * * *

THE BACK BENCH

"If you let it slip, we catch it"

May 3

As we enter May, there are but seventeen legislative days remaining on the calendar.

I point this out because we have yet to see any inkling of an education package from either the Speaker or the E Party. The Speaker obviously wants the E Party to go first so he can have his minions pick it to death. To the contrary, the E Party wants the Speaker to lead because they believe he will have difficulty developing a meaningful product. The Speaker put the bulls-eye on his back, so I suspect he has the ball for the time being.

The Speaker is also facing the extended public notice requirement for passing the budget. Last time I checked the E Party web site, there were thousands of qualified savings ideas posted. All of these newbie economists are also registered voters. Of course, the bigger challenge lies six months from now. The legislative session is merely prologue, setting the stage for the spinmeisters and other political operatives. It will be interesting to see whether the E Party has altered the math or if the Speaker has correctly calculated that E equals minority caucus squared.

In other news…

* * * * * * * * * * * * * * * *

E-MAIL
To: Tom
From: Liz
Sent: 5/4 2:00 p.m. (CST)
Subject: Call With Atlas

Atlas asks that I set a time for the two of you to catch up. Please give me a few days and times over the next few weeks when you will be available. Thank you.

* * * * * * * * * * * * * * * *

"Danny, it's Rae. I'm ready to move."

"Great! I knew I could count on you…if…."

"Wait—before you start running full speed, there are a few conditions. First, I need to see the entire plan—soup to nuts. If I want changes and the Speaker can't get on board, I reserve the right to walk. Next, I need to be kept abreast of any developments. When you know, I know. The Speaker's one thing, but when you tell me Cobb is trolling around, that spells trouble. People around him have a habit of doing time. Finally, I need a way to communicate when I need resources."

"Done. And for the record, Cobb scares me too. More importantly, I'm certain the Speaker feels the same way. There's nothing in this plan you haven't seen before. Just on a much larger scale.

"But I need plausible deniability," he emphasized. "I'll send Jill Siegel with the package for your review. But it doesn't leave her sight and then it comes right back. When you're entirely on board, you own it. Sorry to be such a stickler, but I think you know I'm not calling the shots on this."

"No prob. I'll wait to hear from Jill."

* * * * * * * * * * * * * * * *

E-MAIL
To: Atlas, General, K.C., Lisa, Mark
From: Lauren
Sent: 5/6 8:30 a.m. (PST)
Subject: Budget Recommendations

Last night was the cutoff for submissions. We have approximately 4,000 qualified recommendations on a disk for delivery to the Legislative Reference Bureau. As you may know, the bureau has the unenviable task of turning each idea into legislative ready budget amendment language.

As directed, the list has been collated by legislative districts, by submitter and sitting legislator, regardless of party. Each will get the entire list and their district specific lists.

Anyone submitting an entry that failed for any reason will get an e-mail and a follow up letter thanking them and documenting the reason their proposal was not accepted. In the great majority of cases, the failure relates to either: (1) incomplete submission, (2) duplicate submission, or (3) not a registered voter. All sitting E legislators will also communicate with this cohort in an attempt to soften any harsh reaction to rejection.

Finally, pursuant to Mark's directive, we have begun to cull the voter registration data for the general election.

* * * * * * * * * * * * * * * *

THE BACK BENCH
"If you let it slip, we catch it"

May 8

EXTRA EXTRA EXTRA EXTRA

The E Party dropped two bombs on Springfield yesterday.

In the morning, all legislators in the General Assembly were advised, in agonizing detail, of the budgetary recommendations arising from their citizen challenge. With the seven-day budget notice period set for next week, the action should be hot and heavy as individual legislators jockey for their constituents' ideas. At the same time, the Speaker, the Senate president and their appropriation staffs will have to separate the wheat from the chaff and begin the arduous task of preparing the actual budget documents in legislative format.

I am advised that, in the aggregate, the E Party submission represents a total savings in excess of $6 billion. That's sufficient to cover the revenue shortfall three times over.

Finally, not wanting to leave a complete vacuum on an issue of this magnitude, both candidates for governor issued statements vaguely commending the E Party and promising that their respective administrations will carry on the cause of wisely shepherding tax dollars.

While the budget submission was widely anticipated, not so with the second bomb.

In a press conference that tested the seams of the Blue Room walls, the E Party unveiled a comprehensive education package covering a wide range of issues. Although the E Party was expected to offer a legislative package reflecting the work it began almost ten months ago, the pageantry associated with the announcement caught this reporter totally off guard.

Representative Abernathy of the E Party and Chair of the Committee of the Whole presented two unimaginable documents. One was a Memorandum of Understanding executed by leading education, business, civic, labor and other groups calling for either passage of the entire package or passage of an equally comprehensive package meeting a set of very specific topics and principles. This grouping is very strategic in that it encompasses most of the players the Speaker would be expected to call upon to generate a counter-attack.

The second was a disk containing the signature or electronic authorization of over 20,000 current and retired teachers across Illinois in support of the terms and conditions contained in the memorandum. The magnitude of participation dwarfs any like effort in this reporter's memory bank.

Of course, both of these bombs landed on a well bunkered Speaker. No doubt both were anticipated. MOU's and petitions of this sort don't stay secret for long. However, with the adjournment clock ticking louder than ever, there would appear to be need for immediate damage control.

In other news…

THE BACK BENCH
"If you let it slip, we catch it"

May 11

For the second time in a few short months, the E Party has earned the national spotlight. In an exclusive edition of *Nightline*, the E Party's budget challenge drew attention and accolades.

Because most states across the country are grappling with difficult recessionary budget cycles, the results in Illinois have not gone unnoticed. In states where tax increases have been proposed, governors and legislators are scrambling to replicate the Illinois program.

In a surprise announcement, E Party spokesperson Lisa Boudreau identified four other states in which the E Party will again offer bounty for creative and effective budget solutions. The question she dodged, in a very provocative way, is whether the E Party will be supporting candidates in those states.

In other news…

* * * * * * * * * * * * * * * *

"Mr. Speaker, I have Eddie Cobb on line two. He has been calling repeatedly and demands to be put through."

"Hello Eddie. What's so urgent that you had to call my office a dozen times in less than an hour?"

"What's so urgent? What's so urgent? Is this some fucking game?"

"No game, Eddie. I just don't have time for extraneous bullshit. Yes, I've got a creative, tenacious minority party dropping bombs left and right. But I need sixty seats to control the Illinois House and thirty in the Senate. Which means I set my strategy around those two numbers. All the rest is noise and noise doesn't win elections. Even with all these distractions, our candidate for governor has a seven-point lead. Which means—unless you called to tell me I can't count or you have contrary polling—what's the urgency? If you need to pretend the sky is falling over the E Party's fifteen minutes of fame, be my guest."

"You may think it's that simple, Mr. Speaker. But from where I sit, your firewall is inadequate. I'm looking at a forest fire burning out of control. I was calling to discuss a solution that's in the works. Thought you might offer some input. But as we're not fighting the same war, you can read about it in the papers. By the way, good luck getting to sixty."

* * * * * * * * * * * * * * * *

"Mr. Speaker, I have Danny Ryan on line one."

"Daniel. Eddie Cobb tells me he is working on a solution to what he calls a forest fire burning out of control. Unless our polling is totally off, I'm not reading this situation the same way. Other than calling a meeting of the State Central Committee, do you have any suggestions on how we get an independent read? If we're missing something, we'd better find out ASAP. I'm also more worried than ever that Cobb will totally mess this up. Do we have any sources at the D.N.C.?"

"Mr. Speaker, I am totally confident in our polling. We can always expand the sample size to increase the statistical validity. We can also sub-out targeted issue sampling to test against the larger polls. As to Cobb, let me see what we can uncover. But we're not exactly on anyone's invitation list these days."

"OK. Look at options for adjustments to the polling. When would you expect our recent efforts to be reflected in the polling data?"

"Mid-June, unless we ratchet up the volume."

"Let's keep it where it is for now. Provided the end of session isn't a total disaster, we effectively have the summer to make adjustments."

* * * * * * * * * * * * * * * *

E-MAIL

To: General
From: Atlas
Sent: 5/12 1:15 a.m. (MST)
Subject: Tom

Tom and I spoke for almost two hours last night. Your information was totally on point. We are close enough friends that I could get right at the rumors concerning sexuality.

He's a proud man, and rightfully so. His reputation in the black community has taken a huge hit and he either can't or won't fight back. He decided that time can heal the wound, particularly if he avoids politics.

While I don't agree with his approach, there can be no doubt that Mr. Ryan was behind this effort.

Tom insists he isn't gay, which is good enough for me—as if I care. But they care in the churches and he doesn't need polling to know there is a huge backlash with his kids. That's his life!

He rejected the strategies I offered. He keeps coming back to not being able to disprove a negative. Referred me to a kids' book by Madonna called *Mr. Peabody's Apples*. Said I would understand.

I know we need Tom back. Mark and Lisa both consider him a strategic linchpin for their efforts. Please give this some thought.

* * * * * * * * * * * * * * * *

THE BACK BENCH
"If you let it slip, we catch it"

May 14

The Speaker has sent me scrambling for that copy of *The Art of War* I keep on the shelf. In an act of uncharacteristic weakness, the Speaker held a press conference yesterday and announced he is deferring education legislation until the fall Veto Session and that any and all budget amendments filed by next Tuesday will be heard on the floor.

Regarding education, although he did not mention it by name, he deflected back to the E Party. His exact statement was: "Education reform is critical and essential. It is also deserving of complete and eloquent debate before the General Assembly. In light of voluminous recommendations to improve the state budget, that opportunity will not present itself this spring. The budget and the prudent expenditure of tax dollars must take priority at this time."

Smooth. But will it play in Peoria?

In other news…

THE BACK BENCH
"If you let it slip, we catch it"

May 30

The Illinois Legislature adjourned yesterday. There was a rather remarkable three week sequence surrounding the state budget, including one week of virtual 24/7 debate in the House concerning thousands of citizen-proposed amendments.

The result was also rather remarkable. There was unanimous vote on what purports to be a truly balanced budget, substantially void of the gimmicks we have come to expect. For the first time in anyone's memory, there is also a healthy rainy day fund. Many a sacred cow line item was gored, but in the end, the fury unleashed by the E Party was too much for individual legislators to overcome. No need for polling to tell them which way the wind was blowing, particularly in an election year.

In other news…

* * * * * * * * * * * * * * * *

E-MAIL
To: General, K.C., Lisa, Lauren, Mark
From: Atlas
Sent: 5/30 6:30 a.m. (MST)
Subject: End of Session

A fantastic session! Thank you all for your amazing efforts!

I will have Liz suggest some dates in June for a planning session. No rest for the weary in this crazy business.

Please, in your own way, extend the most heartfelt congratulations to the E team legislators. Among other things, their work in education has been a marvel. However, I fear it could be for naught if the Speaker has his way in November.

For now, let's cherish the moment.

* * * * * * * * * * * * * * * *

E-MAIL
To: Atlas
From: Mark
Sent: 5/30 10:01 a.m. (CST)
Subject: Budget Victory

Congratulations. If this were to be the E Party's only success, I would tell you that you could quit while ahead and declare victory. The final tally of estimated savings from our challenge exceeds $3 billion. I wonder how long it would take Warren Buffet to achieve that return on a $50 million investment?

* * * * * * * * * * * * * * * *

THE BACK BENCH
"If you let it slip, we catch it"

June 2

This will serve as our annual, post session declaration of winners and losers. With this being an election year, a few of the victorious moments may be fleeting. My scorecard reads as follows:

WINNERS:

1. The E Party has to be the BIG winner. Through their education initiatives dating to last fall, in combination with a ridiculously imaginative budget maneuver, they have begun to reinvent government.

2. Representatives Jenkins and Abernathy and Senator Benjamin of the E Party: In a legislature starved for leadership, they brought energy and initiative. The Speaker may have unwittingly christened a new star when he anointed Representative Abernathy to chair the Committee of the Whole on Education. Working in tandem, this trio is being credited with the success of the Memorandum of Understanding and related petition.

3. The Speaker wins, as always, but slips to third for the first time ever. His inspired, last minute budget negotiating was a fete of logistics and hardball. While the E Party provided the inspiration for the budget resolution, the Speaker and his staff provided the perspiration. Then again, this was more an act of desperation than of courage and conviction. Not a good time to disappoint thousands of potential voters awaiting their rewards.

4. For the second year in a row, the taxpayers of Illinois are winners. They have the cleanest, most honest budget in decades. They also have reason for renewed hope in the legislative process.

LOSERS:

1. The Republicans played ostrich the entire session, including Robert Allen, their candidate for governor. I would have expected him to become head cheerleader for the E Party initiatives as they can be expected to generate beaucoup turnout in November. They all lose BIG TIME because the E Party is now the party of fiscal responsibility. Get ready for a rousing campaign of "the Democrats have been in total control and look at the mess they've made." Only thanks to the E's, there may not be a sufficient mess for that pathetic strategy.

2. For the second year in a row, the Speaker is a winner and a loser. Just as the Republicans have ceded fiscal issues, the Democrats have fallen way behind on education. No doubt the Speaker will determine a theme for his flock. But, negative, negative and negative may not be sufficient against the well-funded E Party. He would also appear in need of some serious fence mending with core constituents and donors over his last minute punt on the cusp of an education reform breakthrough.

In other news…

CHAPTER NINETEEN

E-MAIL
To: Bruce Frazier
From: Elizabeth DiMaggio
Sent: 6/3 9:56 a.m. (CST)
Subject: Ballot Case

Now that the session has ended, we are prepared to file as soon as possible. Please update the petition and advise when ready.

* * * * * * * * * * * * * * * *

E-MAIL
To: Atlas
From: Keith Mix
Sent: 6/6 2:01 p.m. (CST)
Subject: Legal Action

As the agent of record for the E Party of Illinois, I was served today with a petition filed by the Republican Party of Illinois before the state's Supreme Court seeking a declaratory judgment requiring the E Party to field a complete slate of statewide constitutional officers.

In Illinois, the statewide constitutional officers are governor, lieutenant governor, secretary of state, attorney general, treasurer and comptroller. They are each elected to four-year terms and all offices are up for election this year. In the case of governor and lieutenant governor, they are elected in tandem.

We have immediately begun to analyze the filing. As you can imagine, this is a case of first impression in Illinois. It appears to be based on a loosely drafted section of Illinois law, 10 ILCS 5/7-2, that reads:

> Sec. 7-2. A political party, which at the general election for state and county officers then next preceding a primary, polled more than 5 percent of the entire vote cast in the state, is hereby declared to be a political party within the state, and shall nominate *[all*

> *candidates provided for in this Article 7 under the provisions hereof,]...* (emphasis added).

Our response is due in 30 days.

* * * * * * * * * * * * * * * *

E-MAIL

To: General, Mark, Lisa
From: Atlas
Sent: 6/6 4:06 p.m. (MST)
Subject: Ballot Case

FYI, see attached e-mail from Keith Mix. We may have to reschedule our retreat, or perhaps schedule as a video conference.

* * * * * * * * * * * * * * * *

THE BACK BENCH

"If you let it slip, we catch it"

June 6

EXTRA EXTRA EXTRA EXTRA

The silly season has officially begun. This time, long before the first parade on the Fourth of July.

The Republican Party of Illinois today sought a declaratory judgment from the Illinois Supreme Court that the E Party must field a complete slate of statewide constitutional officers.

Politically, it may be a brilliant move. If they win, the E Party will be forced to scramble and will have little hope of producing a credible slate. However, the E Party will be compelled to campaign on behalf of its slate and that will undoubtedly take more votes from the Democrats. Besides, based on the campaign to date (or should I say lack thereof) and the most recent polling, what do they have to lose? Stewart is seen as anywhere from eight to twelve points up on Allen.

On the legal side of the ledger, I am told their case is weak, at best. Further, the timing is curious because petition challenges were due last October. Finally, the court is weighted 5 to 2 Democrat and is not inclined to assist Republican candidates for governor. A few well placed quotes in any major paper from Democrat leadership should sufficiently signal to the jurists the direction they want this case to take…not to mention one well placed, untraceable phone call.

In other news…

* * * * * * * * * * * * * * * *

E-MAIL
To: Atlas
From: Keith Mix
Sent: 6/12 1:11 p.m. (CST)
Subject: Ballot Case

We have finished our research and do not believe the Republicans have a leg to stand on. The section of the law upon which the action is predicated is taken out of context and their interpretation is not supported in legislative intent.

However, we did pass the 5 percent threshold and are required to meet various statutory obligations for political parties. We will address those in a separate memo.

In terms of setting our strategy, please note that Illinois Supreme Court justices do not receive life appointments. Rather, they are elected on a decennial basis and the five sitting Democrats (out of seven justices) owe significant allegiance to the Speaker.

Please advise how you propose to proceed.

* * * * * * * * * * * * * * * *

E-MAIL
To: Keith Mix
From: Atlas
Sent: 6/12 2:16 p.m. (MST)
Subject: Ballot Case

Stall! We cannot afford the perception of shirking from this constitutional challenge. However, we need time to put a slate together. What should we anticipate as a reasonable time frame? Also, to what extent is this case open to a settlement?

* * * * * * * * * * * * * * * *

E-MAIL

To: Atlas
From: Keith Mix
Sent: 6/12 4:12 p.m. (CST)
Subject: Ballot Case

We will proceed as directed. However, at some point during the briefing schedule, we will need to advise the court that we will not contest the petition and seek an agreed order regarding submission of candidate petitions. I am guessing you will get sixty days at the outside. Finally, there is no exact avenue for settlement as the court will need to issue a ruling to validate the petition process. All of this presupposes the Democratic party of Illinois does not file an amicus brief challenging the declaration.

* * * * * * * * * * * * * * * *

"Mr. Speaker. I have Danny Ryan for you on line one."

"Danny, we need to determine what course of action, if any, to take in the Supreme Court case. Our attorneys are preparing briefs, both pro and con, so we can make a last minute call once the briefing schedule is determined. That should give us a thirty-day window.

"If the polling trends continue, we may be forced to roll the dice. Given their funding advantage, forcing them to redeploy assets may be to our advantage. You know as well as I that they face a daunting task to field a credible slate. Also to our advantage.

"In addition to our weekly polling, I want to poll on hypothetical slates. Run polls based on both actual celebrity types and candidate characteristics, include the General, although the residency he created to establish the E Party is not timely for the purpose of seeking statewide office. At least he provides a test case against their best candidate. Can you get this done in two weeks?"

"Consider it done. I will have the sample poll on your desk by noon tomorrow."

"Thanks."

* * * * * * * * * * * * * * * *

"Welcome all to our video conference. I wish I was seeing your smiling faces in Aspen, but the Illinois Republicans seem to have found alternative use for our time. I never expected today's agenda to be headed by the topic: Finding Candidates for Statewide Offices. General, where are we?"

"Try nowhere," the General said somewhat dejectedly. "We've become somewhat efficient at finding legislative candidates. But governor, attorney general—that's a tall order. I'm not as concerned with secretary of state, treasurer or comptroller. Secretary of state is a patronage post that basically requires walking and chewing gum at the same time. Treasurer and comptroller are really one job with two descriptions. Integrity and bean counting should suffice for either. In fact, we jettisoned some very talented people when we cut back on legislative races. Depending upon how it plays out, we can pick a lieutenant governor from the group of governor candidate finalists, assuming we get that far.

"That's only the tip of the iceberg. They all need vetting considerably more rigorous than representatives and senators. These races are much higher on the food chain. Our candidates will face daily scrutiny and our candidate for governor will be subjected to constant media attention. We won't be in Kansas anymore. Mark may want to jump in here."

"Happy to, General. For governor, the General and I have begun outreach to the business and education communities. Luckily, we created valuable contacts during the M.O.U. process. K.C. has been working with our legislative team to comb their local communities. In many cases, mayors and councilmen are elected on a non-partisan basis, although they generally have a party affiliation. School superintendents for large districts are another source we've identified. So far, the going is slow. It's also possible that a candidate will find us once the outcome of the case becomes public.

"With respect to attorney general, we've asked Yura, Mix & Eisenstat to quietly research the ranks of the state's attorney and U.S. attorney offices. I'd be stunned if a few solid candidates are not quickly identified."

"As you may suspect," inserted Atlas, "I've been thinking about this non-stop. Primarily with respect to the candidate for governor. In addition to the trials and tribulations of the campaign, overnight that person becomes the face of the party. I think we need more than what you've got in motion. The dilemma is how to broaden the universe without coming across as pandering or desperate. No gimmicks."

"I totally agree," added K.C. "This could be make or break. I particularly like the idea of a college president or school superintendent. They understand bureaucracy, their day-to-day politics are brutal, and they can easily carry the education flag we've been flying. If there is no objection, that will be my focus.

"I also want to put an idea out for consideration. If we can't get to where we want—and on time—Representative Jenkins should be readied to step in. That should apply to lieutenant governor as well. She may not be the ideal candidate, but she is brilliant, dedicated, will run with distinction and we will be well represented."

"Is there a second?" asked Atlas. "Hearing no objection, at least we have a candidate for governor in waiting. K.C., you break the bad news. Mark, what are we missing?"

"At a minimum, I propose we dust off the ASC research department to do some modeling. It would be a huge help if they can identify and prioritize the public's mood on this."

"I agree," said Atlas. "We'll get on that ASAP. Anyone else? General, you've been too quiet. Lisa? Lauren? All right, let's move on. Mark where do we stand on the legislative races in Illinois?"

"If you compare us to two years ago, light years ahead. All incumbents have favorable ratings above sixty. The new group has been riding the coattails of our legislative success, so it's a bit early to get an accurate read. A bit troubling is the fact that, particularly for incumbents, numbers are off of late. Could be any number of things, and we will be watching closely.

"Across the board, our opponents have been aggressively raising funds. The Democrats have been running a virtual shuttle service from D.C. of cabinet officials and other political leaders to headline events. We won't know until the June 30 filing deadline, but I'm guessing their cash on hand will be two to three times the average for this point in the campaign. They can always play the president card to raise three to five million dollars in one night. They won't catch us, even with the added burden of the statewide races. But, I'm certain they will have what they need.

"Although the Republicans were quiet during the session, they, too, have been fundraising aggressively. Most of their events are combos with their candidate for governor, Robert Allen, taking the lion's share, leaving slim pickings for their incumbent legislators. It would not surprise me if Allen has the money lead on Stewart. It won't be determinative, per se, but as we discussed in December, there's no doubt where their priority lies. The Supreme Court case made that abundantly clear."

"Thanks, Mark. General, how are we positioned for the rollout in the other states?"

"I'm very comfortable particularly, as Mark says, in comparison to the last go-round. Petition drives will begin quite soon. We won't have the element of surprise, but our budget challenge contests and the P.R. Lisa has lined up should more than offset any downside effect."

"K.C., I think we'll give you a pass on issue development. The draft position papers are excellent."

"I'll take the pass. But in a few of the target states, there are some local issues that I want in our candidates' quivers. Those papers will be distributed shortly."

"Lisa?"

"I've rewritten the P.R. plan 'til I'm blue in the face. At this point, I prefer to wait until the slate is set. As you said Atlas, it becomes more about governor than legislators. A great deal depends on what we have to work with. Having someone capable of projecting a positive media image is obviously a plus. 'Til then, the General remains available for the interview requests already in the queue. In Tom's absence, we've had K.C., Jenkins, Abernathy and Benjamin on standby."

"So I guess you also get a pass. Lauren?"

"Once again, saving the best for last," she quipped. "I don't need a pass, but I will be brief.

"We have updated all web-based components with state-of-the-art technology. We will be faster and able to handle the increased traffic as other states roll out. An enhanced video component is being tested and will be ready to go. Finally, Mark and the General have made recommendations to upgrade the canvass and Election Day functioning. Field tests on those elements are also in final testing."

"I'm sorry this had to be so rushed," Atlas apologized. "Let's plan to reconvene once the case is finalized. Let's hope we do not have to do another one-eighty. And I owe all of you a trip to Aspen in June. One of our best months. Thanks again."

* * * * * * * * * * * * * * * *

THE BACK BENCH
"If you let it slip, we catch it"

June 24

EXTRA EXTRA EXTRA EXTRA

Briefs have been filed in the Republican ballot challenge case before the Illinois State Supreme Court, and in the new world of political intrigue, the Republicans, Democrats and E Party all concur in the requirement that the E Party must slate candidates for all constitutional offices.

The Republicans and the E Party filed separate memorandums in which they each suggest a forty-five day window in which to complete nominations. It happens to be a ridiculously short period in which to find candidates. Regardless, they won't be able to campaign much before Labor Day.

No doubt there was many a late night session devoted to their respective positions. On the blog, speculation is that the E's concluded their newly won public image would take a hit if they ran from the challenge. They will now have to scramble to meet whatever deadline the court sets. It looks like a suicide mission for their candidates.

With respect to the Speaker's position, over 2,000 rabid bloggers posted their insights before I finally shut things down. The two opposing pieces I liked best came from "Judge Judy" and "I Love Lucy."

The "Judge" writes:

"The Speaker has been spun around so many times by the E Party, he can't see where he's going and is definitely stumbling. The Republican's case was a clear loser. If the E Party statewide slate performs with the same class as their sitting representatives, the Speaker will have just written his epitaph. I'm voting straight E, even if the three stooges head their statewide ticket."

Lucy writes:

> "Once again, the Speaker has made lemonade out of lemons. Where will the E Party find a credible slate in short order? They're more likely to find a bunch of Sarah Palin types that will drag them down. Their funding will now be dissipated in a losing cause. Further, the last thing the Speaker could afford was to look weak. Never lose sight of his end game: a 60-plus Democrat majority in the House and 30-plus in the Senate. Obtaining that result is, to him, easily worth the risk of a Republican governor. Besides, Stewart is the likely winner in any scenario.

In other news…

* * * * * * * * * * * * * * * *

"Mr. Speaker. That call you were expecting is on line two."

"Hello, Eddie. I figured you'd be calling. Let's get this over with."

"I realize," Cobb began without any attempt at exchanging pleasantries, "we have not been on the same page for some time regarding this E Party. You have this horse with blinders view and I'm looking at World War III. If nothing else, I thought you might have heard my expression of concern.

"So imagine my reaction when I look at today's clippings and find a curious set of articles describing how the E Party will now have a candidate for governor and that you, Mr. Speaker, are complicit.

"Now seeing as how I'm now doing my best to stay calm, perhaps you can enlighten me—especially about the part where you don't have the common courtesy to provide advance warning. If I'm not mistaken, you told me that you wanted forty-eight hours' notice before I did anything about Stein."

"Eddie. The one thing you said that I agree with entirely is that you and I are not on the same page. And we won't be. I don't have time to work you through the machinations of Illinois politics, so please excuse me if I don't bother. I've been doing this for over three decades and have never asked the national party for help. You call me when you need money, bodies, jobs, votes, you name it, and I'm happy to assist. But let's not pretend I owe you anything, and if I determine that giving you, or anyone for that matter, notice of my strategy will risk my position, then common courtesy takes a back seat.

"If you have any interest in helping, we may need funds at some point, and as you previously predicted, we may need the president. But that's a call I will make, if and when necessary. So, if there are no further questions."

"No further questions. But know this. There are many people in agreement with my assessment of the risk and we are working on a strategy as we speak. So you will understand if our little play appears in your clippings one morning, common courtesy having taken a back seat. Goodbye, Mr. Speaker."

"Goodbye, Eddie."

* * * * * * * * * * * * * * * *

"Danny, I just got off the phone with Cobb. Any word on what he's up to?"

"Nothing. In fact, my sources are quick to point out that you, me and anyone within an eyelash of the Illinois Democratic Party are all persona non grata. And that's the nice version."

"To be expected. All I know is that his shit-eating-grin was permeating our conversation. So whatever it is, it's coming soon."

* * * * * * * * * * * * * * * *

THE BACK BENCH
"If you let it slip, we catch it"

June 29

On the eve of the state's new fiscal year, the governor signed the various budget bills. This fait accompli is not, in and of itself, newsworthy. What is newsworthy is the anticipated release of the successful participants in the E Party's budget challenge. One lucky SOB (as in "son of a budget") will be declared the winner of a $1 million grand prize.

E Party officials plan a PR rollout in the next week to ten days, with a small grouping of winners released daily based on geographic distribution and with the grand prize winner announced in Chicago at the conclusion of the pageant. To date, they have not been given to self-aggrandizement, so I think we can forgive them this indulgence.

The budget challenge may have changed Illinois politics for the duration. It was a sensational example of democracy at its best.

In other news…

* * * * * * * * * * * * * * * *

"Nat, it's Mark. I've decided to spare you the agony of setting the alarm clock. Tomorrow afternoon I am having delivered to your office dossiers on the E Party statewide candidates for all but governor."

"We anticipate a series of announcements spaced at least one day apart beginning in no more than two weeks. I'll provide at least twenty-four hours' notice in each case."

"Thanks, Mark. But when's the main course?"

"Can't say."

"Can't say or won't say?"

"Whatever—you'll get the scoop. For now, I need a favor. This has all moved at a speed that defies sufficient vetting. Can you do some independent snooping, using whatever sources you deem appropriate, to determine if there's any skeletons we've missed?"

"Sure, I'd be doing the work anyway."

"Great. Call me if and when you have anything."

* * * * * * * * * * * * * * * *

"Hello, Mark?"

"Hey, Nat. That was quick."

"Just goes to show what a dedicated newsman can accomplish with a computer, a Rolodex, a twelve-pack and a quiet weekend. Anyway, I'm not finding any ghosts of Christmas past in this group. Given your accelerated schedule, I'd say someone is either very good at their job or very lucky."

"Well, in this case, that someone is General Smith. Need I say more?"

"The man's a stud."

"As for this group. Solid on paper. But the proof is in the public scrutiny pudding. In fact, you can return the favor. Feed me the exclusive interviews. I'll work them hard and I'll brief you on any blatant faults. Let Lisa sit in if she wishes. Anything they say can and will be used against them, but my rendition will be kinder and gentler than the *Tribune* and *Sun-Times* thugs, not to mention the networks. And you won't be stuck with my rag. The stories will all be nationally syndicated. Deal?"

"I think we've got a deal, but on this one, I'd like to double check. Thanks again for the help. I'll get right back to you."

* * * * * * * * * * * * * * * *

E-MAIL

To: Atlas, General, Lisa
From: Mark
Sent: 7/12 7:15 p.m. (CST)
Subject: Carson Interviews

Worked like a charm. Nat actually proposed the deal. Even invited Lisa to sit in before I could make the suggestion.

* * * * * * * * * * * * * * * *

E-MAIL

To: General, K.C., Mark, Lisa
From: Atlas
Sent: 7/14 8:04 a.m. (MST)
Subject: Governor Candidates

The two candidate prospects for governor are better than I could have anticipated. Not sure how we'll choose.

The ASC research Mark requested has been completed. I will distribute to all of you after my initial review. Hopefully, it will prove to be an effective tie-breaker.

Liz will set a call for Thursday and we'll get this finalized.

* * * * * * * * * * * * * * * *

E-MAIL
To: Atlas, General
From: Mark
Sent: 7/16 5:26 p.m. (CST)
Subject: Recent Polling

I am becoming concerned about the polling trends. As I suggested a few weeks ago, we are seeing an unexpected erosion in favorables, coupled with increased negatives.

I cannot fathom the DiMaggio case is driving these numbers because, for the most part, they are candidate-specific polls and the results lack the uniformity I would expect from a single impact source.

I also went back to study the trends and most of this began post session. This smells like Danny Ryan, but does not reflect any of his known tactics. He's not usually that subtle when he's on the attack.

Then again, maybe I'm paranoid. Part of the job description.

Look at the polling and give me your thoughts.

* * * * * * * * * * * * * * * *

E-MAIL
To: Atlas, Mark
From: General
Sent: 7/17 9:06 p.m. (CST)
Subject: Recent Polling

I'm not sufficiently savvy to interpret these polls and reach the same conclusion. But I am sufficiently paranoid, which also comes with my job description.

And, I've got some ideas on how we can get to the bottom of this rather quickly.

* * * * * * * * * * * * * * * *

THE BACK BENCH
"If you let it slip, we catch it"

July 18

The Back Bench has learned that the E Party will begin unveiling its statewide candidate slate next week. In addition, T.B.B. has been granted the exclusive opportunity to interview these candidates. Over the next ten days, we will dedicate special editions to candidate profiles.

However, it does not appear that the E Party is prepared to announce its candidate for governor. With the court-imposed deadline only twenty-eight days away, General Smith and his search party have to be getting a bit nervous.

In an effort to help the world of Illinois politics stay crazy, I am opening a special section of the blog for nominations to the E Party governor slot.

Anyone posting the name of the ultimate candidate will receive a lifetime subscription to *The Back Bench*. In the unlikely event of a tie, the earliest post will be the winner. Let's have some fun with this. Only, no inanimate objects or barnyard animals.

In other news…

* * * * * * * * * * * * * * * *

E-MAIL

To: Atlas, General
From: Mark
Sent: 7/20 7:00 p.m. (CST)
Subject: June 30 Reports

The financial reports for the funding period ending June 30 have been filed.

As expected, the Democrats have been shaking all the bushes, especially the unions and trial lawyers. When compared to the same period for the last cycle, their cash on hand is up almost 80 percent. For the same period during the last statewide elections, they are up almost 50 percent. Without a doubt, they will have all the funding needed to nuke us.

The Republicans have not been slacking either. They're up 40 percent and 30 percent respectively. More than enough if the trend continues.

One interesting expenditure item in the filing for the Democratic Party of Cook County was a rather substantial consulting fee to a detective agency. Can't imagine what that's about. General, please advise if we have to revise any of our security procedures.

* * * * * * * * * * * * * * * *

E-MAIL

To: Atlas, Mark
From: General
Sent: 7/21 10:11 a.m. (CST)
Subject: Procedures

They can investigate all they want. At this point, they have what they have—which can't be much unless they are somehow intercepting e-mails. I am comfortable in my belief that Lauren's security screens are more than adequate.

Regardless, this might be a good time to consider a few misdirection plays. Let me give it some thought.

* * * * * * * * * * * * * * * *

E-MAIL
To: General, K.C., Mark, Lisa
From: Liz
Sent: 7/26 9:00 a.m. (CST)
Subject: Conference Call

Tomorrow's call to discuss candidates for governor has been cancelled. Instead, the E Party will be holding a nominating session at the Chicago headquarters on Saturday morning, to be led by Representative Jenkins. All of you are invited, but Atlas will not be in attendance.

* * * * * * * * * * * * * * * *

"Atlas," said K.C. in an excited voice. "I just received the e-mail from Liz, and without a doubt, that was the perfect decision. I'm so disappointed that you continue to miss out on some of the most exciting and compelling moments of this party's young history."

"I appreciate you looking out for me, K.C., but I haven't changed my mind about keeping my role as benefactor totally divorced from direct participation in the party's political decisions. This time, however, you should know that I have authorized the General to video the proceedings. So, tell me. Who's your candidate?"

"I haven't made up my mind. Even though I'm responsible for bringing Dr. Ross Hamilton to the dance, Zack Groebe was also a terrific find. I know it's a cliché, but it's a shame either has to lose."

"That's not even a good hedge on your part. I've never known you to be sans opinion. If it will help, I'll go first. I hope it's Groebe. The difference for me was the ASC polling, particularly the section on intangibles. My take is that the citizens of Illinois are screaming for leadership. Not necessarily bold or inventive, but straightforward, trustworthy, dedicated and independent. Characteristics that are in short supply in today's American politics.

"When I was conducting my early research on American politics, my favorites were the presidents who, when faced with the toughest decisions, reached inside and found intestinal fortitude that could rally a nation in its darkest hours. I'm not hoisting Groebe on that lofty pedestal. But, that's how I would distinguish between them."

"Interesting you would focus on leadership. It's probably one of the attributes that is most difficult to project in an election. Does that mean you're resigned to defeat?"

"Maybe. Whereas we've repeatedly discussed our expectations for victory, in this instance, I think we need to be realistic and shape our expectations for losing. And it needs to be more than losing with dignity. It needs to be losing, having gained respect. I believe Groebe will earn that distinction."

"Well," K.C. paused, "I say we have to be able to look back and know that, in losing, there was nothing more we could have done to gain victory.

"Oh, and Alex?"

"Yes."

"Groebe is my pick, too. I just wanted you to go first."

* * * * * * * * * * * * * * * *

"Nancy Rae. You are unbelievable."

"So, you're just figuring that out?"

"It doesn't hurt to be reminded once in a while. The new polling shows significant shifts from late May. Most of the E Party incumbents are down quite nicely in favorables, and for the first time, there is a nice spike in their unfavorables, at least considering the campaign hasn't started."

"Maybe. But we're the only ones in the field," she reminded him. "Sooner or later they'll be onto us."

"Agreed. But your efforts have shaved six to eight points off favorability across the board. Of course, they'll respond. But in the heat of battle, those points don't easily reappear. Had they stayed in the sixties through Labor Day, the lift would be too great."

"What's next, Mr. Ryan?"

"I think you can go back to your seven-figure day job. Seeing as how the legislature is adjourned, what is it you high priced lobbyists do anyway?"

"You know. The usual. Pass out money in paper bags. Attend golf outings, ball games, nights at the opera, the museum, the hot play. Whatever bullshit they can concoct to suck up contributions."

"Be careful. That's mother's milk you're slandering."

"Sure, Mr. Purist. Whatever you say. I know better than to think we can get together before November. Gimme a rain check."

"In fact, I still owe you that Caribbean adventure. Let's plan on it."

"Win or lose?"

"Win or lose."

* * * * * * * * * * * * * * * *

THE BACK BENCH

"If you let it slip, we catch it"

August 2

This is the first installment of *The Back Bench* series introducing the E Party statewide candidates. In all cases, the complete interview will be posted on the blog.

Kellie Morgan is the E Party candidate for attorney general.

Morgan is a career prosecutor, having served in the Tazwell County State's Attorney's Office right out of law school, where she spent the first sixteen years of her career. In 1994, she left the state's attorney to join the U.S. attorney's office for the Central District in Illinois where she currently serves.

The bulk of Morgan's career has been spent prosecuting violent crimes, especially where drugs have been involved. She prides herself on preparation and dedication. She considers herself honored to have spent her entire career in public service.

Asked why she would put her career at risk to run on the E Party ticket, she said they caught her attention early on and have greatly raised her hopes and expectations for participatory democracy.

Other than presenting her outstanding record as a prosecutor, she is not proposing any suggestions for significant changes in the office. In fact, she commends the sitting attorney general for a job well done. The thrust of her campaign will be ethics reform and honesty in government, among the E Party's guiding principles.

She believes the attorney general and the governor should never be from the same political party. How, she wonders, can the attorney general be a truly fair arbiter and watchdog if he or she comes from the same party? She extends the same logic to the president and U.S. attorney general. This notion of checks and balances was obviously endearing to the E Party leadership when choosing their candidate for attorney general.

Which begged the question…what happens if she wins and the E Party candidate for governor also wins? Without hesitation, she said she would resign and recommend the governor appoint whoever finished second in the voting. I think she meant it.

Editorial Note: When you read Kellie Morgan's interview on the web, her answers appear naïve and sophomoric. I assure you, this seasoned prosecutor is anything but naïve and sophomoric. I have a sense that her babe-in-the-woods outlook toward the political process will be adjusted quickly and significantly as the campaign kicks in. If, as I suspect, she makes the necessary adjustments (and General Smith will certainly work to make that happen), the attorney general's race could become very interesting.

In other news…

THE BACK BENCH

"If you let it slip, we catch it"

August 5

This is the second installment of *The Back Bench* series introducing the E Party statewide candidates. As with the first interview, the complete interview is posted on the blog.

Anthony Manzella is the E Party candidate for secretary of state.

Manzella recently retired from the military, where he served as a procurement specialist. We actually diverted from the campaign and spent most of our time discussing his career. It was fascinating to learn about the procurement facet of war. While the network's coverage focuses on the guts and glory elements, there is a vast network of supplies, transport, etc., that supports the entire effort. If nothing else, the logistics of feeding in excess of 100,000 troops during the most recent war was a fascinating study in military efficiency.

It's that same standard of efficiency that Manzella intends to bring to state government. The secretary of state's office is responsible for many areas of compliance, such as the Driver's License Division, and he believes these functions can all become more efficient with some military style discipline.

Manzella also made it clear that he was a protégé of General Smith and, reading between the lines, is only in this because he was asked (or was he ordered??).

In other news…

* * * * * * * * * * * * * * * *

E-MAIL
To: Atlas
From: General
Sent: 8/8 4:22 p.m. (CST)
Subject: Governor Candidate

The session went extremely well. We now have a candidate for governor and a candidate for lieutenant governor. The video is on the way. You can see for yourself.

* * * * * * * * * * * * * * * *

E-MAIL
To: General
From: Atlas
Sent: 8/8 5:27 p.m. (MST)
Subject: Governor Candidate

What? No name? How about some initials?

* * * * * * * * * * * * * * * *

E-MAIL
To: Atlas
From: General
Sent: 8/8 7:30 p.m. (CST)
Subject: Governor Candidate

You'll just have to be patient. Trust me on this one.

* * * * * * * * * * * * * * * *

"Mr. Speaker, sorry to bother you on the weekend," said Danny Ryan. "I think we just got lucky."

"No problem, Danny, go ahead."

"Our man Jacobson followed Stone to the E Party headquarters this morning. While there, he noticed a steady stream of visitors and decided to snap some photos. As far as we can tell, all of the E Party representatives and senators attended. Although we haven't yet identified everyone, there were two very notable guests. I'm thinking they could be under consideration for governor. One is Dr. Ross Hamilton, the former chancellor at Eastern University and currently the head of an education think tank. The other is Zack Groebe. I don't know much about Groebe, but Jacobson thinks he is from a prominent family back East. Evidently, broke from the doctor/lawyer family business model and studied engineering. He has multiple patents and has built a very successful environmental testing and equipment company. One educator and one greenie."

"Makes sense. No harm in getting a jump on opposition research."

"That's what I was thinking. We can hit these guys hard the minute they announce. Let's also think about polling."

"I like it."

CHAPTER TWENTY

"Atlas."

"Yes, Clay."

"Sorry to interrupt, but there's a special delivery and it can only be left upon your signature."

"Thanks, Clay. I've been expecting this delivery. I should have alerted you."

"Should I show her in? She is rather insistent on delivering in person."

"Yes, please."

To Atlas' astonishment, K.C. walked in.

"K.C.! What a wonderful surprise! What are you doing here?"

"I volunteered. Thought you might not shoot if I were the messenger."

"Shoot?"

"You'll see. Where can we watch this tape?"

"Clay. Can you get us set up?"

"Sure. Give me ten. I'll set up in the library."

"Well, what's this all about?" Atlas quizzed K.C.

"I keep telling you that it's a remarkable group we've assembled. Just watch the video and then we'll talk."

* * * * * * * * * * * * * * * *

"Well. I didn't expect that," said Atlas once the video was finished. "Maybe I shouldn't be surprised."

"If you think about it," offered K.C., "it's somewhat ironic it didn't come up sooner."

"Now what?" Atlas asked.

"You have a choice as I see it. Either you honor the group's mandate and choose the E Party candidate for governor or you decline the offer and send the ballots back for counting."

"And?"

"No and. In hindsight, it was logical for them to have thought the General had arranged all the funding. After all, he found them, he groomed them, and he's mentored them. As you saw in the film, once they got on that tangent, the General had no choice but to set the record straight. So, they want their mysterious benefactor to pick their candidate. I think you should be honored."

"Honored? I guess so. But this runs totally contrary to my wishes."

"Wishes, smishes. You saw the tape. Your wishes were well represented in debate. If either the General or I were deficient to that end, blame us. This is what they want. And, you have an out. Just send back the ballots unopened. However, you've now seen them in action and they're moving forward with or without you. As you predicted a few months back, the E Party is all grown up and about to flee the nest."

"And, where is that chicken shit General best friend of mine?"

"Let's just say this is one I had to do. And he wasn't about to pull rank on me."

"In that case, what do you say we continue this over dinner? I'll have Clay make reservations. 7:30?"

* * * * * * * * * * * * * * * *

"Alex, this menu is lovely. Do you eat here often?"

"Not really. Even though it's one of my favorites in town, I save it for special occasions. Actually, you've had their fare on all of your trips. Clay, or should I say Liz, is masterful at ordering in."

"I never did figure Clay for the gourmet chef those meals would have required. What do you recommend?"

"Well, when in Rome. The bison filet and the Colorado striped bass are both terrific. How about some wine? Waiter."

"So, quite the conundrum, hmmmm?"

"Quite. Which is why I'm inclined to send the ballots back unopened. At the same time, based on recent conversations, you know I have a favorite and I desperately want this to work. I don't think I ever told you this, but Mark sent me an e-mail after the session ended and suggested I could call the whole thing off and never have a regret given the great things we've accomplished. But I didn't feel that way then. And I don't now. Those policy victories, particularly our back-to-back budget efforts, make me want much more. I think this little engine of ours can make it all the way to the top of the hill."

"Of course it can," she confirmed. "But what we all realize and are afraid to say, is that it can all come crashing down in November."

"That too. More wine?"

"What!" was all a startled K.C. could say upon seeing the General enter the restaurant.

"Mind if I join you?" he asked upon reaching their table.

"This evening is full of surprises," Atlas responded. "Don't tell me…more bad news?"

"Actually, yes. Otherwise, I would not have flown here unannounced. In fact, this is perhaps the worst news we could have imagined. I received a call last night from John Castellano. He served as my attaché while at the Pentagon. He's now at Justice. Because of our history, they chose him to make the courtesy call."

"They?" Atlas asked. "Courtesy call?"

"In this case, they is the U.S. attorney's office in Chicago, Illinois. It is customary to extend the courtesy of alerting former brass and celebrities prior to receiving service. Avoids undue embarrassment."

"I'm still not tracking," said Atlas.

"I'll cut to the chase. On Monday morning, before the banks open, the E Party of Illinois, Alex Stein of Aspen, Colorado, and yours truly will be criminally charged in the matter of the *U.S. v. Stein*. The complaint will allege multiple violations of the Internal Revenue Service Code and will also allege various mail fraud and R.I.C.O. violations. At 9 a.m. sharp, the U.S. attorney will appear in court and ask Judge Suffredin to freeze the assets of all defendants as well as the assets of those trusts you created. That order will be granted."

"And how do we know this?" K.C. challenged.

"Like I said. I got a call from an old friend who is in the know at the Justice Department. Given my background and given the respect Atlas has earned with both the military and various administrations, we received an alert. We're not exactly flight risks. Only not so advance that there's anything to be done.

"The E Party has obviously come too far, too fast, my friends. We talked about this from day one. The guys that run this country have a vested interest in the status quo. No room for third parties. No room for new ideas. As far as they're concerned, it's all working just fine. For this to happen, the FBI, the U.S. attorney general, and a bevy of very powerful people have to be involved."

"This is still America," said Atlas. "We have rights. We fight—we win!"

"You fight, you win. That should play out over, say six months to a year, if not considerably more. Meantime, the funding is kaput and you, personally, become the poster child for any act of evil they can fabricate and get published. They won't rest until the E Party is six feet under—literally and figuratively. That's their definition of victory."

"So, what's the bad news?" smiled Atlas. "Waiter—a round of scotch for my friends and me. Bring the bottle."

* * * * * * * * * * * * * * * *

"Thanks for being available on such short notice," Atlas said to those on the conference call. "I trust the General has briefed you on his conversation with his buddy at Justice.

"As of sometime tomorrow, the E Party will be essentially penniless, as will I. We are less than eighty days out from the election and we do not have declared candidates for governor and lieutenant governor. The General and I will be dragged through the mud for heaven knows what, and opponents of the E Party will have a field day. So, Mark, how do you make lemonade from this mess?"

"I don't suppose I can pass?"

"No. But you can have a brief reprieve while Lisa jumps on the hot seat. Lisa?"

"As you said. Not only will you and the General face criminal charges, whoever ginned this up has connections. I cannot begin to imagine what they will be leaking to the media. Any and all of their crap might stick. Every other sentence will take your names in vain and use the phrase 'E Party' at the same time.

"At that point, it becomes imperative for you and the General to be visible, cooperative, and presenting one hell of a rebuttal. We'll also be getting blogged, Twittered, and chat-roomed to death. There's no known inoculation for that gibberish.

"At some point, and relatively soon, either the case has to break favorably, or we need some huge diversion. General, can you get us to bomb Iran in the interim?"

"Not any sooner than I can get Judge Suffredin to release our funds," he sighed out loud. "By the way, Atlas. We have to engage counsel."

"At this point, if it's okay with everyone, I plan to let Yura, Mix & Eisenstat handle the preliminary motions. If we're going to lose anyway, let's not make hasty decisions. Since they probably also have a conflict, Liz will immediately get started on a replacement. We'll have to decide if we stay local to the Illinois Bar or go national."

"My suggestion," entered Mark, "is to at least start with counsel who can navigate the media and political angles. Preferably a big name with a stellar reputation. Assuming the charges are totally fabricated, there won't be much court action before the election. In the interim, this gets tried in the court of public opinion. Style points will carry the day.

"On the political front, we abandon the statewide candidates. No way to get any of them in the game. They can play out the string if they wish, but we have to clearly let them know the score. And it's not much better for our rookie candidates. They have a modicum of name recognition and favorables at this point, but that will all erode quickly. The slightest effort by either party and they become pixie dust."

"Well," Atlas thought out loud, "if that's the case, how can we ask either of our proposed candidates for governor to go on the chopping block? I won't allow it. Unfortunately, without a candidate for governor, the entire ticket gets tossed and that's inconceivable."

"The one ray of hope lies with our incumbents," said Mark. "But it all depends on how believable it is that they have no direct ties to the day-to-day workings of the E Party, particularly the candidates. To that end, we will need rather immediate media clarification of the General's role as party leader and your role as funder. You and the E Party need a quickie divorce, while you become the sole bulls-eye. All the while, Danny Ryan will be working to solidify the image as one big Kodak moment.

"If we can isolate the twenty-two and find a way to bring in at least $5 million, we have an outside shot at holding the Speaker under sixty votes. In the interim, we'll need the greatest ground game since the Four Horsemen."

"Five million?" Atlas choked. "We'll be lucky to bring in five cents. Let's get through court tomorrow and regroup on Tuesday. Lisa, good luck on your end. It's going to be one long, agonizing day. Mark, I would greatly appreciate you assisting K.C. and the General in fully advising all E Party players. This news has to come directly from us."

* * * * * * * * * * * * * * * *

E-MAIL

To: Atlas, General
From: Keith Mix
Sent: 8/12 11:16 a.m. (CST)
Subject: U.S. v. Stein

We got our butts kicked today, just as the General predicted. The only ray of hope is that the judge's order limits the funds freeze to fourteen days. He knows he's on thin ice and without a reasonably short time frame, he otherwise risks a stay by the Appellate Court.

Our preliminary research suggests this case doesn't survive summary judgment. In count one, they contend you mixed charitable foundation funds with political purposes during the education forum. Because the foundation funded research and speakers, they allege a taxable event to the foundation and various acts of fraud by the E Party. On its face, the most you could owe in taxes would be less than $10 million, $15 million with penalties and interest, against which they've impounded close to $1 billion. Under any other circumstances, this whole thing is no more than an audit finding.

The counts for mail fraud and R.I.C.O. are there for show. They give the allegations a sense of proportion for the judge to hide behind. Among other things, we find no cases where R.I.C.O. has ever applied to tax withholding.

If the judge continues to restrict funds after fourteen days, we will immediately appeal. With luck, some or all of the funds get released. At any time, we can pay the taxes, etc., and take that off the table.

* * * * * * * * * * * * * * * *

E-MAIL
To: Keith Mix
From: Atlas
Sent: 8/12 10:28 a.m. (MST)
cc: General
Subject: U.S. v. Stein

Can't agree to pay taxes. Any hint of culpability and we're toast.

* * * * * * * * * * * * * * * *

THE BACK BENCH

"If you let it slip, we catch it"

August 12

EXTRA EXTRA EXTRA EXTRA

A criminal complaint was filed today in the U.S. District Court in Chicago. The complaint accuses Alex Stein of Aspen, Colorado, of massive tax fraud in the funding of the E Party of Illinois and other organizations. It also charges General Smith with related offenses.

The complaint was apparently served by U.S. marshals early this morning and by 9 a.m. the U.S. attorney's office was in court seeking to freeze assets of Mr. Stein, General Smith, and the E Party in excess of $1 billion. The order was granted for fourteen days, at which point there will be an additional hearing.

Little is known about Mr. Stein at this point or his ties to the E Party. However, until today, it had been assumed that General Smith was both the mastermind and funding source for the E Party.

Regardless, this legal action will cause severe, if not irreparable, damage to the E Party. They have yet to announce their candidate for governor and it is hard to imagine that any prospects would now be willing to move ahead.

In other news…

* * * * * * * * * * * * * * * *

"Nat, it's Mark."

"Alex Stein, huh? Alias, Atlas. Self-made billionaire, behind the scenes mover and shaker, U. of C. with distinction, attributed with advancing treatment and solutions for large-scale trauma and, to all who know and work with him, to say he is highly respected would be an understatement. How am I doing?"

"Just fine. And I apologize for not calling sooner, but it has been chaos personified the last forty-eight hours."

"I can imagine. Damage control city."

"To say the least. Listen, I obviously don't have time to meet, but I would like to send you some stuff on Atlas. No favors, just straight shooting. Too early to get into the charges. We expect to be vindicated on all counts."

"No doubt. But, when? This is sweet revenge by someone and very well timed. Hijack all the money and do it when the candidate for governor must be announced in less than ten days. That kind of shit just doesn't happen."

"We always knew we would attract attention from the national level boys and, let's face it, they make the Speaker and Danny look like choir boys. It's a very short, very powerful list."

"Now *that*," Nat hyperventilated, "would be an awesome story."

"We're working it. Let's talk soon. Thanks."

"Mr. Speaker. Mr. Cobb called and left a message. He said to tell you 'you're welcome.' Said you would understand."

"Thanks, Dawn."

* * * * * * * * * * * * * * * *

THE BACK BENCH
"If you let it slip, we catch it"

August 14

Mr. Alex Stein of Aspen, Colorado has certainly captured the public's attention. From obscurity to ubiquity in a heartbeat. As I conducted my background research, I was struck by a few things. He comes across as the sort of person who would never tempt the IRS gods. He also comes across as the sort of person who, in league with General Huntington

Smith, Tom 'Jackie Jr.' Robinson and lots of caring, talented, well-intended people, could invent and implement the E Party. In doing so, he is also the sort of person who is capable of attracting powerful enemies that would be all too happy to destroy him.

On the other hand, the U.S. attorney is not one to chase windmills and is known for his independence. He is not likely to stake his reputation on a political boondoggle. That suggests this case has legs and runs deep.

The PR battle has also been joined. Lisa Boudreau was masterful yesterday in separating the charges against Mr. Stein from the E Party. If her assertions prove correct and, in fact, Mr. Stein has had no direct contact or communication with any E Party office holder or candidate, the Stein booster rocket can plummet to the earth while the E Party module continues its flight.

At the same time, a host of national level Democrat officials and talking heads are spreading super glue all over the story. Stories linking Mr. Stein to the General and Tom Robinson, and the E Party in particular, are being aggressively and meticulously orchestrated.

On the other end of the spectrum, the Republicans seem reluctant to enter the fray. When reached for comment, both candidate Allen and leader DiMaggio elected to "wait and see." Without a viable E Party candidate for governor, their game plan becomes quite flawed. At the same time, without some holier than thou piling on, they look weak in the world of political gamesmanship.

In other news…

* * * * * * * * * * * * * * * *

"Mr. Speaker, I have that call with Danny Ryan on line one."

"Daniel, as you know, Eddie Cobb has made his move. And, I must admit, upon first impression, it is quite inspired. I can't imagine the amount of arm-twisting necessary to get the U.S. attorney on board. At the same time, I don't want to know. If and when this gets out, and it always does, it could make Watergate look like a church picnic.

"No doubt Cobb is also behind all the anti-Stein noise. The DNC has someone on their payroll at every major paper and media outlet. From editorials, to op-eds, to syndicated columns, to talk radio, you name it. We just sit back and enjoy the moment.

"As I see it, from this point forward, we're all about issues. As long as the E Party stays impotent, might as well play the education card. Unless and until the E Party demonstrates any capacity to turn their numbers, we're as sweet as sugar. The Republicans are between a rock and a hard place. Let's stay with the weekly polling.

"And, Danny. Thanks. None of this happens without your hard work, especially unearthing Stein."

"I appreciate the gratitude. But it means nothing 'til we get to sixty. The fourteen E Party representatives still poll over 50 percent favorable and, as I see it, their only play is to circle the wagons around them. That's how I read their PR response."

"Correct. I couldn't agree more. But, I am concerned that if we overplay our hand at the local level, we run the risk of making them sympathetic figures. With all their funds coming from Stein, it will take them at least a month to generate any significant outside contributions. And, even then, it may not be enough. The September 30 filing will tell us a lot. Let's plan to talk after the next hearing. I assume Cobb has this locked up for at least another fourteen days. In the meantime, we need to be ready when they announce their candidate for governor. Thanks again."

* * * * * * * * * * * * * * * *

"Good morning, and welcome to this glorious day," announced a much too chipper Atlas. "If there's a silver lining in any of this, it's having my two best friends in Aspen for the past few days to commiserate."

"You seem remarkably upbeat," said the General.

"That's because I am. I woke early and headed for my favorite spot on the Rim Trail. I sat there for the longest time and put this all on rewind. The U.S. attorney has us bunkered down. For the first time in a very long time, I have time to think.

"K.C., as we discussed just the other day, I recently lost my internal compass. We have accomplished an amazing amount in a very short time. Because of that success, I became consumed with the election. But we owe our accomplishments to two important factors. One, we focused on issues, and in doing so, always stayed out front. Two, the general population is sick and tired of politics as usual.

"As I see it, we need to find another way to stay out front. Fortunately, the Republicans have given us an opening."

"Whoa, whoa," interrupted the General. "Did you get enough oxygen up there?"

"Try this," Atlas responded. "Since we're broke and look to remain broke for the duration, how do we stay out front and on message? K.C.? General? I may not have had enough oxygen, but you guys are sleepwalking. The answer is, our candidate for governor, that's how."

"Oh," interrupted K.C. "You mean the candidate we don't have?"

"Exactly. The one we don't have. If we found ourselves on the ballot with a roster of only representatives and senators and no funds, it's over.

"But, since we haven't declared for governor, and knowing that we're broke, we have the chance to build around a strong candidate who is capable of driving the education issue. Of course, we lose the election, but in doing so, we can still try to force the Speaker to honor his commitment to education reform. That's our victory."

"Sure," laughed the General. "In the next seven days, we find the second coming and he or she boxes the Speaker on education. Correct?"

"That's about it. What's your plan?"

"I'm about the money, " answered the General. "If the judge relents, we've taken only a small hit and we immediately get back on track. If not, we open the web site to public contributions. As long as our PR stays strong, I'm betting we collect enough to stay competitive."

"That's two big ifs," said Atlas. "My way, our downside is covered if you're wrong. But things get very exciting if we're both right. As for the money, someone has gone to great lengths to gain leverage over a federal judge and a U.S. attorney. No way that gets unwound in only fourteen days. We could also lose the short term PR battle, in which case there may not be a pot of gold under your Internet rainbow."

"Meaning?" guessed K.C. "You know the candidate for governor."

"Excellent. I do. Remember, the choice was ceded to me. I now intend to exercise that choice. And, I plan to make you guys wait for the video to find out."

* * * * * * * * * * * * * * * *

THE BACK BENCH

"If you let it slip, we catch it"

August 20

The E Party has petitioned the Illinois Supreme Court for an additional ten days to nominate its candidate for governor. Speculation is that the tax case has caused their once imminent nominee to withdraw.

It is doubtful that the request will be denied. The court has nothing to gain by piling on and county clerks have plenty of time remaining to print ballots. It is also doubtful that either the Republicans or Democrats will object.

The Republicans want and need the E Party to field the strongest possible candidate. While the tax case will undoubtedly inhibit the talent pool, it's still their best shot.

As for the Democrats, no sense facilitating a new diversion at a time when you are enjoying the daily onslaught of Mr. Stein and the Stein party.

Speaking of which, we had intended to run features of the E Party candidates for treasurer and comptroller. Instead, the complete interviews are on the blog for anyone interested.

In other news...

* * * * * * * * * * * * * * * *

E-MAIL

To: Atlas
From: General
Sent: 8/22 8:46 p.m. (CST)
Subject: Ground Game

It did not take much to rile up the troops. They smell a big rat in that tax case and have great energy for the battle ahead.

In addition to our rah-rah, I learned something very interesting about our Democratic friends—most likely, Mr. Ryan.

Remember when our polling numbers began falling after session? Turns out the Democrats have been orchestrating a very creative, aggressive, and comprehensive Twitter-based attack campaign. My guess is that he used a similar methodology in efforts to destroy Tom Robinson's reputation.

This Twitter stuff is all new to me. But on the surface, it's just one big fucking game of post office. Start a few tweets about the E Party candidates being this and that, and no telling where it goes or where it ends.

From the small sample I saw, our guys were attacked for a wide variety of frailties. One of my union buddies keeps getting buzzed about the pension legislation, saying we secretly want to also undermine all private pensions. Another, obviously directed at teachers, predicts disaster if our education plan is adopted. But, the worst of all was a personal attack on Senator Cullen, probably not unlike the Robinson stuff. I'll fill you in when we talk.

For whatever reason, they stopped around the time the criminal case was filed. Curious. In the event they begin anew, we will need both Mark and Lauren to help plot a defense.

* * * * * * * * * * * * * * * *

E-MAIL

To: Mark, Lauren
From: Atlas
Sent: 8/22 7:51 p.m. (MST)
cc: General
Subject: Tweeting

Please see the General's e-mail. Contact him if you need any additional information to proceed. Thanks.

CHAPTER TWENTY-ONE

The Speaker knew and understood the symptoms and their implications. They were uncommon, yet also uncanny. They would start with the slightest change in sleeping habits. He would be aroused from a deep sleep and then, uncharacteristically, lie awake, unable to fall back. At times during the day, he would become distracted, if even momentarily. Within days, he would sense a gnawing, a tugging, that would ebb and flow. The symptoms were all present, but the diagnosis escaped him.

He advised Dawn to cancel all his weekend appointments. He needed time and solitude. There was one element of certainty. If he ignored the symptoms, he did so at his peril.

He sequestered himself in his home office, his sanctuary. All machines were disabled: phone, computer, TV, fax, cell, PDA, scanner, digital clock. They were of no use in this situation. He took a legal pad from his desk and began the exorcism.

The election was just over seventy days away, victory was in sight, and yet his mind and body were telling him that something was amiss. But what? The polling was on track, funding was more than adequate, the planning for the ground operations and G.O.T.V. was well conceived, and the team assembled to execute was experienced and tested. The campaign materials were all in production. He well understood from where his opponents would attack and how he would respond.

The Republicans had bet the ranch on the governor's race. Elizabeth DiMaggio was nobody's fool. She understood the importance of the map and, with the insertion of the E Party in the last election cycle, had no realistic play at controlling either house of the legislature. Based on the polling, they would be lucky to see forty-one seats in the House and twenty in the Senate.

She had successfully maneuvered the primary to produce the best general election candidate and they were pursuing a low risk approach in their campaign: marshal resources and institute a campaign targeted to their voter base. Focus on turnout. Let the Democrats and E Party duke it out and hope to sneak in with 38 to 42 percent of the vote.

Recent events had not been kind to the Republican strategy and Allen was now showing signs of issue promotion. But there was nowhere for him to go. They had been neutered on fiscal responsibility and this was not an election for family values. Their best day, at 42 percent, would now come up quite short. Not even the most disastrous mid-terms on record, Clinton '94 included, were going to get them any higher.

E Party. What did Churchill say? A puzzle, wrapped in a riddle, wrapped in an enigma? Something like that. They had more money than the Catholic church and yet had not slated enough candidates to take a run at the majority in either chamber. Until the Republicans forced their hand, they had abandoned statewide offices. They avoided votes on most issues. To what end?

They were imaginative and refreshing. Their work in education was brilliant, but they did not press for a solution when they had the momentum. Their back-to-back budget strategies had reshaped the state's economy.

What are they about? Seeking solutions, but not power. They do not attack when they have the clear advantage. Surely the General knows better.

Now, thanks to Cobb, they would be without money for the foreseeable future. Perhaps they had other resources. Not likely, though. They could not have anticipated this contingency. Too late for fundraising. They can't buy media on credit and the window of open television slots will soon close. All of the available points in the vital markets will be sold. Cobb is pounding them relentlessly on television and in the press. His talking heads are dominating the airwaves.

Does the General have a nuke up his sleeve? What would that be? Can't be negative. They're not positioned for it, and at that point, they lose credibility. They can scream education from the roof tops to no avail. None of their announced statewide candidates are remotely electable, particularly if Danny is right about their options for governor.

That gnawing again? Maybe some fresh air will help.

* * * * * * * * * * * * * * * *

E-MAIL
To: Atlas
From: Liz
Sent: 9/2 11:01 a.m. (CST)
Subject: Don Colletti

Don Colletti has been calling. Insists I set up a call with you. Please advise.

* * * * * * * * * * * * * * * *

E-MAIL
To: Liz
From: Atlas
Sent: 9/2 10:16 a.m. (MST)
Subject: Don Colletti

Set it up at his convenience. Thanks.

* * * * * * * * * * * * * * * *

E-MAIL
To: Atlas
From: Keith Mix
Sent: 9/4 4:56 p.m. (CST)
Subject: Star Power Counsel

We are not faring well in our search for a star power attorney to handle the tax case. The best in class are intellectually giant bean counters. These cases rarely hit the press.

* * * * * * * * * * * * * * * *

E-MAIL
To: Keith Mix
From: Atlas
Sent: 9/4 3:59 p.m. (MST)
Subject: Star Power Counsel

Start over. "If the glove don't fit, you must acquit." Find us a Johnny Cochran! This case has absolutely nothing to do with taxes. It's *Chicago*—all razzle-dazzle. Find Billy Flynn!

* * * * * * * * * * * * * * * *

"You are one crazy mother fucker!" sputtered Colletti. "Next time you want to piss away a billion dollars, give it to me. I'll unionize China! Did you think Eddie Cobb and his henchmen would leave your head attached to your body? By the way, you are also one brilliant son of a bitch."

"Thanks, Don," Atlas said. "And yes, I figured to get hit by a truck. But it's been worth it. By the way, you're welcome for pension reform."

"I just wish I could help. I hate those fucking assholes at the DNC, but they have my guys by the short ones. Where're we going, to the Republicans? No fuckin' way. Your E Party actually gives us newfound leverage. As I'm sure you've already figured out, the judge is in the tank. And the U.S. attorney wants to be the U.S. attorney general. The good news is that it all stops once you get your ass kicked."

"Don, I can't stop. In fact, I think we can fight our way out. Wanna help?"

"You are a crazy mother fucker. Fight back and they will take it all. And I mean all. Your money, your reputation, and your dignity. Don't let that happen, my friend."

"Too late. If we're right, we either reverse course and kick ass or, more likely, we still get our asses kicked but ride off into the sunset having fostered an education revolution."

"I was afraid there would be no talking to you. Fact is, my money's on you. Gimme something to take back to Cobb other than to go fuck himself."

"Tell him to keep the money. That ought to freak him out. By the way, how 'bout Vegas after Thanksgiving?"

* * * * * * * * * * * * * * * *

E-MAIL
To: Atlas, K.C.
From: Lisa
Sent: 9/5 12:12 p.m. (CST)
Subject: Budget Contest Winners

Lost in the shuffle has been our obligation to the budget winners. We promised to have all payments in the mail once the rollout hit Chicago. That's in three days.

* * * * * * * * * * * * * * * *

E-MAIL
To: K.C., Lisa
From: Atlas
Sent: 9/5 11:36 p.m. (MST)
Subject: Budget Contest Winners

We need to come up with just short of $4 million. Any ideas?? This may actually work to our advantage when we go before Judge Suffredin. I will instruct Keith Mix to make an appeal to release funds to the winners under court supervision. It will drive 'em nuts.

In the interim, we need to personally contact each winner and assure them that they will get paid. If nothing else, I might be able to unload some ASC stock once the annual report is released. As an insider, I'm embargoed for the time being.

* * * * * * * * * * * * * * * *

E-MAIL
To: Atlas, General
From: Mark
Sent: 9/6 10:11 p.m. (CST)
Subject: Revisions

As you instructed, attached is a revised election strategy that avoids any additional expenditures of money. We will be relying entirely on free media, the General's volunteer army, and Lauren's Internet machine. It was at least fortuitous that the General was tipped regarding the tax case so we could pre-fund Lauren's operation through the election. That move could prove the saving grace.

The plan for the field operation is predicated on at least 200 volunteer full-time equivalents in each legislative district. Our education reform petition drive will hopefully prove to have been another stroke of luck. If the Speaker passes an education bill in the spring, we never institute that campaign. Still, it becomes the most ambitious person-to-person campaign effort in modern Illinois' political history. But, and it's a major but, every one of their commercials and mail pieces has a reach that dwarfs anything we can accomplish in terms of in-person messaging.

That's where Lauren comes in. It will certainly test all preconceived notions regarding how elections are won. Imagine the campaign commercial joining the newspaper in dinosaur land. Unthinkable! How ironic that we will be relying on TV, radio, and newspapers to supply untold quantities of free PR while an unintended consequence thereof will have been the further sapping of their revenue base. Just remember to send a thank you note if we win.

* * * * * * * * * * * * * * * *

THE BACK BENCH

"If you let it slip, we catch it"

September 7

Alex Stein and the E Party appeared before Judge Suffredin today to again contest the court order restraining access to their funds. Keith Mix, defendant's counsel, was very persuasive in his arguments while Phyllis Ryder, representing the U.S. attorney's office, did not offer the most scintillating presentation.

Nonetheless, in the end the judge renewed his order for an additional fourteen days. He even denied the release of $4 million for the budget contest winners.

This may have been a fatal blow to the E Party's chances in November. Without access to funds, they will not be able to purchase any airtime or printed media. Television, in particular, must be paid before ads can run. Shortly, all of the most sought after time slots will be spoken for.

In a related bit of piling on: shortly after the judge issued his latest ruling, a class action suit was filed by a group of the winners from the budget savings contest. There appears to be no end in sight to the plethora of bad news surrounding Mr. Stein and his E street irregulars.

In other news…

* * * * * * * * * * * * * * * *

E-MAIL

To: General, K.C., Mark, Lisa
From: Liz
Sent: 9/7 4:22 p.m. (CST)
Subject: Conference Call

Atlas asks that we set a call for this evening to discuss options in light of the funds freeze continuation. Please let me know your availability.

* * * * * * * * * * * * * * * *

"Good evening everyone. As always, I'm glad you could be available on short notice. I trust you have had an opportunity to review Mark's revised plan. Mark, before we begin, do you have any updates?"

"Just that we have to set our priorities for both races and resources. At a minimum, I assume keeping at least one House from gaining a Democrat majority is critical. Otherwise, any and all leverage is lost. The best bet is the Senate. As you know, because all senators have two four-year terms and one two-year term each census cycle, only three of our eight seats are up for re-election. So as long as we hold two of those seats and the Republicans can hold serve, the Senate Democrats will not have a majority. Conversely, all fourteen are at risk in the House where we have to hold all fourteen. This analysis also assumes that our new challenger candidates are D.O.A. without sufficient funds to run effective campaigns."

"Thanks, Mark. Anything else?"

"No."

"Then let's understand what we're up against. Whoever devised the funds freeze also understood there would be what I'll call intended consequences. The General and I have been contacting banks and other conventional lending sources to no avail. They're all directly or indirectly regulated by an arm of the federal government. You name it: F.D.I.C., F.S.L.I.C., S.E.C., D.O.C., C.F.T.C., the Fed, Treasury. Which means we can turn over lender rocks for the remainder of the millennium and none of our spineless friends are going to risk a one-way ticket to regulatory purgatory."

"Maybe so," said K.C., "but we don't need them. I would be stunned if we couldn't raise sufficient funds by opening the E Party to public contributions via the Internet. Lauren has already tracked a large number of potential donors and our candidates all deserve this opportunity. We have to find a way to make it work."

"K.C.," responded Atlas. "I figured you would bring that to the table. So I checked with Russell Yura to see what that would entail. As for the E Party, we can't add to our political fund because it remains frozen. We could raise money, but we would not be able to spend it unless Judge Suffredin has an epiphany, which is not likely. The alternative is to either launch a new fund or to have the candidates each activate funds for their individual campaigns. I think a new E Party fund would meet the same fate as our current ice cube. As for the individual candidate funds, it comes down to timing and coordination.

"From a timing perspective, we can probably have them operational in a matter of days. That's assuming the candidates' local banks will not be feeling the political heat. In the interim, Lauren's team will have to set up web sites for each fund. I don't see us having time to arrange fundraisers, coffees or any other classic fundraising format. Nor would I expect that route to produce sufficient sums. It's Internet or nothing. With over seventy candidates in Illinois and dozens more in the expansion states, that's a tall order.

"I also hesitate to go that route because it sets a precedent that runs contrary to one of our most basic principles. It creates a scenario where the individual candidates become free agents, eroding the team concept.

"Having said all that, please know that I told Yura you'd be calling him to get the ball rolling."

"In that case, I assume we're talking about all five states. Correct?" asked K.C.

"If you and Lauren can make it happen…I say go for it! General, it looks as though we won't have an air attack. What about the ground game?"

"I'd feel better if I had conscription," he joked. "But between our petition drive and my army network, we'll stay competitive."

"Lisa?"

"If our candidate for governor sells, we can maintain a strong PR presence throughout. To that end, we need to get moving very soon."

"That we will. I promise," Atlas pledged. "Thanks again everyone. I have a hunch the next ten days to two weeks will be fun."

* * * * * * * * * * * * * * * *

E-MAIL

To: Atlas
From: Lisa
Sent: 9/9 8:30 a.m. (CST)
Subject: Governor Announcement

I am still shopping the announcement. *Nightline* has expressed interest, but won't guarantee the slot if there is a breaking story. I also have concerns about the late hour. At a minimum, we need to make the late night news and the morning papers; preferably the national evening news. We also need a live show. Anything taped will cost spontaneity and control. As much as I hate the word, this has to be all our spin. Neither the Democrats nor Republicans can have the slightest hint or the advantage we so desperately need is lost.

* * * * * * * * * * * * * * * *

"Hello Nat, it's Mark. Any chance we can get together tomorrow. I may have something of interest."

"You bet. This tax case is something else. I've got tons of questions but wasn't going to bother you. What works for you?"

* * * * * * * * * * * * * * * *

"Mr. Speaker. I've got Danny Ryan on line one."

"Danny, I'm glad you called. I'm very anxious about the polling."

"As usual, I will be sending the complete report via e-mail later today. This is one of those, good news/bad news polls. As you would expect, the E Party has taken a huge hit. All of their incumbents are now below 50 percent favorability and their new candidates have taken a bigger hit. However, their negatives have flattened since we halted our Twitter onslaught. We ran polls on their statewide candidates for the first time, and for the most part, no name recognition to mention. They have a long, long way to go.

"The bad news is that we also took a big hit. Almost as though the E Party was floating all boats and their deflation cuts across the board. Curiously, we took a bigger hit than the Republicans. Without much explanation, the governor's race has tightened considerably.

"Finally, we ran separate polling on both of the suspected E candidates for governor. As you'll see, one does significantly better. It will be interesting to see who they finally select next week. No doubt their polling also points in the same direction."

"Thanks, Danny. I couldn't agree more. I don't know if they blundered by extending the announcement. With Cobb's assault continuing unabated, if I were they, I'd be thinking about abandoning the statewide candidates. Makes me wonder if the delay was more about cold feet on the part of their designated candidate for governor. Do me a favor. Go over the entire plan one more time. I have this sixth sense we're missing something. I'll call you if I have any questions after seeing the polls."

* * * * * * * * * * * * * * * *

"Good morning, Mark," welcomed a surprisingly alert Nat.

"You actually seem coherent," Mark observed.

"Coherent may not be accurate for this hour, but I crashed early last night so I actually have a few brain cells operating. Anyway, I was glad you called. This case has been, shall we say, unusual. I can't begin to fit the pieces together."

"In what way?"

"Take your Atlas. Nothing about this guy remotely suggests he fucks up this bad. He has top-notch legal counsel and I assume his tax accountant is no slouch either. Let's face it, scratch any billionaire and there's a good bean counter somewhere.

"But then, Judge Suffredin and our U.S. attorney have always been highly regarded, straight shooters. Almost as though there are some serious facts not being disclosed. Like I said, it just doesn't add up."

"I agree. I've been working with Stein for over two years now. The guy is so good, he's scary. Works around the clock and doesn't miss anything. He's also one of the most, if not the most, honest, straightforward and down-to-earth people I've ever met. Certainly not the kind to have pushed the tax code envelope at the risk of the entire enchilada."

"You must have a theory," pushed Nat.

"We do. And it rhymes with Eddie Cobb."

"Hadn't thought about him," said Nat. "But that would be a fascinating puzzle piece."

"Agreed. Although he's been charged but never been convicted of attempted bribery, we know that cajoling the law has been his trademark. What if the national, big wig Democrats were getting a bit too nervous about the E gang? If we crack a few other states, who knows where this ends up? So how do you stop us? Try freezing all our funds at the most inopportune moment. I'm betting this case quietly goes away if we get dry cleaned and pressed in November."

"So the judge and prosecutor don't really have to miscarry justice, they just have to slow you down enough. Very interesting. You've got my attention."

"That's why we start pushing back tomorrow. I thought a greater reporter, such as yourself, might want to run with the story."

"Flattery will get you everywhere."

* * * * * * * * * * * * * * * *

E-MAIL

To: Atlas, General
From: Mark
Sent: 9/11 10:09 a.m. (CST)
Subject: Carson Meeting

Nothing like a good conspiracy theory to peak the curiosity of a journalist. I suspect that in addition to covering the announcement of our new lead counsel, Nat and his brethren will be working all the angles.

* * * * * * * * * * * * * * * *

E-MAIL

To: General, K.C., Mark, Lisa, Lauren
From: Atlas
Sent: 9/12 7:29 a.m. (MST)
Subject: Operation Comeback

Unless any of you have the least bit of hesitation, Operation Comeback, as the General calls it, kicks off tomorrow.

Phase I. The push back against *U.S. v. Stein* will launch with a noon press conference in Chicago. Lisa will introduce Elaine Richards as our new lead counsel. Lisa has her scheduled for a three-day statewide whirlwind of networks and editorial boards. During that time, she is center stage in a one person show.

Phase II. Introduction of our candidate for governor and his campaign will launch on live national television within a week of Phase I. The timing will depend upon which outlet is chosen. Keep your fingers crossed for *Conversations With Kathryn Collins*. Once timing is finalized, all E Party regulars will be briefed over the Internet. That evening, the General will ready his troops for a campaign field blitz, tied to the launch of another Lauren de la Rosa Internet spectacular, from Twitter to Facebook to YouTube.

Just when Cobb and his cronies are getting ready to bury us, the whole thing makes me feel like the payback finale from a Godfather movie. Let the games begin!

* * * * * * * * * * * * * * *

THE BACK BENCH

"If you let it slip, we catch it"

September 13

Mr. Alex Stein, General Smith, and the E Party announced today that Elaine Richards has been engaged as lead counsel in *U.S. v. Stein.*

The case has attracted unusual national attention for a rather mundane allegation of tax fraud, primarily because Judge Suffredin has twice ordered the freezing of E Party campaign funds along with Stein and Smith personal assets in excess of $1 billion, all at a time when the mother's milk of politics is most desperately needed for the infant political party.

Elaine Richards is best known as the original pit bull with lipstick. She was the first woman U.S. attorney in the state of Texas, serving in Houston. Born and raised there, but for an Ivy League undergrad and legal education, she is all Texas. She was appointed U.S. attorney under Bush senior. She also served under Clinton before leaving over the ubiquitous "philosophical differences."

Speculation attributed these differences to her seeking indictments against leading Democrat party honchos, including Eddie Cobb, only to be rebuked by the attorney general.

Since leaving Justice, she has been a senior partner at the prestigious Keidan, Doolittle & Isaacson firm in Dallas, specializing in white-collar criminal defense. She has also written extensively and is a regular on radio and television talk shows whenever high profile cases capture the nation's attention.

She is smart, slick and tenacious. She may have a score to settle with Mr. Cobb and the Democratic National Committee, which became quite apparent in her opening remarks. She came within a millimeter of crossing the line in suggesting this case never sees a courtroom if the defendants aren't collectively perceived as a threat to the political establishment. When pressed, she used her best southern drawl to tell us good 'ol boys not to get her in trouble.

Her first appearance in court should be a good 'ol Texas barn burner.

In other news…

THE BACK BENCH
"If you let it slip, we catch it"

September 15

In a rather stunning reversal of momentum, Elaine Richards has captured the imagination of the press and TV corps in carefully worded insinuations regarding the Stein case. She has been leaking selective facts like breadcrumbs marking a trail to Eddie Cobb.

Why, she asks, is it necessary to impound in excess of $1 billion in a case where the maximum in fines and penalties is $15 million? Why, she asks, is General Smith a defendant? Why, she asks, was the complaint issued this year when the questionable tax returns were filed in March and it usually takes up to three years for such matters just to come to audit? How is it, she asks, that this case leapfrogs an audit, and at the veritable speed of light, works its way to the U.S. attorney in Chicago, bypassing the courts in Colorado, domicile to Mr. Stein and the trust accused of wrongdoing?

With these and other very leading questions, she has sent legions of press geeks on a fact finding witch hunt.

In other news…

* * * * * * * * * * * * * * * *

"Mr. Speaker. I have Danny Ryan on line one."

"Danny. This Richards could be a game changer. The only positive is that we jettisoned Cobb. Nonetheless, the ooze is headed our way. Put a hold on everything until we can poll. Fortunately, we still have up to ten days before our TV commercials are launched."

"Mr. Speaker, I agree with one exception. I think we should re-engage the Twitter campaign attacking the E candidates. We need to drive their negatives more than ever."

"Maybe so. I never thought they'd be on to Cobb so quickly. No doubt he's been a little too drunk and a little too braggadocio since the Stein case broke. Never could keep his mouth shut. Let's hope this is the worst Richards can fabricate before the election. There's no way we can get involved and Cobb will never understand the virtue of silence at this time."

* * * * * * * * * * * * * * * *

"Elizabeth, it's Scott Grusin."

"Mr. Chairman, what an honor," answered a very surprised Elizabeth DiMaggio.

"The honor's all mine," he responded smoothly. "Unfortunately, you and I don't usually have much to address at this time in the campaign cycle. In fact, I can't remember the last time Illinois was even on the agenda at a Republican National Committee meeting. But in hiring Richards, the E Party appears to have found a way to boost Republican chances in November. And to that end, much more than just the governor's race in Illinois."

"Mr. Chairman, if our polling is off by as much as a standard deviation, we're still in the catbird's seat. Allen's numbers get better every day and Stewart's negatives have been soaring, particularly once Richards arrived on the scene."

"Wonderful news," he exclaimed. "I'm calling to find out if we can do anything for you, particularly funding. I'm prepared to divert significant seven figures your way."

"Thank you, Mr. Chairman. Hard to recall the last time we were worthy of such an offer. By the way, offer accepted. We can also use some bodies for G.O.T.V. But more than anything, is there any way you can help fan the flames surrounding the Eddie Cobb stories? I'm guessing you've got quite the library of vignettes."

"More than vignettes. And, yes, we're quietly and effectively sprinkling gasoline whenever and wherever possible. Don't forget, Richards is a card-carrying member. I have her on speed dial for Christ sake."

"Thanks. That's all I need to know. Keep me in mind if a head's up is in order. And Mr. Chairman, let us know if there's anything we can do for you."

"Will do. Keep up the good work."

* * * * * * * * * * * * * * * *

E-MAIL

To: Atlas
From: Lisa
Sent: 9/17 8:02 a.m. (CST)
Subject: Let's Roll

Our candidate is due at the studio tomorrow at 10:30 a.m. sharp. I assume K.C. will be in attendance as well. She has done an unbelievable job of prepping. No matter how impressive his background, no one is ever truly ready for this stage. But with her amazing determination and focus, coupled with his dedication and attention to detail, we're as ready as we're ever going to be.

* * * * * * * * * * * * * * * *

"Nat, it's Mark. I think you'll find it well worth the time to find your way to the local CBS affiliate studios at 11 a.m. tomorrow. I will leave a pass in your name. Have them bring you to Lisa. Plan to spend two to three hours."

"Eleven? How civil of you. Consider it done."

CHAPTER TWENTY-TWO

THE BACK BENCH

"If you let it slip, we catch it"

September 18

EXTRA EXTRA EXTRA EXTRA

For the small portion of Western Civilization that does not watch or Tivo Kathryn Collins' nationally syndicated talk show, today's program was a ground-breaking event in television journalism. The dialog is so compelling, I am abdicating my editorial proclivity in favor of selected, verbatim narrative. The entire interview will be on the blog this evening.

Collins: This afternoon we are honored to have Thomas "Jackie Jr." Robinson as our guest. For those of you unfamiliar with Tom, he was elected to the Baseball Hall of Fame in 1992 and has spent the majority of his afterlife, if I can call it that, as a goodwill ambassador. In that capacity, Tom travels the country promoting both youth baseball and the value of education. Of late, he has been a spokesperson for the E Party of Illinois, a recent up-start that has captured the attention of the political world for innovation, and as of last month, a fair amount of controversy.

Today, we're going to hear about a rather dark secret that Tom has been carrying for some time and learn about an exciting new journey upon which he will soon embark.

Tom, let me first say how excited I am that you could join us today. Growing up, you were always among the sports heroes in the Collins household. In addition to your great physical talents and accomplishments, you always carried yourself with grace. And in an era when ballplayers were chasing record salaries and jumping from team to team thanks to Curt Flood, your loyalty stood as a beacon.

Robinson: Thank you, Kathryn. It's a pleasure to be on the show. I'm honored that you would give me the opportunity to once and for all clear the air on an issue I should have addressed many years ago.

Collins: Tom, before we get ahead of the story, I think we should set the stage for our audience. As I understand it, you have undertaken a self-imposed exile since late last year. Why is that?

Robinson: (Deep breath) Phew. Sometime last fall, I was in Chicago on a tour of inner-city churches talking baseball and education. One evening, as the question and answer session was drawing to a close, a young man asked me a very pointed question. He wanted to know if the rumors were true that I'm gay.

I was stunned by the question. And although my denial was quick and decisive, I soon discovered that the rumor to which the young man referred was a rapidly spreading virus. The churches, schools and community organizations that served as my platform began cancelling engagements. I found myself being confronted with targeted questions I could not adequately address and a reputation that took a lifetimc to build was rapidly eroding.

Collins: Tom, what do you mean when you say there were questions you could not address?

Robinson: The whole thing felt like an orchestrated attack. Aspects of my life were either redacted or taken out of context and used to paint a damning scenario. Why had I never married? Why did I never appear at any sporting, charity or speaking event with a female companion? Why had I moved from town to town throughout my adult life, never settling roots? Why was I always with young boys, putting my arms around them while pretending to coach them? I learned a very difficult lesson. You can deny rumors, but you can't make them go away. So I decided to go away, hoping time would heal the massive wounds.

Collins: And has your strategy worked?

Robinson: I don't honestly know. Until today, I haven't been to Chicago for quite some time. But, I suspect the questions are still out there, ready to surface the minute I attempt to again address a youth audience.

Collins: Tom, I know this is very difficult for you. But I think that your answers today will go a long way to helping you set the record straight. Let's take the easy one, and the rest will fall in place. How is it that one of America's most eligible bachelors never married?

Robinson: Like most ballplayers, I did my share of carousing. Had a romance or two in the off-season and an occasional one-night stand. It wasn't as if I had to go looking. Beautiful young women would seek me out. Despite the cliché, it was me that felt like the piece of meat. Toward the end of my career, during a preseason physical, I had an unusual finding. Further tests were conducted and I was devastated to learn I had contracted AIDS.

This was prior to Magic Johnson's startling and heroic announcement. Also, baseball does not feature the same degree of contact as basketball. The doctors said it was OK to play as long as the symptoms could be regulated and controlled. I quietly finished my career, and at the same time, avoided any relationships with women. In hindsight, maybe I could or should have handled it differently. But until last year, I had no reason to doubt my course.

Collins: And you've coped with the disease all these years?

Robinson: I've had superb medical care. In fact, one of the reasons I have relocated periodically was to seek new and innovative treatment protocols. Modern medicine has not only kept me alive, but has kept me robust and productive.

Collins: Tom, I know this has been an extremely trying period in your life.

Robinson: The hard part is living a lie. At least now, that's over. I greatly appreciate you giving me this opportunity.

Collins: You're most welcome. I understand there's other news to be shared today.

Robinson: In fact, there is, Kathryn. But first, with your permission, I would like to digress to set the stage a bit.

Collins: Please do.

Robinson: Just over two years ago, my friend Alex Stein invited me to his home to share very exciting news.

Collins: And, Tom, before we go any further. Your friend, Alex Stein, is the same gentleman who has recently been in the news regarding a tax fraud case and his role as the principal benefactor of the E Party of Illinois?

Robinson: That's correct. In fact, that was the occasion for my visit. Atlas, as he's known, brought his best friends together to announce his intention to start a third political party.

Collins: And you and Atlas have been friends for quite some time?

Robinson: Indeed. Atlas is a legend in the Robinson family. Almost fifty years ago, he was part of a team that helped restore a modicum of sanity to families suffering from a school fire tragedy. He was a young man at the time, but he clearly stood out. In those days, for a white man to devote untold hours to poor, suffering black families was a small miracle in and of itself.

Later, around fifteen years I guess, I had two relatives who returned from Nam in bad shape. Not injured. More like psychologically scarred. As it turns out, their mental well-being was restored in conjunction with a new program the Army had just developed. It was my aunt who put the pieces back together. She remembered the name when she learned it was Alex Stein who devised the program. That story continues to make the rounds at Robinson family celebrations.

A few years later, I'm speaking at an event for the Commissioner and lo and behold, Atlas is one of the honorees. I introduced myself and thanked him on behalf of my entire family. We stayed in touch after that. He's a baseball nut and from our common interest, a long-standing friendship emerged.

Collins: So you're invited to his home and he talks about starting a new political party. That had to be fascinating.

Robinson: Quite. As it turned out, he had a role in mind for me. He told me that this new party would be the greatest possible platform for me to reach children, mainly black children, and begin to make a difference. I was hooked.

Collins: I understand you were very active from the beginning.

Robinson: Yes. General Smith and I became the public face during the first campaign. We talked about making a difference. Why the system wasn't working anymore. The potential of the E Party. We had great candidates, mostly educators, and all recognized leaders in their communities.

Collins: There is no doubt the E Party has made a difference. But, as I understand things, the forthcoming election will be a real dog fight and this tax case has been a real setback.

Robinson: One thing I've learned. Politics is the ultimate contact sport; with an emphasis on hitting below the belt. I'll never prove it, but it is not beyond the realm of possibility that my E Party involvement was the impetus for those vicious rumors.

Collins: I would have to think that was the case. I've been in Chicago enough to learn that they play the game very down and very dirty. How do you fight back?

Robinson: Well, I guess I didn't. I ran from the fight. But that changes today. My friend Atlas called me a few weeks back and issued a challenge, if I was up for it. He would guarantee me the chance to set the record straight, and at the same time, embark on the mission of a lifetime.

Collins: And what would that mission be?

Robinson: He asked me to run as the E Party candidate for governor of Illinois.

Collins: To which you said?

Robinson: No, of course. Why would I have any interest in running for governor of Illinois? But Atlas is persistent and persuasive. He quickly pointed out that he would not be inquiring if I had any chance of winning. In fact, the tax case was threatening to destroy the entire party. All of its funds had been frozen and Atlas and the General were being verbally flogged on a daily basis. It was painful to watch. He told me this could be my one and only opportunity to set the record straight regarding my personal situation. He also said that, for six weeks, 24/7, I would be the ultimate messenger for education reform; not just in Illinois, but across the country.

Collins: You have to admit, that was quite a sales job.

Robinson: Which is why I'm here today to announce my candidacy for governor of Illinois representing the E Party.

Collins: Well, that's a first for us. And I think we should advise the audience that we will be extending invitations to both the Democrat and Republican candidates. You don't want to mess with the television gods of equal time. So, Tom, in the few minutes remaining, why don't you tell us about your party and your run for governor?

Robinson: The E Party stands for ethics, the economy, and education. If you check the record, in just two short years, we have pushed the Illinois legislature to achieve much greater financial stability coupled with ethics reform. The big fish is education.

In that first session with Atlas, he challenged me with three statistics: our high school drop out rate, our teen pregnancy rate, and our incarceration rate.

The E Party has worked hard for the last year to put education front and center. We conducted hearings for months and produced some of the finest white papers on a multitude of critical issues. We also proposed a comprehensive legislative package that sits dormant in Springfield.

For the next six weeks, the E Party will be shouting education from every rooftop and soapbox we can find. It will start with our education package and include a concept I am very excited about called "Getting to 21."

It all starts with those horrendous statistics. And it is not a recent phenomenon either. Add it all together and we have failed countless generations. I know we don't have time today for all the details. We'll save that for the campaign trail. It boils down to this: until the youth of America reach the age of twenty-one, not sixteen, not eighteen, the highest priority will be to finish high school and move onto college. Anyone not continuing their education through age twenty-one must either serve in the Armed Forces or one of the various volunteer programs such as the Peace Corps or Americorps, in which case they are still expected to complete their high school equivalency. Another alternative could be apprentice programs sanctioned by unions and business.

Bottom line, we have to end the cycle of failure to which so many of our youngsters are subjected. In my world, you go to the minor leagues to get ready for the majors. Even the greatest ballplayers need that seasoning and maturation.

If adulthood and all its responsibilities are the majors, we need to develop a better minor league structure to cultivate our greatest resource. It can't end once our kids reach drop-out age. Over one million kids each year drop out. Our society has to come to grips with that fact. Without a process for seasoning, which is for the most part education and maturation—putting those late teen years to productive purposes—we are going to continue losing our kids. And, that's what "Getting to 21" will be about.

Collins: Tom, that's a wow. I can't wait to learn more. Also, I've been to the E Party website and I wholeheartedly agree. Those white papers are fascinating. After today, we are going to post a link on our web site. Unfortunately, this hour has flown by and we're out of time. Tom, best of luck. And, win or lose, you have an open invitation to return to talk education and much more about "Getting to 21." Please bring Mr. Stein with you.

In other news…

* * * * * * * * * * * * * * * *

Gnawing had been replaced with relentless churning. Was it only two weeks ago that he was searching, racking the recesses of his brain? Two weeks ago. The polling was moving their way. Two weeks ago. Their candidate for governor was still solidly in control, and with him, the map. Two weeks ago. The campaign strategy was locked and loaded. Two weeks ago. The E Party was a ship in distress. Two weeks ago. Tom Robinson was down for the count living a homophobic nightmare. Two weeks ago. Sixty seats in the House and thirty in the Senate, the Holy Grail, were well within his grasp.

At least all the facts were now squarely before him. The three candidates for governor were known at last, the E Party had openly declared its strategy, and the Republicans were on the attack. Six weeks, plus, remaining. This would be the political fight of his life. He wondered if he was ready. It was a question he had never needed to answer before.

He instinctively understood the appropriate adjustments to plan, and without hesitation or reservation, set his course.

"Hello, Daniel." The Speaker's tone hinted at a sobering return to reality. "I need you to make the following adjustments to plan, confirm when complete, and be prepared to immediately execute.

"The low volume negatives need to be reinstituted as soon as possible. Use any and all personal attacks and push every envelope. In addition to the weekly polling, begin separate issue polling with hard-hitting push questions.

"Start running education commercials. The ones we prepared are too superficial for current circumstances so we need to have a new series cut. The focus will be teachers—it all starts and stops with teachers. The subliminal message needs to be pro-union: 'This is a good place to be a teacher. Don't let the E Party get in the way.'

"Start the constituent focused commercials and mail pieces, rotating issues every four to five days. The E Party is 100 percent about education and the Republicans will be desperately mimicking. It's all they have. Our base needs energizing. Throw them some red meat. Start with pro-choice, gun control, green, green, green, and finally, healthcare. In all cases, we are the answer. The E Party doesn't vote, doesn't care, and the Republicans are the problem.

"As the issues play out, start the letters to the editors and op-eds. Unlike the E Party, the Democrats are not just about education. Blah, blah, blah.

"We also need to shut down Allen. I don't like the trajectory of his numbers. Instruct the 527 organizations to launch their attack pieces, especially regarding his business failures. If he couldn't run his business, how can he run the state?

"Finally, get in the field now. No reason to wait. Every Democratic voter with a pulse has to vote this time.

"As for Suffredin and the tax case. Leave that to me.

"Questions? Call me if you hit any speed bumps. Goodbye, Daniel."

* * * * * * * * * * * * * * * *

Well, thought Danny, that was a short-lived renaissance. Six weeks out. No room for error. Go to the mattresses. But unlike the Corleone's, it was also very personal. He didn't just crave the win; he desperately needed the win.

* * * * * * * * * * * * * * * *

Not everyone's reaction to the Tom Robinson segment on Kathryn Collins' show was as hardened and calculated as that of the Speaker. In fact, he was on the outer banks of the spectrum.

For many, it was an emotional roller coaster ride, from the agony of his personal torment to the sobering revelation of his suffering to the exhilaration of his new mission.

Far from the Speaker, on the soapy, emotional end of this pendulum was Nancy Rae; woman not scorned. Although she and Kathryn Collins were not on the same planet, the replayed segments and news accounts, the water cooler buzzing and web chatter were almost as ubiquitous as the news of Michael Jackson's death, especially in Chicago's black community.

Nancy Rae kept returning to that evening and that momentary embrace. As a flashback, her initial perception of passion was now more than vindicated. Yet the resulting pangs of gut wrenching guilt were the dominating emotion. The pyramid of hotel miniatures she had built that fateful evening was easily surpassed over the next few days with life-sized versions.

For the E Party regulars, the show and the endless reruns were a commutation of the death sentence imposed by *U.S. v. Stein*. It was the doctor saying those initial tests were false positive; there is no cancer. It was the starting gun of a six-week sprint to the election finish line.

* * * * * * * * * * * * * * * *

E-MAIL
To: Tom
From: Atlas
Sent: 9/18 3:01 p.m. (MST)
Subject: Your Conversation With Kathryn Collins

My friend. You can return *Mr. Peabody's Apples* to the library. Welcome back.

* * * * * * * * * * * * * * * *

E-MAIL
To: Lisa
From: Atlas
Sent: 9/18 3:03 p.m. (MST)
Subject: Wow!

Don't know how you managed to get Tom on the show. You saved a life today. Thank you.

* * * * * * * * * * * * * * * *

E-MAIL
To: Atlas
From: Tom
Sent: 9/18 7:14 p.m. (CST)
Subject: Thank you

Thank you. You continue to work emotional miracles for the Robinson family. God bless.

* * * * * * * * * * * * * * * *

E-MAIL
To: State Central Committee
From: Elizabeth DiMaggio
Sent: 9/24 9:04 a.m. (CST)
Subject: Tom Robinson

Thank you, E Party. If Tom Robinson can't steal enough votes from Stewart to put us over the top, no one can.

We will shortly revise and release an education platform for the rest of the campaign. In the interim, we need to energize the base. The attached poll has

Allen squarely in the lead. We need to use this momentum to lock in our votes. Good luck.

* * * * * * * * * * * * * * * *

THE BACK BENCH
"If you let it slip, we catch it"

September 25

All of a sudden, you can sense an energy surrounding the governor's race that has been sorely lacking.

Tom Robinson, the E Party un-candidate, held the obligatory state fly-round yesterday on the heels of his official announcement as the E Party flag bearer. If I had a nickel for every time his face was on the news… well, you know.

Candidate Allen, sensing that Mr. Robinson and the E Party might totally disrupt the Democrat's stranglehold on Illinois government, has gone on the offensive. Without mentioning Robinson by name, Allen is suddenly applauding efforts to advance the cause of education reform. Conversely, while repeatedly referring to candidate Stewart by name, he castigated the Democrats for decades of neglect and dispassion with respect to the children of Illinois.

Stewart, not to be outdone, applauded the great work of the Speaker and the Democrats in the legislature for their ground-breaking education program (failing, of course, to mention there never was one) while praising the work ethic of the fine teachers in Illinois. At each venue, he was also noticeably surrounded by a rainbow of teachers and union leaders, all with their obligatory lapel pins.

Stewart called for three debates. Allen, not to be outdone, has called for four. Tom Robinson merely offered to show up anywhere, anytime, on twenty-four hours' notice.

In other news…

* * * * * * * * * * * * * * * *

E-MAIL

To: Atlas, General
From: Lauren
Sent: 9/26 2:55 p.m. (PST)
Subject: Twitter

I believe we have found a way to re-engineer Twitter signals, allowing us to pirate the sender universe for the campaign of negatives the Democrats have launched and put out an immediate response/rebuttal to any rumor mongering. As to any FCC issues, let's leave this at don't ask, don't tell.

* * * * * * * * * * * * * * * *

E-MAIL

To: State Central Committee
From: Elizabeth DiMaggio
Sent: 9/26 8:30 a.m. (CST)
Subject: Polling

It's one week since Tom Robinson was on the Kathryn Collins show, and as you will see from the crosstabs, there has been a massive shift.

Allen continues to lead for governor. Robinson has shot to the low 20's with galactic favorables, particularly bolstered by inner-city minority voters. Stewart has dropped almost one-for-one in reverse relation to Robinson.

Surprisingly, most representative and Senate races remain constant. No Robinson effect as of yet.

* * * * * * * * * * * * * * * *

"Mr. Speaker. I have Danny Ryan on line two."

"Daniel. I have reviewed the polling and I agree that immediate action is required to bolster Stewart.

"At this point, I do not think he can regroup without immediate star power reinforcements," Danny noted. "Can we get the president? Particularly for a quick city-based tour?"

"Unfortunately," the Speaker replied, "both the president and vice president are out. Cobb has made Illinois radioactive. Focus on Hollywood types and athletes. Get me a list of recommendations as soon as possible. I will also alert our union and other friends to the situation."

* * * * * * * * * * * * * * * *

THE BACK BENCH
"If you let it slip, we catch it"

September 29

EXTRA EXTRA EXTRA EXTRA

Judge Suffredin called an impromptu news conference today to announce that he is recusing himself from *U.S. v. Stein*.

While strenuously denying any outside influence in the case, he neatly spun the situation to the interests of fairness and justice.

Speculation is that the chief judge may take her sweet time appointing a replacement.

In other news…

THE BACK BENCH
"If you let it slip, we catch it"

September 30

Shortly after Judge Suffredin recused himself yesterday in *U.S. v. Stein*, Republican Congressman Simon from the 19th Congressional District of Illinois called for a federal inquiry. Citing rumors with sufficient circulation to have achieved semi-truth status, he attacked Eddie Cobb and the entire Democratic label for hijacking the judicial system.

Elaine Richards, counsel for the defense, applauded Judge Suffredin for his decision, conveniently avoiding her roll in the related character assassination. She made a plea for release of the E Party funds, so as to level the playing field.

Every Democrat this side of the Mississippi was conveniently indisposed and unavailable for comment.

In other news…

* * * * * * * * * * * * * * * *

"Nancy, it's Danny. Sorry I missed you. Can I entice you with a plate of C&C? Say 1 o'clock tomorrow at Leo's? I'll assume we're on unless I hear from you."

* * * * * * * * * * * * * * * *

THE BACK BENCH
"If you let it slip, we catch it"

October 6

With the first of three gubernatorial candidate debates scheduled for next week, the campaigns have slowed somewhat. This is a common pattern for a variety of reasons: (1) the candidates need to devote time to preparation; (2) they need to observe the time honored tradition of allowing their surrogates to set the stage, either dampening or heightening expectations as required; and (3) they want the debate to frame the news. As suggested, surrogates and talking heads have been yakking likely voters to death.

As we have come to suspect, the E Party has broken the mold. Tom Robinson has chosen to signal his first punch. He announced that he will ask each of his opponents to declare if they support or oppose the E Party legislative package in its entirety. Yes or No. If either indicates support, he expects a signed oath to work for passage in the spring legislative session.

Quite the catch-22. If either goes along, they strengthen the E Party message. If they don't, they look weak on education. Allen is a lock. How Stewart handles this is a toss-up. Vegas odds-makers would be at least 7-2 against.

In another pre-debate custom, polls are being leaked. This is usually designed to set the stage for the bounce polls to be leaked post-debate. Whether you are a Democrat or a Republican, you have to take note of the Robinson numbers. Depending on the poll, anywhere from 15 to 20 percent of likely voters support him. More importantly, he has huge favorables and miniscule unfavorables; the kind of numbers from which upsets occur. The unmentionable is whether either the Bradley effect or the more recent Obama effect are at work. Unspoken or not, my political guru friends tell me that race will be a major issue, if not already.

In other news…

* * * * * * * * * * * * * * * *

"Hello, gorgeous," said Danny sweetly.

Nancy Rae chose not to respond in kind. "Hey, champ," she said weakly.

"You, OK?" he asked her, concerned.

"Sure, just been a little under the weather. Who knows, might be that Swine Flu they're talking about. Going on a week now."

"Sorry to hear. I hope you're feeling better."

"I'll be fine. How's the war?"

"Unlike any war to date. Never seen the Speaker so unsettled. We're normally on cruise control at this point. But it's four weeks and counting and he's calling a new play every day."

"I figured he'd be calling my number by now. Needs to run a little misdirection, right?" she guessed.

"You could call it that. It's definitely not fullback off center. Here's the deal. Robinson is killing us. Stewart is dropping fast and it's that base of minority votes we love to take for granted. Inner city minorities, predominantly black. If Stewart can't hold 76 percent of the black vote in a three-way, it's over. Right now, he's only at 65 and fading. We've got every celebrity under the sun dancing and prancing."

"So, where's the president?" she quickly asked.

"I think you know the answer to that. Rhymes with Cobb. And although they're not saying, I'm guessing his own electoral clock is ticking. Supporting Stewart against Robinson is not necessarily the smart play from where he sits."

"So where do I come in?" she asked in her best imitation of the cross-examining lawyer who already knows which answer to expect.

"Your word: misdirection. We need to take Robinson down. Quickly, quietly, and without fingerprints. But the Speaker's not calling your number. I am."

"Danny, I wish this was about the Speaker because I've never said no to you in twenty years, no matter how crazy the ask. But I came here today knowing that this is the one time I can't be there for you."

"You've got to be shitting me. This is for the map and who knows what else. This is Gettysburg. We win, it's over. We lose and…" he hesitated.

"Stop, Danny. If it's about getting to sixty, I'm on the program. But Robinson is off limits. In fact, I want you to tell that to the Speaker for me. If you can't, give him my cell. I don't think either of you want to face the consequences. Go back and read Senate Bill 986: Ethics Reform. It requires legislators to report all contacts with lobbyists. Then check the reports your guys have submitted and tell me how much reported time was spent with yours truly. In case the Speaker is interested, I've taken the liberty of keeping track."

"Jesus Christ, Nancy, not you. You can't be buying his bullshit."

"It's not that at all, Danny. But it's off limits. And so's Robinson. End of conversation."

* * * * * * * * * * * * * * * *

E-MAIL
To: Atlas, General
From: Mark
Sent: 10/9 6:03 p.m. (CST)
Subject: September 30 Campaign Financials

As we expected, based on their September 30 reports, both parties are adequately funded. Even if it's not optimally distributed among the candidate field, as you well know, there are no impediments to reshuffling in Illinois. We can expect maximum TV buys, radio ads, etc.—the full Monty.

The trick for the Democrats will be how to best protect all flanks. Based on current polling, it's hard to see them getting to sixty without abandoning Stewart. That should be the Speaker's favored bet. If the money starts to move in that direction, we will have to consider Plan B.

* * * * * * * * * * * * * * * *

E-MAIL
To: General, Atlas
From: Mark
Sent: 10/10 8:47 p.m. (CST)
Subject: Weekend Canvass

Until you experience it, you can't overestimate the power of Kathryn Collins, Tom Robinson, et al. We scored more pluses from just two days in the field than in the entirety of the last campaign. If the polls match, we are back in the game.

* * * * * * * * * * * * * * * *

THE BACK BENCH
"If you let it slip, we catch it"

October 11

On the eve of the first debate among the candidates for governor, Republican candidate Allen announced that he accepts Tom Robinson's challenge. He will support the E Party education package and will sign the oath.

This preemptive strike is drawing cynical, but congratulatory, blog support. Allen gets out in front of Stewart on education and can join Robinson, if the opportunity arises, in taking him to task for being weak on education.

Robinson released a statement commending Allen for his bold commitment.

In other news…

THE BACK BENCH
"If you let it slip, we catch it"

October 11

EXTRA EXTRA EXTRA EXTRA

Democratic candidate for governor, Stewart, just released a statement joining Republican candidate Allen in support of the E Party education proposal.

More to follow in tomorrow's debate wrap-up.

In other news…

CHAPTER TWENTY-THREE

THE BACK BENCH

"If you let it slip, we catch it"

October 12

It wasn't the knock down, drag out variety of debate we anticipated, but it had its share of body blows, and on occasion, both Stewart and Allen were staggered.

Neither took on Robinson directly, but in a bizarre twist, Robinson came close to suicide by refusing to respond to questions not focused on education, ethics or the budget. In a move reminiscent of the E Party legislators, particularly in their first legislative session, he declared all other issues to be moot points until the education reforms are enacted. That left the door open for Stewart and Allen to pander to their respective bases on abortion, guns, the environment, ad nauseum.

However, Robinson's advantage on education was so dominant, it may have overcome his misguided obstinance. With both opponents having committed to the reform package, Robinson was free to pound away regarding his "Getting to 21" initiative. His command of the facts, and from the heart sincerity, produced the debates' finest moments. In his closing remarks, he paraphrased the Gipper with the line of the campaign: "When it comes to education, have your children been better prepared to face life's challenges than you were? If not, join with me to make that happen."

Stewart and Allen were not without their fifteen seconds of sound bite fame. Allen scored heavily by linking Stewart to Blagojevich, while Stewart vigorously invoked George Bush.

It was ugly, but seemingly effective. Sometimes I think we should just let the pollsters debate.

In other news…

THE BACK BENCH
"If you let it slip, we catch it"

October 16

The first post debate polls are out. In a joint *Chicago Sun Times*/Better Business Bureau poll, Allen holds a decent lead over Stewart, with Robinson creeping into the low 20's. The complete results are posted on the blog.

This is also the first poll to track all the statewide races, and somewhat surprisingly, Robinson's not keeping the entire E ticket competitive.

If the election were held today, the Speaker would be at or about sixty. It's not clear why Robinson is not providing legislative coattails. However, the blog commentators are reporting some of the nastiest stuff ever being used in legislative races. Or, do I say that in every election cycle?

In other news…

THE BACK BENCH
"If you let it slip, we catch it"

October 17

EXTRA EXTRA EXTRA EXTRA

In a move that defies all political logic (oxymoron intended), Lisa Boudreau of the E Party today announced that it will not press to have Judge Suffredin replaced prior to the election.

Tom Robinson spoke at the conclusion of her remarks and upped the ante. He announced that the E Party would not be running any commercials nor mailing any political literature in this campaign.

They will be relying solely on their field operation and earned PR, whether through newspapers, TV, radio or Internet. They are, in his words, "taking back democracy by engaging the voters one-on-one."

Given that they probably wouldn't have gained the release of their stash in time to make a difference, it is a somewhat hollow gesture. But, once again, they have captured the imagination of the reporting syndicate. This is the third straight week they have dominated all news outlets.

In other news…

* * * * * * * * * * * * * * * *

"Mr. Grusin, I have Elizabeth DiMaggio for you. Do you wish to take the call?"

"Elizabeth. What a pleasant surprise. Allen's numbers are looking good. Let me guess—money?"

"No, actually the funding is solid. It's the polling. Tom Robinson's numbers are gradually climbing and getting a little too strong for comfort. I would have bet my life that the Democrats would be in full attack mode, but they're clearly not. If Stewart keeps sinking, Robinson becomes a solid threat. As things stand, if the undecideds break big for the E Party, Robinson can sneak in. If the Speaker won't attack, I'm afraid it's on us. So my question is this: Can you develop an effective 527 organization attack on Robinson without entangling Allen? Even better, can it look like Mr. Cobb is the source of mischief?"

"Elizabeth, I like it. Let me work on it. Give me a few days."

* * * * * * * * * * * * * * * *

Atlas was not pleased when Clay advised there would be company for dinner. He was further annoyed when Liz did not immediately respond to his e-mail inquiry. But he was overjoyed when Clay returned from the airport with K.C.

Her occasional trips to Aspen had managed to keep him in perspective. The world of politics had proven more challenging and debilitating than he anticipated. But she was continuously able to direct him to the silver linings.

For K.C., the trips were part of the healing process enabled by the E Party experience. And above all else, they meant time with Alex; always the homecoming.

"This better be good," he teased her. "Last time you showed up unexpectedly, I lost all my money."

"Well," she laughed, "I was in the neighborhood and felt like dancing. I asked Liz to book us at the Caribou Club. As I recall, last time we never even made it to dinner. So I figured you owed me."

"Done," Atlas said and smiled at her warmly. "Can't disappoint Liz, can we? I'll get changed while you unpack and freshen up. Remember, Colorado chic."

* * * * * * * * * * * * * * * *

"Perhaps we should order quickly before the General appears with more atrocious news," quipped Atlas.

"Quite," said K.C. "But I have it on good authority that we won't be bothered tonight. I've left strict instructions."

"You make it sound so serious."

"Actually, Alex, I came to be wined and dined, but I do have a rather serious agenda."

"In that case, let's put business before pleasure. Dancing starts in just over two hours and I took that as an order."

"Very well. Alex, I have a proposition regarding political contributions. And I want you to hear me out before you interrupt."

"Then you have my word. I'm all ears."

"Thank you. As you know, we now have individual campaign web sites established for all individual E Party candidates, save Tom Robinson and Barbara Jenkins."

"Outstanding! Sorry, continue. More wine?"

"Yes, please. Mark thinks the average legislative campaign needs at least $100,000. In districts where our opponents are particularly well funded or other extenuating circumstances exist, as much as $200,000. The statewide candidates require $1 million on average to remain competitive and at least twice that to have any chance of winning. Having said that, at some point we need to assess our expectations for that group. Ballpark—I estimate $8 million on the low end and $16 million on the upper end.

"As you are well aware, Lisa and Elaine Richards have done a masterful job of rehabilitating public opinion in the tax case. You are now the world's most sympathetic billionaire. Tom has done an equally wonderful job of carrying the campaign on his shoulders. I don't know what ASC research would predict, but Julie Kersten-Covington predicts that the undecided voters of Illinois are clamoring to get on board. I also know that public funding at the party level, particularly in the wake of the tax case, is anathema to you. In addition to realizing Atlas-style victories into the future, I understand the importance to you of keeping the "E" in team as the saying goes. Agreed?"

"Agreed."

"So, here's my proposition. I am prepared to fund the entire campaign and settle all debts from the budget contest."

"But…," started Atlas.

"Ah, ah," she cautioned. "I finish, remember? I can easily afford it. It solves every issue we face from a financial perspective. I am not party to *U.S. v. Stein* and they'll really look like assholes if they go after me. It honors and fosters all of the goals you have set down. It gives us a chance to really push the envelope. And, the General says if you don't take the deal, he'll kick the shit out of you. Now…you can have the floor."

"Somehow I'm sensing 'let me think it over' is not an option."

"Not necessarily," she grinned. "Think it over all you want as long as you say yes before the music starts."

"K.C., I don't know. It's a truly wonderful offer, but it's too much to ask. I don't know that it's legal and I would not be able to pay you back…not even when my funds are released. I'm fairly certain that would violate campaign finance laws."

"Alex, I'm not asking to be paid back. I want to do this. And, I need to do this."

Even in hindsight, he would not have expected tears to begin flowing uncontrollably. But K.C. became inconsolable and left the table.

"Is this seat taken?" she joked upon returning. "After that display, I wasn't sure you'd be here when I got back."

"And miss dancing?" he smiled softly.

"Alex. Let's try something one more time. I talk and you listen without interruption. Deal?"

"Deal."

"It's been just over forty years since Patrick and I wrote that letter. In all these years, you never asked for or even hinted that an explanation was due and owing. Patrick and I thoroughly discussed this situation and we decided that I could and would pick the time for that explanation. That moment has come."

"But…," Alex attempted to speak.

"Ah, ah…," she again cautioned.

"When your father died and you went to Chicago, Patrick and I became close friends. Certainly, the odd couple, but nevertheless, our bond was unbreakable. All the while, our relationship remained platonic. I was in love with you. One night, during the Kennedy campaign, we attended a fundraising event at the home of Patrick's parents. It was one of those, 'I don't remember what happened' kind of evenings, and Patrick and I awoke in his bed. That evening was anything but platonic because, soon thereafter, the rabbit was dying and my life was turned upside down.

"We were in our twenties. Things were a mess. You were in Chicago. *Roe v. Wade* was light-years away. And, my dear friend chose chivalry. With you, we chose cowardice; a decision that we woefully regretted until the day you rang our bell. And God bless that day.

"I must tell you, and I'm sure you know, how blessed I was to marry Patrick. As fine a man as I have ever known and the greatest friend any woman could have. We were very happy together and I cherish his memory.

"But I also must tell you," she said while again fighting back the tears, "I have never stopped loving you. To this day, I still carry the stupid pen from Intro Psyche class at Harvard. I have every letter you ever sent, every gift, no matter how trivial. And, most importantly, I have Patrick's blessings.

"So, it's actually a package deal. The money comes with me."

* * * * * * * * * * * * * * * *

E-MAIL

To: General
From: K.C.
Sent: 10/18 11:14 p.m. (MST)
Subject: You Win The Bet

We're eloping to Vegas. As you suggested, I made him an offer he couldn't refuse.

* * * * * * * * * * * * * * * *

E-MAIL
To: General
From: Atlas
Sent: 10/19 5:18 a.m. (PST)
Subject: What Happens In Vegas

I need a best man. Liz has you booked on the 11:36 a.m. Southwest flight. The ceremony is set for 5 o'clock. Thanks for everything, old friend.

* * * * * * * * * * * * * * * *

THE BACK BENCH

"If you let it slip, we catch it"

October 20

The second gubernatorial debate produced an interesting juxtaposition. In the first, Tom Robinson played offense, whereas last night he was forced to play defense.

Jeff Stewart, the Democratic candidate, launched an attack on the E Party. He said it is a secret cabal funded by a billionaire from Colorado and lead by a secret team of decision makers, most of whom have no ties or loyalty to Illinois.

Robinson deflected this attack by refocusing on the individual legislators elected by the citizens of Illinois and their great work to date, citing ethics reform, budget reform, and education reform proposals.

The rebuttal was effective, but Stewart shot back that this group was merely a group of puppets led by a secret puppet master. Borrowing from *The Wizard of Oz*, he alluded to Stein as the man behind the curtain. To make his case, he declared the environment, healthcare, and gun violence also to be great issues of the day, but said the E Party puppets refused to vote because the great and powerful Oz told them not to.

Robinson deflected to the E Party paradigm that, as a minority, they have chosen to prioritize their focus elsewhere. On this point, he was less than convincing. Look for increasing attacks from the Democrats on these themes.

Allen tried to gain some moral high ground on education. He reminded the audience of his commitment to education, including the E Party legislative package. At the same time, he also went back to his Republican roots and attacked Robinson's "Getting to 21" initiative.

In his finest Republican-speak, he said the costs would be excessive, requiring tax increases to implement, *and* that it would be one more large government take-over attempt.

Robinson was, again, weak in response. The Republicans will undoubtedly use these points as a beachhead.

To his credit, Robinson scored points of his own. He spoke passionately about what the E Party represents, pointed to changes in Illinois government and politics that would not exist without the E Party, all the while reinforcing with sports analogies that resonated in the initial post debate polling.

In other news…

* * * * * * * * * * * * * * * *

E-MAIL

To: Speaker
From: Danny Ryan
Sent: 10/21 5:06 p.m. (CST)
Subject: Polls

As indicated in the attached, the governor's race continues to trend against us, although Robinson's ascent has abated some. However, almost all of his gains continue at our expense. Fortunately, we still retain separation between Robinson, the E Party, and their legislative candidates.

To that end, I am suggesting a reallocation of resources. Most, if not all, of the new E candidates are foundering without funding. I suggest we halve our field component in all of the races where we are up with at least 55 percent based on likely voters. My recommendations for reallocation are detailed in the attachment.

Finally, the negative campaign against Allen has not produced. His unfavorable ratings jumped three points, but his lead over Stewart remains disturbing. Please advise.

* * * * * * * * * * * * * * * *

THE BACK BENCH

"If you let it slip, we catch it"

October 22

I have often found the vice presidential debates to be more insightful and informative than the presidential debates. Last night's lieutenant governor candidates' forum was no exception.

For the uninformed, the candidates are: Kyle Witte (D), Judith Wimmer (R), and Barbara Jenkins (E).

Witte, the Democratic candidate, is the sitting mayor of Decatur, Illinois, a position he has held for more than ten years. Although his place on the ticket makes the Democrat pairing devoid of racial or sexual diversity at the top, he brings many pluses: downstate to Stewart's Chicago base; executive experience to Stewart's legislative; and an extremely solid union background, having spent his entire career in the workforce with the UAW. During his tenure as mayor, he has leveraged his union and political relationships to bring significant economic development to Decatur. Finally, he offers a bit of philosophical diversity in that, given downstate roots, he is decidedly pro-gun.

During the debate, Witte stuck to the Democratic script, but brought a passion that Stewart sorely lacks. He features a Southern style of straight talk that connects well. He also sufficiently honored the tradition of attacking both Allen and Robinson in ways that Stewart has proven either unwilling or inept to date.

Wimmer, the Republican candidate, is a sitting state representative from Will County, just south of Chicago. Although not providing meaningful geographic diversity, Will County is quite different than Allen's Northwest suburban base. She is also more conservative, in a Palin-like outreach to that subset of the Republican base. Whereas she is known as a tough negotiator, her public persona is lipstick sans pit bull. Not unlike the Democratic team, no doubt a gaggle of political consultants spit her out after digesting reams of polling data.

During the debate she advocated leadership and education themes and stressed the importance of her legislative experience, while also walking that fine line of not wanting to be an insider. Her attacks were more subtle and directed at "years of stagnation," as she called it, on the part of the "democratically controlled government." At the same time, she was profuse in her praise of Tom Robinson and the recent accomplishments of the E Party. No doubt, all gaggle driven.

Barbara Jenkins, the E Party candidate, has been the caucus chair for their brief encounter of the third kind. Given that the E Party still defies the stereotyping we journalists are so desperate to impose, she does represent the themes of recognized leadership and dedication to education its base generally reflects. Of course, the most unique feature of their ticket is that both the candidate for governor and lieutenant governor are black, a fact that has not escaped their adversaries, who embrace stereotyping as a way to introduce negativity.

She was particularly well prepared, and consistent with her running mate, preached their education platform. Whereas Tom Robinson leans emotionally toward "Getting to 21," Jenkins was focused on the work of the E Party legislative team. Also consistent with the E Party mantra, she sidestepped the usual Democrat v. Republican dueling issues related to guns, abortion, etc. She also sidestepped when given the opportunity to either praise or damn her opponents, choosing instead to emphasize the record and vision of the E Party.

All in all, a lively evening with sufficient sound bites for the participants and their sponsors to breathe a collective sigh of relief.

In other news…

* * * * * * * * * * * * * * * *

E-MAIL

To: Atlas, General
From: Mark
Sent: 10/23 7:17 p.m. (CST)
Subject: Polling

With just under two weeks remaining, we continue to tread water. Our incumbents are viable, but the trending of the unfavorables continues unabated. The field operation is valiant, but can't support the numbers. At a minimum, we have to find a way to fund phone banks.

The new candidates can't catch their breath. The negative campaigns are daunting and they do not have a sufficient voice to respond. In almost all cases, they face a seasoned incumbent calling in all chits.

Take the 83rd Legislative District. Richard Hollis is the incumbent. He has held the seat for fourteen years and in the last four cycles he has not been challenged.

He votes with the unions 97 percent of the time, and is rated B or higher by the pro choice, green and anti-gun lobbies. He had $167,000 reported at September 30, and has been on cable with fluffy stuff for four weeks. His first three mail pieces played to the Democrat's base. His favorables/negatives are 53/21.

Our challenger, Will Reimers, has lived his entire life in the district. He is a successful businessman and has held leadership posts in the Rotary, Scouts and PTA. He and his wife attend the Presbyterian church and their children are exemplary in education and sports.

We have a field operation in excess of 250 volunteers, but over the course of a weekend, they are managing less than 100 meaningful engagements each, generally resulting in ten or less plus encounters. At the rate of 2,500 plus encounters per weekend, we are not in the game.

The demographic is more suburban and the average voting age is just under forty. Tom Robinson does relatively well, but the percentage of minority voters is below 20 percent.

At this stage in the last cycle, we would have already delivered five to seven positive mail pieces and phone banks for three to four weeks. On his best day, our boy scout candidate and family only polls 38 percent name recognition among likely voters.

If Elizabeth DiMaggio were running an opponent, she would be attacking on at least ten very defective votes Hollis has made, including two significant tax votes and a bill in 2002 that allowed a connected Democrat fundraiser to work a significantly advantageous sale and leaseback deal with the state.

The shame is, another quality candidate is losing to a political mope who, to date, is outspending him $87,000 to $3,500, the latter amount being a candidate loan to keep the campaign office open after the tax case was filed.

Change the name; change the district. The results are the same. Unless the cavalry arrives soon, he loses at least 60-40.

At some point, we either have to cut the Reimer's of the world loose or honor our commitment: beg, borrow or steal.

* * * * * * * * * * * * * * * *

THE BACK BENCH

"If you let it slip, we catch it"

October 24

Tom Robinson has more than held his own in the campaign for governor. He is eloquent and passionate when he talks education, his "Getting to 21" initiative in particular. He has been tireless and ubiquitous.

Yet, in most polling, he is still in the low to mid-20's, and without funds, not poised to move up sufficiently to be competitive.

Regardless, a little known 527 organization calling itself the Crusade for Campaign Reform has launched a series of attacks on Robinson and the E Party.

The attacks are consistent with some of the themes raised by Allen in the last debate, but as the Republicans need Robinson to stay viable, it is unlikely they would lead this charge. The Democrats need an effective response to Robinson, but this is not Democrat scriptology. All rather puzzling.

In other news…

THE BACK BENCH

"If you let it slip, we catch it"

October 24

EXTRA EXTRA EXTRA EXTRA

The E Party's financial prowess has again manifested itself. It was reported yesterday that each E Party legislative candidate received at least $100,000 in campaign contributions while each statewide candidate other than Tom Robinson received at least $1 million. In total, close to $10 million in contributions were reported.

Even more curious than the amounts was the donor and the donor's address. All funds were received from the Estate of Mr. Patrick Covington, New York, New York. The executor of the estate, a New York attorney by the name of Sarah Kane, could not be reached for comment.

This reporter has never known a contribution to be made out of an estate. *The Back Bench* contacted attorney Alyssa Rowley, an estate planning expert. She indicated that this was a highly unusual circumstance and could only be undertaken if the Will included a specific bequest.

Lisa Boudreau, spokesperson for the E Party, called an afternoon press conference to head off any controversy at this late date in the campaign. Any further financial irregularities by the E Party, real or imagined, could doom their entire ticket. She indicated that the funds were released only after the E Party obtained opinions from both New York and Chicago counsel that the transfers are legal under the laws of both jurisdictions. She further indicated that the written opinions would be publicly released.

In addition to fielding questions concerning the contributions, Ms. Boudreau spoke to the inconsistency between Tom Robinson's recent comments and the use to which these funds would be put.

Mr. Robinson recently declared that the E Party would not be running commercials nor mailing any political literature in this campaign. His comments were made following the E Party declaration that it would not press for expedited release of its frozen funds.

Ms. Boudreau said that neither the party nor Mr. Robinson would accept contributions. However, in fairness to the other individual candidates, they were free to make their own determinations with respect to accepting and allocating contributions.

In a separate legal opinion that was released, Elaine Richards, counsel to the E Party in the Stein case, indicates that these funds are not subject to the judge's freeze order. The donor has no ties to the case and the contributions are being made to separate and distinct political funds.

Although it is extremely late in the campaign, seasoned wonks we contacted said the funds might be timely assuming the candidates had been active in the field and previously developed campaign materials that could be quickly produced and distributed. Given the sophistication of the E Party, it is hard to imagine that they would lack that discipline.

In other news…

* * * * * * * * * * * * * * * *

"Mr. Speaker. I have Daniel on line one."

"Daniel. I need an instant analysis of every legislative race involving an E Party candidate. We have to assume they have mail pieces ready to go and pre-arranged media buys.

"Ignore any race where the polls have us at plus 20 or greater. But give me your gut on any race where a huge pop from an E candidate could create a risk, particularly where we have high negatives.

"Finally, start pounding on the source of their money. Play on any weakness for the district's likely voters. Remember F.D.R.—give 'em something to fear. And, crank up that Twitter network. No telling how convoluted this can get—all to our advantage.

"Call me tonight as soon as the report is ready—no matter what the hour."

* * * * * * * * * * * * * * * *

THE BACK BENCH
"If you let it slip, we catch it"

October 25

Last night's final debate among the candidates for governor will long be remembered for both its intensity and late drama.

Stewart, now as many as eight points down with likely voters, launched an all out attack on Allen. It got personal and then it got ugly. In all, it smelled of a desperate candidate. Had some of these attacks been leveled earlier in the campaign, particularly by a surrogate or two, this last debate may have presented as a way to close the gap. Coming at the end, Stewart came across as too desperate and too harsh.

Notwithstanding, Allen has not run a substantive campaign and the attacks do have a basis in fact. He did fail to pay income taxes on a controversial swap transaction and ultimately paid significant fines and penalties. His business also did once hire low wage foreign workers at a time when the local work force was experiencing unusually high unemployment because of a plant closing.

All of which might inure to the benefit of Tom Robinson. Robinson, however, appeared to snatch defeat from the jaws of victory. In response to a question from Brian Staples of the *Decatur Tribune*, one of the debate facilitators, Robinson stated that he was not qualified to serve as governor. I believe the question was intended as a softball so Robinson could respond to a recent series of commercials from a hostile 527 organization. Instead of hitting it out of the park, Robinson swung and missed. There were enough awful sound bites in his answer to float an armada of swift boats.

So who won? Beats me. More like a three-way tie for last.

In other news…

* * * * * * * * * * * * * * * *

E-MAIL

To:	Speaker
From:	Danny Ryan
Sent:	10/25 6:30 a.m. (CST)
Subject:	Final Push

The attached memo reflects our recent discussions. It contains the plan for the last ten days, G.O.T.V. and polling operations. Among the prominent changes are the following:

Legislative Candidates: All will see at least four mail pieces drop. Two negative, one positive and one closing piece; endorsement based if we capture sufficient editorial support. We will be in the field both weekends canvassing plus/minus and dropping pieces based on the most recent polls. In any race within five points, either way, we will be running cable in all markets.

Statewide Candidates: We will be running statewide cable and targeted network featuring the "Tom Robinson says he isn't qualified" piece, and the "There's more to governing than education" piece. In a break from our historic statewide media outreach, we will also be using targeted mail; hard hitting negatives where we are weak to help to suppress turnout and wave the flag stuff in our core areas to drive turnout.

At this point, it's safe to say there will be no Air Force One sightings. However, we have various surrogates, including cabinet officials and celebrities scheduled for a series of rallies and demonstrations across the state. All have been matched to maximize demographics based on likely voter profiling.

Finally, if needed, we have the infomercial set to run the last three days. Depending on polling, we can pull it back to hold down costs.

G.O.T.V. and polling operations are pretty much status quo. On the plus side, we have significantly enhanced our runner capabilities, supported by vehicles, to get the elderly and no-shows to the polls.

* * * * * * * * * * * * * * * *

THE BACK BENCH

"If you let it slip, we catch it"

October 27

EXTRA EXTRA EXTRA EXTRA

One mystery solved. A new one surfaces.

The E Party today released legal opinions, probate documents and legal memoranda to support the recent contributions from the Covington Estate. I'm sure there are myriad attorneys combing every verb and participle to find either a news story or a political attack piece. I subscribe to the "it looks thick enough to be legit" school of journalism.

What caught my attention, however, was a new name: Julie Kersten-Covington, wife of the deceased. It was apparently Mrs. Covington who directed the executor to cut the checks. To me, that becomes the story. "Widow parts with $10+ million." You know what they say, follow the money.

In other news…

* * * * * * * * * * * * * * * *

"Sherlock, it's Mark."

"Hello, stranger. I thought my wise-assing might earn me some cell time with you."

"So nice of you to keep the cauldron stirred."

"Sorry. End of campaign fatigue."

"Breakfast?"

"How's nine-thirty? End of campaign fatigue."

* * * * * * * * * * * * * * * *

THE BACK BENCH
"If you let it slip, we catch it"

October 28

This may be a little too soap opera for my tastes, but Mrs. Covington is apparently now Mrs. Stein. However, before you conspiracy theory my blog to death, read on.

Alex Stein, Julie Kersten and Patrick Covington, the deceased, were life-long buddies. Covington, playing Crosby, got the girl after college. But, Stein, playing Hope, also gets the girl after her husband succumbs to a tragic illness. In between, it's one long, happy road movie with the E Party being the last scene. Among other things, "K.C." as she's known, has been the mastermind behind all of the candidate issue development, including the staging and rollout of the education package.

There is obviously a marvelous story here somewhere, but not the makings of a last minute voter backlash. At least not until Mr. Ryan does his best spin-mongering.

In other news…

* * * * * * * * * * * * * * * *

E-MAIL

To: Atlas, General, K.C., Lisa, Lauren
From: Mark
Sent: 10/28 9:01 p.m. (CST)
Subject: Final Sprint

I keep thinking of that great scene from *Hunt for Red October*. The Soviet captain has launched his torpedo at the Red October with the safety mechanism disabled. All of a sudden, the Dallas draws the torpedo away from the super secret Soviet submarine about to defect and the torpedo ultimately blows up the Russian attacker.

When they make the movie about this campaign, let's hope that K.C.'s heroic diversion allows us to avoid disaster while the Democrats sink themselves. After just two mail pieces and moderate cable, our legislative candidates, particularly the new challengers, appear to have dodged the torpedo. The undecideds have been breaking 4 to 1 in our favor. If the weekend canvass confirms this data, we can hold the majority of our incumbents and possibly look to gain seats.

The statewide candidates have gained some footing, although not enough in any one race to hint at victory. But certainly enough to give some Republican candidates a chance to upset the Democrat's apple cart.

Tom's race is extremely difficult to read. He still hasn't broken 30 percent in any poll but his favorables jumped after the last debate. The voters seem to appreciate his honesty, but at the same time, also took him at his word that he is not qualified. I expect a televised double whammy attack about to unfold. This is likely his high water mark.

His only hope lies with Lisa and Lauren. Lisa is pushing the editorial boards and has scheduled some star power events with former ballplayers. Representative Jenkins has appealed to Billy Shakespeare for a YouTube based E Party tribute. If only the 18 to 24 crowd would vote. They may be Billy's devotees, but less than 70 percent were alive when Tom was playing. Still worth the shot, especially to boost the legislative candidates.

The General and Lauren are ready for G.O.T.V. Lauren has super-teched the field operation and the General has the troops primed and ready to go. Once data from the final weekend canvass has been input, we will make any necessary last minute adjustments to resources. Anyone not within ten points will have to be cut loose.

* * * * * * * * * * * * * * * *

E-MAIL

To: Scott Grusin
From: Elizabeth DiMaggio
Sent: 10/29 11:56 a.m. (CST)
Subject: Last Call

One week to go and Allen is well-positioned. The 527 organization stuff, both the originals and the follow-up pieces, has halted Robinson in his tracks.

Thank you for suggesting and funding the G.O.T.V. phone banks. We just don't have the manpower to match the Democrats on the street.

At this point, anything that can call attention to the Eddie Cobb connection will help. In addition to getting our voters to the polls, dampening Democrat spirits and influencing the undecideds is welcome.

Let's plan to talk election night.

* * * * * * * * * * * * * * * *

"Danny, it's Nancy Rae. I thought we had a deal."

"Nancy! We have an understanding, yes."

"Then pull your ads."

"What ads?"

"Don't be fuckin' cute with me, Danny. Sometime in the next ten minutes, and at least every ten minutes after that, I'm gonna see

Tom Robinson in a commercial, paid for by the Democratic Party of Illinois, announcing that he is unqualified to be governor. That fuckin' ad, Danny."

"Whoa Rae, take a breath. Calm down. Yes, that's our ad. But that's Robinson, in his own words, at the debate. It's not Willie Horton or anything. It's not fear and loathing. It's not even near the line. It's your guy, his words, public forum."

"And, it's negative, negative, fucking negative! Should I spell that for you? It's there to bring him down. End of point. End of story."

"Settle down. Let's talk. Meet me at Leo's this afternoon?"

"Danny. I'll meet you anywhere, anytime. You're my best friend. But Danny, the ad goes or I go off."

* * * * * * * * * * * * * * * *

THE BACK BENCH

"If you let it slip, we catch it"

October 31

Endorsement week is upon us. Although *The Back Bench* does not endorse, we always report on endorsements by the press and other legitimate, independent third party media and other organizations.

This year, for any number of reasons, people seem to have kept their powder dry to the very end. The *Tribune* broke this morning and I suspect most will follow in the next few days. Our state's leading paper and traditional Republican cheerleader endorses…drum roll…Tom Robinson.

Sure, the *Tribune* has broken ranks before. Usually to back a sure winner. Endorsing local favorite Obama over McCain was a no-brainer. But Tom Robinson is third in the polls and, according to politically induced web chatter, a carpetbagger to boot.

The Tribune has declared editorial war on politics as usual. They have demanded ethics reform; open and honest government; and legitimate, no nonsense budgeting. Not a good time for "do what I say, not what I do." They also broke from tradition in not praising the non-endorsed with faint damn. They gave both Stewart and Allen a blast for being "business as usual, unimaginative and uninspiring party hacks" who "fail to understand the E Party is trying to take politics and government to a new and better place."

As for Robinson, they totally unwound his recent self-deprecating comment.

"Governing is about leadership and trust," they wrote. "**Tom Robinson** may not have the political pedigree we have come to associate with governing. Unlike Stewart, he hasn't worked his way up the party and held numerous figurehead committee and blue ribbon task force positions. And unlike Allen, he hasn't run a business or championed local charitable causes. **Tom Robinson** leads by example. He quietly inspired his teams with day-in, day-out perspiration and dedication. He has been inspiring children and parents for decades with honest, straight talk about sports, education, and the perils of the streets. And, he has boldly and proudly embraced education reforms that others avoid or ignore for a variety of parochial reasons. At a time and place where our electorate is begging for honesty, integrity and fresh ideas, **Tom Robinson** is totally qualified to serve as governor of Illinois and he is our endorsed candidate."

In other news…

CHAPTER TWENTY-FOUR

"Mr. Speaker. I have Danny Ryan on line three. He says it's urgent."

"Daniel. What's so urgent?"

"I just heard from Nancy Rae. She is all worked up over the latest Robinson ads. Says they have to be pulled as soon as possible, or else."

"And you think she's serious?"

"Very."

"What are our options?"

"You mean other than pulling the ads?"

"Exactly."

"Not many as I see it. If the press buys her story and it gets any kind of coverage, the damage could be insurmountable. Our negatives are too high already and we would have no time to respond. This would make that last minute Bush DUI story look like thumb sucking."

"That bad?"

"That bad. I shutter to think what Nancy Rae does while lobbying after hours. But I have a very good idea with whom."

"And she's willing to risk her career and livelihood? Not many make that kind of leap when they look over the precipice."

"In her case, I think it's safe to assume there are emotional blinders. I've known her for twenty years and you do not want to get in her way when she's on a mission."

"So Robinson gets a pass and Allen becomes governor? That is not an acceptable scenario for redistricting. My friend Elizabeth will jam this up our ass."

"Mr. Speaker, Stewart may not win even with the ads, but Nancy Rae will definitely jam her story up our ass. She can cost us ten to fifteen seats in each House. That scenario frightens me more than any other."

"Maybe there's another way. How much time can you buy me?"

"I've talked to the networks. Nothing can be done about today's programming, but we can pull anything for tomorrow as long as they are notified by midnight."

"Alright. Try to work some magic with your friend. Otherwise, unless you hear back from me by ten o'clock tonight, pull the ads."

* * * * * * * * * * * * * * * *

"General Smith, this is Dawn Eckersley calling for Speaker Kennedy. Would you be available for a call early this evening? Say seven o'clock? Thank you. I will place the call to this number."

* * * * * * * * * * * * * * * *

"Atlas, I hope you're sitting down because I just got off the phone with Speaker Kennedy. He's offering a deal."

"What are you talking about?"

"He called this afternoon to set it up and we just talked. He thinks Stewart is dead in the water. At the same time, the thought of Allen as governor is seemingly repulsive to him. He's willing to throw his support to Robinson."

"That's awfully generous of him. The Democrats go to great lengths to bribe a federal judge and coerce a U.S. attorney to stop us and now they want to be our friends. I can respond to that right now. Is 'fuck you' strong enough?"

"Let's not shoot the messenger. In fact, he apologized for Cobb up front. Says nothing would give him more pleasure than to defeat every one of our candidates. But he claims to have had no role in Cobb's scheme. Calls him a miscreant. When it's over, deal or no deal, win or lose, he will help us see that Mr. Cobb is drawn and quartered. I've only dealt with the guy once, but I'm giving him the benefit of the doubt."

"OK. So 'fuck you' may not be the socially acceptable response in this case. How 'bout 'up yours'? What does he want in return?"

"He essentially wants the same deal he has now. Assuming the Democrats do not achieve a majority in either chamber, we give them the votes. He stays Speaker and Fred Welk stays Senate president."

"Only if Tom wins?"

"Only if Tom wins. But practically speaking, he'll ask for the same deal if Allen wins."

"Sounds easy. What's the catch?"

"That's what I can't figure. I have a call in to Mark. If you're at least willing to consider, I'll get back to you after we talk."

"OK. Get with Mark and call me back. I'll talk this over with K.C."

* * * * * * * * * * * * * * * *

"Atlas, I've got Mark on a three-way."

"K.C. is on with me."

"Mark," started the General. "Why don't you tell Atlas and K.C. what you told me."

"Sure, thanks. Quite an interesting proposal from the Speaker. As I see it, this can only be about the map. If Allen becomes governor, he vetoes anything coming out of the legislature. At that point, unless the legislature overrides, which is doubtful, the map drawing process is delegated by lot. Should the Republicans win the draw, they have an excellent chance of producing a map that maximizes their power, especially for congressional candidates.

"We're the unknown. But he must figure on having a better chance of forging a deal with us than with Elizabeth DiMaggio. It's that simple. In the meantime, he also takes off the table any possibility that we cut bait with him and fish a few Republicans into Speaker and Senate president. From where he sits, not much downside."

"What about our downside?" asked Atlas.

"That's hard to gauge. We haven't contemplated a map strategy. We could be giving up a lot there by not working with the Republicans. If he can't envision a deal with the Republicans on the map, well I'm not about to out think the Speaker, especially on a moment's notice.

"The bigger risk, and this has to be your call Atlas, is that the E Party could be governing. That may be a one shot ticket to oblivion if we screw things up. On the other hand, if Robinson wins and he's effective as governor, well, you tell me."

"I've said it before," the General jumped in, "I'll take a chance at leading over following any day."

"K.C.?" summoned Atlas.

"Like Mark, I could use much more time. But my gut's with the Speaker."

"In that case," Atlas thought out loud, "what else do we want in return?"

* * * * * * * * * * * * * * * *

"Hello Daniel. How did it go with Ms. Mitchell?"

"Not well. We walked through a few alternatives, but she's dug in."

"From the picture you painted earlier, that's what I expected. Pull the ads. But here's what I also want you to do…"

* * * * * * * * * * * * * * * *

THE BACK BENCH

"If you let it slip, we catch it"

November 1

One weekend and four days total until the election. It's been quite a week.

For starters, Tom Robinson and the majority of the E candidates have swept the newspaper endorsements. Even the *Chicago Sun Times*, bastion of Democrat flag bearers, has spoken out for Tom Robinson. The Speaker's pipeline to the editorial board must have sprung a leak.

It's not only the unanimity; it's the quality of the appeal as well:

Chicago Sun Times: "…time for a shake up in Illinois politics."

Peoria Journal Star: "…bringing fresh ideas and idealism…"

Rockford Register Star: "…from the Blagojevich ashes, the State of Illinois has a chance to embrace lasting and meaningful change."

Decatur Tribune: "…the E Party has earned the chance to lead Illinois, and Tom Robinson has shown qualities we desperately need in our governor."

Chicago Defender: "…Illinois once again has an opportunity to stamp greatness on the political world…"

Daily Herald: "…Tom Robinson and the E Party deserve the chance to reshape education in Illinois and across America."

In a world where newspapers may have lost their place, it still remains to be seen what impact this will have.

If the polls are any indication, Allen heads into the final weekend with an almost insurmountable lead. Not surprisingly, there do not seem to be any Robinson coattails as the Democrats look to maintain their stranglehold on the balance of the statewide officers. If lieutenant governor weren't legally joined to governor, that would go Democrat as well.

Depending on which polls you trust, the legislature is too close to call. Several polls show the Speaker gaining enough seats to re-establish a true majority. The Senate, with less seats at risk, will likely settle close to the current breakout.

In the legislative races, one significant statistic is an unusually high number of undecideds. They usually break against incumbents. Combined with the late infusion of funds to the E Party and the resulting media flurry, don't be surprised to be surprised.

Three snores in congressional races where, in the absence of E candidates, no changes are expected.

In other news…

THE BACK BENCH
"If you let it slip, we catch it"

November 4

What a crazy last weekend, even for Illinois politics. We'll take it party by party:

Democrats: Danny Ryan unleashed one of his patented blitzkriegs on the legislative front. From robocalls, to tweeting, to mail, to door-to-door frontal assaults, the political blogs were awash with stories of libel, slander and other classless, verbal rape. The type of stuff that, in perpetuating the harsh realities of American politics, suppresses turnout and favors the entrenched Democrats.

Curiously, fewer public punches were thrown in the governor's race. A few attack pieces against Tom Robinson and the E Party that started to run mid-week were mysteriously deep-sixed. Most likely, the overnight polling told them this was a non-starter. There was another late round of 527 organization attacks against Robinson.

Republicans: Where the Democrats lacked negativity, the Republicans filled the vacuum. They repeatedly attacked Tom Robinson on TV and radio. Consistent with their approach throughout the campaign, all efforts were focused on the governor's race.

E-Party: They stuck with Tom Robinson's pledge and remained media-free with respect to the governor's race. Their other statewide challengers bought what little media was still available and were true to the E playbook. In a unique and apparently hugely effective effort, Billy Shakespeare released a new rap song on YouTube in support of Robinson and the entire E Party. Today's *Tribune* reports that web and YouTube records were shattered over the two-day weekend. I found the entire presentation quite intriguing, and if the web response is any indication, turnout, at least for Generation XXX, could be significantly elevated. As you can't do justice to rap in print, the full video is posted on the blog. But here's a stanza that I found very compelling:

You gotta think E So you can be E Then you should vote E
Think E Be E Vote E E Partee
Think E for Educate, Elaborate, Elucidate, Elevate,
Extenuate, Envision, and Epitomize.

Think E Be E Vote E E Partee
So you can be E to Electrify, Exemplify, Enhance, Enjoy,
Evolve, Embellish and Exhilarate.
Think E Be E Vote E E Partee
Then you should vote E to Enrapture, Enhance, Empower,
Enable, Expedite, Energize and Emancipate.

Think E Be E Vote E E Partee To VictorEE.

Heading to Election Day, it will be very interesting to see if the polling has changed in any significant way.

In other news…

* * * * * * * * * * * * * * * *

"As always, let me start by thanking everyone for their time this evening," Atlas said to the usual conference call ensemble. "If you had told me, after roughly thirty-six months and two election cycles, that we could be on the verge of electing a governor and disrupting majority rule status quo in five states…well, that would not have computed. For that matter, if you had told me the same thing a few weeks back after that first hearing in *U.S. v. Stein*…I would have said, in fact I did say, we're toast.

"Yet, here we are, no longer on life support and with decent odds to add legislative seats and for a major upset by Tom. I want to thank all of you for an amazing run. Well, enough from me. Mark, walk us through tomorrow."

"Happy to. Let's take a snapshot.

"Allen still has a comfortable eight point lead on Stewart. Let's call it 39 Allen, 32 Stewart, and 29 Robinson. If Stewart's numbers hold, it's virtually impossible for Tom to catapult ten points in less than three days. No matter how much pixie dust the Speaker sprinkles.

"However, we've come up close to two points on each day following the editorial sweep, coupled with Lisa arranging Tom's face on every network of consequence. Kudos to Lauren as well. She has literally reinvented our web presence on a daily basis. And of course, no matter how you feel about rap, the PR benefit from Billy Shakespeare's newest production has been astonishing. We have a metric that puts us within reach of Allen if the 18 to 24 cohort increases their turnout by 10 percent and breaks 80-plus percent for us.

"Going into Election Day, our preparation for voter turnout is the only other potential difference-maker. I'd like to think we've grown light-years since last time. There are just under 8,000 polling places in Illinois and about half are included in our legislative races. Up until last Friday, we were spread thin. However, after the General cut his deal with the Speaker, we decided to roll the dice and go bare at all polls where there is no E Party legislative candidate. We're relying on the Democrats to have that covered for Tom. With redeployment, we are now adequately staffed in all precincts where we have a competitive legislative candidate.

"Field operations in the other states more closely resemble our last run. In an odd sort of way, the funding hiatus may have positioned us for another sneak attack. Billy might just rap a few across the finish line. Although these new frontiers have been the lowest priority, there's still sufficient voter resentment for us to catch some late lightning.

"In addition to the technology from last time, we will Twitter an update to the field team every ten to fifteen minutes. The General and Lauren have developed abbreviated message codes for all scenarios to pinpoint and update all voter turnout data in real time.

"From our canvass, Internet data sources and phone banking, we have identified sufficient pluses to achieve victory in all of our tier one races. At the risk of getting shot later by the General, I just want to add how exceptional the preparation has been for the Election Day field operation."

"Thanks, Mark. Lisa?"

"Most media outlets are preparing for their Election Day rollout. Notwithstanding, I'm working a long shot to have Billy perform via live feed on either the *Tonight Show* or *Letterman*. Other than that, the candidates are primed for local news interviews as results come in. Our headquarters in Chicago will be the Sheraton Hotel. Win or lose, Tom will be the story of the evening. Needless to say, we have two speeches written."

"Thanks, Lisa. Lauren?"

"Like Mark, I'd also like to bring everyone up-to-date on recent progress. Until then, in almost all legislative campaigns, we were significantly down in web traffic across all mediums when compared to the last go round. However, once the ads hit, and to a lesser extent the mail, the uptick has been remarkable. Based upon the measuring we can do regarding the time of the visit and the depth of the materials examined, the response has been uniformly positive. By far, we had the highest percentage of surveys favorably completed by undecideds than during any other period, including the budget competition.

"The General and I developed a rating system for various response categories and we have begun Twitter follow up to encourage turnout. This methodology applies to all states and all races. It's been stressful, but quite a wild ride."

"Thanks, Lauren. General, tonight you get to be last, but not least."

"We're ready. My ass is in bed. Reveille's at three-thirty. Atlas, bon chance my dear friend. You deserve it. Good night, everyone."

* * * * * * * * * * * * * * * *

E-MAIL
To: State Central Committee
From: Elizabeth DiMaggio
Sent: 11/4 6:03 p.m. (CST)
Subject: G.O.T.V.

Depending on the polling, Allen has anywhere from a 6 to 10 point lead on Stewart. Robinson has momentum, but according to our own polling, he would have to move at least 8 points to catch our guy.

It is imperative that our turnout is stellar. The phone banks were fully operational as of noon today. All of you should have rehearsed the G.O.T.V. plan over the weekend with your field organizations.

Copley is predicting a 62 percent turnout of registered voters. Should that hold and we hit at least 76 percent of our plusses, Allen is the next governor of Illinois.

The Democrats were uncharacteristically quiet over the weekend, which only means that Mr. Ryan is hatching something. Please keep me posted of anything out of the ordinary. We will immediately dispatch an attorney and alert the attorney general's or U.S. attorney's office.

Above all else, make sure your closers stick with the ballot count to the end and confirm all final totals. We can't afford to have Danny Ryan steal votes. Each poll-watcher is expected to produce a tape of the results before they get paid.

This is a once-in-a-lifetime opportunity. Imagine capturing governor and possibly the map with 38 percent of the vote total. Good luck everyone.

* * * * * * * * * * * * * * * *

E-MAIL
To: Danny
From: Black Pearl
Sent: 11/4 11:47 p.m. (CST)
Subject: Operation Robinson

Next time you need a miracle, give me four days instead of three. Even the big guy gave himself seven.

All kidding aside, “Operation Robinson” is gaining momentum, especially on the South Side. Thanks to you and the Speaker for the confidence and the opportunity. I’m all over this. I’ll see you at headquarters after the polls close.

* * * * * * * * * * * * * * * *

“K.C., my love. How’d you like to go to Chicago tomorrow?”

“Mr. Stein, I thought you’d never ask. I had Liz make the arrangements weeks ago. We leave at ten o’clock.”

CHAPTER TWENTY-FIVE

THE BACK BENCH
"If you let it slip, we catch it"

November 5

Election day, with all the trimmings. The only thing that's certain is that all the polling, all the campaigning, and all the drama means nothing. John and Jane Q. Voter get their day in court as prosecutor, judge and jury.

The only other person that matters is Mother Nature and the weathermen tell us she plans to cooperate. Mostly sunny across the state and relatively mild for early November. Perfect weather to boost turnout.

High turnout favors incumbents with favorables over 50 percent and strong name recognition and also favors non-incumbents with undecided voters.

Statewide tallies for absentee and early voting are complete through Sunday. No remarkable findings to report. Most likely because the E Party candidates came so late to the television.

Finally, I don't know if you caught Billy Shakespeare on *Letterman* last night. If the E Party does well today, he could just be reasons ten through one.

We will update throughout the day on *The Back Bench* blog. Just remember, the stuff we report on election day is even less reliable than our usual news. The comment section will be closed today. It will reopen tomorrow for all the Wednesday morning quarterbacks.

In other news…

THE BACK BENCH BLOG
"If you let it slip, we catch it"

November 5

10:18 a.m. NBC Chicago reports that turnout is running at a 70 percent pace. That would be unheard of for Illinois, especially in a non-presidential election year.

11:06 a.m. WBBM Radio Chicago is also reporting large turnout statewide. Regional breakouts should be available early this afternoon.

11:14 a.m. There are unsubstantiated Twitter reports that, in the predominantly minority wards of Chicago, Democrat precinct workers are passing palm cards with Tom Robinson's name posted for governor; otherwise all other names are Democrats.

12:06 p.m. The palm card rumors are surfacing in Democrat stronghold districts statewide. Something is up.

12:46 p.m. The web site for the Chicago Board of Elections reports that over 98 percent of polls opened on time. The State Board of Elections reports 97.3 percent. Both average to good. There are only a handful of sites indicating openings delayed more than one hour. In almost all cases, the delays are attributable to voting machine failure.

1:27 p.m. WGN Chicago ran a feature on the noon news with voters displaying the Tom Robinson name on Democrat palm cards. They were, however, unable to identify or produce a campaign worker willing to say if they were with the Democrats or the E Party. Either way, WGN just gave an unsuspecting boost to Tom Robinson.

2:17 p.m. Elizabeth DiMaggio has apparently asked the attorney general to confiscate the confederate palm cards and investigate their origin. Not sure if this is purely for PR effect. As far as the law goes, all's fair in love, war and palm cards. At least she is getting some late airtime on radio to signal her Republican voters that something's amiss.

4:22 p.m. Just under three hours to polls closing. Statewide turnout is projected in the high 60's. Totally unsubstantiated are reports that turnout is very heavy on college campuses. Should that prove true, it could be the Billy Shakespeare effect.

6 p.m. Polls close in one hour. CBS Chicago has just run a citywide spread showing long lines at a host of polling places. Everyone in line at 7 p.m. gets to vote. If the lines hold, the reporting of results could be delayed. No word yet if

anyone has gone to court to have any polls remain open late for any reason.

7 p.m. All polls should be closed. I will be making the rounds and updating throughout the evening. I have provided links above to all known election board and media outlets that are expected to present running totals and commentary.

* * * * * * * * * * * * * * * *

What had started with a bout of escape thinking by a lonely figure on a park bench perched at 10,000 feet in Snowmass Village, Colorado, was now playing out on national television and the world wide web. The core group of five that kicked the tires three years earlier on a veranda overlooking the Roaring Fork Valley was in the Sheraton Hotel, Chicago, Illinois.

Lisa Boudreau, a late entry to the group, was in the ballroom presiding over countless media and news reporters, and an estimated assembly of at least 3,500 from General Smith's voluntary army of campaign workers.

The General, Mark, and Lauren were squirreled away in a non-descript war room surrounded by countless phones, computers and support techs. Calls, tweets and e-mails of campaign results were filtering in, logged, and being immediately analyzed against pro forma models based on historical voting data, polling results, and voter registration data. Victories and losses were estimated, confirmed, and reported to Lisa for public distribution.

Tom Robinson, K.C., and Atlas were housed in the Platinum Suite, a three bedroom behemoth complete with kitchen and sufficient space for entertaining the entire E Party statewide ticket, their spouses, families and close friends—a fairly typical choreographing of election night festivities, with one unusual exception. In a scene cast from a Nora Ephron script, for the very first time, Alex Stein was meeting candidates from the E Party of Illinois. It wasn't exactly an introduction; it was a warm, loving, respectful reunion.

One additional special guest was in attendance off and on throughout the evening. Nat Carson had been granted exclusive access.

With each television in the suite tuned to a different channel, results of individual races were often known before the call came from Mark or the General. Each E victory was celebrated with toasting and hugs; each defeat with remorse and grace.

By the relatively early hour of 10:30 p.m., the Illinois Legislature was taking shape. The twenty-two seats held by the E Party would grow, slightly, to between twenty-eight and thirty. This news was tempered somewhat by the loss of five incumbent House seats, one being the seat vacated by Representative Jenkins. Pending the outcome of the governor's race, the Speaker had been wise to call the General to preserve his place in history.

The statewide races were all uncharacteristically tight, taking much longer to project winners. Mark called four times between ten-thirty and eleven, each time handily beating the networks to the punch. Remorse and grace for Anthony Manzella in the race for secretary of state and then for Kellie Morgan in the race for attorney general. The three other races for statewide office remained too close to call, with all E candidates holding their own.

At 11:47 p.m. and 12:18 p.m., respectively, toasting, hugs and voluminous cheers as the E Party claimed comptroller and treasurer. The contest for governor was heading for Bush/Gore, Coleman/Franken territory with less than 2 percent of the votes outstanding.

Mark and the General finally arrived at the suite at 3:15 a.m. Each wore his best poker face and asked permission of the remaining diehards to meet alone with Tom, Alex, and K.C. For one final time, the Aspen Five were assembled.

"First," began Mark, "we've had a great night! Not only did we have a net gain of eight legislative seats in Illinois, the E Party now has a working toehold in Pennsylvania, Indiana, and Iowa. There was no way in hell that Eddie Cobb was going to take a hit in Texas. Maybe we'll have a shot next time when he's in jail. And, as you know, our Olivia Van Straten is the treasurer elect of Illinois and Paul Richmond is the comptroller elect. Could have knocked me over with a feather."

"And, governor?" Atlas snapped with apprehension.

"As you know from television," Mark calmly continued, "it has been too close to call almost all night. With 2 percent of the vote outstanding, Allen was ahead of Tom 37.8 percent to 37.5. The bulk of the outstanding vote was from the South Side of Chicago, but we needed to carry at least 75 percent of that vote to win. Not impossible for Democrats in predominantly black wards, but nowhere near any of our polling."

"Is there an end to this lecture?" an agitated Atlas demanded.

The General did not respond, instead handing him a tally sheet.

Atlas looked at the sheet and passively handed it to K.C.

"Tom," Atlas said, taking a long, deep breath, "I guess you were the secret weapon after all. Just don't expect me to call you governor!"

LaVergne, TN USA
08 April 2010
178593LV00003B/7/P

9 781600 474279